MERCY ASKED
MERCY FOUND

MERCY ASKED MERCY FOUND

a novel

Karen McGoldrick

Deeds Publishing | Athens

Published by Deeds Publishing in Athens, GA
www.deedspublishing.com

Printed in The United States of America

Cover and interior design by Deeds Publishing

ISBN 978-1-961505-13-1

Books are available in quantity for promotional or premium use. For information, email info@deedspublishing.com.

First Edition, 2023

10 9 8 7 6 5 4 3 2 1

To my "Wahoo" husband Lawrence. He is always and forever my Virginia Cavalier.

Betwixt the stirrup and the ground,
mercy I asked and mercy I found.

—William Camden

1

Betsy pointed to the sign over the interstate, "That's your exit dear, nearly home now."

Eloise put on her turn indicator and gripped the wheel tightly. "I'm nervous."

Betsy said, "Understandably. I know you feel that you are beneath the sword of Damocles. You have some repair work to do. Our words and deeds carry consequences to ourselves and others. No outcomes are certain. That's life."

Eloise said, "Even thinking about seeing Joe, giving him his dog back, well, it makes me sick."

Betsy said, "You are ashamed, I understand, but you must get past that."

Eloise said, "And I won't blame Doc if he fires me."

Betsy replied, "No use dwelling on that now. Look on the bright side, we just had the trip of a lifetime visiting Dabs. He's a dream. I always liked his online persona, but who knew he was going to be that handsome and charming and generous in person? Exploring Ivy Creek Plantation, revealing the headstones, and transcribing the journals of Louisa Robertson, they made the visit magical. I'm now totally invested in the story of Louisa Roberts and her gallant Hessian soldier as well as the other members of the Roberts family at Ivy Creek. They are real people to me now. We've walked in their footsteps! We've experienced 18th century Virginia. We discovered the slave graveyard of Ivy Creek for goodness' sake. That was thrilling. We came about as close to time-travelling as is possible. So, something wonderful came out of you bolting from Atlanta."

Eloise said, "But Pinky? She was my best friend. How does she feel about me now?"

Betsy said, "Whatever Pinky may feel, Pinky is who sent me to check on you. Goodness, I had no idea I was about to go on such a grand adventure though. Life is full of surprises."

Eloise took a deep breath.

Betsy continued, "So, now you must face the music back in Atlanta and make things as right as you can. But regardless of the outcome, there's a real live handsome man in Virginia who is interested in you, and that's no lie."

Eloise said, "He is. Oh my God. That's true Betsy. Hard to believe."

"And we aren't finished learning about Louisa Roberts and Ivy Creek Plantation. There's still more journal to be transcribed and sent to us. The story continues. The American Revolution has yet to come to Virginia. We know Buck will be going into battle. You have some trials ahead of you here in the present, but at least you aren't marching into battle."

Eloise sighed and exited I-85.

Eloise nodded, "No battles. No retreats. But I'm waving a white flag. It's just, I have no idea what the terms of my surrender will be."

Betsy said "Since you kept the dog under false pretenses, you have no room for negotiations. Try and show some grace."

"I hope I still have a job."

"Not my place to say."

"Plus, I flaked out on Bev. Going to her barn and riding Red, well, it's meant the world to me."

"Just tell her the truth."

"All of it?"

"Time for full disclosures. You must be the new Eloise, the changed Eloise. Make something good come from all your failures."

"People trusted me."

"So, return the favor by becoming trustworthy. It doesn't mean you won't suffer more losses, dear. Life isn't fair. But in time, if you keep the faith, in yourself and others, people will stick with you."

"How do you know that?"

"Well, I'm still here, aren't I?"

Eloise smiled and felt her grip on the steering wheel relax.

Betsy looked at her phone, "Oh Eloise, Dabs has sent us another journal entry!"

Eloise made a happy sound and stepped on the accelerator.

Betsy raised her voice in alarm, "Eloise, slow down. You aren't galloping a horse in some race."

Eloise said, "Oh, please read it to me! Read it to me now."

Betsy said, "I respectfully decline. I intend to read it in my own home with a cup of tea and Marilyn purring in my lap. But first we must arrive alive."

May 31, 1780

Charleston fell. It now, like Savannah, lies in enemy hands. Major General Benjamin Lincoln surrendered. Many brave Americans were taken prisoner, although I am assured that Lincoln orchestrated a mass escape so that many men will fight on. Lincoln himself was given parole, and perhaps will be exchanged. But who would want to fight under his command? Not brother Buck.

Buck now waits until the new southern command is announced. There is much concern the British mean to take the South entire, cutting us off from the north. Virginia is General Washington's home. With Savannah and Charleston taken, I pray the good General will be alarmed enough to bring himself, along with the French navy, back to free the southern states, and chase the scoundrels out to sea.

Then came news of the Waxhaw's Massacre. What sort of commander allows his men to disregard a white flag, butchering those begging for quarter? Banastre Tarleton. His was the command, but the bloody work was carried out by American Loyalists. Americans butchering Americans. This news fills me with horror and shock. In this massacre, Tarleton's horse was shot and fell upon his master. Tragically, the horse was killed but the master survived.

Buck and father meet behind the closed study door, and voices can be heard raised in passion. Father protects his sole heir by restraining him from the battle still. Buck obeys but spends much time practicing his rifle skills in anticipation of killing more than game. The threads of love and duty that bind Buck to father are frayed and near to breaking. They cannot hold much longer. I do not fear for Buck on his own account as much as on behalf of father, and even more so, Aunt Bess. Buck has been coddled and spoiled by Aunty and she will grievous mourn should any harm come to him. Aunt Bess makes a point each day to fill Buck's plate and create some new sweet that will elicit his praise. Her efforts are performed with a sort of mania, as if her food and affection given now, can shield him from the uncertain dangers ahead. We all benefit. I note that Major Schmidt's form has softened round the edges. Father however remains whipcord thin.

Buck mentioned taking Henry as his servant. I asserted I would not allow this. He will not take my Henry and misuse him as he must have done Sammie. Father backs me up.

Not three days have passed since I came around

the barn to find Priscilla in the arms of Sammie. I backed away double-quick.

Priscilla was wailing. "I cannot bear to live."

Sammie was speaking urgently, "It will come right, gal. You swear you do naught and let your ole Sammie make it come right."

I thought I should not hear more and fled. It was not that I did not have the right. I have the right. It was that I did not want to know. You cannot reveal what you do not know.

Priscilla's wailing was animal-like and sickening to hear. I think I shall have a hard time forgetting the sound of it.

June 1, 1780

I admit a twinge of guilt over eavesdropping. But I assuage such guilt by thinking myself here an historian. Who will one day read these words? Well, God willing, I will make old bones and someday read the words of the young woman I was. I hope that fate will be kind to me and my household in those intervening years, Though, I have no expectation of dispensations awarded. Certainly not if we lose this struggle for indepedency.

The Major and I stay within our proper boundaries. Does my older self, approve or feel regret? Sometimes I feel the Major's gaze upon me. I try not to show recognizance of his admiration. One day he

will leave us, and he and I can then part with fond
memories of our friendship, without shame.

The Major does shower his affection upon young
Henry, who follows at his heels like a faithful dog.
Henry is spoiled. Yet, Henry has blossomed. His music forms the center of his world. His instrument he
talks to like a companion. Henry talks to Lady Jane
too. But then I talk to Beast, and I talk to the horses.
"Judge not..."

We are a fine band, the three of us, and Beast
and Beauty and Fashion and whoever we put
young Henry on for the ride. We still ride out in the
morn. Father is selling a few of the young horses. I
dread this but come summer we bring up the three-
year-old horses to train, so we must sell riding horses
to devote ourselves to the next generation. The cycle
continues.

Father sold Fanny to Mr. Bell for supplies. Henry cried. I thought Henry disliked the filly. He will
never forget nor forgive Fanny for baptizing him in
the creek.

The Major came to aid in loading and unloading the wagon. I begged father for scented lanolin
soap balls. There is nothing to compare for washing
of hair. Such items are rare as hen's teeth. I promised to be frugal. He sweetly purchased that and
other things for me and Aunty. I did see Mary
and Jane and Sophia, who were agog at the sight
of the handsome Major. Once they heard he was
a prisoner of war from the Barracks, they looked

sorely disappointed. Even though the Major is unavailable, their envy I confess to have enjoyed. I am a shallow young woman.

* * *

Bev met Eloise at the car.

Eloise had tried to explain everything that had happened on the phone. Bev had interrupted her to tell her stop her yapping and to come get her ass in the tack. They could catch up face to face.

Eloise still had Prince, which Doc reminded her was temporary. It made the last couple of days feel like a long and painful goodbye.

Bev asked, "How's your noggin'?"

Prince bounded out of the car, spun, then leaned against Bev's leg, looking up into her face, panting with excitement.

"Head's okay."

Bev stroked the dog and then looked back at Eloise.

"So ya' messed up, Didja'?"

Eloise exhaled, long and slow. "In a major way. Doc is calling Joe, the dog's owner, and setting up a meeting. What to say?"

"Might try begging

"And if that doesn't work? I want to keep Prince."

"That the hill you want to die on?"

"No. I don't want to die on any hill. I just want to keep my dog. Maybe I can prostrate myself on the hill."

Bev put a bony hand on her shoulder, light, and brief. "You go give Red a pipe-opener on that back hill. It'll do you both a world of good. Might even buck up your courage to call your old man and make demands on getting something you lost returned to you."

Eloise frowned, "Jock may have possession of Whiplash, but she's my horse, and he needs to return her."

Bev grunted, "Might be what that feller says about his dog come tomorrow."

Eloise's face must have shown that she heard Bev's words loud and clear.

Bev saw she had hit the bullseye.

Bev said, "Seems like God has a mean streak, don't it? Well, I got one of my own. It's gotten me into more trouble than I care to think on. But here's the truth girly, we don't own a damn thing. No, we don't. But if we can get up in the morning, eat when we're hungry, shit when we got to, and got enough money to keep us out of trouble, well, that ain't too bad."

"That's a low bar, Bev."

"I'll be long dead before you realize it ain't. But that's okay. Now go on and work the starch out of Red."

Red was in the crossties, saddle on. The mare wobbled her nostrils making a "whu-whu-whu" sound in greeting when she saw Eloise.

Bev said, "Ain't that sweet? I been longing her, so's you wouldn't get launched when you got back on."

"Thanks Bev."

"Give her a good twirl on the longe. Looks real innocent standing there, but she'll have a cold back from not carrying no weight for a week. Red won't feel a bit guilty if she unloads you in the dirt."

"I'll be good. I can't afford to knock the old melon again."

Bev grunted.

Eloise did as she was told. She gave the mare "a twirl," then mounted and worked on basics to warm her up. Red was fresh, but not naughty. Prince was waiting at the gate to the pasture, watching the preliminaries. When Eloise finished, she dropped the reins and gave the mare a rub on her withers. Prince hopped up and barked and was off, leading the way, just as he had done every day in Virginia. Eloise walked the first circuit, with Prince running back to check on her before bounding off again.

Eloise got into jumping position and gathered the reins, starting off at a jog. Eloise felt a tremble in her legs, a shudder up her spine, because she knew she could hit the ground again. She was breathing too shallow; the familiar flush of dizziness came but washed over her as she regained her focus. Red lowered her neck and pulled into the reins. She allowed the mare to lengthen the trot strides up the hill. Eloise felt a good sort of stretch in her calf muscles. They had gotten tight from all the walking in Virginia. The next loop, Eloise allowed Red to break into canter, still holding the mare in check, letting her find a rhythm, "puff, puff, puff," the exhalations coming with the landing of the mare's leading leg. It was sweet music, music that filled her with anticipation. Eloise knew she would never settle for Bev's modest list. It was not enough. It was not this.

Eloise skimmed along the bottom land, flat and wide, another turn, and then by simply pushing the reins toward the bit, Eloise let Red know it was her chance to "let 'er rip."

The kick against the ground behind the saddle changed to the rhythm of a boxer attacking a punching bag, "wham-wham-wham!" Red accelerated up the hill passing Prince who, paused, and watched with approval, before following them.

Eloise and Red were both breathing hard as they walked back, Prince trailing after them. Eloise's tight calf muscles were screaming, full of lactic acid. Red was relaxed, her ears swiveling in the sockets, flicking back and then flopping to the side. This view of her ears made Eloise yearn for Whiplash and brought back the image from the dream she had while in Virginia, in a way that was physically painful. Overcome, she stopped and turned the mare around, away from the barn. Eloise needed another lap around the field. This time at the walk, so she could cry in private, mourning ahead of the loss of Prince, the loss of Whiplash, the damage to her friendships, the damage to her job at the clinic. And even though she would like to blame it all on her Dad, Jock, and on the unfairness of losing her mother, well, the time had come to accept her part in all of it. She had come back to Atlanta resolved to be a truth-teller, and to make amends where she could. But more importantly, to accept with grace her reality. But there was no getting around the fact that it was all going to be painful.

* * *

High on Eloise's to-do list was having a heart-to-heart with her dashing, unreliable, hot-shot dad, in Ireland, who had promised to send her back her horse. But hadn't. She needed to get a spine and say what needed to be said. Jock was five hours ahead of her. If she was going to call, it needed to be now. But instead of calling Jock, Eloise called her financial advisor, Ralph. She called expecting to leave a message but was startled to have him pick up on the first ring.

Ralph was breathing so loudly that Eloise went to speaker and set the phone down.

"Eloise, how incredible. I was just about to call you. I called the clinic to make an appointment for Murtagh and Doc picked up. Well, he filled me in on your little, ahem, accident. Dear one, I am so sorry. Are you okay?"

Eloise took a breath and steeled herself. "I'm okay. Mostly it was embarrassing. I called because I'm finally sending you a budget on the costs associated with getting and keeping Whiplash. I'll need the money to ship her, and money to cover board and the farrier and the vet and supplies. I still have her bridles and saddles and stuff like that. But at least I know where I want to keep her and have specific numbers for you."

"Well, Eloise that is good news. I didn't think Jock

was going to ever relent. I mean, that man is slippery. Oh, dear, I'm sorry. I shouldn't have said that."

"It's okay. It's true."

"I should get back to my work out. But you email me the details, and I'll figure out the money. Let me know when Whiplash is arriving. I want to be there to greet her when she steps off the horse van back here in Georgia."

"Really? But you're not a horse person."

"I'm not, but I want to see your happy face when she is returned to you. Now, I've got to get back to sweating this belly off. I'll see you at the clinic when I bring Murtagh in. Ta-Ta, darling."

Eloise couldn't believe it, she said, "Ta-Ta."

She felt fortified. She was calling Jock, regardless of the hour.

The rings sounded distant, foreign, more like an alarm than a ring.

Jock sounded annoyed. "Everything okay? You're calling pretty late."

Eloise lied, "Sorry I forgot how many hours later you are."

"Five. It's five hours."

"I'm sorry if I woke you up."

"Let me go into the other room, hold on."

Eloise waited a few beats. "I've done some thinking and I've made some decisions."

"Phone calls late at night usually mean someone's died."

Eloise felt a small chill pass over her, remembering

that she had made the call to Jock when her mom had died. The thought made her dizzy, but no, she couldn't let Jock do that to her, not now. She got straight to the point. "I want Whiplash returned now. I don't want to wait any longer. She can rest in a field at Bev's if she's not sound yet. Ralph says I've got the funds. I'm past ready to have her back."

There was a long pause, long enough that Eloise looked at the phone to be sure the call hadn't dropped.

"Lulu, I bred her."

Eloise's mouth went dry. Her tongue felt foreign in her own mouth. Her brain went foggy.

He continued, "When she got hurt, well, I thought we might as well try. She's no spring chicken, those kinds of injuries are tricky to heal and frankly, too easy to re-injure. She had a super career but it's over Lulu. Breeding her was the best direction, and I wasn't sure she would even catch, she's old for a maiden mare. I didn't want to say anything in case she didn't, but we just had her ultra-sounded, and she's confirmed in foal. We can alternate foals, Lulu. You know, one for me, and one for you. She could provide us with top sport horses. I'll send you the link to the stallion I chose. Next year the choice can be yours."

Eloise could hear her tongue unglue itself with a little pop as she pulled it off the roof of her mouth. "Jock, you never asked."

Jock changed the subject, "Hey, that red filly of Bev's? She ever going to sell it to me?"

Eloise's voice was flat, "No. She never will. Never."

"Too bad. No one else is going to give her that price. Totally inflated."

"But you were going to pay it."

"My client's money. I make my commission on the purchase price. You know that."

"The client you're planning to marry?"

Jock showed zero shame as he said, "It will never be my money, Lulu. Besides, the horses are my real treasures."

"Clearly."

Jock either missed the irony or did not care.

"And Lulu."

"What?"

"Bev is an old piece of shoe leather, tough and worn out with one hell of a mean streak. She used that filly to settle an old score. Got me to commit and then pulled the rug out. Sorry I sent you down there for nothing. But remember, there's always another fish-in-the-sea."

"I guess there always are."

"Call me earlier in the day next time and we can catch up. I'm dead on my feet."

"Sure."

Jock lightened his tone, "Don't worry about Whiplash. Your old man has her looking like a million bucks. You and Suzy had good runs with her, but it's best for the mare now not to have to run and jump that hard. Let her be a Momma horse. It's for the best. It wouldn't be right to do otherwise. Now, you let your old Dad get some rest. Sweet Dreams."

Eloise was able to make some sort of noise that Jock took as a goodbye.

And then there was dead air and a blank screen.

She marveled at the person who was Jock Robertson. Jock had just made perfect sense. And yet. She had been screwed. Meanwhile in Ireland Jock had left the bedroom so as not to disturb his sleeping "sponsor" while admitting he had been willing to gouge her on the price on Red to score a bigger commission.

It took Eloise a full fifteen minutes to find that she was furious. She went to the closet and looked for the sack of letters from Jock to her mother. To hell with privacy. She intended to read every single one of them. And then burn them.

Eloise got the bag of letters out and dumped them on the bed. She began to sort through them. A few were those old air mail letters, thin like onion paper. Some were on hotel stationery. And the last six were in pre-printed business envelopes, the farm logo and address of the place Jock lived and worked in Ireland.

When Eloise picked up the oldest, the envelope had re-sealed itself. She went to the kitchen and got a butter knife.

She was intruding on her parents' personal lives from anger, from weakness, from frustration. These letters were not written to be shared. These were letters between a husband and a wife, between two lovers. And if the letters weren't proof of their love? Did she want to discover why the marriage was never going to work? Was she hesitating to protect herself, or them? She had believed she had the perfect family, no better than perfect, before it all had gone to shit. Maybe this was just another step toward grace, toward acceptance of reality.

Eloise tapped the tip of the knife against her bedspread. So typical of Eloise, she thought of famous letters of history.

Jefferson had betrayed his friend Adams, lied, and slandered him in the press. When Jefferson and Adams reconnected as old men, laid aside their anger and political grudges to write, it was with a full understanding that these letters were for the ages. They were meant to be read by strangers. Copied and saved, the two old lions of the American founding were writing to explain themselves to each other but also to explain themselves to future historians. This was their chance to be sure they had a hand in influencing the opinions of those future writers.

And these letters? Had Elly saved them for Eloise? Did Jock explain himself? Missing from the collection, though, were copies of what her mother had written to Jock. This was a one-sided conversation. But then maybe Elly had said what she needed to say to Eloise. It was Jock's words that had been saved.

Eloise kicked off her shoes and sat down on the bed leaning against the stack of matching pillows. Prince hopped up on the other side, turned a few times and plopped down on his side.

Eloise used the butter knife and opened the oldest one. It was one mailed from Europe, years and years ago. Jock's print lettering was tidy. He never wrote in cursive, Jock, but spaced his letters evenly in a hand that was child-like. It reminded Eloise of the lined paper with the broken line between two solid lines used to teach children to write. The lowercase lettering went to the broken line, the upper case to the top line, all arrow straight. It meant that when Jock wrote, he wrote slowly, and sparingly. It was out of character for a man who liked a speed horse. Jock was not known to be a careful man, but his lettering struck Eloise as careful. Or to be less generous, calculating.

It was hard to hold on to her anger as she worked her way through the oldest letters. They were full of dreamy plans, where Jock planned the layout of the farm, spoke of horses that Eloise had never met, purchasing fencing, paying for injection seeding, staying ahead of the fire-ant mounds, while trying to qualify for national teams or impress sponsors. Some of the concerns seemed mundane. Some of his words incredibly egocentric. But all his desires and plans included Elly. Jock was charming.

Eloise looked at the collection of letters on the bedspread. She saw the letters as a three-act play, a tragedy. These oldest letters were the first act. The play had yet to turn dark. She knew how all tragedies end. Eloise jumped to act three.

These envelopes had not resealed themselves. The paper was of high-quality stock. The logo was professional. Jock's printing was the same. The letters were short. They were no longer aspirational. The crisis had arrived.

El,

We had a great run. We gave our daughter a happy home. She's become a lovely adult. She loves us both. But right now, you need her more than she needs either one of us. Now we must trust that she will be able to bear what is coming. I wish you'd let me be there. But I will carry on here the best I can.

J

And then the last one of them all, painful to read.

El,

I think it's wrong to continue to keep the serious-ness of your illness from Lulu. While I am grateful you have not dragged my name through the mud, by keeping her in the dark, you prevent me from providing emotional support.

The mare arrived, safe and sound. I'm sorry you didn't want Eloise to continue riding. She'll come back to it. It won't be on the mare, and it won't be under my guidance. I'm sorry you feel that strongly about it. But if that's your wish, I won't challenge you. Neither will I show up in Atlanta if that's what you want. But if you change your mind, I'll be on the next plane out.

J

Eloise did not burn the letters. She put on her pajamas and brushed her teeth. She missed her mother intensely in that moment, but she was angry at her and ready to fight, needed to fight.

Jock had thanked her mother for not dragging his name through the mud. That was not exactly true. The story was that Jock had left them. Jock had replaced them with another family. And he had. For God's sake, Jock had found a substitute daughter to ride her horse. And he knew her mother was sick when he moved to Ireland. He knew and he still left them. What kind of person does that?

But it was Elly who had wanted Eloise to stop riding, had sent her horse away. It was Elly who had not wanted Jock to come back home. Elly had let Lulu believe it was all Jock. All Jock. Because of Jock they had to sell their home. Eloise had to come home from college because of Jock. Because of Jock, her mom said, they had to send Whiplash to Ireland while they sold the farm and all the other horses.

Elly wanted Lulu to finish college, make friends outside of the horse world, to "take a break" from the horses while they reorganized their lives, their new lives together without Jock. Once settled, Eloise could go spend a summer with Jock in Ireland, and then bring her horse back.

None of it was ever going to come to pass. Her mother had known all along.

What had Elly done? She had died. There was no new life together. She had died and left Eloise alone in this strange town home. Alone. Not even a dog for company.

Eloise sat back down on the edge of her bed, and redialed Jock. She knew she was going to make him angry, calling at such a terrible hour. An hour that no one should be awake.

Jock picked up after a long buzzing ring, a ring that must have been an electronic glitch it lasted so long.

"Lulu? Did you mean to call again?"

"I read the letters."

"What? What letters?"

"Your letters to Mom."

Eloise heard nothing in reply, but in her mind's eye she saw Jock run his fingers through his hair, his mind working to formulate a plan, a story, a way to smooth the waters.

Eloise yelled into the phone. "I lost my home, my horse, my dad, and then my mom. Fuck, Jock."

"Eloise! Your mother would hate to hear you use that word."

"She's not here to hear it."

"Have you been drinking?"

This made Eloise snort. "Are you kidding me? No, I've been reading."

"Why did you call, Lulu?"

"You left your dying wife alone with your daughter to put her affairs in order. You divorced her and replaced her. You replaced your daughter and took her horse and lied about it. You kept telling lies. You're still telling lies."

Jock's voice was stern, parental, lecturing, "I'm not

going to replay all those tough calls we had to make, because frankly, those decisions were never yours to make. They were hard ones with no happy endings. Neither of us could bear to tell you the truth. Maybe that was cowardice. Maybe it was to try and prolong whatever innocent days you still had. I did as I was asked. I'm sorry Lulu. No one could stop what was coming. All I could do was honor Elly's wishes. I can't make it better."

Eloise felt stunned, "That's it?"

Jock softened his tone. "Elly and I, we had a wonderful love affair. And then we had you. And our world revolved around loving you, being amazed by you. And then we got run over by a freight train. I had the option of running away. Elly didn't. The one person we couldn't bear to hurt, we ended up hurting anyway. We both of us need to figure out now, how to regroup. You love your stories, and so do I. But we can't change the endings. We only get to choose what comes next."

The truth of those words filtered through to Eloise.

There was a long silence. Then Jock said, "I guess I'm getting up now even though it's still dark as pitch out. You think you can sleep?"

"I'm so tired."

"Please try to be at peace."

Eloise couldn't think of anything to say.

2

The next morning when Eloise got herself and Prince in the car she thought of Dabs. He would be getting up, starting the coffee, and then heading out to the barn to feed his geriatric herd. Eloise had a fleeting urge to turn her little car up I-85 and make another run for it. Afterall, this could be her last day owning Prince. She reached over and stroked "her" dog on the top of his head, then ran her hand over one silky ear. He panted, his mouth hanging open in what looked like a smile. She fought down the instinct to flee.

Eloise sighed. "Well, Eloise, you tried that number." She imagined one of those Amber Alerts going out except it would be for an animal abduction. Dabs was a good egg, but she didn't mean for him to aid and abet a dognapping. Besides, he'd likely turn her right around and give her the boot. Like other horrible days she had lived, other losses she had experienced, she had no option left but to live it, experience it.

The night before, Eloise couldn't remember feeling as exhausted as she felt after she had hung up with Jock.

Not even the exhaustion she remembered feeling after a long weekend at an event.

She remembered that overwhelming fatigue, pulling in with the horse trailer, unloading the horses and getting them settled before being able to take a shower and fall into bed. How she remembered the heaviness of her legs, the sense of disorientation as she unpacked. Her mom would be forcing her to drink water, to "fill up the tanks" after sweating all weekend. But that was an exhaustion from physical exertion, from being outside in all weather, and usually carried with it a feeling of satisfaction.

Eloise also remembered how she felt after her mother's memorial service. That too was a sort of exhaustion.

This was something different, although getting into bed last night she had welcomed the oblivion of swiftly falling, falling, falling down the downy rabbit hole into a deep sleep.

But she had woken up early, with the sun barely breaking the horizon, no quarter given. The day was today. Joe was coming to the clinic. Nowhere to run, nowhere to hide. She went through her morning routines, fed Prince, who was always eager for his breakfast and greeted each day with unbounded energy and cheer. This could be another day of loss, likely would be. She should "gird her loins." Then she snorted to herself. She wasn't going into battle. She had no weapons, no armor. And whatever she had to face that day, it would not challenge her existence or anyone else's for that matter. Prince was not going to die, was not going to be harmed. His owner, his rightful owner, wanted him returned.

Eloise grimly returned in her mind to her two conversations with Jock. As if that would be a helpful distraction. Eloise was no match for Jock. And what about her mom? Did she even know anything about either one of them? She wasn't too sure she did.

Eloise had a pain in her chest. She knew now it was not a heart attack. Not in the medical sense. She turned and looked at Prince who looked at the road, sitting up like a person in the passenger seat. Eloise had put his seat belt on, pulling it across his chest. She thought to herself that if she had been a responsible person, Prince would have been in the back seat with a proper dog restraint. If she could keep him, she thought, she would research online and find him the safest dog restraint on the market. She loved this dog. She wanted to keep Prince. She knew she was bargaining with fate. As if making such internal declarations would influence future outcomes.

Bev had said we don't really own anything. But then if we don't really own anything, what is left to us? What IS ours?

Eloise felt the pain in her chest sharpen as she heard in her head the words, "Love." It sounded trite.

But the thought that came next was this, and it did not sound trite, it sounded real, because it was real. Eloise thought, "I still love my parents. I can't help it; I love them, and I can't stop loving them. I'm so angry at them both, but it changes nothing. My parents were the center of my universe. And they loved me back because for a time, a golden time, I was the center of their universe too. I did not own them, I do not own Jock, but I do own my love for them, and I own that forever, and nobody, damn it, nobody can ever take that away. I own that." Eloise's declaration, unspoken, but clear in her mind, gave her something to grasp.

The pain in her chest began to ease as she pulled into the clinic. Eloise realized too that she loved her job. She hated that she had disappointed Doc. He had always been so kind, so good to her.

Another voice, a different voice inside her head said, "What now, brown cow?"

It was Jock's voice. It was the light but serious tone he used when he coached her. She closed her eyes and there he was. She was looking down from her horse, getting her last instructions.

"Out of the box, you find your pace, breathe when you can, if you don't see a distance to the obstacle, take another breath, don't panic, don't rush, but no pussy footing either. Steady as you go."

Eloise opened her eyes, took a deep breath, then a longer slower one. She spoke to Prince as she unbuckled him, "Steady as you go, steady as you go."

* * *

Eloise had finished the morning chores and was having her quiet moment with Prince and a freshly brewed cup of coffee, trying her best to distract herself. Would she still have a job? Would she still have a dog? Would she have friends? Or would she be toxic, the unhinged employee that everyone had to tread lightly around until she could be dismissed?

She drank her coffee and went to the Extreme Readers website, reading the long essay Betsy had posted about their trip to Monticello. Betsy had uploaded a photo of the two of them someone had kindly taken standing in front of the iconic home. They looked rosy-cheeked and merry. It made their bolt up I-85 look like a vacation taken to further their education on Jefferson.

Then Eloise reread the latest journal entry that Dabs had sent. She still had the journals. She still had Dabs. She still had Betsy. Bev had not disowned her. She still had the ride on Red. All of that was not nothing. Those things were enough even if she had to lose Prince and all of this. Steady as you go. Breathe.

She read the journal entry differently knowing now that Louisa's brother Buck would not survive the war. Finding Buck's grave had made his life real to Eloise. This was no work of fiction. Buck's death would deeply injure those who loved him. But how would his death change the fate of Ivy Creek and Louisa? This was yet to be discovered.

Doc walked into the lounge with a box of donuts. He opened the box to offer her first dibs. The room was filled with the scent of icing and warm bread. Prince was thumping his tail, hopefully.

Eloise took a deep breath. She thought again, "Steady as you go. Steady as you go."

Doc poured himself a coffee and grabbed a donut, taking a sip of coffee first and then a big bite of the donut, saying, mouth full, "I shouldn't eat these anymore, but they are too good." He studied Eloise for a moment, swallowed and then said, "You still having headaches?"

Eloise tore off a piece of her donut and handed it to Prince, who had collected drool on his chin while staring at the donut. "No."

"Good, good. That's good. Did you get back on Red yet?"

"Yeah. It felt great to get back on."

Doc finally got to it. "I thought it best to have Joe come later in the day when things are winding down here. Hope it won't interfere with getting out to Bev's."

Eloise felt her heart dip in her chest. "Do you think there's any chance he might let me keep Prince?"

Eloise focused again on the donut, taking a little bite.

"Can't say. I thought it best to let the two of you discuss it. I've said my peace."

Eloise had trouble swallowing her donut and had to take a big swig of coffee. After she felt the lump of donut slide down her throat she asked, "Did he seem like a nice person?"

"Eloise, he put a lot of effort into searching for his dog, and then like a miracle, after he had lost hope, he found his dog. He was thrilled at the idea of having his dog back home. Which, by the way, he still hasn't accomplished."

Eloise frowned. "You have any suggestions?"

"No. I'm sorry, but I don't."

Eloise couldn't look at her dog, who she knew was staring at the half of a donut she was gripping in her fist. Prince wasn't worried about the future. He was only worried that Eloise was going to eat the last bite without sharing.

She gave him the rest of the donut.

* * *

When Pinky came into the basement, she had her puffballs Ying and Yang with her. The Shih-tzus made little screeching noises all the way down the stairs which set off the other dogs, the barking echoing off the walls. Prince was excited to see his friends and broke his "down-stay" bouncing around the puffballs while they spun circles getting their leashes tangled.

Pinky scooped them up and tossed them into one of her grooming cages, leashes still attached, she said, "Oh for the love of all that is sacred, will you dogs please shut your traps!"

And like turning off a tap, it was quiet. "Ah, that's better."

Eloise should have greeted Pinky. But instead had that weird sensation again of her tongue being stuck to the roof of her mouth. She found herself dropping her gaze, as if she had spotted something on the floor.

Pinky said, "Sorry about the noise; grooming day for the puffballs."

Then Pinky said, "You look like someone shrunk you in the laundry."

That made Eloise look up. "I look like what?"

"Shrunken. You know, like a rabbit does. Like you think you see a rabbit in your yard, but then you don't, because they know how to shrink."

"I'm still 5' 6"."

Pinky shifted gears, "I noticed your little friend Murtagh is coming in today. Seems like he'll be a regular."

"Oh? Yeah, well, you did a great job. You always do a great job, that's why he's back."

Pinky looked thoughtful. She said, "I like Ralph. Kind of like your weird uncle or something, but nice. Personally, I think he wants to check up on his weird niece."

Eloise said, "I don't think I have the energy for jellybean Ralph today. Joe is coming later today. I've got to live through that."

"Ah. So, you *are* hunkered down in the grass, little rabbit."

"I can plead to keep Prince, but I don't have the moral high ground here and Doc didn't give me any hope either."

"Well, you're right about that. But either way, you can choose to be grateful, you know. That dog has been an angel, sent to you. But he's his own dog. He doesn't really belong to anyone."

Eloise closed her eyes hard. She thought to herself, "Breathe. This is Pinky. You love her. Oh my God. You do. You want whatever can be saved here to be saved. Steady as you go. And really, isn't she saying what you know to be true. We don't own anything. Not really. You've just said so yourself."

Pinky continued, "Dog gave you something you needed, and you needed it pretty bad. Don't go back-sliding if he is needed elsewhere."

Eloise's voice was raised more than she meant it to be when she answered, "You're right. I know you are. It's just that *I need* Prince more than Joe. Joe's done fine without the dog all this time. And Jock told me last night he's not sending me Whiplash. I've lost her to Jock."

Pinky shook her head, "I don't get how you lost your horse *last night*. Your horse has been gone for years. And I thought you didn't know Joe. I mean, if you think Joe has done fine without his dog, why couldn't your dad make the same argument about you and your horse?"

Eloise opened her mouth. But nothing came out. Damn tongue was paralyzed. But maybe that was a good thing. Because of course, Pinky was right.

Pinky continued, "I hope Joe lets you keep the dog, by the way. But don't look too needy when you make your case. I don't want him to think you're mental. And be sure not to stand too close. I mean, he might still be a little creeped out from last time."

Eloise felt herself shrinking as she remembered her stupid fantasy, her lies, her manipulations to keep Joe's dog. How she had literally knocked herself out, and then kissed Joe and called him by name, when she should *not* have known his name. Doc had witnessed it all, too. Oh, and handsome, handsome Joe. Her fantasy lover.

But someone she had never met in person, just the man on the lost dog flier, searching for his missing dog. Joe had plenty of reasons to be creeped out. She had kissed a perfect stranger and called out his name, this after evidently keeling over and whacking her head on the floor. She was not only a creep, but a klutzy creep.

Pinky was right, she *was* that crouching little rabbit, hoping she could hide in the tall grass, and no one could find her.

She nodded and said, "Okay."

Janet rang for Eloise to come take a grooming job down to Pinky. She specifically asked for Eloise.

It was Murtagh wearing a plaid doggie raincoat with a matching red collar and leash. And there was Ralph beaming at the end of the leash. There was no place to hide.

"Eloise, there you are. I hope you can tell Murtagh is excited to be here."

Murtagh looked up at Eloise and mechanically tick-tocked his stubby tail back and forth a few times in greeting.

Eloise gave Ralph a weak smile, steadied herself once again, then knelt and slipped the clinic leash onto him, unbuckling all his clan tartan for Ralph to take with him. "Nice to see you again, Murtagh."

Then Eloise affected a breezy tone and asked, "Any special instructions for Pinky? Same as the last cut?" She stood up and handed Ralph Murtagh's coat and leash and collar, carefully not making eye contact. She knew Janet would be listening, watching. She thought Janet didn't really care about her but working the front desk could get dull.

Ralph felt no compunction to keep up appearances for Janet. "You should have the money before the end of the week Eloise. I trust that will be soon enough."

Eloise unstuck her tongue to say, "When Jock was here, I thought we had made a deal. That he had agreed that Whiplash would be returned to me. But then the deal fell apart for him to buy Red. I think he blames me. And maybe that's why. Or maybe not. We've had some words. But now, well, everything's on hold."

"On hold? Do you mean temporarily on hold or on hold until Hell freezes over?"

Eloise looked at the floor and pulled at her ponytail before answering. "The latter. Yeah, definitely the latter."

"Look Dearie, we can make a new plan. I'm sending you the money regardless. Game's not over yet."

"I can't think about that today."

"No pressure. No pressure from me that is."

Ralph looked down at Murtagh and said, "Don't be a dour little Scot. Chin up and all that. We have wild caught Salmon for dinner."

Tick-Tock went the stubby tail.

Ralph began to turn but stopped himself. "Do you eat Salmon?"

Eloise shrugged.

"I've this gigantic piece of fish marinating in the fridge. Please come and join us, won't you? Casual, casual, casual! But we do need some time together to talk, you and I."

Eloise hedged, "I have to go ride at Bev's after work, and I certainly don't want to keep you and Murtagh from your dinner."

"Nonsense. You must eat. Doc told me you get off around three or four at the latest. That should leave you time to ride before dinner. I won't ask for a time certain now but do expect to hear from me after you finish your ride this afternoon, so I won't overcook the salmon. Terrible sin that would be."

And with a fluttering of his fingers, Ralph was out the door.

Murtagh watched Ralph leave, seemingly only half interested. Eloise said, "Well come on then. It's a rainy day and we can all be glum together."

The day stayed dark and chill. It was raining on and off. Eloise did manage to get all the dogs out for walks between showers. Prince seemed to sense her mood although he wagged his tail and gave her a play bow once, as if to say, "lighten up." But of course, he did not know what she knew.

Pinky even was quieter, humming to herself as she worked. Eloise helped her brush out dogs after lunch and told her about Ralph asking her to come to dinner. Eloise didn't feel up to discussing the letters with Pinky, or the upcoming meeting with Joe. But it wasn't necessary. There it was. the awful anticipation of what was to come.

When Janet buzzed later for Eloise to go up to Doc's office, Eloise's mouth went dry. Janet said, "Doc said not to bring the dog."

Eloise felt a wave of dizziness wash over her. The moment was at hand. Prince got up from his bed and trotted over to her. He thought somehow that he was going with her. She once again stroked the top of his head, felt the silkiness of his ears. They gazed into each other's eyes. In her head she repeated Jock's last-minute advice, "Steady as you go. But don't pussy-foot either. And then said to herself again, "Don't pussy-foot."

She said to Prince, "I have to leave you."

Pinky said, "Eloise, don't make the dog anxious or sad. Besides, we don't know for sure yet."

Eloise nodded.

Pinky said, "Remember, ask him about himself. Let him talk, Eloise. Don't stand too close either. Whatever happens, happens, but we can still hope for the best, okay?"

Eloise nodded.

Pinky said, "Best of luck."

Eloise pulled off her smock, that was covered with dog hair, pulled at her ponytail, and drew herself up. She gave Pinky a nod, grateful for Pinky. Grateful to feel she still had a friend, and ally, even though she wasn't sure she deserved it. And although her heart was beating fast, she thought she would at least look composed.

Bev had asked Eloise if this was the hill she wanted to die on. Eloise did not want to die on this hill, she wanted to run from it. It was the nature of all living things to move away from pain. And this was likely to be painful. But she had no choice. Eloise's steps were slow and heavy. She felt she should have heard music as she ascended the steps, a dirge. But there was just the occasional meow from the cats housed upstairs.

Doc's door was mostly closed, and Eloise had the feeling she should knock, but Doc was there to open the door as she lifted her hand.

"Come on in Eloise." Doc opened the door wide, then closed it behind her. He also pulled the rolling chair to Eloise, holding it for her to sit down.

"Not taking chances with me and that chair, are you?"

"Nope."

Eloise got a good look at "Joe," who had also played the role of the Hessian "Major Schmidt" in her mind as she read the journals. She was able to nod. But it was still a shock to see "Joe/Major Schmidt" in-the-flesh, looking right at her.

He said, "How are you feeling, Eloise?"

"Fine. Fine. Thanks for asking, um, Joe."

"I understand you and Jaeger had a week in Virginia."

"Jaeger?"

"I'm sorry, I forgot that you call him Prince."

Eloise said, "That's German. German for Hunter."

"Yes. You speak German?"

"No. I know the name because the Jaeger troops were the Hessians that were mounted infantry. In the American Revolution. I'm kind of into history."

She remembered too late; Pinky told her to ask him about himself." Um, you speak German?"

"No. He came with that name."

She realized she had revealed her weirdness. Then

she thought how 'that ship had sailed' already. Would they bring it up? She was dying inside. But "steady-as-you-go."

Eloise tried to start again, "I can tell you put in a lot of time training him."

Joe shook his head. "Jaeger did get a lot of training, but my sister acquired him when he flunked his exam as a police dog. She and her husband were stationed in Germany."

Eloise said, "Oh. That explains a lot."

Joe continued, "Kind of surprised me he took down that shoplifter because he flunked the attack dog test. He did show promise as a drug detection dog. But he gets distracted too easily, goes off and steals stuff and then plays keep-away. He's not one to take things seriously."

"I noticed."

"When my sister and her husband were redeployed, she sent him to me. Now she is back in the US, and she got herself a female. She asked to borrow Jaeger to breed to her dog. He's a well-bred Giant Schnauzer. People here don't recognize he's a purebred. They don't cut the tails or ears in Germany. It's my fault he got lost. I had no idea the crate was damaged."

Doc grimaced. "I'm sorry that breeding him is now out of the question. We searched for his chip, couldn't find him in any registry."

Joe shrugged. "I can't explain that. But I'm glad he is safe and sound."

Eloise felt her mouth go dry again. Guilt. She was

shrinking again. Rabbit in the grass. Except there was no place to hide here. Why was Joe so handsome? He was looking at her now. His eyes were soft, pitying her perhaps? She tried to swallow, but gosh her mouth was so, so, dry.

He addressed Eloise, "Thank you for taking such good care of my dog. I'm so sorry about last week, but I'm relieved you weren't seriously injured. I hope you and Jaeger had a good week together while you recuperated in Virginia."

Eloise realized all was lost. Lost.

"I'm sorry for everything. I fell in love with your dog. And I really have no excuse for my, um, other, um, odd behavior. But I am sorry. He's different. Prince. Magical. A rare spirit. Prince and I have had amazing adventures."

Joe looked sympathetic when he said, "I know you've grown attached. But please know I am grateful that he was cared for and loved. I've felt terrible for so long about what happened to him. And my poor sister too."

Doc looked on anxiously, ready to close the deal, "It's an incredible story. Really astounding. Well, let me ring Janet and you can finally see your dog again. If you don't mind, Joe, I need to talk to Eloise. Janet will take care of you downstairs. And of course, if we can be of help to you in the future, you have my number."

Joe rose and so did Eloise. He gave Doc a firm handshake, but Eloise simply nodded to Joe with a weak smile.

Once the door was closed, Eloise slumped back down in her chair. And Doc did the same. She felt hollow. It was done. Her dog. Her dog was going home with Joe. And now finally, she would face whatever Doc had to say to her.

She said, "You didn't tell him that I hid the flyer? Or, um, anything else?"

Doc shook his head, "Why would I? He has his dog back. All because of the reporter interviewing you on TV when Prince tackled the shop-lifter."

Eloise squinted at Doc. "He never asked why I knew his name? Or why I kissed him?"

Doc shook his head, "I expect he wonders about all that. He alluded to your head injury, as well as your mental health. I made a few apologetic noises and mentioned this was not your first concussion."

"Really?"

Doc raised his eyebrows.

Eloise said, "I guess I deserve that."

Then Eloise asked, "Is it possible he's forgotten?"

Doc's eyebrows went up higher, "Eloise, you were the only one who hit their head that day. Let's not go there."

"Thank you."

"Eloise, this time you did the right thing, hard as it was."

Eloise started to rise, but Doc said, "Sit. Please. I don't want you to go down until I'm sure Joe and Jaeger have left. And then go ride. Get a dose of equine therapy."

Eloise was amazed. As hard as it had been. Doc had not fired her. Maybe he would never feel the same about her. But even though she had lost Prince, and she had lost Whiplash, she still had a job, and she still had friends. And now she just needed to hang onto them with everything she still had left.

Eloise sat, crouched down low and still, Doc sat across from her, looking much the same. She might be like that rabbit in the grass, on that proverbial hill, waiting, waiting, until it was safe to flee, but she was not alone.

3

Traffic was horrendous. It was raining. Eloise passed her third wreck on the way to Bev's. Why was it, that every time it rained in Atlanta people crashed into each other? And why was she even driving to Bev's? It was going to go from rainy to stormy. Red was probably deadly to ride in a storm anyway. Horses didn't like the "boom-booms" any more than dogs did. But here she was, sitting in a line waiting for a cop with a flashlight with one of those red cones on the end of it, to wave her around traffic cones blocking off a crunched-up sedan.

She should have just gone home. But it would be a home without Prince in it. She wasn't ready for that yet. And then she had dinner with jellybean Ralph. Eloise did not want to see Bev or Ralph or Pinky or Betsy or anyone. They would feel sorry for her. And sympathy made it harder to be strong. Sympathy had a way of peeling back one's protective bandages, exposing all the wounds, allowing them to be probed. Ugh. No way. She needed time to recover without all the probing. She realized that she *did* want to be that little rabbit, crouched down into the grass, safe where no one could see her.

The farm gates were open when Eloise made it to the farm. Odd. They were never left open. Eloise pulled through the gates and then stopped. Should she get out and close them? The rain was coming down hard, so Eloise didn't. She pulled up to the barn and felt uneasy. She parked as close as possible and then jogged the short distance to the doors. She had not brought a raincoat.

The barn lights were off. As she walked down the aisle, she noted that it had been swept.

Eloise stopped to look at each horse as she walked. They looked content, munching hay. When she looked in at Red, the mare had a huge mouthful of hay. Red looked at Eloise with interest, but then put her head back down for another bite. Eloise was running late, but this was the first time she hadn't found Bev in the barn, waiting for her arrival.

Eloise tried to call Bev on her cell phone, but it went to message. This made her nervous. Eloise grabbed a stable towel and put it over her head and marched up the drive to Bev's house, getting soaking wet in the process.

It was a modest brick ranch house but had a large covered front porch so thankfully Eloise was out of the rain. She hung the wet towel over the railing. She knocked timidly. Eloise went to ring the doorbell, but the button was missing. She tried the door. It was unlocked.

Eloise stepped into the foyer and called out, "Bev?"

The foyer had a large ceramic fox on the hall table.

And over the fox hung a watercolor, humorous in tone, of dogs and horses sailing over a brush fence, with a fox sitting against the base of the jump, licking its paw like a cat. Two upright upholstered chairs flanked the table. the floor was black slate. There was an attractive arched opening to each room, one to a formal dining room, one to a living room, and one to a hallway.

Eloise wandered down the hallway, calling for Bev.

Bev answered, "In here. I fell asleep or I'd a called you."

Bev was in bed. Eloise was surprised to see that Bev had a large plush animal in the bed with her. A fox with a bushy tail.

"Are you sick?"

"Naw. I just get these spells from time to time. I'll be right as rain by tomorrow."

"Oh, good. Who did the barn?"

"Caroline called in Miguel. He come on back and did 'em early."

"Why didn't you call me? I'd have done the chores for you."

"Cause Miguel don't mind, and you live down there in Buckhead, and a big storm is on the boil. You got Prince still?"

"No. Joe took the dog. By the way, Prince's name was Jaeger."

"Jaeger?" She sniffed, "Ain't that a foreign name?"

Eloise nodded. "German. Prince was bred in Germany."

Bev said, "I thought he was a mutt. Didn't know that

dog was some special breed, and you'all went and cut his nuts off! Well, what's done is done."

"I guess that's my fault too."

"I've done worse."

"I loved that dog."

"Yeah, well, in my long life, I've let more than one love slip away."

There was a moment of silence, then Eloise sighed, "Prince isn't the only one I've let slip away. Jock's never going to let me have Whiplash. Now he says she's in foal. He had no right to do that."

Bev frowned, "If he's keeping your mare, then he ain't never going to get Red neither."

Eloise smiled, "That's what I told him. But, Bev, he was going to give you a lot of money for her. Maybe you should reconsider."

Bev grabbed her stuffed fox, tucked it against her side and then stroked its' tail, She muttered, "Money only matters when you ain't got enough of it."

Eloise pulled up the little chair that sat next to Bev's bedside table and sat down. "But you were going to sell Red."

"What do I need with that five-year-old firecracker? Besides, when Jock called, I pulled that number out of my ass. I figure he's got some sponsor he's soaking anyway."

Eloise put her elbows on her knees and her chin in her hands. She had nothing to say. But the word "incorrigible" did pop into her head. Jock and Bev both, well they had a good handle on each other. Better than good.

Eloise sat back up and asked, a bit shyly, "So, you have enough? Money, I mean?"

"Sold off the back half of this farm years ago so's I could feather my nest. I had some young friends that told me to invest it in some stock called Yahoo. Well, I'm an old yahoo myself. Kind of liked the name. It's done mighty good."

That made Eloise sit up taller. "Good grief! I hope you thanked them."

"Done what I could for 'em."

Eloise saw out Bev's window that the wind had picked up. Soon she heard the roll of thunder. Bev read her thoughts.

"Best not tempt the devil. You go on home. Not sure why you made the drive."

"Oh, Bev, I forgot to mention, your front gate was open when I came in, can I at least close it on my way out?"

Bev nodded. "Miguel's gonna' hear from me. He knows better. Might as well pull the doors on the barn too. Weather's going to get rough."

Eloise rose and looked at Bev in the big bed with her stuffed fox. She didn't really know this woman, but she sure as heck could see she and a wily old fox had a lot in common.

Eloise asked, "Can I get you something to eat? A drink? Turn on your TV for you? Anything?"

Bev smiled, "That's real sweet. But no. The one thing you can do for me is drive slow. Driving down 400 in bad weather is a test of nerve. Watch out for the idiots."

"I hope you feel better tomorrow. I'll be back."

"And I'll have the indoor ready. It's been dragged and I got them sprinklers working last week so you and Red won't choke on the dust. Maybe Miguel will take a broom to them cobwebs if I give him a kick in the butt. I ain't gettin on no ladders no more."

Eloise had an urge to give Bev a kiss on her cheek, or at least squeeze her hand before she left. But she didn't. Instead, she put the chair back and gave a small wave.

There had been no pity party. Eloise had lost the hollow feeling inside. Bev's matter-of-fact tone paired with her self-deprecation, well, it didn't let Eloise off-the-hook, but didn't rub her nose in it either. It was already an accepted fact that Eloise had messed up. Eloise had suffered a loss. Bev knew about both of those things. They had plenty of reasons to feel a kinship, even though they were not blood relations.

But even as Eloise felt better about her own recent loss of Prince, she wondered about Bev's "spells" and if they were serious. Bev was an old woman who evidently suffered "spells" whatever that meant. Eloise realized she cared for this tough-as-old-shoe-leather horsewoman. She needed her rides on Red. But maybe she needed her time with Bev just as much or more. There had been no ride tonight. Eloise had barely even looked at Red. But the drive, treacherous as it had been, and would still be getting back to Buckhead, had been worth it.

Now she felt obligated to have dinner with Ralph. Duty called. Ralph had been a childhood friend of her mother's and had managed her mother's financial affairs.

That had evidently included more than a few contentious rounds with Jock during the divorce. And then along with the bulk of the estate, her mother it seemed had bequeathed her Ralph, the jelly-bean addict. Ralph managed her money, and deposited money into her account, and now that she was 21, he was officially her financial advisor, rather than her mother's. Ralph was odd, but Ralph was okay. And now that she had seen Bev, Eloise felt calmer. She could manage to chit-chat and eat dinner with Ralph. Besides, she really did like Salmon.

* * *

Ralph poured Eloise a glass of wine and then donned purple rubber gloves.

"Murtagh and I both love grilled Salmon, but you know it often has those tiny bones, and I live in horror of him getting one stuck in his throat. So, I carefully feel through each bit that goes into his bowl."

Eloise took a sniff of her wine before sampling it. It had a nice mild fragrance that matched the flavor. 'This is good."

Ralph had called her as she had made her way down the highway and said, "I won't take no for an answer." Why did people say that? It was pushy, wasn't it? But she had simply told him she was on her way. So, here she was taking a sip of wine while watching Ralph, who looked ridiculous wearing purple rubber gloves, finger bits of expensive grilled salmon he was going to feed his dog.

Said dog was sitting erect, staring at Eloise. Pinky had done a bang-up job on his hairdo. Although Eloise thought the cut of his eyebrows made his gaze seem like he was scowling at her.

Ralph was chattering away happily. "Murtagh gets the full menu, well, I don't feed him the dessert course. But he does get the roasted sweet potatoes and asparagus. I put his dish down right when we sit down too."

Eloise wondered briefly if Ralph would add a garnish.

Ralph did take off the rubber gloves before serving the plates. Regardless, when they sat down at the dining table, set with flowers and candles, he said, "Beware of bones, Eloise since your portion has not undergone the glove treatment."

Eloise could see Murtagh in the kitchen, nose down in his bowl, polishing off his dinner. Then as she began to sample it herself, she could hear Murtagh getting a drink. Soon, the dog was stationed between them.

Ralph addressed his dog, "Now young man, simply take a seat and enjoy the conversation."

Murtagh sighed and made himself comfortable, his stubby front legs pushed out in front, his chin resting on them.

The salmon was good. The roasted veggies too.

"This is delicious. Thank you. I seldom cook for myself, although I ate well while in Virginia."

Ralph replied, "You're welcome. I'm sorry about all that, Eloise. I mean, with the dog and the horse."

Eloise shrugged dismissively.

Ralph pursed his lips and there was a long pause that began to make Eloise uncomfortable. She did not want this man she hardly knew to play "Uncle Ralph."

Eloise had not realized how hungry she had been. Bev had done her a world of good, and now the food and wine were also fortifying her. Now she wanted to go home, get into her pajamas, then into bed, and read. She wanted to read Louisa Robert's journal. But first she had to stay a polite amount of time enjoying her dinner, because, well, because her mom would have wanted that. But the tension of the day, the drive, the meal, the wine, well, Eloise was tired.

Ralph said, "Jock and I never liked each other. That doesn't mean I was unable to see his charms."

Ralph twirled the stem of his glass.

He continued, "When Jock entered any room, he was the center of attention. I can't imagine what that must feel like. So handsome, tall, and confident. If you could bottle that and sell it, oh, my, wouldn't you be rich?"

Eloise nodded in agreement.

He continued, "Everyone enjoyed having Jock join their gatherings. He even had the men enchanted. That's a trick, isn't it? The women thought he was handsome and funny and daring, and the men thought he had everything all figured out. Why do people assume that someone who is charismatic is also wise?"

Eloise said, "Because things always did work out for Jock. They still do."

Ralph frowned, "That's not exactly right, Eloise. Jock ran out of luck. Elly, well, I think they did have some good years, certainly. She enjoyed building the farm and of course she loved you to the moon and back and that's what her life became about; you. But Jock had to start over from scratch because that's about all she let him walk away with."

Eloise made eye contact with Ralph. "She let him walk away with my horse. She let him walk away from me. And the thing is, he went. He didn't fight for me."

Ralph looked like he was going to cry. "Eloise, know this, you were adored by both your parents. And by adored, I mean loved, cherished, wanted. The reason they stayed together as long as they did."

Eloise said, "Jock's luck has not run out, by the way. He has this amazing ability to turn his back and walk away from stuff. He's made a new life in Ireland. He's landed on his feet. He's planned his future. I think he considers me taken care of financially, so he's looking after himself like he always does."

Ralph tipped his head and gave the wine glass another turn. "Hmmm. I suppose there is some truth to that. But, Eloise, there's something else. I have a confession to make. Because of my history with Jock, I thought to make further inquiry on the horse you want returned, Whiplash."

"Thanks. You didn't need to do that. I already got the bad news. Jock dropped the bombshell that he has bred her. She's in foal. Of course, he had no right to do that without my permission. Now he insists on keeping her there, and he tried to tell me she's not ride-able anymore and needs to be retired."

"Hmmm. I suppose that could all be true. But there's a bit more that I know for certain is true. I didn't want to mention any of this at the clinic. I contacted Jock's employer, the farm owner, there in Ireland. She is a big fan of Jock's. She couldn't stop bragging about him. Her daughter rode Whiplash to some sort of championships. Anyway, I told her I was managing the assets of your mother's estate, and I was unclear about the ownership of said horse. Sorry to be so bold, but I had a hunch."

Eloise was in awe of Ralph's hutzpah but said nothing.

Ralph said, "She told me that they had been leasing the mare from Jock, but after those championships they bought the horse. I asked if she could fax me a copy of the bill of sale for my records, as well as a copy of the horse's papers."

"Oh my God! And did she?"

"Yes. Jock was listed as the owner-of-record on all the horse's paperwork. Eloise, neither your name or Elly's name appear anywhere. And of course, this woman is now the legal owner."

Eloise leaned forward in her chair; her face felt slack. "The reason Jock can't send my horse back is because neither one of us owns her?"

"That appears to be the case. And since I can find nothing to prove you, or your mother, were ever the owner-of-record, I don't see a way forward."

* * *

Eloise finally made it back to the townhome. It was so quiet inside the house that even the sound her keys made as she dropped them on the kitchen counter seemed unnaturally loud. There on the kitchen floor was Prince's rubber toy, the one she used to stuff with peanut butter to keep him occupied while she sat at her computer. Eloise picked it up along with his bowls. Eloise dumped the water out, and then took all three items into the laundry room, placing them on top of the tub that held his kibble. Prince's things, few as they were, had joined the museum of lost pets in Eloise's laundry room alongside Whiplash's tack. Eloise went to her bedroom to collect his bed, that he rarely used, and a squeaky toy. Then it was done. She closed the door to the laundry room, feeling very sorry for herself, but still dry-eyed.

Pinky had been right about Prince, about her, in ways that Eloise had not wanted to admit. She had needed Prince to "heal her." And in many ways, he had. But having to give him up, well, it was a new wound. She wanted him back. And in some secret corner of her mind, she believed she would still get him back, because stories should have happy endings. But that was the old Eloise, the child Eloise, the Eloise steeped in romantic fantasy. She was trying hard now to be the adult Eloise, clear-eyed, honest and trustworthy. But although she was doing it, being a full-fledged responsible adult, facing her losses head-on, she still badly wanted her Prince. She still wanted Whiplash. Honestly, she badly wanted her mommy and daddy, too. Irrational. But feelings have so little to do with being rational.

Eloise checked her email, hoping for a new journal entry to settle her. She was relieved to find an email from Dabs.

Eloise,

Betsy brought me up to speed. I'm so sorry about Prince. I can only imagine how you are feeling.

I have been working hard on the transcriptions. Please let me know when you've read this one.

I haven't been up to the cemetery since you left. I started to go up there with Dude but found I hadn't the heart to turn him up the trail.

I feel a stranger in my own house these days, an interloper, and rather lonely since you and Betsy left. I think I may get a dog.

Dabs

Poor Dabs. Eloise finally felt the tears flow down her face. She had not wanted a pity-party. Not one with guests. But crying while alone, reading someone else's words was something she felt totally comfortable doing. Even if she was mostly crying for herself.

Eloise now wanted nothing but to be asleep, to be flat and face down into her soft pillow.

But before she did that, she would read Louisa's latest journal entry.

* * *

August 25th, 1780

*Priscilla has been breeding. It was soon no secret that
the joining of Sammie and Priscilla was formally
acknowledged, although among the servants this
meant little but new sleeping arrangements. Sammie moved back into his sick cabin here at the home
quarter and Priscilla was moved from her pallet in
the kitchen house to join him. The two got the cabin
cleansed, under Aunt Bess' direction by the appli-
cation of lye soap and scalding water and scrubbed
down with brooms and brushes. The Major did aid,
and little Henry gamely toted the hot water from the
wash pot in the yard. The chimney smokes terrible
and will need repair. While all is now sodden within the cabin, it is sunny and hot as Hades all day
long, so it shall air out and be dry in no time.*

*I caught Aunt Bess scolding Buck once again
upon the subject of trespass. Whether he obeys her
directives I cannot say. I shall leave that topic there.
He shall soon be away. Buck is now a man in search
of an army. Who knows where he shall find his
brothers-in-arms nowadays, but he will not tarry
here much longer.*

*General Gates has been a disaster. One thousand
men taken prisoner at Camden and the entirety of
the artillery now in the hands of Cornwallis. It is*

only due to Father's staying hand that Buck is not among them. Dear Lord, why are such calumnies sent upon us! We need a southern man to protect our home country, not some dandy from the north. "Granny Gates" they call him. I say that Granny needs to retire to his rocking chair post-haste.

Father has taken to long talks with the Major upon the back porch in the evening to catch what breeze they may. The days are long now and the porch cooler than the house. I open my bedroom window and listen. Tonight, they spoke of how the British provision their army through pillaging. The villains take what they will as prizes of war and officers turn a blind eye. They descend like a swarm of locusts, oft leaving the farmers bereft of any way to survive the coming winter. The Major warned that once an army moves through, you will not be able to find a squirrel in a tree or a fish in the streams. But worse still, this Cornwallis who is now occupying the Carolinas is reportedly a cruel man. The monster Tarleton of whom we hear is merely this man's wicked accomplice.

I nearly revealed myself with a gasp when the Major confessed that should the armies come this far West; every riding horse would be taken. The Major had heard in the Barracks tales of young horses, even mares and foals, having their throats cut in the fields, simply to teach the rebels not to defy the King. This did make my blood turn cold. The Major stated this in tones most ordinary.

But here we are on the frontier, so far west that General Washington thought it a place to secure the prisoners of war from recapture. My head calmed my heart. Considering this fact, the Major's talk seemed alarmist.

I was pouring water from my pitcher upon a handkerchief to dampen my arms and face before trying to lie down in my shift. The open window and door provided some movement of air, and I was tying my hair up off my neck when I heard a cough behind. I turned to find Aunt Bess too, standing in her own shift her hair up in her cap.

She said, "I suppose you, like I, were listening."

She came closer and whispered. "We must prepare for the worst you know."

"What does that mean, Auntie?"

Aunt Bess said, "If the enemy should make it this far West, they will do so to capture Jefferson. He is too juicy a prize. And we my dear, are proximate."

I answered, "Jefferson will not sit upon his little mountain and wait to entertain them."

Aunty said, "All will be laid waste in the hunt, regardless."

I stated with more authority than I felt, "The reason we house prisoners of war here in Albemarle, is that our dear General Washington believes this to be a site where recapture is unlikely."

Aunt Bess nodded, "Still, I will ask your father to have some furniture constructed with secret shelves. Clever ones mind you, nothing so ordinary

*as we've seen from England. And we must dig a
new root cellar and disguise it. I will not starve
next winter nor see our servants starve to feed the
King's soldiers."*

*"Aunt Bess, mayhap we drive our best stock to
High Meadows if the danger approaches? We could
not drive them all, but we could take ourselves,
our home servants, and a selection of our best stock.
Father could drive the wagon with Isaac, and we
could leave the overseer in charge until the danger is
past."*

*Aunt Bess snorted in indignation at the thought.
"It would take the devil himself to make me seek
refuge at that place of horrors."*

*I was surprised at her vehemence. Aunt Bess oft
joked about the lack of love between herself and her
Carter relations, but this was no joking tone.*

* * *

Eloise read the journal entry several times. Then she
looked at her watch. Every inch of her was exhausted. It
seemed like a week since she had left in the morning for
work, her dog, yes, damn it, her dog bouncing happily
around her. She had no other heartbeat now to help
regulate her heartbeat, no warm soft creature to pull
against her chest. She thought of Bev and her stuffed
fox, something to at least hold onto. She had nothing.

Eloise got into her pajamas and into bed. The room
had an odd mechanical hum she did not recognize. The

bed looked foreign. The sheets felt cold. She was observing her surroundings instead of being in them. A weird sense of dislocation. It must be from exhaustion. Nothing looked familiar. This townhome was still not home, and this room had been her mother's room, not hers. But she'd been using it for a very long time now. Still, on some level, she was a squatter here. An interloper. For some reason, Eloise opened the top drawer of her bedside table, strangely, she had never done that before.

And in that drawer was a framed photo, placed face down. Eloise turned it over and recognized it. It had once sat on her mother's desk at the farm. There was that pain in her chest again, that familiar wave of dizziness. She gazed at the photo of her parents. They were so young and beautiful. Their smiles radiated with genuine happiness. Eloise placed it on the bedside table where she would see it.

Eloise turned off her light, and stretched out on her stomach, face down. The bed seemed to float off the floor and slowly turn in the air as she sank into the pillow and mattress and began to drift into sleep.

Her last cogent thoughts were of Jock. Oh, Jock! Jock could have returned Whiplash to her after her mother had died, but instead had used her horse to feather his own nest. In more ways than one. But those were her feelings. She needed to be rational. Jock needed a job, and Jock needed money. And she could hear Jock saying, "Lulu, if someone offers you big money for a horse, you take it. Some opportunities only knock once on your door, and then they're gone forever."

Jock always answered the door. She vowed that one knock he would never need to answer, ever, was hers. Eloise, like her mother before her, made a pledge to herself. She was done loving the living, breathing Jock. It was just too hard. She would love the memory of Jock, but not the man. Eloise would simply keep her distance, because of course, Jock had chosen that distance by design already.

She only felt a momentary pang for his newly acquired, soon-to-be stepdaughter, Suzy. But then she remembered the kid had enjoyed her good horse, would enjoy more good horses under Jock's expert guidance. Suzy would have her golden hour. Until Jock heard another knock at the door.

4

Eloise woke up before the sun and rolled over, reaching for her dog who was not there. For one indulgent moment her eyes filled with tears of self-pity. Then she lectured herself to get a grip and get up, wash her face, and shore up the courage she needed to just get on with it. She turned on her bedside light, and there was the photo, her parents smiling at her. It did not hurt this time to look at it. There they were. Jock's smiling face telling her to not pussy foot, her mom encouraging her to be a part of the bigger world out there. And so, Eloise got dressed and decided to just go to the clinic, no matter if it was hours too early.

The stars and the moon were still visible as she pulled into the parking lot. She fed the animals, then did her cleaning, then settled into her quiet time in the lounge. The coffee warmed her, and a much-needed feeling of peace came over her, as she opened an email from Dabs.

Hi Eloise,

I made a visit to Henry. His granddaughter has

*moved in to help care for him. She told me he had
been doing poorly, but evidently, he perked up for
my visit. That made me feel good for coming, and
guilty for not coming enough. Betsy was right. He
gets confused about the present, but his mind is clear
about the past.*

*I was shocked by how his condition had deteri-
orated. He seemed ageless to me for so many years.
But I've lost track of time too. Henry was Mom's essential man. I think of him as someone who could do
whatever needed doing. And even toward the end
of her life he was at her beck and call. He was not
only good with the animals, but a shade tree me-
chanic. He learned his skills at his father's knee. He
shares my last name, by-the-way. But so far back he
cannot say where the lines crossed, as surely as they
must have crossed. Although, slaves were often called
by the name of their masters, even if unrelated. But
Henry's features and complexion tell a more likely
story and he considers himself "kin" and always has,
and we have always felt the same.*

*I asked Henry if he knew anything about the
slave graveyard. His first reaction was to say, "Why
you asking about that?"*

*I told him about what we had found there, in-
cluding the field stones and the angel we unearthed
pointing toward heaven.*

*You should have seen his bushy white eyebrows
shoot up. "They ain't going to be no ways pleased to
see a white man traipsing on their sacred ground."*

61

I was stunned. "Henry, you knew all about it? Mother knew all about it?"

He made a grunt. He said, "Ivy Creek been around long enough to have a passel of secrets. I ain't saying I knows the half of 'em. Don't get too many ideas 'bout that."

I said, "Mother and Daddy always kept the old family cemetery taken care of. If they knew about the slave graveyard, why in the good Lord's name did they let it go wild and get covered up with earth and leaves?"

Henry looked me full in the eyes and said, "It be full of haints. Everybody who know anything 'bout it, know that. Long before your Mama's time it was given over to the poor souls resting there. Nobody living knows who down there, they all from slavery days, but we never had any trouble from 'em. Daddy told me weren't always so. Best let them be, Mister Dabs."

I then asked Henry if he didn't think there were a couple of "haints" in the white man's cemetery. And he took my question seriously. He said, "I 'spect there are. But that stone wall is there to keep 'em from leaving. Keep 'em from going down that hill and troubling the poor souls they troubled in life."

Then I said, playfully, mind you, "Or keep those down the hill from getting in."

Henry was serious when he answered, "Spect you right about that too. Them days were kept by

*violence and fear. Lordy, lordy, justice can't sleep
forever. That's Jefferson said that."*

Well, you can imagine that made me sit up
straighter.

I asked Henry if he had studied Thomas Jefferson. He grinned and said, "Ain't I born and bred
here?"

Then Henry proudly told me that he had a
grandson who just started at UVA. I listened to
him brag on his children and grandchildren. He
had five kids of his own, and he has a huge number
of grandchildren. His wife has been gone a long
time.

Henry asked me some questions then. He wanted
to know if Miz Freddy was gettin' on okay. He said
she wasn't right in her mind last time he saw her.
Damn. He had forgotten she had passed. I told him
as gently as I could, and he started to cry. He apologized for crying. Nearly made me cry too. But what
consolation could I offer him? I told him how I was
fixing up the house. He seemed genuinely interested.
I detailed how I had fixed the sagging floors at great
expense. All the plumbing and electric were up to
snuff. I told him I had moved most of the clutter up
to the attic space and the house was finally neat and
clean again. Henry said he wanted to come see for
himself.

He said, "Miz Freddy, I can't believe she went
on before me. You know, I be seven year older. I
knew her all her life. Except when she went off to*

that school. Took her horse with her. Did you know that?"

I told Henry about the journals. He wanted to know if they were Miz Freddy's words. And I had to tell him they were the words of a Miss Louisa Roberts. He said he did not know who that was. He didn't know Roberts were any kin of "our'n."

He then said that old house was full of stories and secrets, and he thought Miz Freddy had written down some, 'cause she was always scribbling.

I have no idea what he was talking about.

Enjoy the attached transcription. Fascinating.

Dabs

* * *

October 7, 1780

Buck is finally gone in search of the Continental Army. Granny Gates has fled to North Carolina to lick his wounds after the disaster of Camden. We hear that Cornwallis has followed him and settled into the town of Charlotte. Near in name to our own Charlottesville. What finally made father release Buck to the fight was Morgan coming out of retirement. The old wagoner has been given a command. Morgan is someone father cannot fault as a soldier and a Virginian. He may be rough, *but he's smart, a good shot, and will look after his men. Auntie commenced to knitting stockings. She gave a lecture before us all on the importance of dry feet. She delivered it with great authority as if battles were won by stockings. Buck left home with his bag bulging with stockings. Father became tender as soon as the decision was made, touching his son on his arm or shoulder at every opportunity for days on end. Even I had a tear in my eye at our farewells. Buck and I disagree on nearly everything. I do not approve of his hard use of our horses, but he is my brother. He was not always the man I struggle against today. He was a boy once. I remember the day Mother died, although I would like to forget it, because no one was as visibly distraught as Buck. Weeping does not describe his tortured agony. Mother's death did change Buck. I think his grief wrung him dry. Like a river gone to silt and stone.*

Now that we are without Buck's agitations, I feel the air itself is calmer. Priscilla and Sammie have settled into their cabin, although the chimney is not right yet. Isaac and Henry and Lady Jane live in their cabin, and Major Schmidt and Cleopatra have quarters to themselves. Cleopatra's kits are now relocated at the barracks yet pay social calls to their mother on occasion. In this calm I find myself drawing again. Any creature who is still for longer than five minutes I make a subject of study. I fear drawing interferes with the keeping of this record. *I nearly forgot to report the shocking news of the day in the treason of General Arnold. I fear this indicates our ship is sinking and rats will jump upon any floating timber rather than drown. Major Schmidt and I have worn out our tongues on the topic.*

Aunt Bess has got the field hands up to the house to dig her hidden root cellar. It is to be disguised above as a privy. She will post a sign on the door warning of venomous snakes within. She thinks herself the wiliest vixen.

Auntie awaits her new furniture which has not yet met her design requirements. She has sworn the cabinet maker to secrecy. All this seems to me to be extreme measures. But Aunt Bess appears in my doorway some nights with furrowed brow unable to sleep. She sees this as a time of preparation. She frets over what we may have forgotten. She has asked for father to give Isaac and Sammie weapons. She made a right good argument for them being armed. Those two can use the guns to hunt as well as for defense. Father obliged. We do trust them. Father trusts them. We need not, dare not, tell anyone. Sammie was given Buck's old rifle. Isaac was given Father's. Father takes the two of them to the woods for prac-tice. This has helped to settle Aunt Bess. Father says Sammie is a right good shot and Isaac is improving.

Beast has got a terrible case of vermin and Henry did carve a fine-tooth comb. It took him many tries. But it is well done. He sits for hours

with the comb and a dish of vinegar to kill the pests
and when he has done Beast, he works on his Lady
Jane. Henry's violin playing has reached the level of
nearly tolerable. Major Schmidt beams with pride
as if Henry was a prodigy.

This is about as lovely a fall as we see in Albemarle. The foals will soon be weaning. The mares
moved where the little ones cannot see them. The
babes will scream and run, but then they will settle
and seek comfort from each other.

Hog killing time approaches, which I hate but
admit I do not shrink from greedily eating ham at
table. The apple crop came in aplenty, and father
puts up a special barrel with my name upon it,
because I love them so. Beauty shares in my bounty. Buck will have none of them this season and he
loves them same as I. I will think of Buck when
Aunt Bess bakes them into pies. Buck does love her
apple pie. He counts those orchards as his own. I do
wonder when next Buck will see them.

* * *

October 17, 1780

I have been beyond indolent of late. I ride and
I draw, and I eat apples. The Major and I with
Henry along use whatever ruse we can to lengthen
our training rides. The air is sweet and cool, and

the harvest done, and we tarry. We ride past the young horse field and admire and discuss the best features of the weanlings. Soon the colts will need to be sorted from the fillies. They have formed naughty gangs that torment the fillies. We do not geld our non-breeding males until they are well past yearlings. Father believes too soon cut makes for weaker development. We ride down to visit with the overseer, chat about the harvest and the mill. We have even dismounted to taste the butter at the dairy. The Major takes interest in the details of our enterprises and enjoys the patter with the servants. He even stopped to admire some fancy chicken seen strutting about. My time with the Major is held dear. Dearer for rumors that barracks may be abandoned, should the enemy come up the James. This is old talk that I have not, until now, given much credence. I had thought to have the Major for the duration of the conflict. I admit my motives are selfish. He has made our days something fine. Now that Buck has left to be a soldier, I find everyone here vies for his attention. And so, I linger in our rides while Henry and I have him to ourselves. If he must be moved to be kept safe from liberation by British forces, I have no power to change that action. I try not to dwell on it.

We have received news from Buck. Buck located Dan Morgan who has claimed Buck and his rifle for his own company. Father and Aunt Bess whooped with joy at this. Morgan has removed to a town called Hillsboro. So, it matters not who Washing-

ton gives the command now. Buck will answer to
Morgan. We are relieved to see Gates replaced. Bess
remarked, sagely I think, that there will be no large
action until the new commander, whoever he be,
is settled in. It's a fine fall, but winter comes apace.
Auntie stated that Buck will not see action this year.
Hearing Aunty say such would make him spitting
mad, were he to hear it. Father quietly agrees with
his sister.

Between Henry and I we have "soothed the
savage Beast" and I am not referring to Henry's
violin playing. Henry plucked the vermin off Beast
with his comb, and I bathed the dog with my finest
soap. I then rinsed the dog with a tea I brewed with
ground rosemary. This is something I was told to
try by the Major. I declare it seems to have worked.
In addition, my friend's natural aroma is much
improved. If the pests try to take me next, I will use
the same concoction upon myself.

Priscilla has taken up singing. She sings while
she stirs the washpot. She sings while she works
the dough. She sings while she plucks the birds for
our supper. Her songs are not loud, just constant.
We control our smiles as we pass each other. It is, at
least, preferable to seeing her darting about like a
scared cat or throwing the apron over her head and
wailing. I suppose her present condition may have
something to do with this change in demeanor.

The Major has also now taken on teaching Hen-
ry his letters. I asked father if this was not unwise.

69

Plenty of folk around here would declare that a let-
tered negro would forge papers for nefarious reasons.
Father brushed off my concerns. When I brought
them to the Major, he looked disappointed in me
for even suggesting the dangers. How, he asked,
could we claim the negro inferior in intellect, if we
starved their intellect by design? He then went on
to insult me by asking, how we could claim they had
stronger body odor when we gave them no soap, or
that they perspired more when we put them into
the hot sun all day long whilst we sought shade?
I answered him with no ire. His questions rang
with truth and justice. But I also told him that I
never wanted to see a hair on Henry's head harmed
by jealous men, who would not stand to see him
bettered, because they did not have the same intellect
or gifts as our Henry. Major Schmidt nodded, then
said, "Should fear be an obstacle to justice?"

All I could say was, "Few can surmount such
an obstacle. We are not all warriors." I disappoint
him. I cannot help it. He nodded in acceptance of my
answer. But he continues to teach Henry his letters.

* * *

Eloise had just finished reading the journal entries, and
was still mulling over them *and* Dabs' letter about Henry, when Janet arrived, and then Suzy. They came into
the lounge and filled their coffee mugs. Neither one had
said anything to Eloise about her troubles, but Eloise

felt their pity. It was obvious in the way they looked at her, the tip of an eyebrow, stolen sideways glances at each other, the tone in their voices. Clearly, they thought she had gone 'round the bend to keep the dog. They knew she had been deceitful. Perhaps they gossiped mostly about her romantic fantasy about the guy in the flier. Maybe Janet had circulated gossip about her financial status. Eloise was a loopy rich kid with a horse in Ireland, a college degree, but one who could only get a job scooping poop because she was damaged goods. Or maybe they said none of those things.

Self-pity (and a good imagination) is its own hair shirt.

So, Eloise put in her earbuds and listened to a new book from her reading list on Jefferson and waited for Pinky to arrive.

This one was pointedly apropos to the journals. It was about the triangle of Jefferson, Sally Hemings, and Jefferson's daughter, Patsy. The premise was great, but Eloise thought the book so far, was loaded with historical inaccuracies. She wasn't going to be able to stomach the poor writing. This triangle deserved a more capable author. At least in Eloise's opinion. Both Sally and Patsy spent their lives orbiting Jefferson, neither one necessarily by choice. Sally Hemings and Patsy both outlived Jefferson. Both were present at Monticello when he died. Patsy left enough of a record to be an historical figure of interest. Sally was a character one could only speculate about with no record, no voice of her own. Well, what the record did show is that on the day of his death Jefferson, "called in his domestic workers." His last words were uttered to them, not to his daughter or other white relations, at four am, on July 4, 1826. He never spoke again and died at 12:50pm later that same day.

Jefferson's last words, words that could have included words for Sally, were never recorded. What were they, and to whom were the words addressed? Instead, the words we know as Jefferson's last words were, "Is this the fourth?" Those words were uttered on July 3rd, not 4th. He was told "no", but it would soon be. And he hung on until it was.

We, as a country, know that Jefferson and Adams both died on July 4th, 1826, the fiftieth anniversary of the Declaration of Independence. Fifty years prior was the day we became a nation. They used the power of their formidable will to live to see that notable anniversary before granting God his due. Amazing story.

Yet, more poignant to Eloise was the knowledge that Sally Hemings was called into the room along with the other "domestics" to hear Jefferson's final words upon this earth. That fact had been obscured. Such is the importance of who writes history. Legacy is often a carefully crafted tale. Eloise asked herself, "Who writes your story, Sally Hemmings?" And the answer is "No one." The story of Sally was never meant to be told. Not by anyone who cared about Jefferson's legacy.

Eloise was folding towels deep in thought when she had a wet towel land next to her on the top of the washer. She looked up to see Pinky shaking her head. "Earth to Eloise!"

Eloise reluctantly hit the pause button and pulled out her ear buds. She had somehow missed the fact that Pinky was there and had started work.

"Look, I get that you are burrowed in, but the dogs and I are running out of topics of conversation. What's going on?"

"Oh, man, sorry. I guess I was in a sort of trance. What's going on? Okay. Well. Let's see. I had some interesting stuff from Dabs about the history of his plantation. Plus, I haven't been contributing to Betsy's page on Extreme Readers for ages, so I'm trying to get caught up and participate more there by reading a new book and reporting back to the group on it. Super interesting stuff."

Pinky shook her head and used her hands to mime someone talking. "Eloise, you're talking but not saying *anything*. What's going on in *your* life. Not the lives of fictional characters in some story."

"Not fictional. Historical."

"And you? Are you fictional or historical?"

Eloise smiled, "I'm not historical yet. I have to die first."

"Can we not do that anytime soon?"

"I have nothing planned."

"Well, praise the Lord on that one. I see that to get anything out of you, I may need to ply you with truth serum."

"You have truth serum?"

"No, but I know where to find some and I intend to administer a dose to you tonight. You and me. Bud can stay home with the puffballs. After you get back from riding that bottle-rocket you call a horse. Tonight. Call me. I'll be waiting. No excuses."

Eloise simply nodded and said, "Yes ma'am."

Eloise stuck her earbuds back in. But she didn't re-start the audiobook. She marveled at the fact that she suddenly was getting one-on-one dinner invites. That was something to ponder. She found she couldn't focus anymore on her book. So, she just walked around the rest of the day with the buds in.

* * *

When Eloise got to the barn after work, she was re-lieved to see Bev who acted as if her "spell" had never happened. She was full of energy, telling Eloise to pick up the pace and take Red to the indoor arena.

Eloise did a "lick-and-a-promise" grooming job and a speedy tack-up. She then led Red into the small in-door. Today it was not only dragged but watered. The lights were on, and someone had washed down the mir-rors that lined the short end. The rafters still sported dust laden cobwebs that hung down like flags. Well, it was still a vast improvement. There was a plastic green mounting block in the corner too. Eloise led Red over and snugged up the girth. Bev, who had followed her, stopped her up short and handed her a longe line. It was stiff and full of knots that would never be undone as they had nearly petrified.

Bev said, "It'd be too easy to hop on up, but she still

needs her twirl, even though you two are on best of terms. She can't help herself. Remember she missed her ride yesterday, had a shorter than normal turn-out, and those storms make 'em anxious. Bet they didn't sleep good neither."

Eloise smiled, "She seems so calm."

"That's when they get ya'. Never get too comfortable."

Eloise unbuckled the reins, tying them to the girth, not too tight just as Bev had shown her. Then Eloise sent the mare out on the circle. Red trotted around lazily.

Bev was leaning on the kickboard looking pensive, arms crossed, likely getting the back of her shirt filthy. She said, "I can see that hump in her back a mile away. She ain't going to let it go trotting. Ask for the canter and then hold on."

Eloise gave the voice command, "Caaan-ter!" with a hard "t" sound and an upward lift to the last syllable. Red launched herself in the air with a grunt at that second syllable, then hopped on her hind legs looking like Peter Cottontail hopping down the bunny trail. Eloise had a clear view of Red's bellybutton. As soon as Red's front feet found the earth, Red added flourish to the performance with a second leap. Red grunted with each hop and leap. The mare at least had the courtesy to stay out on the circle away from Eloise during her fireworks display.

Bev hollered, "Keep her moving forward now 'til she settles into a canter. I 'spect she's feeling a might better."

Eloise did as she was told and the "Red Devil" finally cantered, adding a few less dramatic bucks to finish shaking off the evil demons. Eloise held on to the stiff old line, feeling one of the petrified knots dig into her palm, and thought to herself that it was a good thing that the mare hadn't shown this side of her character up until now. This maniac she would never have tried riding. As the mare began to slow, and Eloise thought maybe she was finally safe to get on, something else set Red off. The mare's tail went straight up in the air and Red began to trot around like she was on pogo sticks. This felt even crazier than the hopping and leaping. The mare had a faraway look in her eye and Eloise realized she now had no control.

Bev hollered, "The flag is up! Reel her in if you can."

Eloise had a moment of panic because if Bev wanted her to "reel her in" there was a good reason.

Eloise steadily shortened the line, saying "whoa" in soothing tones. But it was hard to sound soothing when your voice was quaking. Red was slowing down, but her tail was still up, as she arched her neck and sent the air through her nostrils deep from her chest, making those distinctive loud "whufffff-whufffs." Jock had called it the "danger call" a horse made to alert the herd. The horses in the barn were likely standing at attention by now, wary, and nervous. Eloise got her stopped. Red stood alert and searching with her eyes for something. As if she were scanning the horizon. Except in the indoor, there was no horizon to scan. The mare whinnied loudly, and from the barn came a chorus of answering whinnies.

Eloise put her hand on the mare's neck. It was hot

and wet, the veins standing up and showing under the skin. Eloise breathed deeply. Red turning her head as if finally noticing that Eloise was there. Eloise tried to slow the quickness of her own heart and her breaths.

Bev said, "Well shit. Untie those reins and see if she settles if you hand walk her round the arena."

"Has she never worked in here before?"

"Only the first day she come here. She done better than this."

Eloise walked one direction, around and around, then walked the mare around and around the other way. Eloise felt herself getting wearier by the minute. She was thinking to herself how much work young horses were. How long and fraught with danger the whole process was. And especially when the horse was quick in their reflexes and athletic like this one. Like Whiplash. Except Eloise had weathered that long process with Whiplash. And now that horse was experienced and trained. And Eloise would never reap the rewards now that she was an older, wiser, experienced horse. The thought brought a tear to her eye. She wiped it away, hoping Bev wouldn't notice. In that moment, Eloise wondered if she could do it all again. Did she want to do it all again?

Bev interrupted these thoughts. "Get on up. She only needs twenty minutes. She'll be all right. And better still tomorrow."

Eloise felt slightly ill. As she pulled her stirrups down with a loud snap to test the mare's reaction, her hands were visibly shaking. Even though Red did not react badly, Eloise still turned to Bev and said, "I don't feel brave tonight."

"Fake it."

Bev sounded exactly like Jock. And Jock knew what he was about. She swung up. Eloise gave Red a sugar cube she dug out of her zippered pocket in her breeches. And then the mare stepped off as if nothing had happened. Horses never had agendas. They just were. They reacted and those reactions could be deadly, that was true. But, as prey animals, once the perception of danger was past, so was the reaction.

Oh, if only people could be the same. Not have agendas. Let go of the past. Eloise took a deep breath. She knew she and Red would be fine now. Those red ears had been loosened right down to the base. They bounced along with the trot; they swung a bit in the canter.

Eloise could hear Jock's laugh in her mind. "Your horse just gave herself a chiropractic adjustment. Got all those kinks out. She's good to go now."

When Eloise pulled up and scratched Red on the withers as a reward, she realized she and Red were alone. How long they had been alone she did not know. But Bev had felt good enough, sure enough about them both, to walk away.

* * *

Pinky said, "Pick your poison."

Eloise sat down and leaned back, squinting at Pinky she said, "You started without me."

"Maybe. I love this place. It's cheap, the margaritas are strong, and the chips are always hot and so is the dip."

Eloise asked, "How's the guac?"

Pinky waved a waiter over. "A big margarita for my friend, make it like the one you made me. Yum. And guac and queso and a fresh bowl of chips right out of the fryer. When he started to turn, she added, "Oh, oh, oh, you have that lime-marinated grilled shrimp? The kind with the Habanero dipping sauce? Yeah, two of those too."

Eloise grinned. "You know the menu?"

Pinky grinned back and took a slurp of her ginormous margarita. "Best Mexican food ever. Some, okay, is too hot for us gringos. But I promise you will love the grilled shrimp. The guac is the real kind made fresh, all lumpy. Not that thinned down stuff."

Eloise was presented her own ginormous margarita. The glass was nice and frosty, the rim salted. She took a bigger slurp that she meant to, and Pinky began laughing.

"Makes my heart sing to see you do that."

"It is delicious."

A hot bowl of chips arrived along with the guac and queso dip and salsa. Pinky applied a liberal shake of salt to the basket, and Eloise dove in. She realized she was both thirsty and hungry and in a few minutes the basket of chips looked like a pack of wolves had descended upon it. A fresh basket of hot chips appeared like magic. Then came the shrimp. Pinky was right. They ordered more.

Pinky said to the waiter. "Can we get fresh drinks?"

The half-consumed margaritas were replaced with frosty new ones.

Pinky was ready for her interrogation. Yup. Truth serum had been administered. Patient was stupefied and would reveal anything.

Pinky said, "You going to bring me up to speed on the latest developments?"

The weather outside even seemed in on the deal. The storms had returned. It was raining hard. Eloise was going nowhere. There would be no escape. The room got darker, the canned light shining down on Eloise like a bare bulb.

Eloise giggled. She said in her gruffest voice, "Where were you on the night of the murder?"

Pinky got the joke and laughed. "So, what? What's going on?"

"Where do I start?"

Pinky said, "I'll make it easy for you. What happened with getting your horse back from your dad. It was on, it was off, it was on again. Where are we now?"

"Well, believe it or not old jellybean Ralph did a bit of sleuthing."

Pinky raised an eyebrow. "For God's sake Eloise, spit it out."

"Ralph, said eater of jellybeans, went the extra mile for his client, that would be me, and discovered that Jock sold my horse. He's been stringing me along, making stuff up, because he couldn't fess up. Ralph even got a copy of the bill of sale."

"Wow. Can Jock do that? Legally?"

"Ralph said my name did not appear on Whiplash's papers. My name isn't on her passport. But why would it be? My parents bought the horse for me. She was my horse. But I was never the owner-of-record. I always understood that I would have her back, could have her back, when I was ready for her. But none of that was true."

"Do you think your mom knew? That you would never get your horse back."

Eloise shrugged. Then she took another sip. Her voice was raspy when she answered, although she did not feel upset, just resigned. "Yes."

"What did Bev say?"

"She has no intention of ever letting him have Red now. But when I told her he'd sold Whiplash for a chunk of change, she wasn't surprised. She said, it made sense he would wring as much money as he could from the new squeeze. He's got a retirement to fund. That's what she said."

"Bev's a trip."

Eloise nodded. "She is. I like her."

Pinky paused a moment then said with conviction, "Now I want to hear everything, and I mean everything about Dabs."

"Ah, the interrogation has changed focus."

Pinky laughed too. But she also was tenacious. Eloise would give it up.

Eloise did not even have the energy to be coy. The truth serum had done its magic. Eloise would even reveal the journal. (And feel guilty about it, swearing Pinky to silence.) Eloise let it all pour out. Pinky made sympathetic noises and ordered flan.

As the floodgates opened, as Eloise found herself telling Pinky stuff that she hadn't even told herself, well, she began to understand that Pinky wasn't going anywhere. That Pinky, for whatever reason, had not given up on her. That Pinky instead was investing herself even more in Eloise, into their friendship, and Eloise realized that she loved her for it.

5

"I don't think Buzz would want you to drive."

Pinky answered by touching her nose. She was spot on. She said, "I think I stretched it out over enough time."

Eloise examined her own state of sobriety. Likely better than Pinky's. How many margaritas had she had? Pinky had made the waiter replace drinks that were only partly consumed. On the other hand, they were big drinks.

Eloise said, "Still, I think I'll follow you home just to be extra sure you get there."

"And who is gonna' follow you home?"

"I'll call you when I get home. How about that."

Pinky said, "Deal."

Pinky had picked up the tab, refusing to let Eloise even leave the tip. She said, "It was worth every penny." Eloise made a mental note that she had accumulated quite a social debt to Pinky. Somehow, she was going to pay her back. She wasn't sure how.

It was quiet on the streets of Atlanta as they drove home. What was surprising, was how empty tenth street was along Piedmont Park. The rain had finally stopped but the streets were wet with runoff filling the gutters. Eloise was following Pinky who was driving slowly. Eloise noticed trash caught in a storm drain but did a double take when she saw the trash move. It was not trash. She put on her flashers and pulled over. She dialed Pinky to explain. Eloise ran back to the grate. There was a black plastic bag stuck in the grate. But it was torn open and sagging between the metal slats. Sitting atop the plastic was one tiny kitten, bobbling weakly. Eloise immediately scooped it up. It was grey with a skinny white blaze down its face and white on its toes. Its eyes looked newly opened, with a blue cast to them.

Eloise pulled the bag out of the grate. It was empty. The horror of the moment struck her. This little guy had been part of a litter. Whoever had put the bag down, had torn it open by design to drown the kittens as they would be swept down the storm drain in the heavy rain. The litter of kittens had gone down the drain. Except this one tiny survivor.

Pinky was now by her side. "Shit like this slays me."

Eloise handed her the kitten and found herself on her stomach, as close to the opening as possible, listening, listening. Nothing. She heard nothing but the sound of rushing water.

The others were gone. As she got up, soaked and filthy, Pinky was on the phone. The realization that the rest of the litter had drowned caused Eloise to feel weak and clammy. But as much as her heart was breaking, she knew what mattered now was to save this one.

Pinky was saying, "Yeah. Eloise will let us in. You want to come? That would be great. We'll clean it up and try some kitten milk replacer. You're the best, Doc."

Eloise said, "Doc?"

Pinky hung up. "Turn around. I'll call Buzz."

* * *

Doc took one look at the two of them and shook his head. "You two do get into trouble. Even without the dog."

Pinky said, "It's not me. But, Eloise, yeah, she's a lightning rod."

Doc went to work. The kitten got a blood transfusion and intradermal fluids. A blood donor 'volunteer" was found among the boarders.

The kitten got deloused and bathed and dried with a hair dryer while sitting on a blanket covered heating pad. Doc monitored body temp. Evidently, you never feed a cold kitten. Pinky found a neonatal kitten bottle, and the clinic had a case of KMR powder in stock. Pinky was an old hand at mixing the formula, getting it the right temperature, and testing it on her arm to check both flow and temperature. The little patient, though a bit dazed, had brightened up, and managed to latch on to the bottle while Pinky steadied the kitten's head with one finger gently on the throat so she could feel it swallow. Eloise bent down to watch. The kitten seemed to be in a trance, its tiny ears wiggling with each swallow.

Eloise said, "Horses wiggle their ears when they

swallow water. I had no idea that cats did it too. Man, it's adorable. How often does it need the bottle?"

"Pinky said, every three hours. You also have to stimulate the kitten to pee and poop and clean them up afterward, keep them warm and safe until they are weaning age and eating wet food. About five or six weeks. Since the eyes are open, I'm betting this one is only two weeks old. Being a Mama cat is a full-time job."

Eloise weakly said, "Every three hours? Oh." After a pause she added, "I can't help thinking of the rest of the litter. Was there something else we should have done that we didn't do?"

Doc said, "Don't torture yourself. As a vet, you can't let yourself dwell on all the times you fail. Because if you did, you couldn't go on. And if you don't carry on, then that's when you do fail."

Pinky said, "Well said, Doc"

Then Doc added, "That little one isn't out of the woods yet. But at least it has a fighting chance. Orphan kittens are a lot of work. You two going to take turns?"

Pinky teased Doc by looking like she was about to hand him the kitten. He put both hands up and backed up a step. "Nope. I'll do the doctoring. You lucky two get to do the nursing."

Pinky looked at Eloise. "I'll take tonight. Tomorrow night is yours Eloise."

"I don't know how to do any of this."

Pinky said, "Tomorrow you learn."

* * *

Eloise awoke earlier than ever. She felt ill. Why, oh why, had she not had a cup of "Sleepy-Time" tea before she crashed? Then she remembered she didn't have any Sleepy-time tea. Pinky was the one with the tea. What she had was gas and heartburn. She vowed never, ever, to have another Margarita. She did manage to find an old, way past expiration date, bottle of chewable antacids in her mom's medicine cabinet. Eloise chewed them slowly and belched loudly. She tried to go back to bed, but soon realized, being upright was key to avoiding heartburn. She might as well have a shower and get on with it.

By the time Eloise was out of the shower, she felt a bit better. She went on Extreme Readers to talk about her newest read and to acknowledge and comment on Betsy's latest entry. By the time she had finished her entries and caught up on comments, some by Dabs, the sky had lightened. She'd still be early.

When Eloise pulled into the parking lot, the sun was barely up, the sensor over the front porch light had not yet been triggered to turn off the light. She still had an ache in her chest. Maybe the ache was for Prince. Or maybe it was for Whiplash. Or maybe it was for her happy childhood that had ended with her parent's divorce and then her mother's death. She admitted to herself that she also missed Dabs, the characters from the journals, and Ivy Creek Plantation itself. She supposed the pain in her chest was from knowing she had only been able to save one kitten in a litter. And that she lived in a world where someone had tried to drown babies.

She shook her head. She was being a drama queen. The ache could certainly have something to do with her hangover and its subsequent heartburn.

Eloise snapped out of her obsessing when she saw a shape by the front door. The moment delivered a jolt of adrenaline to her bloodstream, her chest pain forgotten.

In the next instant, she realized nothing was there. A breeze had moved storm-bent branches, that made shadows cast by the light. Shadows. Just shadows mixed with litter from last night's big storm. She sighed and realized she needed to sweep off the porch.

She let herself in and began her routine. Feed the animals, sweep, mop, empty trash, wipe off counters, tables and sinks, check supplies. She swept the porch then went inside and made coffee. She had her cup of coffee in the stillness of the room, quiet but for a buzzing in her ears. With a full mug of coffee in her stomach, caffeine reawakening her pickled brain cells, Eloise released one final monster belch. A deep breath and Eloise considered never having another alcoholic drink in her life.

Eloise went to her email, and reread Dabs' last email about visiting Henry. His note had been niggling at the back of her mind, her thoughts unformed, until now. She wondered if Dab's mother had written all those journal entries? Were they all an invention? His mother's "scribbles?" Had the thought crossed Dab's mind? Eloise began to compose an email to Dabs. She erased it and started over. Then she erased the second one and began anew. She did not know a way to broach the topic. So, this time she started with the antics of the previous night. Eloise was smiling as she wrote of her evening with Pinky. Until she described finding the neo-natal kitten.

What about the poor little kitten? The kitten who was not yet "out-of-the-woods." She stopped writing. She knew nothing about neonatal kitten care. Eloise had a six-week commitment ahead of her. On her turn she would have a kitten attached to her that would need attending every three hours. How would that work with riding Red? Eloise made herself a second cup of coffee. She wanted Prince. Not a kitten. Tears stung her eyes. Again, her heart physically pained her. Well, that could still be heartburn.

Heartburn or not, she acknowledged she was sad. Oddly, she spoke these words out loud into the buzzing stillness of the empty room, "I'm sad." She sounded like her four-year-old self, telling her mom, and seeking her comforting words.

And weirder still, the buzzing ceased, and her mom answered her back, her voice clear and real in Eloise's mind.

"It's okay to be sad, Lulu. It's part of being a good and loving person. Always be that good and loving person that I love. Just know that sometimes you will feel sad."

In her mind, not out loud this time, Eloise said, "But I don't want to feel sad anymore, Momma."

Eloise closed her eyes and could nearly summon the feeling of being pressed against her mother's chest.

She heard, "Do something special for someone. That's the magic cure, Lulu. Do something kind for someone else. The sadness will get better, I promise."

The silence returned, still buzzing in her ear like a dropped connection on an old-fashioned telephone line. Eloise thought of the kitten. The magic cure was right in front of her.

She was going to take good care of that tiny kitten. She made a pledge to her mother.

* * *

Eloise heard Pinky before she saw her coming down the stairs with a sherpa pet carrier. The kitten was mewing, mewing, mewing. The sounds carried the edge of panic in them and triggered in Eloise the urge to grab the pet carrier from Pinky.

Pinky was talking to the kitten, "Did the alarm bell go off in your belly? No worries, your Aunty Eloise is right here."

The intercom buzzer went off. It was Janet. "Pinky, come and get your grooming client, and tell Eloise to bring the kitten up for Doc."

Pinky handed Eloise the Sherpa-bag carrier. "All yours."

Pinky set her other bag down and grabbed a leash and headed back up the stairs. Eloise wondered if Pinky felt as rough as she had this morning. Then she remembered that Pinky had gotten up every three hours all night to care for the kitten. Poor Pinky.

Doc was chatting with Suzie, a cup of coffee on the counter behind him.

Doc straightened up when she came in, "mew, mew, mew, mews" were coming in a steady rhythm from the carrier.

Doc said, "So, here's our little survivor. Did you two name it yet?"

Eloise set the carrier on the exam table. "I don't think so. I forgot to ask if it's a boy or a girl."

Suzie said, "I can ID the sex, if you want."

Eloise heard herself say, "Oh, I can do that."

Suzie looked doubtful, "It's actually not that easy."

Doc said, "If Eloise says she can do it…"

Eloise blanched, realizing she had never, ever, done such a thing. She'd only read what Henry had said to Louisa.

She said, "I've been reading an old journal and they discussed how to do it. I'm not claiming any expertise."

Suzie said, "So, you've never actually done it? Interesting."

Eloise said, "Very. The journal is from 1780. But I'm guessing nothing's changed in kitten anatomy since then."

Doc smiled. "Now I'm curious."

"It's cute. The little boy called it 'a matter of punctuation.'"

Suzie laughed, but Doc just raised his eyebrows.

Eloise continued. "So, if the kitten is on its back in

your lap, its head toward your knees, you simply lift the tail. If it's a girl, you should see a tiny exclamation point. If it's a boy, you'll see a larger punctuation mark of a colon.

Now Doc guffawed, "Let's go from theoretical to practical. You go first Eloise, but don't say what you find. Then you go next Suzie. I'll look last."

Eloise took the mewing kitten from the bag and sat down on the floor. She gave the kitten a few strokes on its back and then cupped it in her palm. She saw a flea as she rubbed its tummy but tried not to get distracted. Then she lifted its butt toward her and pulled back the tiny little tail. She saw the exclamation "slit" instantly, tiny as it was. Eloise tucked the kitten into her side and got up and handed it to Suzie.

Doc nodded, "Decisive."

Eloise nodded back, suddenly doubting herself.

Suzie took a moment longer. Then Doc took the kitten and surprisingly took the longest of all three, then he pulled open a drawer and removed the flea with a comb. He also took his stethoscope and listened to the heart and lungs, examined the eyes and ears too. He looked satisfied.

He handed Eloise the kitten, "Eloise, pink or blue?"

"Pink. Definitely pink."

Suzie looked disappointed but said. "Yeah. Pink."

Doc, put his lips like he was going to say "Buh" but changed it to "Pink!" Then "Well done ladies."

Eloise said, "I hope Pinky won't mind if I name her after the grey kitten in my read."

Suzie said, "And what name would that be?"

"Lady Jane."

"Well, at least this Lady Jane escaped the fate of the other Lady Jane."

Suzie sneered. "You named the dog Prince, and you named the cat Lady?"

Eloise did kind of see her point. "Not original, I get that. I'm currently riding a horse named 'Red' too."

Doc said, "My best dog was named Pooch."

Suzie said, "Pooch? Did you name it?"

"Yeah. I did. I'm afraid I named my cat Blackie and my horse Star."

Now Eloise and Suzie were both laughing.

Eloise said, "Thanks Doc. You always make me feel better."

Doc added, "TS Eliot I am not."

Eloise thought Suzie likely didn't get the allusion. But she did. She loved, "Old Possum's Book of Practical Cats" way before she ever watched the musical. Eloise enthused, "I love the poem about the naming of cats!"

Doc winked at Eloise, then he added, "Suzie, let's start on the in-house patients."

Doc turned to Eloise. "Have fun with the kitten. Lady Jane needs to have her bladder and bowels emptied and then her bottle. An old toothbrush makes a good substitute for the tongue-baths that her mother would have given her."

Eloise thanked Doc and waved at Suzie. Eloise felt proud. She had been able to tell the sex of the kitten from the advice Henry had repeated from Major

Schmidt and Louisa had written down. And wasn't that something?

She couldn't wait to tell Dabs and Betsy.

"Lady Jane" had recommended her mewing. It was loud and annoying, well designed by nature to get a nurturing response. Except Eloise had no clue what to do.

But Eloise had made a pledge to her mother. Or at least that is how it felt. And she would try her best to keep her pledge. But first she needed Pinky to show her what to do.

* * *

Dabs typed, "You named the kitten Lady Grey?"

"I could hear Henry's voice. Isn't that cool? It was a matter of punctuation! Naming the kitten after his kitten, was the least I could do."

Dabs replied, "You seem to have a knack for finding animals."

"Prince found me. That was a little different. I can tell Lady Jane is going to wear me out. Thank God Pinky is taking shifts with me. I learned today how to properly mix up the special kitten formula and warm it just so. It's more work than a human baby I think since those pee and poop on their own. I have this big wad of TP and I have to kind of go pat-pat-pat to get things moving, and then clean her up."

"Send me some photos."

"I will."

Then Dabs added, "At least no one else will claim this one."

"True, but first I have to keep her alive. What if I don't? What if she doesn't make it? "

"Eloise, don't go there right now."

"You're right."

Eloise hesitated again. She typed into the message bubble and then erased it. Finally, she wrote. "Your visit with Henry, well it must have been hard. To have to tell him again that your mother, his friend, was gone. But, Dabs, have you never found any of your Mom's writings?"

Dabs was one step ahead of her. "There is no way that my mother wrote those journals. I know her handwriting for one thing. And for another, the ink is old and clearly not from a modern pen. If they were hers, it would mean that she had been producing an elaborate hoax. And that was not Mom."

Wow. Eloise felt hurt just reading those words. She sat back in her chair, her face feeling slack. What to say to that?

She said, "I certainly don't think the journals are a hoax, or fraud. I think though that your mom likely knew about the journals just as she knew about the slave graveyard. She might have been writing about it all. Just a thought."

The little dots were floating across the field. Dabs was on a roll. Finally, he finished his thought.

Dabs wrote, "Why would she not have told me? I was clearly the one who had to step in and continue to care for the land and the house. If she was working on a project, then she should have shared it with me, instead of hiding it from me."

Eloise asked, "She may have planned to tell you. If she did write about it, it was for someone to read. That someone is probably you. Henry seemed to think she wasn't right in the head at the end. Her illness could have prevented her from sharing her writing with you."

"I suppose that could be true. I wish you had known her. She was a wonderful woman, my mother. Well read, athletic, smart, with a dry sense of humor and wit. She and I shared our love of riding. She was an avid fox-hunter. Looked great on a horse."

"You said her name was Freddy. Short for Frederika?"

"Yes. Always called Freddy though."

"Of course, you know that was the Baroness's first name?"

"Mom said it was an old family name, passed down through the generations. Mom gave me a nudge about it when I married. She said, if I were to have a daughter, she would be most pleased if I would name her Frederika. Dad was horrified. But mom shushed him and looked at me as if we were making a solemn vow."

Eloise said, "I wish I had known her."

Dabs said, "She was at Rocking Horse that day. The day I caught Whiplash and returned her to your mom. If I was competing, my mom was there, too."

Eloise typed, "Wow. Still blows my mind that you

caught my horse and met my mom. I have many regrets. One is that I never spoke to you in all those years."

Dabs said, "On another topic, I thought I should confess, Betsy and I now text and call each other frequently. I value her friendship. She's such a good friend to you too, you know."

"Should I be nervous?"

"Not at all. But we do speak of you often. I was sorry to hear that Jock pulled yet another fast one. This guy Ralph went the extra mile for you. I've never heard of a financial adviser doing that kind of digging."

"Ralph was a childhood friend of Mom's."

Dabs said, "So it's over? I mean, getting your horse back? I guess I shouldn't even ask."

"Jock can't send me a horse he doesn't own. He cashed in."

"He still marrying the owner?"

Eloise said, "Well, Jock hasn't exactly invited me to the nuptials."

"I think Ralph still has more sleuthing to do."

Eloise was perplexed, "Really? I don't understand where you are heading with this?"

"I guess nowhere. Just forget it. I'm sorry about the whole thing. I'm glad you are riding Red, and that Bev has no intention of selling the mare to Jock."

Eloise said, "Red is still the 'Red-Devil' though. She reminds me so much of Whiplash. It was a good three years before Whiplash was reliable. Some days I just don't think I can go through that long process again."

"You did it before, you can do it again. Only better.

And faster. That's what your experience with Whiplash will have done for you."

Eloise sat at her keyboard feeling spent. She heard her kitten begin to stir and make a little mewling sound as if looking for her.

"Gotta' go. It's show-time for Lady Jane."

"Go mix your formula and feed your kitten and do your drill with the TP. I'll be working on a new transcription. Interesting stuff, I can't wait to share with you and Betsy."

Eloise typed, "No fair. Tease."

Dabs finished with, "Plus, I want to talk to you about dogs."

Eloise typed, "Dogs?"

Dabs said, "So, Pinky and Doc are part of a group called 'Good Stewards?' A rescue?"

"Yes."

"I want to rescue a dog. And I want you guys to find me the perfect dog for this farm. Frankly, having you and Betsy and Prince here, well, it was hard when you left. Strange, isn't it? I had been perfectly satisfied working and living here, me and the old geriatrics outside and my keyboard. But when you three left, it hit me like a ton of bricks, that it wasn't enough. I found myself saying out loud to the universe, "I'm lonely." Isn't that odd? I wish I could have kept Prince. He was a special dog for sure. I know they broke the mold after they made him, but I'll take something close."

Dabs was lonely, she was sad. What a messed-up pair of people they were. Instead of telling him about her own revelation, she joked with him. She said, "How about an adorable little grey kitten?"

"I wouldn't mind that too. But the dog first."

"You better be certain, because once I tell Pinky, there will be no stopping her."

"I've heard enough about Pinky, that I have no doubt what you say is true. In fact, I'm counting on it."

6

Aunt Bess bakes an apple pie like no other. Priscilla is her accomplice in this major undertaking as we are experiencing a bounty of fruit. Her secret lies not just in the excellence of the fruit, but in her pie's distinctive flavor. I suspect our hard cider is involved.

I have been tasked with delivering pies. I find the task most gay. Sammie drives and I descend from the trap to distribute the gifts to our nearest neighbors, who appeared delighted, and pumped me for news of the war and of Buck. Several sweet young things, very young indeed, seemed keen for news of Buck. I note, those whose ears pricked at the name of my brother, seemed especially solicitous of my attentions. I accept that I am pegged as the old maid. And suspect I am viewed with both pity and fear that they may find themselves as companions in my boat.

When rounds were completed, Bess gave a pie to

Isaac. Priscilla would later bring a pie to her cabin. I was handed a pie to take to the Major. Aunt Bess raised an eyebrow and said to me, "If you tarry, you sit out on the stoop where I can see you."

Aunt Bess is nothing if not direct. I nodded back dutifully. The Major was sitting on a stump in his little dooryard his fiddle across his knee. Henry sat on the step, working at his fiddle while the Major observed. When Henry saw me coming bearing a gift, he stood up and so then did the Major. As I came even with Henry, I was struck by his height. I was still taller, but I could see that condition would be temporary. What he was gaining in height however, had not impacted the rest of his frame. Henry was all long bones and angles with no meat upon him. His feet appeared to have been stretched, long and narrow, as were his hands, too big they seemed for the slender bones that met them. Henry's face had also elongated yet appeared closer to the baby than the man he would become. I felt relief gazing upon his still innocent face. He was yet but a boy, just one in an awkward phase.

The Major accepted my gift from Aunty and took it from my hands. He found a rough stool for my seat. Then he disappeared, reappearing with a knife. I mentioned Bess had saved us pie for our supper, and that this pie was meant only for the Major. The Major asked Henry to put away the instruments. Henry handled the Major's with the reverence one would expect for a holy relic.

Then the two sat at my feet and devoured that pie with knife and fingers! Even though I mentioned that Isaac was given a pie for Henry to enjoy later, no matter. Both Cleopatra and Lady Jane got wind of it and appeared at a trot, tails held high. Soon both cats were purring and rubbing up against the men, until they too enjoyed Aunt Bess' pie. I wondered if she was watching and fussing. Imagine cats eating Aunty's pie! But I saw it with my own eyes.

I managed to make polite sounds while those two ate like pigs at a trough! Henry looked stupefied as he looked up at me and told me to tell Aunt Bess it was the best pie he had ever put in his mouth. I did not mention to him that he was wearing half a slice upon his face. Lordy, a smear was on his nose! Lady Jane found his lap and was purring loudly. Henry got heavy against my leg as the Major and I chatted, his eyes drooped and soon his mouth was hanging open as he melted in place. He lowered himself and ended up circling his arm around my ankle like hitching up to a post, finally resting his head on my foot like a pillow.

Major Schmidt was grinning at the sight of Henry. I told him that he too was wearing crumbs in the corners of his lips. Oh dear, I looked at his lips too long and felt the gaze returned. But there we were sitting out front with a child anchoring me to the ground. If Aunty was peepin, I knew she was laughing. There was no chance for mischief.

I said with feeling, "That pie hadn't a chance!"

The Major looked embarrassed, which was not my intent. He said, "Forgive my poor manners. Sometimes, I feel that I may never eat again."

I asked him what he meant.

He said, "Starvation changes a man. We went seventy days without meat here. We went weeks without bread. All we were given was a little corn meal. We were given no winter clothes and had but rags upon our backs when we marched in winter to come here. When we arrived, we had no shelter and no provisions. And then the illnesses began."

I weakly answered, "But Jefferson..."

And the Major interjected, "Promised to do better than Patrick Henry."

The Major shrugged, "I had funds. When I could get them. In time I bought myself a fine horse and dined at fine tables. And then perhaps because of Jefferson, I was allowed to labor for your family, here I have been sheltered and nurtured. But the memory of lack, it comes on me in waves yet. Your home has provided more than food and shelter. But I fear this time of plenty is not to last."

A feeling of dread left me tongue-tied.

The Major said very quietly so as not to wake Henry, "The British prisoners march next month to Maryland. It is yet another betrayal. The Continental Army broke the provisions of our Convention of surrender at Saratoga. They agreed to send us home under paroles, but instead have held us. They broke all agreements to provide for us. And now, after we were told we must remain here for the duration and are finally settled by our own labors, we are once again betrayed. Forgive me please, I should not speak of such things to you."

I asked, "What about the Hessian prisoners?"

Major Schmidt grimaced, "We are not told. But we will not march with the British. We are not considered as valuable. Washington knows that an invading force of British cares not to risk anything to liberate us. And to be fair, many of my soldiers have slipped away."

I asked, "You will not slip away?"

He most firmly answered, "No."

I could not help the poor Major. Nor did I fully understand the depth of his sufferings, nor the anger that clearly simmered so near the surface. I changed the direction of our exchange. Henry had curled himself tighter and placed his thumb near his mouth.

I looked down at the boy and said, "He did suckle his thumb for years. He knows it is not allowed. But still, you see he dreams of it."

Major Schmidt looked sad. He said softly, "I feel for the boy. I believe one never recovers from losing a parent at a tender age. I know you understand that more than I."

The Major did touch a nerve. I simply nodded.

Very softly he said, "I worry what becomes of him."

I tried to reassure the Major, "You need not worry about Bud. I mean, Henry. He has been under my protection since a babe, and I would not remove it for any reason."

He nodded, I think somewhat reassured, but then he said, "When I leave Henry, the injured party I fear will be me."

I could see the Major was under a dark cloud today, and I brightened my voice and said, "Perhaps you and your men will be allowed to remain. The Barracks are now completed. Such a large investment surely must be utilized to justify the cost."

The Major said with doubt in his voice, "Perhaps."

Instead of brightening us both, I found anger welling inside my breast, feeling this was all due to the terrible loss by General Gates. I said too loudly, "Damn Granny Gates for Camden!"

Major Schmidt looked shocked. Then he laughed. Henry stirred, then sat up and rubbed his eyes. Lady Jane squeaked in protest as she was bumped from her spot.

Henry looked startled and alarmed and said, "Miss Louisa, I heard you curse. Aunt Bess won't like that."

I narrowed my eyes and he quickly, in earnest tones, amended his statement. He said, "Miss Louisa, I didn't hear nothing."

And finally, like music to my ears, we all three of us laughed.

* * *

Eloise drove to Bev's, her mind filled with thoughts of Dabs and dogs, little grey kittens, Louisa Roberts, her Hessian, her Henry, and her apple pies. One very real little grey kitten was in her Sherpa bag on the floor of the front seat, full of formula and quiet.

Once Eloise got Lady Jane settled in the tack room, she tacked up Red for their ride. Eloise went back into the indoor arena with Red. Eloise could have chosen to ride outside. She would have preferred to ride outside. The footing was still wet in the outdoor arena but pounded down enough that it had a firm feeling, not mushy or slick. She knew she couldn't do field work today. She and Red would damage the grass and make the turf footing "cuppy" if they did. But she took Red to the indoor because she knew that the mare needed to learn that wherever they were, the rules were the same. Routine was the bedrock of relaxation for a horse, or really any creature. With repetition came ease. With ease came relaxation. Not the sort of relaxation of rest, but the sort of relaxation that comes from the absence of anxiety, tension, and fear. The alarm that Red had shown in the indoor was connected to anxiety and fear.

Eloise put on the dressage saddle and brought along a better longe line. Bev made no recommendations, but about ten minutes into her longing session, Eloise noticed Bev had joined her, was leaning again against the kickboards, right next to the spot from yesterday where Bev had left an imprint in the dust.

Eloise called to Bev, "If you keep moving to a new spot each day Bev, you'll have dusted off the entire kickboards in no time."

You're Jock's daughter all-righty. Smart-ass."

Eloise had no reply but returned Bev's smile.

Red started to rev herself up again in the canter in an ominous way.

"Don't be lettin' her take no off-ramp to crazy-town. Pull her up. I got other ideas for ya'."

Eloise obediently reeled in Red. Bev left her newly dusted off spot on the rail and began pulling jump rails off the wall where they were hung in racks. The polls were frosted with dust, the paint on them chipped away. Bev was grunting loudly as she dropped each into the sand with a thud.

"If you hold Red, I'll come do that."

Bev waved her away. "No need."

Eloise said, "They sound heavy."

"I been toting jump poles since before you was born."

Eloise zipped her lips. She and Red both stood quietly while Bev made a fan shape out of the poles and used her feet to step off the distance between them.

Bev barked, "Don't assume she's gonna' trot nice and quiet over these. Assume' is just a way to make an ass out of you 'n me."

The first few attempts were comical but not explosive. Red ducked to the left of the poles, stopping abruptly facing Eloise, a confused look on her face. The next try, Red moved to the right of the poles, enlarging the circle. The third attempt Eloise got her lined up better and gave a cluck as Red went over the first pole but then launched herself over the rest of them. Eloise reeled her in before the mare could take off bucking.

Bev grinned and spoke to Red, "You're running out of options girlfriend." Then to Eloise, "Why don't you lead her through once?"

Eloise jogged along with the mare through the poles. Bingo. Red kept a wary eye on the poles, but made it through them all, lifting her legs dramatically, but rhythmically.

Bev hooted. "Now yer cookin'. Let her out some and give her a few minutes each way. She'll be like butter when you get on."

Red did have the hang of it now. And if Red met the first pole well, then all the poles were good. The mare picked up the rhythm with her breathing too. The sound of her breathing reminded Eloise of how Red sounded galloping in the field, the magical trilling of air through her nostrils, in rhythm to the beat of the stride. This is what the expression "finding your stride" sounded like. It was musical. At this point Red's tail danced along with a side-to-side swing going in its bottom half.

"You get on now 'for she's tuckered out."

Eloise mounted and went through the poles in rising trot. Red DID feel like butter. The mare took the contact in a steady but soft way that felt different, but good different.

After a few minutes, Bev said, "Now cross them stirrups and go through in sitting trot."

Eloise stopped, pulled the buckle down and crossed

her stirrup irons over in front of the saddle. She couldn't remember the last time she had ridden sitting trot without stirrups. It had been years and she knew it would put more stress on her hip joints. But she did as she was told. The first time through the poles she felt herself stiff and against the mare and briefly thought, "no way."

Bev yelled, "You aint got no arthritis to blame. Sit on your ass."

Bev was in full coaching mode now. Eloise did need to sit on her ass, relax her thighs and sit with the mare. A couple more times through and she found her seat and followed the swing. And it was a lot of swing. Red was still lifting her legs more than she needed to, but her neck was long and low, and the reins filled out and steady. This was the feeling of the swinging back of the horse being the bridge between the hind legs and the front legs, not a stiff bridge but an elastic one that conveyed the thrust in a continuous cycle. In the books this was called, "The circle of energy." It was also called "connection." Eloise remembered. And Eloise was now part of it, not against it, but joined to that circle.

But as much as she wanted to keep going, she was cooked. She was using a whole different set of muscles from her galloping muscles. These were her dressage muscles. Very different. Right under her ribcage, right about in the middle, she was feeling that familiar buildup of lactic acid. She would be sore tomorrow. She pulled up the mare, rubbed Red's withers, and cooed "good girl" to her.

Eloise looked over at Bev who looked thoughtful,

arms crossed, once again leaning on the kickboards, in a new spot. Dusting.

Bev pushed herself off the kickboard, "Don't never forget that lesson. That's what a back-mover feels like. A horse who uses his whole self, that develops that whole self, he don't wear out the parts so bad trying to do for his rider. Sometime canter gets that back unlocked, but it wasn't gonna' do it for this one today. Remember, if one tool in your toolbox ain't workin' you don't keep pounding away, you reach instead for a different tool."

"Thanks, Bev." She added, "You do coach a lot like Jock. And I mean that in a good way."

"Used to help Jock some. Mostly give him a good kick in the rear when he needed it."

"So, Jock sounded like you, instead of the other way around?"

Bev shrugged, "Might be so."

"How'd you two get on the outs?"

"Well, that's a tale. We did some mighty big deals. One in particular went bad wrong. I drew a line in the sand after the FBI came a' callin'."

Eloise felt a wave of shock pass through her.

"Now, don't worry yourself. It's ancient history and we didn't neither of us go to jail, now did we? But that's more than I should say."

"Bev, you can't drop a bomb like that and then clam up!"

Bev pressed her lips together hard, considering, then went on. "I put my foot down. See, I owned the horse. So, he was not well pleased with me. But let's just say that when someone comes to a closing with a suitcase full of money, you ought to walk."

Eloise couldn't believe her ears. This sounded like gangster stuff. She asked, "Did my mother know about all this?"

"She should have. We fought about that. Jock wanted her left in the dark. That weren't right. I wrote her some coded notes. By that time, I was gettin' paranoid. Ashamed to say I let the first deal go through. But it set wrong in my gut. So, I pulled out on the second sale. Glad I had when the FBI told me where that money come from."

Eloise had felt tired, but now she felt shaky. She felt like Bev was talking about other people, not her parents. But she needed to hear more. "Don't stop now Bev."

Bev frowned. "I've said too much. So, listen. I'm only going to say this much, Missy. That money was from another country and that money come from the people of that country, for that country, not for to buy some spoiled kid a fancy jumping horse to try and make a team."

"What happened?"

"If I say one more thing, you promise to seal them lips of yours? Especially don't need you tellin' Jock I'm leaking like an old sieve, "cause I am."

Eloise drew her gloved finger across her lips.

"All them horses got seized and auctioned off. I bought mine back for half of what we got paid. Jock wanted to find a new buyer, that way he'd make a new juicy commission. Could have done. That horse had a big jump. But it all sit so wrong with me that I turned that horse out to chew grass. Jock was hot. That horse mowed the grass 'til he got too old to stand on his legs. He's buried in that land I sold, back there in that fancy subdivision. Don't be tellin' nobody that neither."

"I'm confused. Some foreigner absconded with money from his country? Like embezzled?"

"Some places, when a government gets toppled, them's that's fleeing, take everything they can on the way out. So, as a general rule, you don't sell to people fleeing dictatorships with cash spilling out of their pockets. If the FBI or Interpol don't get 'ya, there's always the possibility that something bad comes at ya' from the other side."

"Bev, you could write a book."

"I could, but I won't. I don't need to keep diggin' up old bones and pickin over 'em. Problem is that I got a mean streak so if I get a chance to get even, it tempts me sorely."

Eloise swung off the mare, ran up her stirrups, loosened her girth, and pulled the reins over Red's head. She had heard enough. Enough for today. It seemed that Jock, the Jock of her childhood, had never been just the perfect dad and coach, handsome and talented and funny, her idol. He had even then had this other, far more problematic side. And Bev? Wow. The two of them together must have been both powerful and a powder-keg. They were both, in their own ways, "too much."

The two women walked side-by-side back to the

barn. In that moment, Eloise felt close to Bev. They were very different women. But Bev had trusted her. Bev had revealed something about herself as well as Jock. Her revelations were not all admirable. But revealing both the good, and the morally ambiguous side of herself was an act of trust. You did not tell just anyone such things. Eloise savored the feeling.

Eloise got Red into her halter, and hooked up to the crossties, and began to untack. Riding Red, and getting to know Bev, had been a lifesaver for her. By riding Red and spending time with Bev, in a way far different from saving the kitten, she was doing for others. The weight of her sadness had lifted, her chest pains had disappeared. Her mother was right. Then Eloise thought of Doc. He loved horses. He really liked Bev too. Maybe she could do something for Doc, too.

Eloise asked Bev, "Do you have anything safe that Doc could have a lesson on? He rode for years and years until he went to vet school. He would be rusty. But I think it would be so good for him."

Bev nodded, "Sure. I got Jethro."

* * *

Bev watched as Eloise pulled Lady Jane from her Sherpa bag along with a roll of extra soft toilet paper. The bottle of kitten replacement milk was warming in a coffee mug of warm water.

"Mew, mew, mew, mew." Lady Jane protested as Eloise stimulated her to empty out her bowels and bladder.

Then Eloise cleaned up the mess, carrying the kitten with her as she flushed the TP down the toilet.

Eloise got the kitten positioned properly on her knees, supported by a towel, her finger lightly on the kitten's throat like Pinky had taught her. Lady Jane was eager, butting with her head, her tiny pink paws kneading the air. She latched on, and Eloise felt an incredible satisfaction in each swallow.

Bev watched with interest. "Nothin' cuter in this world than a kitten or a pup."

"Can you believe someone meant to drown them all? Did drown most of them."

Bev said, "Sure I can. Lot of meanness in this world. Folks who think of animals as disposable. Good only for what they can do for them."

Bev and Eloise watched the kitten slow down, a rapturous stupor beginning to envelope Lady Jane. Eloise said, "I'm just happy that I could save this little one."

"Some days when you feel low 'bout things, you think on that. It's no small thing to save a life."

Those words stuck with Eloise all the way home. She didn't even register the bad traffic; she was absorbed in thought. She missed Prince. Her home felt empty, cavernous, hollowed out. But Prince was alive. He was safe. He was likely doing fine. It was her own heart that had been broken. She had lost Whiplash. But her beloved horse had made someone else happy. Whiplash was loved. Whiplash was cared for. She should not think of her animals only in terms of what they could do for her.

They could have good lives, happy lives, healthy lives, without being in her life.

And now she had this tiny, fragile creature who needed her. She and Pinky would share this burden. And it was a burden. Not just the lost sleep. That was the smallest part of it. The larger burden was the stakes, the worry, the investment of self. It was a set up. Nature meant it to be. Otherwise, all baby creatures would perish. It mattered not what species. It was a set up for loss. If it wasn't the worst sort of loss, death, it was the natural and positive outcome of letting go, job well done. This sort of loss was not to be mourned. She should not mourn Prince or Whiplash.

But this kitten was a throwaway, tiny and fragile. Eloise and Pinky had to be successful. This kitten had to thrive. Had to live. Because Eloise needed one to keep, to cling to and not have to let go.

Eloise set an alarm on her watch for Lady Jane's next feeding. She went through a drive-through and ordered a salad and headed home. She sat on the floor to eat her salad, putting the kitten on the floor to wobble around. Then she got an old toothbrush as Doc had suggested and gave the kitten a brushing. It was supposed to replicate a mother cat's tongue washing. The kitten mewed and wobbled and looked up at Eloise with out-of-focus eyes.

Eloise said in a high-pitched voice, speaking for the kitten, "Why is my mama so funny looking?" Then thought, the real mama cat must have been desperate looking for her kittens. That choked her up. Bev was right, there was indeed a lot of meanness in the world. Best not to dwell on that fact.

Lady Jane went back in her Sherpa bag for her nap. Eloise had her shower and changed into her pajamas. She was ready to settle into bed with her Kindle when a couple of thoughts came to her. First, she thought of Bev and Jock and the weirdness of what Bev had described. Then she remembered those unsigned notes that her mother had saved. A lightbulb turned on inside her head. The dots began to connect. She went into the closet and found the bag. There were four sheets that had short, scrawled messages on one side only.

7

Eloise crawled into bed with the four sheets of paper, propping herself up with pillows and did her first read through. It took no time. The notes were short. She had previously skimmed them, but at the time they meant nothing. One thing was now clear. These handwritten notes were from Bev. Even if Bev hadn't mentioned it, the lack of punctuation was a tip off. By the time Eloise had read all four notes, she was certain. Bev was the author. Other than that, though, little else was clear. She found the first note she read especially cryptic.

It read:

There's a tugboat down by the river dontcha know
where a cement bags just a droopin on down
Oh that cement its there for the weight dear
Five will get ya ten old Mackys back in town
Now did ya hear about Louie Miller
He disappeared, babe
After drawing out
all his hard earned cash
And now Mack he

spends just like a sailor
Could it be our boy's done somethin rash

What the heck? Was someone going to disappear? Or had "our boy" done something rash? Eloise tossed the note aside and moved on to the next note.

It read:

Pirates. I notice that the worst of the bunch send
there kids to the best schools money can buy. They
teach em good how to mix talk and dress sharp fit
in good with the money crowd. But they also teach
em the crowd is full of suckers. If any of them so
called friends get wise to the game, then look out. I
saw that movie, Gatsby. It ain't old news. It ain't
yesterday. It's right under our noses. Those kids know
its blood money buying all them things. Things like
horses. They know.

Eloise thought there was nothing especially damning here. Although it was at least plainly stated, if lacking punctuation. Bev did not like spoiled rich kids. It did surprise Eloise that Bev, not someone she would have pegged as a fan of The Great Gatsby, had at least seen the movie and recognized the themes. Bev got it. Gatsby's money came from the mob. It gave Gatsby entrance to the richest old money society. But why had her mother thought the note important enough to save?

Eloise picked up the next note:

Fanciest stable I ever saw. Air had a strange feel
to it. Gave me the heebie jeebies. The horses there
don't come to the front of the stalls, don't look at you.
Course, I've had horses like that from Europe. They
don't pet on em and spoil em like we do. They look at
em like sports equipment. But I got the same feel off
the guy clippin the bushes as I got from the horses.
Could be he aint' legal. Same deal when I smiled at
the groom. No eye contact. I always thought smiles
were bi-lingual. Something ain't right. Them stalls
were huge. Footing that new hi-tech stuff. Horses in
good flesh and all that. Still. I got things to say that
Jock don't want to hear. If you looked into it. Maybe
you could calm me down. I don't feel right about
backing out of the deal. Still, I got alarm bells going
off in my head.

Bev was enlisting her Mom's aid. Jock would be angry at her for pulling Elly into the deal.

Eloise was still in bed, but no longer leaning back into her pillows. Her face felt hot and slack as she leaned forward, fingering the edge of the paper. Eloise read the next note:

Wish you had come along. Jock jumped the moon.
Looked ready for the biggest arena anywhere.
Tight turns and speed too. Made me want to buy
the horse, and I own him. Kid got on and the horse
did for him. Flashy people. Flashy cars. Smooth
talkers. Big grins and shook Jock's hand real long

and grippy. You would have told me what kind of expensive watch was hanging on that tanned arm. Barn could have been in one of them TV shows on the rich and famous. People scurrying all over the place. Even had fresh flowers in the tack room. Orchids. That's a first for me. They feel fake. Not the orchids. They were real. Kind of the reason I'm writing this down for your eyes only before I turn out the lights. Jock's been shooting me looks all day that mean I should just let him do his thing. I handled the horse and played groom. Jock never told I was the owner. So, who is the real fake? Ha Ha They got the vet coming in the morning to vet the horse. Was happy to haul back to Jill's so we could get out of there. I hope they don't take him, but I don't want the vet to find nothing wrong neither. He's a good horse. I don't want no monkey business at the vetting. I'll stay right close for the whole enchilada.

Ah. Eloise realized this last note was likely the first note written. After that, the order wasn't clear. But it seemed all four notes were based on the one sale. Or at least, three of them were. The one about the tugboat was just weird.

Eloise's mind wandered to the good news that Bev was willing to give Doc riding lessons on Jethro. The thought alone made Eloise breathe and let go of some of the tension she realized she had been holding onto. She couldn't wait to tell Doc.

Her alarm went off on her phone. It was time for Lady Jane to have another bottle.

Eloise marveled at the stream of urine coming out of the tiny kitten. And then the poo. Lady Jane sang "the song of her people" through the entire procedure. Next came the bottle. When the kitten had finished, Eloise gave her one more chance to empty out, then brushed her with the toothbrush, and put her back in her bag.

She felt the need to talk to someone. But it was late. The beauty of texting or email was that you didn't impose yourself on someone's time. They could respond or they could not respond. So, she texted Dabs.

"Such a weird couple of days. Bev told me some things about Jock that are disturbing. She swears she won't tell me another word. But remember those hand-written notes I found along with the letters? They didn't mean anything to me, but they do now. They must be from Bev. One is just cryptic as all get out. They aren't dated or signed."

Dabs immediately answered, "I'm up. Why don't I call you? It's kind of old fashioned, I know."

"Ok."

Eloise had on her pajamas and was sitting in bed. It seemed . . . Well, she wasn't sure what it seemed. Dabs couldn't see her. She went and picked up the Sherpa bag and placed it on the bed next to her, unzipped the top and stroked the kitten who rolled over and stretched and yawned. Eloise took a couple photos before her phone rang.

She told Dabs *all* about the kitten. She told him all

about Red. She told him about Bev being willing to teach Doc. She told him all about what Bev had said, and then she read him the hand-written notes. Eloise had to check a couple of times to be sure Dabs was still there, because she hadn't given him a moment to insert a word.

Eloise had emptied out. Whatever Dabs said now hardly mattered. She felt better.

Finally Dabs said, "You lead an eventful life."

"I do?"

"Well, maybe just compared to mine."

Eloise said, "What about that bizarre note about the tugboat? What the heck?"

"That I can help you with. Those are song lyrics."

"I guess that makes sense. Bev doesn't strike me as a poet, but you never know."

Dabs continued, "You never heard of 'Mack the Knife?' Creepy song, but it was a big hit for a bunch of crooners. Not my generation. More like my grandparents. It's about a hit man. You know, cement booties and all that."

"Oh my God. Leave it to Bev not to use quotation marks."

"Bet your mom understood."

"A song about a hit man? Geeze, Dabs. Was Bev saying they were dealing with a hit man? Or the mob? All they did was sell some shady characters a horse. Why would Jock or Bev have anything to worry about? They didn't know the money was, um, embezzled or something like that. Bev said something about it being foreigners."

"Still. Better off keeping far away from gangsters from all points on the globe, right?"

Eloise, "Bev called it blood money in one of those notes. Bev pulled out of a second deal; I think, anyway. I guess she found out when the FBI came calling. But the notes proved her initial vibes were correct. Mom likely took the notes seriously."

"You neglected to tell me about the FBI. Well, none of it affects you. I mean you and your efforts to get Whiplash back. This is just old history between Jock and Bev."

Eloise sighed. "All true. I have to let Whiplash go. I have to let Prince go. Both aren't coming back."

Eloise was shocked at her own words both because they rang true, but also because her words were a declaration of submission, submission to fate, destiny, whatever. History was history, but history did affect her, closed doors, changed the direction of her path ahead. It made her sad. It made her tired.

"You have every right to be angry at Jock. And disappointed in Jock. Heck, I'm disappointed in Jock. I always admired him."

"I shouldn't let Jock take up so much space in my head."

"He's your Dad."

"I demoted him from Dad-ship long ago."

"Not possible."

"I'm so tired."

"Give yourself a break from your own story. I've got a humdinger of a journal I'm transcribing. Then there's the project of finding Dabs the perfect dog. Don't forget about that."

"I'm afraid the perfect dog is taken and gone."

Dabs laughed. "Okay. It can't be the perfect dog, as he is evidently unavailable. But maybe something almost perfect."

"Big and hairy?"

"Just smart and friendly and athletic enough to go on rides and walks."

"You better be serious, because once I tell Pinky, she'll be on it."

"I'm counting on it. And Eloise?"

"Yes."

"I confess I'm jealous. I think of you riding Red and having so many wonderful friends. And now you saved that kitten. Your very own "Lady Jane." You send me a photo, okay?"

"I just took a few. I'll send them tonight."

Dabs added, "And then you and Pinky bring me my new dog. Stay the week. I'd like to meet Pinky. She sounds lively."

Eloise smiled into the phone. "Lively? Really? Lively? Dabs, this is why I thought you were seventy years old!"

"I don't see how the word 'lively' makes me sound seventy. It seemed apropos. Oh no. I did it again. How about 'fitting?' God. I do sound seventy. I guess I qualify as eccentric. Or just stuck in the 18th century. I'll stop now. I'll be looking for the photos. Plus, I'll have the next journal entry for you by tomorrow."

"Don't worry Dabs. Remember I've met you and know you aren't seventy even though you sound like you are."

"Just eccentric, then?"

Eloise was smiling into the phone again. "No comment."

* * *

Eloise dreamed of Ivy Creek Plantation again. It was the first time since she had returned to Atlanta. She was happy to be there. She dreamed of the long stable row of standing stalls. The box stalls were gone, with only standing stalls remaining. She eyed horse after horse, standing in a row, tails toward the barn aisle. She could hear the horses chewing their hay. And a new sound. What was it? Erratic. Unfamiliar. A "rrrrrrr" and a "thunk." It was the tie-bobbin and tie rope, sliding through the hole cut into the manger. It worked just as Dabs had said it would, giving the horses the freedom to move, the tie rope playing out if a horse wanted to bite at a fly on their sides, and then when the horse straightened out, the bobbin taking the slack out of the tie rope with a little "thunk" as it hit the stall floor. It was then that she noticed the grey. Yes, there she was. Louisa's mare Beauty. So pretty. A perfect gift for a horse-loving daughter: delicate, not too big. The mare had a large, dark, placid eye. Eloise did not want to leave but clung to her dream and willed it to stay. But eventually, the scene faded, grew dark, and Eloise slept.

Eloise awoke to find Dabs had kept his promise.

* * *

November 25, 1780

The British prisoners have been marched away.
But not before setting the buildings afire. How is it
that the guards allow such destruction? Not only is
the air befouled with black soot and ash that blows
across our lands, but cats that kept the vermin down
are now abandoned, run to the woods. Before the
cats run rats. I've never seen so many in our barn.
Our neighbors have gone to killing the cats they
catch along with the rats. Foolish and cruel. I think
of Cleopatra's kits, but Major Schmidt says they are
with his men in the Hessian section of barracks. I
wonder if he says so to calm Henry who is beside
himself with worry.

Aunt Bess predicts doom arriving at our door-
step shortly. She talks of flight. But where to flee?
She will not hear of High Meadows. She rambles so
about the Carters and how they had wanted to place
her out of the way by means fair or foul. I always
dismissed such talk as yarn spinning. No doubt she
was never fond of their company, but now I see
though she made jests, she is serious that fleeing Ivy
Creek, High Meadows would be no refuge.

Priscilla is in her own world and Sammie looks

at the conflagration and soot and is, I fear, quietly
satisfied. Father is anxious and looking for news
of the war and of Buck of which we hear nothing.
Isaac is ever present at father's side and watchful
but speaks little and what he says is to father only.
Those two, I swear, know the mind of the other
without speaking. I do believe that father trusts
Isaac with his life. With the young horses, especially
those new to harness, this is literally true.

Father forbade us to ride out. We only ride in
the field next to the house. My wings are clipped.
Training the horses continues, though who shall
buy our horses? If the British thieve them, they
will thieve the finest trained mounts in the state.
Fashion, under the Major's steady hand, is beautiful
to behold. I confess, I listened in from my opened
window as father and the Major had an earnest
discussion in the stable yard. The Major stated that
his fate depended on the decision of the Continental
Congress. He feels things, as we do, come to a head.
If he should be marched away, he would take only
his violin. He asked that we keep safe his horses.
That we could breed the mare and keep the foal as
payment. If he should not survive, to please sell the
horses and put the money in trust for Henry. Well,
I never. What would Henry do with money? But
father agreed. Or at least it seemed so, for the Major
thanked him. I feel the Major avoiding my gaze
these days. He and I now have no time alone in
which to speak candidly. Henry spends much time at

end of day at his violin, and likely at his bit of slate and chalk. I read my books and draw but do not join them.

Aunt Bess is filling her secret larder. She leaves space for us to hide should it be required. I did make Aunt Bess laugh to conjure a scene of invading soldiers relieving themselves only to have it splash right back, and we, below, stifling laughs at the sounds of their curses.

I do have trouble sleeping. It seems I cannot get warm at night. I invite Beast up into the bed, vermin and all. He is happy to oblige. I worry about the horses. I try not to think of our people down the lane who tend our fields and other livestock. Would they stay? If our cause is lost, what retribution will be imposed on all those who took up arms against the King? Would our property be seized and given to a family who stayed loyal? Would we be left paupers? I would never entertain such thoughts in daylight. But I could not keep them from forming in these long cold nights.

Addendum: I know it indelicate of me, but I finally found my opportunity to speak to Major Schmidt alone. The Major's cabin has a privy behind the old poultry yard kept by the negroes who once lived there. Beast walked with me and finding something of interest trotted happily ahead to browse among the scrub. Soon he found a cat and chased it up a tree. It was not one of Cleopatra's as it was yellow. I've always been partial to yellow cats, so I called Beast away. Just then the Major came out of the privy, looking surprised to see me.

I said, "Beast has chased a strange cat up that tree. I feel for these abandoned pets. Might we save it do you think?"

The Major looked up at the feline, and it stared down at him having settled comfortably on a branch. He said, "If it is wise, it will not trust us. The locals have been killing the strays."

I said, "That cat poses no threat to anyone. To kill it is pure wickedness."

The Major nodded. "It shall not suffer harm from me. I'll set out a bit of food, should hunger bring it down."

I then confessed, "I did come this way, with Beast, in hopes of speaking to you. We never have a moment alone, by design, I realize."

The Major nodded. "Everyone sees how it is between us. But we cannot indulge our desires, you understand. Louisa, once I am gone from here, I may not be able to return."

I swallowed hard hearing such harsh words. I said, "Is that your wish?"

He shook his head firmly, "You misunderstand. I have no desire to leave here. I have no desire to leave you. But fate may have other designs for us both. There are trials and tests ahead. I have passed through many. There have been many times before we met, that I thought I should not survive. So many around me did not. And what lies ahead, I still may not survive. "

I said, "Then stay! We can hide you well until all have marched away." But as soon as the words had left my lips, I realized how utterly useless, even insulting they were to the Major.

He said, "That is something I would never do."

My eyes heated up and a tear spilled over before I could wipe it away. I nodded. "Indeed. I did not think you would, it was a moment of pure fantasy."

He continued, "Dearest Louisa, I want all the good things for you that life can hold. If I can return to your side, I will. But I cannot promise you anything, I do not want you to promise me anything."

I said, "If you are marched into Maryland, into a camp for prisoners, at least you will be out of the fight."

He nodded, "That is true."

I said, "At least Buck will not have an opportunity to shoot you."

He said, "I do not fear Buck. Although I understand he is a very good shot. I fear starvation and illness more than I ever did fear your brother, though he never liked me, nor approved of my working for your father."

I stepped closer, letting go of Beast. He trotted lazily back to the bottom of the tree, looked up and whined. Beast liked to chase things, but he never would have harmed the cat. I looked back up into the face of Major Schmidt. I said, "You call me by *my Christian name, but I call you by your rank. I should like, just this once, while we are alone, to call you by the name your parents gave you. The name your sisters and brothers use. The name an intimate would use."*

He nearly whispered, "Yo."

He saw my confusion. "You American's say it differently. You would, I think, say Joe."

I whispered it back to him, but as we would say it here, "Joe."

Then we embraced and kissed far too passionately and for too long. He gently pushed me away. I confess I liked it far too much to want to cease. But he did say that Bess would soon find me gone and be sending Henry to locate me and report back. I knew he was correct.

He sheepishly added, "That must be the last embrace until after…"

I answered, "I will not forget it."

And he said, "Nor I. I will dream of it."

I smoothed my bodice, feeling like I might burst right out of it and tried to compose myself, my heart thumping in my chest, I added, "I will write to Jefferson regarding the treatment of prisoners. He surely wants to hear that you and others from his camps are well fed and clothed and kept from illness."

Just then I noticed that the yellow cat was on the ground, its tail held high, with Beast sniffing at it in a friendly manner.

* * *

Eloise finished reading the entry with her heart pounding and her face flushed. She should have felt happy for the two lovers that they had at last declared their love, although so much still lay ahead. But she could not. His name, "Joe," pulled her from their story, right back into her own.

Major Schmidt's name was Joe. What were the odds? And like a movie scene playing in her mind, a scene that caused her intense discomfort to watch, she saw herself kissing another Joe. It filled her with shame. She *had* kissed a shocked modern-day Joe, a stranger, but a stand-in for the Major of the journals. She had kissed him in front of Doc in her confused, dream-like concussed state. She had said his name as if she knew him, the man of the lost-dog flier she had hidden away. The flier with Prince on it. She had, in that moment, exposed herself as a nut-job. Eloise found herself closing her eyes and tapping her forehead, as if trying to turn off the movie. Strangely, it seemed to work. But she wasn't done thinking about the strangeness of it all.

She had just learned the Christian name of the Major *was* Joe! The Major's name was the same as Prince's real owner, the handsome, handsome, Joe of the flier. It was disorienting to have, once again, fantasy bleed into reality.

She had fallen in love with the long-dead Major Schmidt. She had fallen in love with the image of handsome Joe. She had fallen in love with Joe's dog, who at least had loved her back. She was still in love with all of them.

And then there was Dabs. What about Dabs? He had become such an important friend to her. He cared for her, and she cared for him. But something was holding her back. Oh, Dabs! What was she afraid of?

Eloise needed Betsy.

Betsy talked her down off the cliff. "Eloise, really. It's not as if the name Joe, or Johann is an unusual name, for goodness' sake."

"I guess I'm still feeling ashamed about the flier, kissing Joe."

Betsy chuckled. Eloise heard it over the line. She felt her face get hot and was lucky no one could see her.

"Well, don't forget, you had hit your head."

"I wish I hadn't told Dabs. About Joe, I mean. He must think I'm damaged goods."

"You shouldn't regret being honest. That's a good thing, a brave thing, to show someone who you are. And isn't it sweet that you care? Despite all the revelations, he welcomed us both, invited us back, and we had the most wonderful time, beyond incredible really. And now we have him as our friend. Aren't we lucky?"

Eloise began to feel better. "Thanks Betsy. I needed to hear that. I do have a strong attachment to that place, to that journal, to those people. And I have the Robertson connection, whatever it is, it's something tangible. And now Dabs has asked if Pinky can help find a dog for him. He's invited Pinky and me to come visit when we bring him his dog. So, I get to go back."

"He told me. And you know what, Eloise?"

"What?"

"You're a damn fool if you don't jump right on that project. Don't delay. You may have a strong attachment to the place, and to people long dead, but if I were you, I'd go for the tall handsome guy who is very much alive."

8

It had been Pinky's night for kitten duty. There was a small part of Eloise that felt guilty. She had not told anyone yet that she intended to keep the kitten. If it was now her kitten, then she should not have been foisting night duty on anyone. But she had desperately needed sleep, glorious uninterrupted sleep. Did that make her a bad kitten-mama? A bad friend? She thought the answer was yes on both counts.

She and Dabs had talked on the phone for an hour while she lounged in bed, her light already turned off. Eloise thought of the term "pillow talk" and the thought made her slightly uncomfortable. Maybe that's why she purposefully kept the talk impersonal, and why she did not bring up "the kiss" or the name Joe.

They had been reading about Jefferson, but they had also been looking stuff up about the revolutionary war in Virginia. Then they talked about dogs, and Dab's hypothetical dog, before Eloise and Dabs wished each other good-night, and hung up.

Eloise woke up with the warm fuzzy feeling that she had dreamed of Prince.

It would soon be Thanksgiving. Betsy had offered to host dinner for Eloise and Pinky and Buzz. Buzz had insisted that he bring all the fixings if Betsy did the bird. Eloise could bring dessert. Betsy assured her that anyone could make a pumpkin or a pecan pie. If Eloise also served heavy whipped cream, she couldn't fail. Eloise had accepted the challenge.

Rested and thinking of pies, Eloise pulled into her parking spot at work. The sun was just coming up when she was jolted out of her reverie. The shadow on the front porch was no shadow. It could not be. But it was. Prince was bouncing up and down and barking like a madman. Eloise ran up the stairs and Prince nearly knocked her over. His barks turned to whines and then shrieks of excitement, his entire body trembling in her arms as she sat down and hugged him fully. He had on the same collar, but a new tag hung from it. Eloise stood up and looked around her, sure that Joe was standing to the side, watching the happy reunion.

Eloise called into the empty space, "Hello? Anyone here?" No reply. For a moment she was frozen in place with apprehension. As soon as she and Prince got inside, she called Pinky.

The phone rang and rang and then went to message. Eloise redialed.

Pinky picked up sounding groggy. "Eloise, what the hell? Are you okay?"

"You are not going to believe this. Prince was at the door of the clinic. Just like before. "

"Like before?"

"No. I mean he's well fed and this time he's clipped out like a Giant Schnauzer. But he's alone. I called out, no one is with him. And come on it's ..."

Eloise looked at her watch to check, "It's six-forty-five."

"He's clearly gotten out."

"I guess I'd better call the number on the ID tag."

"No. Wait. Let me get dressed and come over. It shouldn't be you, Eloise. Let's not borrow trouble, okay?"

"I don't understand."

"Look, we don't know how long he's been out, but what if they think the crazy girl at the clinic is stalking them or stealing the dog or some-such."

"I would never stalk anyone or steal their dog."

"I still think it shouldn't be you who makes the call. Sit tight sunshine. I have to feed your kitten and pull on some clothes."

"Maybe I should call Doc."

"I'll call Doc. You do whatever it is that you do there in the mornings."

After a short pause Pinky said, "It's 6:45? Good grief!"

"Okay."

Eloise hung up and then looked down at Prince who was grinning his great big happy grin. She said, "Well, I guess you can join the pack for breakfast."

It was deja vu all over again.

Eloise opened the basement door. Prince thundered down the stairs and the entire kennel erupted.

Eloise made Prince a bowl of kibble and water and

put it and a dog bed in his "place" by Pinky's grooming station. He grinned up at her and dove in. Eloise left him in his spot as she fed the dogs. Then he followed her upstairs as she set out food for the cats. She left him loose in the clinic as she swept and mopped and emptied trash, cleaned off the counters and exam tables and made sure all the supplies were ready for the day.

Eloise was cleaning kennels and walking dogs when Pinky came sweeping down the stairs, mewing emanating from the Sherpa bag. Prince froze and tipped his head at the sound, even while madly wagging his tail.

Pinky said earnestly, "Prince, what the hell are you doing here?"

Prince bounced up to Pinky, twirled then performed a huge play bow and stretch. Then he stood up and craned his neck toward the bag.

Pinky laughed and said, "Okay? Be gentle. Very, very gentle. It's a little baby."

Pinky unzipped the bag and pulled out Lady Jane, cradling the kitten carefully in two hands, she showed Lady Jane to Prince, who was indeed very gentle as he sniffed the kitten who was mewing loudly.

Eloise said, "What did Doc say?"

"We are both off the hook. He has Joe's cell number. I told him what had happened, and he agreed with me that you should not be seen or heard. He's going to handle it."

Eloise gulped and nodded. Pinky said "Go walk dogs. Prince and Lady Jane and I are going to hang in the lounge and have breakfast."

"Prince just had his."

Pinky nodded, called Prince, picked up the Sherpa bag and the three of them marched back up the stairs.

Eloise grabbed a leash off the wall and fetched her next walk.

Eloise thought, "Here I go, Eloise Robertson, suspected dog-thief, stalker or perhaps just plain old nuts trying to stay off the radar."

Finally, Pinky came down the basement stairs, Prince thundering ahead of her and twirling once in front of Eloise, before sitting on her feet and leaning against her legs, smiling like an idiot. Eloise placed her hand on top of his head, "I'm happy to see you too!" But her throat constricted at the end of the sentence.

Pinky placed the Sherpa carrier on top of the washing machine. It was quiet now. Lady Jane had been fed and cleaned up and groomed and now she was tucked into her lambswool bedding with her tiny stuffed animal dreaming sweet kitten dreams, whatever those might be.

Pinky said, "Doc wants to see you in his office."

Eloise flinched. "Am I in trouble?"

"No, of course not. But, hey, at least in Doc's office you guys can speak without, um, you know, the big ears around here listening in."

"Good point."

"Hey, I'm sorry you have to go through this another time."

Eloise nodded, sighed, and pulled her foot out from beneath Prince's butt.

Pinky said, "I'll stay down here with Prince and oil

my clippers. I don't have any jobs for at least another hour."

As Eloise passed through the lobby, Janet said, "Too weird about the dog. Sorry."

She passed Suzy who was putting packs in the autoclave. She said, "What are the chances? Sorry."

By the time Eloise was climbing the stairs, she was fighting back tears. It was not that they weren't sincere. Well, maybe they were and maybe they weren't. It was that she was weary to the bone of being an object of pity.

When she got to Doc's office the door was closed. She tapped on it timidly. Instead of telling her to come in, the door opened briskly, with Doc holding the phone to his ear and waving her in. He motioned to a chair. When he put his hand on the back of the chair, Eloise grimaced.

Doc spoke into the phone, "We'll take care of him until you get here. He doesn't appear any worse for wear."

Doc hung up. "Joe just got back into town to find that Prince had gone AWOL. His girlfriend was supposed to be looking after the dog."

"Prince doesn't like her, does he?"

Doc said, "Evidently not." Then added, "I'm sorry that you have to be separated again from Prince. I've been thinking about you. In fact, I was just talking about you. Were your ears burning?"

Eloise shook her head, puzzled.

"I had a nice chat with Bev. She invited me to come

out on Sunday and ride. She's evidently got some old packer even I can't fall off."

"Oh wow! Can I come watch?"

"Nope. No spectators allowed. I'm only revealing this much because I thought it would make you smile. But on a different topic, Pinky tells me you two are looking for a dog for your friend in Virginia. But I was wondering if first we should find a dog for you."

"Right now, my plate is full-up with that kitten."

"You want to keep the kitten?"

"Yes. I haven't told Pinky yet. It's a little scary to admit I want the kitten. Like admitting I want her, will mean something bad will happen that takes her away. I'm afraid to want anything."

"You should not be afraid to want things for yourself."

Eloise thought her words, though honest, sounded nutty, even to her own ears. Enough to shock poor Doc. She only said, "Thanks." before heading downstairs.

* * *

Eloise came down the stairs into the basement to find Pinky with a hairy Old English Sheepdog in the tub, and was wet as a dishrag trying to get the huge dog lathered up. Pinky had put Prince into a run as the Sheepdog was none too pleased to see Prince.

Pinky still managed to yell at Eloise, "Everything okay?"

Eloise nodded but felt the urge to go outside with

Prince, to have one more moment alone with her dog. She said, "I'm taking Prince out for a walk. Let him empty out before Joe gets here to pick him up."

Pinky frowned and said, "Make it quick," while giving the huge dog a push on its chest to reposition it in the tub.

Prince was gleeful to see Eloise and bounced happily at her side. She loved this dog. She loved looking at him. He wasn't worried. He wasn't sad. He lived in the moment. And for Prince, the moment was good. She took him on the usual loop that ran around the perimeter of the building and parking lot. Pinky had told her to make it quick. She had not. She had, at least, ignored the urge to put him in her car and make a run for it.

As Eloise started for the basement door, there stood Joe. He had spotted them from the parking lot. A leather leash dangled from his hand. Eloise couldn't help but notice that he was still just as incredibly handsome as ever.

Eloise felt her mouth go dry and her heart start to pound. Prince began to wag his tail wildly but made no move to leave her side.

"Hello Eloise. Thank you again for saving Jaeger. He must have climbed out of the yard. He can climb fences you know. I'm surprised he found his way here."

Eloise said, "He's smart." And then felt embarrassed and added, "But you know that."

Joe nodded and held up the leash, "Shall I?"

"Of course, of course."

Joe stepped forward and clipped on his lead. As Eloise pulled off the clinic lead over Prince's head, it got caught in Joe's lead. Their hands touched as the two of them sorted the leashes. Joe's eyes met Eloise's and Eloise felt her stomach do a flip-flop."

Joe said, "I should go inside to say thanks."

Eloise nodded. And Joe walked into the clinic with Prince at his side. Eloise stood and watched them go, leash hanging from her hand. Eloise hadn't expected to be there for the hand-off. And she shouldn't have been there. But that was how it had gone down.

When she walked into the basement without Prince, Pinky said, "Where's the dog?"

Pinky added, "Please tell me Joe wasn't out there?"

Eloise nodded. Pinky frowned, then did her best to squeegee all the excess water off the sheepdog. She said, "I was wondering why you were gone so long. Help me get Goliath here out of the tub. My back is killing me."

Eloise got nearly as wet as Pinky lifting the large wet mop of a dog out of the tub. Eloise wondered how the heck Pinky had gotten the massive dog *into* the tub. No wonder her back was killing her. Once on the ground, he did a full body shake to give them an additional baptismal.

Pinky put her hand on Eloise's shoulder. "Thanks friend."

"You're welcome, friend."

Eloise felt a little bit better.

* * *

After work, Eloise fought the terrible traffic up 400 to go ride Red. She needed this ride.

Bev was waiting with Red tacked up and straining at her crossties. She had her jumping saddle on

"Put that kitten up somewheres safe. Caroline set up jumps for herself this morning. I told her to keep 'em up for you."

Bev was all business. "I'll make sure she ain't got no hump in that back of hers today."

So, while Eloise got the kitten situated, and carefully zipped up her old boots then pulled on her fancy helmet, Bev took Red to the arena and longed her.

Eloise felt "empty" walking to the arena, no Prince, no Sherpa bag, no Red. It was like being dressed for the ball with no date. But her date was in the arena being warmed up for her.

Eloise sat on the mounting block to watch. It was like seeing Red again for the first time. But now, she knew those ears, that neck, those eyes, the sound of her breathing. It made her eager to get on.

Finally, Bev said, "You'll be fine now."

Bev fixed the reins, but let Eloise snug up the girth, saying, "You got young hands."

Eloise set her stirrups on the hole she imagined was right and swung up.

Bev said, "Get your sea legs, I'll lower them poles. Caroline's horse is further along than Red."

Bev set the jumps ridiculously low.

Bev said, "Now listen here. You trot this line, then turn and go on that line, double back and do the line with the oxer at the end, and finish over there yonder at what's gonna' be an easy six stride later. Then go on out the gate to the field, go once around and loosen her up in canter. Then you trot on back real casual like and do it again."

Eloise felt there was nothing challenging ahead of her. Red was alert, flicking her ears back and forth waiting for something, knowing the jumps were up for a reason. When Bev let her start the tiny course, Red over-did every element landing in canter, so that Eloise had to bring her back to trot. They did it once more then Bev said, "Grab a lap, then come on back."

Red scooted out the gate with joy, slapping her tail once as she accelerated. Eloise was happy too, to head out on her path, but felt a brief pang at the absence of Prince. But Red allowed no loss of focus. Once Red turned up the hill, the mare kicked into gallop without any direction from Eloise. Eloise quickly bridged the reins and pushed her heels down, the wind making her eyes tear up. At the top of the hill, Eloise brought Red down to trot instead of their usual walk. They shortened the trot stride down the incline, Red leaned against the reins, asking to accelerate. Eloise was glad of the added support of the bridged reins and kept her in trot. Fortunately, those ears swiveled back to listen.

As they entered the arena at trot, Eloise noticed right away that the jumps had been raised. But still they weren't very high. They could do this.

Bev said, "Trot the first one, then let her canter the rest, just don't let her get too long in the stride."

Eloise could feel Red's eagerness, her ears pointing hard at the jump and over jumping the first element.

"Bev was bellowing, "Good God. Don't give me no

more grey hairs. Get your hands up off her neck and shorten that stride! "Whoa, whoa, whoa, whoa!"

Eloise did as she was told. And they met the next jump perfectly.

Bev whooped. "Now you're talking"

And finally, "Come to the bottom on the vertical, then give the mare her head and keep your leg on for the oxer."

And before it had begun it seemed, it was over. Eloise felt the happy rush that comes from a good go, rubbing Red in front of her withers to congratulate the mare on a job well done.

"Looky how proud that mare is of herself! See, I made it easy for her. And then 'fore she knew what she was doing, the harder bit, was easy as the easy bit."

"This mare doesn't say 'no' does she?"

"She's a tiger. Don't mean she can't be ruint."

Eloise nodded.

Bev continued. "She got faith in you, cause you nor nobody else give her a reason not to. That's the tough part, sometimes we make mistakes, bad ones too. And then a horse don't know nothing about the word, 'sorry.' They just know not to allow nobody to hurt them like that again. The damage is done."

Eloise thought that maybe, when it comes to breaking trust, horses and people were not that different.

9

When Eloise got home, this was waiting for her. She felt the familiar relief and release of falling into someone else's story.

Dec. 26, 1780

Major Schmidt has been ordered back to Barracks by January first. He and the remaining prisoners will be marched to Maryland, but he knows not when. There are disputes still to be settled between Jefferson and the Governor of Maryland, who is distressed to be burdened' with "Virginia's" prisoners. Major Schmidt worries that once again they will be deprived of food and shelter and proper clothing.

Yesterday Aunt Bess gave the Major as many stockings as she sent off with Buck. The Major nearly cried in gratitude, and was rendered speechless, which in turn made Aunt Bess cry. Aunt Bess will also send food back to the Barracks with him, salted meats and a barrel of apples, and as much flour as she can spare.

I gave the Major paper, quill and knife, and packets of powdered ink with the hopes it will find its way back to us with reports of his well-being. Henry had learned some Christmas tunes, and we assembled by the fire for his performance. Priscilla gave the boy a plate of molasses cookies and a large mug of milk as reward. I felt cheered by the music and proud of his improvement. I believe the Major played every note in his mind with his pupil and looked right relieved when the performance ended. The Major demurred to play for us. I think he had no wish to outshine his student.

Father gave the Major a packet of letters. I have no idea what they held. But they were graciously received and put away without further comment. I believe the two men have made a settlement agreement regarding the Major's horses. But I do not pry.

I was but slightly wounded to receive nothing as gift from the Major. This I have tried to chase from my thoughts. He has given me a multitude of happy memories that I will cherish always. God only knows if I will ever have the pleasure of his company again. I must not think of more foolish notions than that. He has been the best of friend and his horsemanship and animal husbandry an inspiration.

Priscilla and Aunt Bess outdid themselves with our Christmas feast. Much fervency was added to our blessing with prayers for Buck. I do not fear for Buck, although perhaps I should. Buck has no trouble living rough. His constitution has always been strong. I fear for the horses. I pray Buck is seeing to their feet, as well as their feed. I pray that he takes care to see the girth does not pinch, nor the saddle chafe. Aunty Bess should have knit something for the horses. Ah, how she would laugh at me for that thought. Father I do not think would laugh.

Aunt Bess, at last, received her cleverly designed chest. The craftsman finally satisfied her requirements. She has reserved its place of honor in her bedroom. She will not say what treasures are to be stored therein. But we are all duly warned that as only we know of the secret shelf, if anything should go missing, her list of suspects is short. Our grandest gift, to no one's surprise, is our new cellar. It is barely finished but has sturdy stone walls that shall keep it cool year-round. The steps are steep down, but a handrail was installed. Father had the servants' sand it fine, so no one need fear getting a splinter. What made me draw breath was the sight of a bench. A bench in a cellar? I did not ask why fore. I only noted that Aunt Bess had her hand upon her chest and her brow was smooth. This cellar, with the long bench for seating, would help dear Aunt Bess to sleep at night. It would not have that affect upon me.

Addendum, Dec. 27, 1780

I have my gift from Major Schmidt. Yesterday,

when he left to return to his cabin, he carried one of Priscilla's baskets laden with a feast to her cabin. It was time for the servants to enjoy their Christmas bounty in private. I assumed I would see no more of him that evening and found my book and candle and chair in the parlor beside Aunt Bess. Shortly he stood in the hallway. Aunt Bess surely heard his steps. But she did not look up, and the Major, gestured to me to come. I rose and followed him down the front stairs, a direction we rarely turn. We must have walked halfway down the carriage road before he spoke. The night was chilly, and I had only my shawl to pull around me.

He said, "We have said much to each other. But certain thoughts do torture me at night."

I nodded to encourage him, as he seemed to stop talking altogether. Finally, I said, "There is not a soul here who does not toss and turn. Priscilla perhaps for reasons that differ from our own."

That helped. He smiled and said, "You do lighten my burdens, and perhaps some distant day I can be equal to you, what you are to me."

That astonished me. As I thought my passion far more obvious than his own. I said in a teasing tone, "Well, Major, do say what it is that I am to you, for you are oft inscrutable."

He reached for both my hands with his and spoke low and serious, "You gave me courage to keep alive, Louisa."

He looked so solemn that I teased him, "I mean

150

to hear from you Major, words more specific of my charms."

"Is that not sufficient? It is no small thing to save a life."

"Have you no love sonnets?"

He pulled me then tightly into his arms and we kissed. Oh, there was no misreading his feelings.

Then he said, "Was that eloquent enough?"

I saucily said, "And what then is the second stanza?"

The Major pulled an ebony signet ring from his smallest finger and held it between us. He said, "I have little to offer. I shall not make promises I cannot keep. But if you will at least wait to see if I live or die, if you will wear this ring, to think of you doing so, will give me strength should my situation become desperate. It will give me courage to fight my way back to you and, God willing, to make you my wife."

It was a heavy ring, and a bit too large upon my finger. I must ask Aunt Bess for a bit of yarn to wrap around it.

We then enjoyed a second stanza. But resisted the urge, strong as it was, to finish the sonnet.

It was indeed no small thing to save a life. Hadn't Bev just said essentially the same thing, even though Bev was only referring to a kitten. Louisa would have her Major, should he survive. He had to survive.

* * *

Eloise's pies looked just like the photos online, with golden crusts that had remained intact without any broken bits. Of course, along with her pies, she had to pack Lady Jane in her Sherpa bag, along with a "diaper bag" of bottles and formula and a roll of toilet paper. The pies would be protected on the journey in plasticware. She made multiple trips to the car before she was ready to roll. It wasn't until Eloise got to Betsy's condo and unpacked the pies, thrilled to see they had made the journey unscathed, that she realized she had left the whipped cream. She had whipped it up herself, nice and stiff, with her mother's big electric mixer and packed it on ice in a small cooler.

Betsy had calmed her down. "Eloise, let it go. I've got a half gallon of vanilla ice cream in the freezer."

Lady Jane had begun to mew loudly from her bag.

"Take care of your kitten, and don't let Marilyn bother her. I'll pour the wine."

Eloise started to warm formula.

Marilyn had positioned herself next to the Sherpa bag, her eyes narrowed as she peered through the dark mesh to examine Lady Jane. Once Eloise pulled the kitten out of the bag, a big wad of toilet paper in hand to stimulate the emptying out process, Marilyn hissed, jumped down and backed up, looking alarmed and disgusted.

Betsy spoke to the cat, "Do try using your company manners."

No cat takes orders. Marilyn left the room. And she never came back out the entire evening.

The kitten protested loudly while Eloise patted her bottom and cleaned her up. After Eloise flushed the mess down Betsy's toilet and got the kitten settled with her bottle, Betsy handed her a glass of wine and watched the proceedings with interest.

Eloise said, "Marilyn isn't maternal, is she?"

"Well, no glamour-puss likes being upstaged by an ingenue."

Eloise finally had the leisure to look around the room. The upholstered furniture was beautiful, but too big in scale for the room. The walls were nearly all floor to ceiling heavily carved bookshelves, neatly lined with both books and photos. Where there was room for artwork, there were multiples hung in groupings, like you see in the great houses of Britain.

Betsy noticed. "I had to downsize. Just like you and your mother. I'm a terrible pack rat. Dabs and I have spoken about how his mother went from packrat to hoarder. Please feel free to intercede on my behalf should I cross that line."

Eloise said, "There's nothing wrong with holding on to the things we love. I wish Dabs' mother was still alive so I could ask her questions. I have so many questions, and I bet he does too."

Lady Jane had finished her bottle. Eloise gave her another chance to evacuate, and then flushed that away and sat on the floor with her kitten and the toothbrush while she and Betsy drank wine and chatted, and the kitten purred and wobbled her way around to explore."

Lady Jane was soon ready for her post-prandial nap. Once Eloise got her tucked into her Sherpa bag, she got up and examined some of the photos.

Betsy explained, "I used to lead student trips. I'd teach a course and then we'd travel. It was wonderful."

Eloise pointed at a group photo in front of the Eiffel Tower. Betsy said, "The course was 'Paris in the 1920's.'"

Eloise raised her brows, interested.

"Hemingway, Fitzgerald, Cummings, Dos Passos, as well as Gertrude Stein, and so on."

The doorbell rang and Betsy swung it open to welcome Pinky and Buzz. Betsy pointed Buzz to the kitchen to unload his food which came in an interesting rolling case that looked like it belonged to professional caterers. But the scene stealer that had them in stitches was Pinky.

Pinky, unburdened by any packages whatsoever, had constructed some sort of square white cape for her shoulders, wore a white apron and a poster board version of a pilgrim's hat tied under her chin with string.

"Ta-da! I'm Pinky the Pilgrim! Happy Thanksgiving!"

Buzz stepped back into the room to add, "I told her she looks like Offred from the "Handmaids Tale."

Betsy and Eloise were laughing so hard they had trouble replying to Buzz. But Betsy finally said, "Pinky I'm afraid Buzz is right. I can't see you as a Pilgrim."

Eloise added, "I'm guessing that dress doesn't qualify as part of the Pilgrim costume."

Pinky's dress, though black, was not a heavy woolen sack, but clinging knit with a low-cut neckline.

"So, I'm a Pilgrim with style. Sue me."

Betsy had pulled out her fine china, crystal, and silver, and lit a huge silver candelabra in the center of the table. When the turkey, casseroles, and rolls were placed on the table it was photograph-worthy. Betsy delivered the blessing before they tucked in. Pinky had removed her costume, including the hat, to reveal a wild topknot of pink hair that resembled a fountain.

Table talk soon turned to Dabs and the journals and it was soon apparent that Buzz was up to speed on it all.

Pinky exclaimed, "Well, you can't expect me to keep Buzz out of the loop, can you? I mean, really Eloise, who is he going to tell anyway?"

Eloise moaned, "My secret-keeping skills are pathetic. Dabs is going to kill me."

Betsy said, "Dabs is certainly not going to kill you. He knows our little circle has grown. And it's wonderful that Dabs and I are now the best of friends. How would that have ever happened if you hadn't confided in me? Now Dabs is looking forward to meeting Pinky, once you two find him a dog."

Buzz chimed in. "Once Pinky cracked, I kept after her until she told me everything she knew. To be honest, the journal thing is freaking cool. And how wild is it with the characters? Like it's a past life thing. Eloise is Louisa, and Betsy is Bess. The dog is even there."

Pinky said, "I'm kind of bummed that I'm not there."

He turned to Pinky, "Honey, you're not there, 'cause you're an original."

"Ah, that's so sweet."

"What about you Buzz. Who were you in a past life?"

"I come from criminal stock shipped over here by Great Britain. You won't find me in those journals."

Betsy said, "No worries Buzz, I think my roots are similar."

Eloise said, "What about you Pinky?"

"Heck if I know. Prior to an Alabama trailer park, it gets kind of murky."

Betsy said, "Well, it doesn't have to be my past-life to enjoy the journals. But I do like Aunt Bess. I appreciate her role as housemother. She is kind to the slaves and devoted to her niece and nephew. Would I have her foresight to prepare as she is doing? Would I take action steps?"

Eloise answered, "Yes."

Betsy said, "How can you be so sure?"

"Who came and got me and took off a whole week to care for me? When I needed you to be my honorary Aunt Betsy, you volunteered. I guess Thanksgiving is as good a time as any to let you know I'm really grateful."

Betsy said, "We had a memorable trip, didn't we? And I have a new friend in Dabs."

Buzz, seeing the female emotional level going up, looked slightly uncomfortable, and changed the subject. He asked Eloise, "Does your Dad celebrate Thanksgiving even though he's across the pond?"

"I doubt it."

Buzz said, "You going to call him?"

Pinky blurted out, "Maybe when hell freezes over."

Buzz said, "Did I just step in it?"

Eloise said, "No. I guess Pinky told you all about the journals but left out my current family drama. I'll try and summarize. Jock sold my horse, put the money in his pocket, and then didn't have the guts to confess. He just kept making up stories. But my financial guy, Ralph, he made a few inquiries and yeah, Jock's been putting off my requests to get my horse shipped back because he sold it to his wealthy client, currently his intended next Mrs. Robertson."

Buzz said, "I think I processed all that. And wow, that's shitty. I hope he feels guilty about that for the rest of his life."

Pinky waved away Buzz' remark. "So, Eloise, what's the next step?"

"I don't see a next step."

Betsy lifted her brows, "Pinky, do you see a next step?"

Pinky changed tack. "Why did Bev want to sell Jock that mare?"

Eloise said, "For a big pile of dough. And because Jock is for real, a good trainer and rider. The mare would do well under his care and direction."

Pinky nodded with interest. "I guess you don't have to be a good person to be a good rider."

Eloise grimaced, "I guess not."

Pinky asked, "So, Bev and Jock used to be tight?"

Eloise nodded again. "Evidently, she mentored Jock. They partnered on horse sales. All before my time, or when I was too young to know her. She and Mom were friends too."

Betsy added, "I do wonder, like Pinky, why Bev would contact Jock now. But I know nothing about the horse business. Do you think Bev was looking for some sort of rapprochement?"

"I haven't given enough thought to it all. I don't know. But, Bev, she's hinted at some pretty dark things."

Betsy cleared her throat, "Dabs told me about the warning letters Bev wrote your mother. Something about a horse sale to a person who had embezzled funds from a foreign government."

Buzz loudly said, "Holy shit!"

Pinky smacked his arm.

Eloise grimaced and said, "Dabs told you? Wow. I guess I won't feel guilty anymore for having leaky lips about the journals."

Betsy shrugged. "I hope you don't mind Dabs sharing with me. I don't know any of the people involved. The only person I care about is you, and these old notes don't reflect in any way on you."

Pinky asked again, "Why would Bev have summoned Jock back into her life? I don't get it."

Betsy added, "Bev's been so very generous with you Eloise. And now you say she's agreed to teach Doc? Regardless of past dramas, she sounds like a lovely person."

"Lovely?"

That made Eloise smile. "Bev is awesome. But lovely? That word doesn't work for Bev. But I do like her. And I love riding Red."

Buzz said, "Pinky says she's an old gal."

Eloise nodded then said, "It's hard to say how old. She's thin as a rake and wrinkled up like an old apple. But full of energy, loud, brash, and funny, and she's an excellent horsewoman, too."

Pinky added, "Maybe she's got some unfinished business with Jock."

"She does keep telling me she's got a mean streak. But I sure don't see it."

Pinky said, "Well, I say, you should still get your mare back. Don't you give up. Never, never, never, never give up!"

Eloise nearly yelled out, "Winston Churchill!"

Betsy exclaimed, "That's right."

And Pinky said, "Who?"

10

Eloise had volunteered to do kennels over the long holiday weekend. She didn't mind. She owed Doc for her time off after her "incident."

She woke up Friday morning ravenously hungry. Why was it that the day after a huge meal you were so hungry? There would be no donuts from Doc today, so she had pulled through the drive through and was thrilled to find someone to sell her a dozen hot donuts right out of the fryer. She didn't care that they didn't have her favorites. Any hot donuts were good donuts.

It was still dark when she pulled into the clinic and shut off her engine. The clinic was full of boarders. She had a full day ahead of her. Eloise fished the keys from the bottom of her bag, put her bag over her shoulder, and grabbed the flat of donuts, swinging her car door shut with her butt. The donuts were so fresh the smell was making her mouth water. She almost dropped the box when something banged against the backs of her legs and made her knees buckle.

And there he was.

"Prince! Oh my God! Not again!"

Prince ran up the steps to the front door and did a dance, looking pleased with himself, as if he'd just yelled, "Surprise!" He certainly had surprised her, too. And of course, Eloise could not be angry. "Her" dog had once again found his way back for a visit. He did not look any the worse for wear either.

Eloise put down the donuts in the lounge and decided. She would call Joe herself. By now surely, he would realize this wasn't because of her. Eloise found Joe's number on Prince's new ID tag. Still, she kept hitting the wrong keys as she tapped his number into her phone. So she double-checked before hitting the green button. It didn't occur to her that most people would still be asleep. It took a few rings before Joe picked up.

Joe's voice was deep and husky, "Hello?"

"It's Eloise. I just got to the clinic, and Prince was at the front door again."

There was a pause. Then, "I'm out of town for the holiday. No one told me he was missing. Let me call my girlfriend and have her come get him. I'm so sorry, Eloise."

"Don't apologize. It's all good here."

"I'd better call her. If she is out scouring the neighborhood looking for him, she needs to know he's safe."

Eloise said, "Well, he's perfectly content, and I enjoy his company, so no rush."

Joe said, "Thanks, Eloise. I'll give you a call."

Eloise hung up and looked at Prince. She thought he looked pensive. She enthused, "Hey, don't worry. You can stay!"

Prince started barking and twirling circles. Eloise added, "For now."

Prince ran to the basement door. Eloise opened it, and Prince bounded down the stairs, predictably setting off the packed kennels. There would be no free space in a run for Prince today. But Eloise made him his bowl of kibble and water and put down a blanket for his bed and told him to stay.

After Eloise got her chores done, she took Prince with her to the lounge to make coffee and enjoy those donuts.

She had downed one donut when Joe called.

"Hi Eloise. I'm afraid I'll need to board Jaeger there if that's allowed. I'll be back Sunday evening."

Eloise felt a surge of joy. She tried to sound casual, but her heart was pounding. "Oh, you don't have to board him. I mean, he can stay here with me while I'm working, but he's used to coming home with me, so of course he can go home with me. Mi casa, su casa. I don't mind at all. Really, it's nothing, I'll enjoy his company, and he can eat here with the gang. And …"

She paused. She realized she was talking too much.

"Well, I suppose this one time. It's just I worry that he'd just run off again. Evidently, Jaeger asked to go out in the yard early. And then she fell asleep. My call woke her up."

Eloise said, "Oh. So, she wasn't out looking for him?" Eloise realized her tone sounded judgmental. So, she added, "Well, Prince *is* an early riser!"

Joe made a little noise that Eloise thought was annoyance, and she was not sure who Joe was annoyed with as there were multiple candidates.

He said, "True. She had no idea he had taken off."

Eloise found she couldn't shut up, saying, "If he wanted to get out of the yard, he would find a way. He's a genius. I've never known a dog as brilliant as he is."

"My girlfriend did not use those words to describe him."

Eloise tried to sound breezy, "Well, enjoy the rest of your vacation. I'll keep tabs on him. See you Sunday."

And they hung up.

Eloise said, "So, you ditched the girlfriend? Clearly, she doesn't appreciate you like I do. Well, it's you and me, Prince! This is the best Thanksgiving I've had in years. The best, best, best, best, and you are a big part of the reason! Tonight, we can go to Bev's, and you can run with the Red Devil!"

Prince knew that whatever it was that Eloise was saying it was good and it was reason to get excited and bark and twirl. For a few seconds they danced a cross-species happy dance.

Eloise opened a bag of Dental chews and got Prince settled on a blanket by Pinky's grooming station in the basement, while she cleaned and walked. Prince seemed satisfied to watch Eloise parade in and out with dogs as he gnawed at his chew. It took longer than usual to finish kennel duty with a full house. Finally, she could release him from his spot and let him come up with her to clean the litter boxes and give the boarding kitties some love.

When Eloise finished, she took Prince back down to the basement. She got him into Pinky's tub before checking out all the shampoo options. After giving all options the sniff test, she picked out one that reminded her of both her mom and Ralph. Cinnamon.

Eloise announced, "Prince, it's spa day!"

Prince, ever cheerful, enjoyed his bath, even making happy moans. Eloise gave him a vigorous toweling off, letting him play tug of war with the towel. Then it was lunch time. Eloise had packed a sandwich and planned to attack more of the donuts. She shared with Prince because any decent surprise party ought to include good eats.

Later, Prince stretched out with her on the couch and they napped. It was almost time for second walks when Eloise was roused by knocks on the front door.

Pinky was peering through the windows. Eloise unlocked the door and let her in. Pinky was carrying a picnic basket. Of course, Prince was there to greet her too, having a happy fit.

Pinky shrieked, "Oh my God Eloise, what have you done?"

"I did nothing! He was waiting for me again. I swear it."

"Did you call Doc?"

Eloise frowned, "I didn't see any reason to bother Doc. I called Joe. Joe is out of town for the holiday. He'll come get him Sunday."

Pinky looked sympathetic now. "Are you okay?"

"Why wouldn't I be? I get three days with my best buddy!"

Pinky stroked the top of his head. "You gave him a bath. Coat feels great."

Eloise pointed at the picnic basket. "You and Buzz are so great to think of me."

"I'll put it in the fridge. Thanksgiving isn't the same without leftovers."

Eloise and Prince followed her back to the lounge. Eloise said, "I'm thinking of this sort of like visitation rights for divorced parents. I get Prince for Thanksgiving!"

Pinky said, "Except you don't even know Joe. Not the real Joe anyway."

Eloise nodded, "Said plenty of women in divorce court."

Pinky started to unload the basket into the fridge. "Cute. Now, if you share this with Prince, only the white meat, okay. No skin or fatty stuff to upset his gut."

"I just fed him a donut."

Pinky rolled her eyes and said, "I saw a dog that might work for Dabs. It looked big and athletic, like it would enjoy all that space. But the foster said he was shy and fearful. And then I thought, 'no' since Dabs needs a dog that would stick around off leash. A shy dog might get scared and bolt. I mean, a hundred acres with Dabs riding a horse and the dog running free and all. He needs a dog that comes when he calls."

Eloise narrowed her eyes at Pinky. "Is there a point here that I'm missing?"

Pinky shrugged. "I've got a feeling about the girlfriend. That's all. Let's see if they can keep Prince from making another unannounced visit. And if that happens, well…"

Then she held her index finger in front of Eloise, "You say nothing. But if Joe is coming to pick the dog up, I'd love to be here. As a bystander."

Eloise began to say something, but Pinky held up her finger again. And it was like she had cast a spell. Eloise couldn't make a peep.

* * *

Bev hollered, "Well, that's a sight I never thought I'd see again," as Eloise let Prince out of her car. The dog was nearly shrieking with joy and Eloise ran after him, concerned he might knock Bev over. Instead, he ran zigzags around her with his tail tucked and his haunches lowered, burning off the excess energy stored from a day at the clinic.

Bev said, "'Silly' don't quite conjure up the right image of that display there, but it's the only word I got. That there is a silly dog."

Prince finally slowed down and came up to Bev and nudged her leg gently with his big hairy nose. He then plopped his butt down and leaned into her, looking up at her with adoration.

Eloise said, "He's clearly happy to see you."

"Feelings mutual. So, what ya' do, sleep with the guy?"

Eloise was speechless. She shouldn't have been of course. This was Bev.

Bev said, "Course you didn't. But wouldn't judge ya' for it if you did. I dun worse for less."

Eloise laughed. "Prince found his way to the clinic this morning. Joe is out of town for the holiday weekend and well, the girlfriend can't seem to keep tabs on him. I offered to keep him until he gets back on Sunday."

"Hmmmm." then nodded, "Well, go on and work the sass out of both the horse and the dog. A tired dog ain't likely to roam."

Prince had trouble staying put while Eloise did her short longing session with Red. He'd get up, wag his tail madly, wander around then go back to his spot and sit back down. He didn't stray though. But once she and Red stepped through the gate into the field, he was off like a rocket. Eloise would lose sight of him, then see him flash across her path, and be off again. Red never batted an eye at the darting big black dog. Red knew him. Eloise did her trot sets, and then made Red stay to pace in a canter circuit, though the mare was on the muscle. Eloise checked her watch to see how long they had gone. She listened to the mare's rhythmic breathing, steady and long. Red had plenty of gas in the tank. Eloise pushed her heels down and stabilized herself for the big surge and allowed it to happen. Boom. They were flying. Exhilaration. She caught sight of Prince in her peripheral vision, coming out of the grass, trying to stay with them. For a few strides the two animals were in a race. Red pinned her ears, then kicked it up a notch. Eloise lost sight of the dog. It wasn't until Eloise had pulled Red up and was walking on a loose rein, that Prince zoomed past them, and ran all the way to the gate, then waited for them, victorious. Technically, Prince had won the race. Silly dog. Silly, silly, silly, wonderful dog.

Eloise lingered at the barn, giving Red an extra good grooming, and then putting on her stable sheet and watching her munch her hay back in her stall. Red was a different horse after her work. The mare was content. Content with her work. Content with her life.

Eloise said out loud, "Well done, you, you Red Devil." And as she stood there, she felt Prince nudge her leg. She looked down to find the dog looking up at her, wanting her praise. She added with a stroke to his head, "Well done you too, you wonderful, silly boy."

Bev spoke up behind them. "Best feeling in the world."

Eloise nodded at Bev, who was shutting up the barn for the night. The two women, and the dog walked out, Bev pulling the barn doors shut. Eloise opened the back door of her car, and Prince jumped in.

Bev's parting words were, "You don't need to give nothin' away to git what you want. Don't give nothin' away. Do right. Do your best. Things always sort themselves."

Bev chuckled; her eyes crinkled up like she'd told a funny joke. Then she gave the car a slap, like it was the butt of a horse that needed to move.

So, Eloise put it in drive. And went home.

11

Jan. 1, 1781

The Major and I have had our last interview for who knows how long. I fear it was not as tender as it should have been. I find myself twisting the ring upon my finger as a worry-token.

I said, "I cannot spin nor weave nor make a tidy stitch. I cannot knit a stocking. I paid no heed to cookery or receipts, nor how to roll out dough. I paid no heed to brewing, preserving, washing nor making of soap or candles. And you say we shall not own servants? All I know to do is read and write, draw and ride my horse."

The Major did not comfort me. Instead, he said, "And I, Louisa, am no farmer. I know nothing of cultivation. I am by necessity adept at living rough, but I would not ask it of you. My best talents are riding and training horses and my violin. We are poor candidates to survive by our own skills. But I will not own a slave. I will not."

I said, "My father would not let us want."

169

He answered, "You would have us live as children then? Dependents?"

I said, "You would work for father. As you do now."

He considered that for a moment, then said, "Buck will, in time, inherit Ivy Creek Plantation. He will not suffer to have me about as a stakeholder. If you tie your fate to mine, Buck will have no qualms to turn us out."

The Major was correct. I finally answered, "We must speak to father."

He said, "Louisa dearest, I never would have offered you my ring had I not done so. Though, we have not settled all, we have spoken well and straight. This sin of slavery though, it nettles me. I see how deeply it is rooted and I fear for your country as well as for us both."

And then he changed the subject in all too airy a way. I could not turn him back to my agitations. Instead, he prattled on about how he had made a wooden case for transporting Cleopatra's kits back to us from the Hessian section of the Barracks. We are to keep them trapped inside the cabins until the troops are securely away and the kits reclaim us as their home territory. The Major fears for their lives should the kits be startled as the men march away. The cats that fled the burning British Barracks were thus destroyed. This worried Henry to distraction. I doubt we can long succeed in keeping them confined. Cats are stealthy creatures. But Henry will oversee these feline prison-ers-of-war.

Poor Henry. I did catch him crying into his elbow, squatting behind the new false privy. I em-barrassed him mightily by calling his name. I tried my best to rouse his courage. "We must all be brave soldiers," I told him. I reassured him, "Our Major Schmidt would be kept safe, likely by some other kind family in Maryland.

Henry brightened a moment then said, "The girls do go on about Major Schmidt, they do. I sup-pose you may be right, Miss Louisa."

Now Henry had introduced a concern I had not considered prior. I think he saw me frown, he said, "You suppose those ladies in Maryland are as pretty as you?"

I said, "As I've never been to Maryland, I can't say."

Henry continued, "I knows they don't have horseflesh like we got here. Ain't no horses pretty as the ones we got. And Mr. Roberts, he gonna' save Major's horses for him. Major'll come back for that mare. Fashion she the finest horse in the country. I feel that certain."

Henry wasn't sure that I could compete with the ladies of Maryland, but he felt sure that the Mary-land horses held no threat to ours. It would be Fash-ion that brought our Major back! I let myself laugh. And laugh. It was a great relief to laugh. And my laughter made Henry laugh too.

And soon the two of us were laughing so hard that we were discovered by Aunt Bess who had a chore for Henry and was looking for the boy. We tamed our jollity. And Aunt Bess was kind enough not to ask particulars.

January 2, 1781

Now that the Major has returned to barracks, I think of how my words failed me at our parting. We have no rosy view before us, that is true. But what a bleak aspect is before me without my dear Major! If we have hardship ahead, should it not be shared? I said naught in this vein at our parting. All we two recited were the obvious deficiencies of our match. As heir to nothing, we are dependents. I have faith that the inequity will be leavened by father now that Jefferson has eliminated the absurd rule of entail. Buck will resent losing anything to his wartime prisoner. There will be trouble there. I trust in father to arrange things. I dare not mention it at present. We have the business of a war to settle.

I presume Buck thinks of me as something to be rid of, like a disobedient slave, traded for goods or land that enriches him or adds luster to our name. But life is not made only by meeting basic needs, or material gain, no, it is made fine by feeling and beauty and devotion. Thank God for Father who is not so base as Buck. Father has approved of the Ma-

jor because of the Major's qualities of character. How foolish to doubt father's judgement for a moment! When I entertain doubt, I do disservice to father. As far as this matter of slavery, well, it must not be a wedge that keeps us apart.

This afternoon, the Major has sent over a note by the hand of a young soldier who had no over coat and was rail-thin, with lips pale and cracked. The note was addressed to father.

I took the note, while Aunt Bess gave the soldier bread slathered in apple butter, and had Priscilla heat up a mug of milk. He said, "Danke, danke, danke, Frau Carter" so many times I wanted to tell him to shush. Instead, I carried the note to father's office door and knocked gently.

Father had on spectacles. A new habit caused I believe, from straining his eyes by candlelight in the evenings. I handed him the note with no intention of leaving the room until he had shared the contents. Father scanned it with raised eyebrows and pursed lips, and then simply handed it back to me.

It read:

Dear Sir,

I am notified that we march not to Maryland, but a destination in Virginia known as Winchester. We shall not go to Fort Frederika. The squabble between the Governors has blocked admission of prisoners unto the Marylander's care. So, my friend Jefferson is not shed of me yet. Although it appears

173

he is under much pressure to cease paying for what scanty, moldy, or rancid provisions have found their way to my fellows. However poorly the situation here, my men are anxious. They and I too, imagine a harsh winter ahead with little comforts. I had sent word to my parents that I would be in Maryland. I send word again, that I am to be in another area of Virginia. By the time they receive such news, who knows where I shall be? Such are the vagaries of war.

I have been informed that the Baron and Baroness were given parole in New York. General Phillips has been returned to the field. This comes as a great shock. They were exchanged for your General Benjamin Lincoln. Cornwallis will make great use of Phillip's knowledge of your countryside and of that I feel certain.

I gave Mother and Father your name and location and told them of the love and care I received under your protection. Also, of the fragile hope that I hold for the future. If you should receive correspondence from Gustav and Frederika Schmidt you will know it was by my direction, with assurances given by me that such correspondence would be welcomed.

With gratitude and affection, Yours truly, Major Johannes Schmidt

Well, there it is copied into my little book before I returned it to father. Not one word to me, or of me, in his note. I find myself twisting the ring upon my finger. When will I be spared from this constancy of uncertainty?

* * *

Jock's voice was cheerful, "Lulu! Funny you should call; I was just bragging on you. Were your ears burning?"

Here she was calling Jock. Bev had motivated Eloise, sending her off with a slap to her car like a jockey going to the stick. Like getting what Eloise wanted would be as simple as urging Red into a gallop. But Eloise wasn't Bev. Just hearing Jock's voice made her lose momentum. In that moment, she felt more kinship to Louisa Roberts, twisting her ring as a worry token, as she faced the "constancy of uncertainty."

Eloise was distracted by her thoughts as she answered, "That's nice, but no."

Jock continued, "Atlantis is already killing it here. I won an Advanced Horse Trials last weekend on him. He's got just enough fitness and fire to run the big stuff, but he still has the gaits and temperament to win the dressage. Good work kiddo. I may just let you be my new talent scout."

"But I don't want to be a talent scout. I want to ride. Well, actually I have been riding. Just one horse after I get off work. Not like the old days. I'm only jumping once a week, and it's pretty small stuff on that red mare at Bev's."

Jock said, "I wish you'd find a better place to ride."

"Didn't you and Bev train together?"

"Yeah. That's why I'm saying..."

Eloise interrupted him. "I knew it! Bev sounds just like you. Her mouth opens and your words come out. Even her sense of humor and her catchphrases are yours. So, what's the deal?"

"Well, back in the day, she found my best jumper for me, and helped me a lot. Then we were business partners, scooping up horses for next to nothing and selling them for a lot. But honey, that was a million years ago. Lots under the bridge since then. She still has an eye. That red mare was exactly the kind of horse I expected from Bev. It's not the horse I worry about. And Bev's a good coach, too."

"So, when you say I should find a better place, what do you mean?"

"Lulu, we lost trust in each other for reasons that don't involve you. I don't know why she contacted me. I thought maybe it was an olive branch. I guess not. I'm just telling you, don't trust anything she says or does. But hey, it's a free country. You do what you want. Just know it makes your old man uneasy."

Eloise said, "You were the one who told me to go there to try that mare."

"I guess that's true."

Eloise sighed, " Riding that mare is a bright spot in my day, especially since I had to give the dog back. His previous owner showed up and took him back."

"Sorry to hear that. I'm sure that was hard."

"It was. But then I found a tiny kitten in a storm drain. The rest of the litter had washed down the drain."

"Oh, wow, that's sickening."

"I'm feeding it with a bottle every three hours."

"That young means it's fragile. Hope it makes it. But life is cruel, sweetie."

Eloise said, "Yes, I've figured that out by now."

The line was silent for a long beat.

Jock's voice broke, "Lulu, please. Don't make your old man cry."

Neither one spoke for a moment.

Jock recovered his voice and pivoted, "So, what'd you name the kitten?"

"Lady Jane. She's grey."

Jock snorted, "Okay, that's gallows humor."

Eloise took a deep breath and finally said what she had wanted to say, "Jock. I *still* want Whiplash back."

"I thought we had come to an agreement on this."

Eloise felt the blood rush to her head, then the familiar wave of dizziness. No, she wasn't going to retreat. Bev had urged her not to give up anything.

She said, "We? I've never agreed to any of this."

"Lulu, I realize that you want what you want. But I'm going to manage this mare until at least the foal is weaned. Then we can revisit this. But, until then it's not negotiable."

Eloise said, "You're not telling me everything."

Jock countered, "And you're not telling me everything, either."

That exchange was followed by a long silence. Because both knew that was the truest thing either of them had said in the whole conversation.

Jock pivoted again. "Sorry about the dog. We always had great dogs, didn't we?"

"Yes."

Jock said, "Great memories, huh?"

"Yes."

Jock softened his tone further, "There will be other dogs, Lulu. There will be other horses too. Those days on Whiplash were fun, and you learned tons from her. But those days are gone. Just because you've lost some things, it doesn't mean you can't gain new things. And have fun. Fun is allowed. And it wouldn't hurt for you to date either. Elly was hoping you'd meet someone outside the horse world. Someone who wasn't all consumed by horses and the horse industry. This horse world can swallow you up whole."

Eloise asked, "Did it swallow you up whole?"

"No. Chewed me up first, then swallowed. I've got the x-rays to prove it."

"But here you are. Still climbing back on."

"I've got no other options at this point, and I'm not getting any younger."

Eloise had one more question. "And you're counting on this marriage? Are you sure it's going to happen?"

"Well, your old man kind of did a 'thing' as you kids say."

Eloise was shaking her head. "And you didn't think to even tell me?"

"I guess I'm telling you now."

Eloise grimaced into the phone, once again thinking of the constancy of uncertainty. Bev had urged her not to give away anything to get what she wanted. What the heck had Bev meant? The thing was, everything she wanted had already been given away. She just wanted to reclaim from the rubble what could still be salvaged.

Still, she managed to say, "Congratulations."

"Thanks Lulu."

* * *

She and Pinky had been in the lounge waiting when Joe came to pick up Prince. Lady Jane was on her lap and Prince was gently nosing her and wagging his fringed tail with delight. And then there was the knock on the door. Prince went bounding out into the waiting room and barked like mad at the door.

Eloise put her kitten back in her Sherpa bag. Before Eloise could make it down the hall toward the waiting room, Prince had run back at her.

Pinky said to Eloise, "You okay?"

Eloise took a deep breath and shrugged.

Pinky went to unlock the door and greet Joe.

Eloise said to the dog, "You had to know he'd come back for you."

Prince looked up at Eloise and his tail drooped. Surely Prince couldn't understand her words, but he understood her tone, he understood her body language.

Eloise and Prince made it to the waiting room in time to see Joe step through the door.

Eloise was trying her best to be cool. But just seeing Joe made her feel clumsy, like she would fall and hit her head again, and she wouldn't have a rolling chair to blame this time.

Eloise had an awful surge of adrenaline. Even though she had told him she would be fine keeping the dog for him, she was not fine. Her knees had gone weak, and her mouth had gone dry. Damn. Damn. Damn. Eloise was able to spit out, through dry lips and a tongue that felt too large for her mouth, "Hi Joe."

Neither one extended a hand.

The voice in Eloise's head was whispering, "Don't fall down, don't fall down, don't fall down."

Pinky was cheerfully yakking away. Eloise put her hand on top of Prince's head. It felt oddly hot to the touch. Like his brain was working at high revs, and for a moment she wondered if it would overheat. Meanwhile, Pinky and Joe were having a conversation. It sounded like a pleasant one. But Eloise was having trouble taking it in.

Then she heard Pinky say, "Wow. You really do live close."

Joe said something, something, something, something.

Pinky said, "Sometimes dogs that have been the center of attention, get their noses out of joint when you know, they now have competition."

What was Pinky up to? Eloise refocused on their conversation. This seemed important.

Joe was saying his girlfriend and Prince had gotten off to a rocky start. Prince had stolen her very expensive sunglasses and it took them days to find them and when they did, the lenses were scratched.

Pinky made sympathetic noises then said, "By the way, I have a friend looking for a large athletic dog if you know one. He's retired and lives on a hundred acres in Virginia."

Joe said, "Virginia? Would that be the place where Eloise took Prince to recover from her concussion?"

Pinky said, "I didn't realize Doc told you about that, but yeah, that's the place and the guy. He was impressed with your dog. Not many people are familiar with the breed."

Joe said, "I'm not the one to ask, but my sister might know of one."

Pinky continued, "He wanted to adopt Prince, I mean Jaeger. I mean, we would have hated to part with the dog, but it was such a great home. Well, obviously that didn't work out, but he'd like a dog exactly like Jaeger."

Eloise realized she was expected to say something, do something instead of once again growing roots. She found herself stiffly pointing to the leash and saying, "Shall we?"

Joe looked confused for a moment, then embarrassed. He said, "Oh. Sure. Here." Except no one moved. Prince had not moved off her feet or stopped leaning on her legs, and Joe too looked incapable of moving toward Eloise.

Pinky smoothly took the leash and clipped it onto Prince's collar and handed the leash back to Joe.

Joe said, "Clearly, he has a wonderful time here. I can't thank you two enough. And I can ask my sister about finding a puppy for your friend."

Pinky said, "Oh, no. I forgot to say. He'd prefer an adult dog if you know of one. Puppies are cute and all that, but boy aren't we always glad when they become dogs!"

Pinky said all that with a straight face.

Joe gave the leash a tug and said, "C'mon Jaeger, let's go home!"

Prince did not move. Instead, he leaned harder into Eloise and began to pant. Joe pulled harder, and Prince unlocked himself. He took two steps forward and then stopped and sat down. He was voting with his feet.

Joe pulled harder, "Jaeger, come!"

Ever obedient, Prince complied.

As they got to the door, Joe turned, thanked them again, and said something about Jaeger enjoying his visit, and was gone.

Eloise's wooden legs, that had just been rooted to the ground beneath her feet, instantly turned to jelly. But it was done. There was a measure of relief in that.

Pinky locked the front door, then turned and said, "He'll be back. Don't give up yet."

12

Our hopes are brought low by war news, and then in turn they soar with news that heartens. Hoof beats pound down our drive, messages are relayed and then the rider is swift away to alert our neigh-bors, with nary a step inside to take a hot drink.

My dear Major is near, yet far, out of sight, but not yet on the march. The weather grows no better and we are kept inside by torrential rains. We are no longer allowed even the slightest communication with the prisoners as tensions mount.

That traitor Arnold has savaged his own peo-ple and country and burned down our new capitol at Richmond. Jefferson has made away safe, as have our Assemblymen. But just barely. Poor Mrs. Jefferson. Jefferson did send her to safety ahead of him. How terrified she must have been. She is yet in danger, having given birth to another girl they have named Lucy. Mrs. Jefferson had to rise from her birthing chamber to flee. This business of war is too cruel. Our General Washington had placed a bounty on the head of Arnold. I am not vengeful by nature, but in this case, I should like to see him caught and pay the ultimate price for his treachery. We hear that Jefferson's house servants in Richmond were stolen by the British. I hope they find their way back home.

Arnold leaves a swath of destruction and thievery in his wake as he fled his carnage. General Phillips is landed with more troops. How dare he come to destroy those who made him welcome here? It seems Jefferson entertained vipers in his nest. May God strike Phillips dead for his ingratitude.

The destruction of Richmond put Aunt Bess into a frenzy of hoarding and hiding. Most of our silver is boxed and stored below ground. I would not let her remove our china service. I will not eat from wood troughs like the livestock. We have little jewelry or cash, but all has been gathered and stored in her secret shelf or in the excess storage space under our rafters, but Aunt Bess thinks that garret space too easily accessed by a raiding party. Father put his foot down to her notion to unstitch our mattresses and put inside them bags of wheat flour and sugar. What a lumpy mattress that would make!

When the weather is this wet and cold, we struggle to keep the stock watered in the barn. Sammie and Isaac and Henry must haul water to them in buckets, muck stables and groom the riding horses. We have turned out all the excess riding stock and await the Spring to bring them back up to our stables. Beast suffers from boredom, pacing, whin-

ing, sighing. I laugh and tell him he must learn to read or draw as both are fine ways to spend a rainy day. He does not get the joke. So, when he becomes too restless, I send him to Henry who serenades him on his violin while Beast torments his clutter of cats.

Priscilla is most miserable. Her belly is bigger than she, and the bulk of it rides so high she can barely draw breath. Aunt Bess says the babe is not ready to make an appearance. Once the bulk shifts downward we should man our stations. We have an old negress who has much experience bringing babies into the world. She is on notice. She attended my mother with obvious success. Priscilla looks terrified and has reverted to her prior habit of throwing her apron over her face to have a come-apart. I try to stay out of the way at such times. I have begun to include Priscilla in my nightly prayers, such as they are.

I come back to my scribblings with astounding news. We have received word from Buck. Our Buck has been in an extraordinary battle! He is unhurt. Morgan conducted a brilliant maneuver that has annihilated Tarleton's troops and sent his battered remnants fleeing. Buck's task was to perch in a tree and take down as many British soldiers as he could before being ordered to fall back. He writes that it wasn't much different than shooting into a herd of beeves, since unlike deer, the soldiers seemed too dumb to run. They came at a slow march, and he just kept shooting. He forgot to count how many he

185

took down, but he boasts that he has gotten light-
ening quick at reloading that long rifle. He claims
he heard bullets whistle, but none even damaged
the branch he sat upon. I expect Buck was still flush
with the excitement of battle when he did write.
Bragging as if he had killed a deer. And yet these
were not deer he has killed.

Can it be that this conflict is ending? That my
Major may still be so near when it does end, that he
can simply walk back to me? Dare I hope so much?

Buck writes that it's a mighty cold wet down
there, with roads that are mud soup and creeks and
rivers swelled. Sounds just like here. He writes that
Morgan used his wiles to trap Tarleton in a maneuver that worked like a pair of jaws. Those jaws
closed on the Brits and chewed them up. It's taken
a lot out of the old wagoner though. Buck said he's
so down in his back that he can't straighten up, nor
walk, nor sit a horse. He may have to be carried to
Virginia. Buck says this battle knocked the stuffing
out of the Brits and is the start to the end. We shall
win.

How I yearn to speak to my Major. Father
forbids all attempts. He says we are in a dangerous
moment in time. He does not share Buck's certainty.
We must show forbearance and wait for better days.
Housebound by rain, battles raging south of us, our
city of Richmond in ashes, and a babe refusing to
come out of the womb, our forbearance continues to
be mightily tested.

* * *

Eloise was not enduring the tests that Louisa endured, yet, December had become a dreary test of endurance. Atlanta humidity made the summers feel hotter and the winters feel colder. Unless Eloise was running up and down the stairs at the clinic or riding, she was cold and stayed cold. Especially her feet and hands. She still enjoyed her time at Bev's, but it took a long hot shower to recover from each ride.

Once out of her shower she noticed a group text had gone out from Pinky.

Pinky wrote, "How about Buzz and I do a Christmas Eve dinner and a gift exchange? Anybody up for it?"

Eloise had a rush of guilt and shame. They had done so much for her. She knew it was time to do something, a down payment on a debt she knew she could never repay.

Eloise bravely stated, "It's my turn. We can do it at my place."

Pinky said, "Great idea! And you have the perfect house for entertaining."

Eloise shook her head, realizing Pinky had set her up. She said, "Pinky, did you just bait me into hosting a party?"

"Moi?"

Betsy said, "You don't have to Eloise. I don't mind doing it here."

Pinky added, "Buzz would do the cooking."

Betsy added, "I like to cook, and I love Christmas, and all the decorating, and the music and just everything Christmas. I don't mind doing it here, but if you decide to host it Eloise, I'm volunteering to help you all the way."

Eloise caved. She owed them, plus the two of them together were a mighty force, and resistance was pointless. She said, "It's settled. Christmas Eve is at my house."

Betsy said, "No fear Eloise. It will be fabulous. I have ideas!"

Pinky said, "I love that!"

Eloise thought, well, there it was. All without any real thought or intent on her part. Eloise was hosting the holiday dinner at her house. She found that she was already proud of herself. And she hadn't done anything yet.

Eloise decided to invite Jellybean Ralph to join them, wipe out her dinner debt to him.

Eloise invited Bev who evidently had no plans. She owed Bev a lot!

Eloise invited Doc, but Doc had regretfully declined, as he had a prior engagement. That was a disappointment.

It had begun to dawn on her that they were all orphans of a sort. Well, not Pinky and Buzz. But she was pretty sure Ralph was a singleton. This dinner, even if the idea had come from Pinky, well, it was a good idea.

Once Eloise had decided to host a Christmas Eve dinner, the decorating tasks at the clinic (that had been mostly up to her and Janet to implement) seemed less of a chore. Doc brought in a live tree, the kind in a big pot.

From somewhere up in Doc's office there appeared a large box of ornaments. There were dog and cat and bird and mice ornaments as well as garlands of plastic beads in the shape of dog bones and strings of tiny white lights. Some ornaments had names of pets on them, sent in by grateful clients. Of course, one strand of lights refused to work and was discarded. As the Christmas cards of clients arrived, they were pinned to the bulletin board.

Even though Christmas in Atlanta could be dark, damp, and cold, the Christmases of her childhood had been magical. Her favorite memory was getting Brighty as a Christmas present. Jock had her open a box with nothing in it but a brass halter tag that said, "Brighty" and a note with instructions to follow a trail of carrots out the back door. Eloise had picked up each carrot along the way, to find herself face to face with her new horse, a big red bow tied to the front of her stall. She had sobbed with excitement and promised perfect behavior and straight A's in school. She had meant those promises too and mostly had kept them with few infractions. She wanted to please them. She wanted them to be proud of her.

Their barn tradition included a group ride to Christmas music with Jock leading in a Santa Claus outfit. He always finished by leading the group over a small jump. Later in the tack room "Santa" had gifts for all the good boys and girls, generally a bottle of something for each of the adults. In the picture in her mind was always her mother, who had certainly planned and arranged everything. She would be laughing. It was a golden time. And perhaps all children feel the same way. You can never replicate as an adult that brief time when Santa is real, and the entire season is infused with magic.

Eloise had not "done" Christmas since her mother's death. It would have made her sadder. But this year, she went to the nursery and purchased a humongous wreath. She was stunned at the cost but handed over her card willingly. She also hired a maid service to clean the townhome. That too was surprisingly expensive, but it made her feel good. Eloise seemed to notice, maybe for the first time, what a pretty dining room table they had. She even had enough chairs for everyone. And the living room was pretty, with a large and colorful oriental rug and old furniture that her mother had sent off to be reupholstered and refinished. Her mother had done all this for her. Had done the things she would have done for Eloise in later years to help her set up a home of her own. Her mother was a planner. And even though these thoughts made Eloise a little tearful, she was also grateful.

Eloise was still toting Lady Jane with her to the clinic every day, although the kitten was now eating soft kitten food. Her eyes were now bright, and she had begun to play like a kitten ought to play, spending more time loose in the house and cautiously exploring her environment. Eloise still put her into the Sherpa bag for safety when she couldn't keep an eye on her. But Lady Jane was flourishing. There were reasons to be hopeful.

* * *

It was pitch dark when Eloise got out of her car at the clinic. So dark, she never saw her attacker. She was knocked from behind, shoved to the ground. Eloise, who had the Sherpa bag in one hand and her pocket-book in the other, went down hard on her knees and then to her chest. She threw her pocketbook with all her might toward the clinic steps and cradled the Sherpa bag against her body.

Her voice came out shrill and panicked. "Take it, take it all!! This one's just a cat carrier."

But no one moved toward the pocketbook. Instead, the assault became one of wet beard and gigantic tongue. It was Prince, again. Eloise rocked back on her butt and rubbed at her knees which were wet and muddy and throbbing.

"For God's sake! You scared the hell out of me! Plus, that hurt."

Prince twirled and barked and then sat down on her lap and leaned against her, which unbalanced her again, but he couldn't stay that still for long and jumped back up to do butt-tucking zoomies. Eloise had such a flood of relief that she began to cry.

Once she was inside, she "ripped off the band-aid" and called Joe. He took a few rings to pick up. His voice nearly growled into the phone. "Hello?"

Eloise's voice came out raspy. "Joe? It's Eloise." She took the phone away from her mouth and cleared her throat.

He seemed to adjust his voice too. "Eloise? Oh, Eloise at the animal hospital?"

She said, "Prince was waiting in the parking lot for me this morning."

"What?" Then, "Hold on a sec."

When Joe came back on the line, he sounded annoyed. "Give me ten. I'll come get him." And then he hung up.

Eloise grew increasingly agitated at the thought of facing Joe alone. She charged up and down the stairs to get the dogs fed. She skipped feeding Prince who barked at her.

"Look, I can get you a biscuit, but your Dad is on his way." Eloise got a few biscuits from the jar on the front desk, which he wolfed down without chewing.

"You didn't even taste those."

She ran up the stairs and was feeding cats like she was competing in a timed event. She had done all the wet food but still needed to give out dry food when she heard knocking at the front door. Prince began barking.

Eloise yelled, "Coming!" She was frantically doling out dry food, pouring way too much into small dishes. When she was done, she spun around too fast and dropped the whole bag on the floor. It spilled everywhere.

Prince forgot all about barking, instead he frantically worked to vacuum up the spilled dry food, while Eloise snatched at the bag and scooped up loose kibble with her hands. What Eloise could not grab, Prince had scarfed down in about three seconds flat. Meanwhile, Joe was still knocking at the door.

Flying high, Eloise and Prince thundered down the stairs and made it to the front door. Joe with his hands cupped on either side of his eyes, was peering into the waiting room. He jumped back when Eloise unlocked the front door and swung it open a little too fast and a little too wide. Eloise grabbed Prince by the collar and pulled him into the room to make a way for Joe, blabbering apologies as she did so.

Joe came in and closed the door behind himself. He was unshaven and wearing black sweatpants and a dark grey hoodie, looking more like this morning's imagined mugger than someone coming to pick up his dog. He looked tired. He also looked angry; his dark eyes had a strong crease between his heavy brows.

He shook a finger at Prince, "BAD DOG!"

Meanwhile Prince did what Prince often did. He sat down on Eloise's feet, tipped his head back and looked up at her. Then he belched loudly.

Eloise giggled nervously, and Prince wagged his tail thumping it against the floor and leaning harder on her legs. Eloise said, "I'm sorry but Prince just got into the cat food. I spilled it and he sucked it up before I could get the broom and dustpan."

Joe still sounded irritated, "He's got a talent for trouble. He's too smart for his own good."

"He *is* smart."

Joe shook his head, "I know better than to let him out. He didn't need to go out. I would never have let him out like that. But he knows how to get my girlfriend to do it."

He looked directly at Prince and commanded, "Come!"

Prince leaned harder against Eloise's legs looking up at her, looking at Joe and then once again back at her.

Eloise said, "Hand me that leash and I'll snap it on for you."

Joe took a step toward Eloise and handed her the leash, which she clipped onto Prince's collar. Then she handed the handle end of the leash back to Joe.

Joe said, "Jaeger, come!"

Prince did not come.

Joe said with disgust, "So, that's how it is, then." And pulled harder.

Jaeger pulled back harder, making a strangling noise, and then all hell broke loose. Prince began to shriek in ear piercing tones, struggling against the pull like a fish on a line, flopping back and forth and all while leaning harder against Eloise. Eloise felt the world begin to tilt and for the second time that morning, she soon found herself knocked to the ground, flailing her arms to break the fall, this time landing on her butt rather than her knees.

Joe made a lunge for one of Eloise's hands to pull her upright, but by the time he had grabbed onto her, her other hand was supporting her body weight. Joe yanked Eloise onto her feet so strongly it made her yelp in surprise and stumble forward, falling for a third time that morning, this time on top of Prince and crashing into Joe. The three of them then found themselves in an awkward sort of scrum.

That's when Prince bit Joe on his forearm, hard enough to elicit a string of expletives. It seemed to echo in the quiet room. Eloise jumped back and found herself in possession of the leash and the dog who once again was pressed against her, this time his hackles raised.

Prince. The dog who had failed his personal protection training because he didn't like to bite, had just bitten his own master.

All motion stopped. The only sound was the panting of the dog. Prince's hackles lowered. And then Prince stepped behind Eloise's back. He was hiding. He was ashamed. Eloise reached behind herself and put a hand on the top of his head. It felt hot to the touch. She knew not to say a word to the dog in front of Joe. But Prince understood her touch. It said, "You are not in trouble. You are a good dog."

Eloise said to Joe, "Let's examine your arm."

And the three of them walked into an exam room and Joe peeled the sleeve of his hoodie back. The clothing had provided some padding, but the dog had still broken the skin, just not deeply.

Eloise said, "At least you know he has had all his shots and is current on rabies."

Joe snorted. He wasn't amused.

Joe washed the wound with antiseptic soap, then slathered it with antiseptic ointment that Eloise offered.

She said, "It's not deep. I think he misread your body language. He's pretty embarrassed about it."

Eloise found the gauze and the tape and did her best to model Doc's bandaging skill. It wasn't too bad. She'd bandaged horses for years. But Joe was too silent. He was stewing.

He said in measured tones, "The dog is too big for you, you know."

Eloise was dumbstruck.

Joe continued. "He knocked you down like a feather. Took down that shoplifter because you lost control of him."

Eloise opened her mouth, but nothing came out.

Joe tucked his damaged arm under his other arm, as if to protect it further from her touch and from the dog. He was controlling his voice, but he was incredibly angry.

"I'm not giving the dog to you. I'm sorry, I know that's what you want to happen, but God, Eloise, every time I see you, you're falling down. And to be frank, you appear to have issues."

Joe pulled his injured hand out and rubbed at the bandage, eyes downcast he growled, "My girlfriend wants him gone and I see her point. And I'm not dense about Pinky's scheme for the dog to go to your friend in Virginia. But Eloise, as much as you want the dog, you have too many red flags. Sorry, but that's the truth."

Joe sighed dramatically, now looking at the ceiling, "You women are killing me. But he's *my* dog, and it's *my* decision. My girlfriend is fed up with him, and Jaeger doesn't need to be roaming the streets of Atlanta, I get that. And like I said, I don't think you can manage him, so a farm in Virginia would be the better place for him. Pinky made it sound like a great place for an active dog like Jaeger. I'll leave him with you today and call Pinky to discuss it further with her. If Jaeger runs off from that farm though, I hope like hell he doesn't make it all the way back to Atlanta. But if he does and shows up here, don't call me. I'm done."

Eloise knew the last thing she should do is seem happy about Joe's decision, because Joe did not want her to be happy about this. Eloise wanted her dog back and Joe wasn't going to allow that. That was just mean. But if that wasn't to be, well, Dabs would be the next best thing. At least her dog wouldn't be flown off to another country like Whiplash. Eloise could still see him and Prince would be happy with Dabs.

Joe was understandably upset. And so, she just nodded, unclipped the dog, and handed the leash back to Joe. He took it without looking at his dog, but instead glaring at Eloise as if this was all her fault. As if she had forced his dog to choose between the two of them, as if his dog had betrayed him, and she, as the other woman, the seductress, was to blame. Joe was just being spiteful, he couldn't have Prince, so Eloise couldn't have him either. It was petty, it was mean, it was absurd, and *besides*, it was Joe who chose a girlfriend who disliked Prince. Eloise thought she would hate the unnamed girlfriend as much or more than Prince did. Eloise, of course, was mute as these thoughts ran through her head.

Eloise asked, "You won't change your mind?"

"This time, I won't change my mind."

They exchanged solemn nods.

And as Joe turned to go, Prince once again sat down on Eloise's feet. He had confirmed his vote.

As soon as Eloise knew Joe was gone, she joined Prince on the floor, put her arms around his neck, and cried.

* * *

Pinky sounded rough. She heard Pinky say to Buzz, "Go back to sleep, babe. It's Eloise. No, I'll handle it."

Then Pinky said, "Is the clinic on fire?"

"No."

"Kitten emergency?"

"No."

"Grooming emergency?"

"No."

Eloise drew a deep breath and tried to settle herself. Pinky said, "Hold on."

It seemed like forever before Pinky came back.

"Sorry. I had to pee. I'm in the living room now and I closed the bedroom door, so we won't disturb Buzz. So, what's up?"

Eloise blurted into the phone, "Prince bit Joe."

"Get out!"

Eloise added, "Broke the skin, too."

"Wait, why are you calling me now at, um, 7:45 in the morning? You need to back up the bus, girl. Like, context?"

Eloise sighed, "Sorry, sorry. He's going to call you. I have Prince here, but he wants Prince to go to Dabs."

Pinky said, "Prince is there?"

"I swear. In my possession."

Pinky said, "Joe brought him over?"

"No. Prince brought himself, again, just like last time. Well, not exactly like last time, this time he knocked me down from behind and I thought I was being mugged."

Pinky said, "What? Oh, never mind, just explain to me why in the world Prince would bite Joe?"

Eloise had to stop and think about that for a moment. "The situation deteriorated rapidly."

"What the hell does that mean?"

Eloise added, "Jock used to say that you always had to be careful with animals not to dip into the panic zone. That's where wrecks happen."

"So you're saying you dipped into the panic zone?"

Eloise said, "It was a group swim."

"Shit. That was good advice from Jock. Too bad you didn't follow it."

Eloise just said, "Hmmmm."

The line was quiet as both thought about that for a moment.

Pinky said, "I had a feeling. But man, I didn't call it to unwind like this. Joe is pissed?"

"Yeah. He had a few choice words for me. Bottom line is he doesn't want me to have the dog. He said the dog was too big for me and that I couldn't control him and that I had issues, but I suspect it's even more complicated than that. By the way, he was onto you and your spiel about Dabs and his farm, knew exactly what you were suggesting. But his girlfriend wants the dog gone.

He made a big deal out of Prince being his dog, and the decision being his to make. He was pretty worked up and I think he was angrier at Prince than me, like angry that Prince loves me. He didn't say goodbye to his own dog."

"Well, it's touchy territory, y'know, being bitten by your own dog, for God's sake. Listen, the important thing is to let me handle it, okay? He can't connect Dabs too much to you or Dabs won't get the dog either. Of course, he knows that's where you went after the, um, prior incident. But if he thinks that giving the dog to Dabs is like giving the dog to you, we could be in trouble."

"Will you talk to Doc? I just can't. I don't think I can talk to anyone about this right now. Not if I want to follow Jock's advice."

Pinky said, "Please, no panic zone. And Eloise?"

Eloise said, "Yes?"

Pinky said, "You know what this means?"

"No."

"Road trip! We go deliver Prince. We make it a total surprise. It's always dead right after Christmas, right? I'm clipping dogs like crazy up to the day and the kennels are full. Then we have that dead spell right after. Let's play Santa."

Eloise said, "If Joe doesn't change his mind."

Pinky said, "Another reason to not say anything to Dabs because that would be awful if Joe did change his mind."

"Okay."

Pinky added, "We tell Dabs we have the perfect dog for him. We don't want him going out and getting impatient and adopting something else. Can I trust you not to leak?"

"I have a terrible track record."

Pinky agreed, "Yeah. You are a terrible keeper of other people's secrets. But you keep your own secrets too damn well, even from yourself."

Eloise did not disagree with Pinky.

She said, "Okay, I'll stay out of the panic zone, and at least this time I'm bringing him the dog, something I know he wants."

"Eloise you are too cute. You still are hiding shit from yourself. But, hey, I'm going to let you unwrap your own packages."

Pinky hung up. Eloise had absolutely no idea where Pinky was going with that last remark, but she looked down at Prince who thumped his tail, completely over the trauma of the morning.

13

Eloise felt like a thief taking home stolen goods. But Doc and Pinky both agreed, even though Joe didn't know about it, she could take Prince home with her until he was delivered to Dabs. It was a challenge not to mention any of it to Dabs, but she didn't. Instead, she cherished their time together, cherished being back in her bed, her best friend stretched out beside her while she read. Every so often she reached over and stroked his silky ears, which made his tail thump. And then she was drawn back into the world of Louisa Roberts.

February 20, 1781

I write to keep the memory fresh. How he looked and smelled and how his coat button pressed uncomfortably into my cheek. The Major did fervently pull me into himself and hold me for a long embrace, yet all too brief. Henry jumped down off Fashion, and the Major embraced him next. Henry did bawl like a calf. The Major took time to stroke the neck of

Beauty and to do the same to young Fashion who champed her bit and fidgeted most anxiously. To Beast he gave instructions to watch over me and the dog did whine before he too enjoyed an embrace from the Major. My Major. Then he gave Henry a leg back up, and then he was lost to us in the sea of men marching in the muddy road.

It had been Isaac who had run into the house out of breath, his hat in his hand shouting, "Miss Louisa, hurry down to the big road. They's on the march!"

I put Beast on a lead, knowing he would follow even if I commanded him to stay, and I began to run on foot. I had no stamina to keep the pace for long. And bye the bye, Henry caught me up, riding Fashion bareback and leading Beauty who had on saddle and bridle. I unclipped Beast and climbed up and we made tracks. When we got to the big road, I got off and put Beast back on the lead and stood by the side of my horse, searching, searching the faces of the passing soldiers. I feared we had missed Major Schmidt.

Beast spotted him first, barking excitedly. Fashion lifted her head and froze, then wobbled her nostrils in recognition. Henry and I exchanged glances, and the boy said, "They knows. We ain't missed him, Miss Louisa."

Henry let out a whistle I had never heard. A whistle came back in answer. Fashion began to fuss, and Henry did his best to regain control. Beauty had lifted her head and pricked her ears. Yet all *forms trudging through the mud were in a way alike. All were in battered uniforms; all wore packs upon their backs. Until one was not the same but had a violin case sticking up. Henry and I whooped with joy. The Major spotted us at about the same moment, and broke away at a jog, grinning widely. Before I had a thought in my head, he had pulled me into him. Yes, wool, the smell of wet wool, was strong, yet beneath that was a signature distinct. An elixir quite masculine, yet not like any other males I have known. The embrace was brief, and he broke away before I could hold him to me, and with him went that heady aroma. Elusive, fading. If I write it down will these words summon the scent of him back like a witch's spell? I should like to preserve it, like the dried herbs that our old cook used to hang from the rafters, then I could make posies that I could hold to my nose. Foolish. A scent is but a scent. Even if I could preserve it, it would not suffice.*

I had few words to share with the Major. When I write, I have an endless flow of words. But in that moment, all I could say was, "Come back." It sounded more like a command than the tender hope I tried to convey. He will write, and then I will have a chance with ink and quill to find fluency.

I have neglected to report here of Priscilla. She is this past week delivered a healthy son. Aunt Bess summoned an old woman from the quarters to attend to the birth. Aunty thought I should show curiosity, as she assured me parturition for women is not quite like it is for Cleopatra or the horses. However, since my attendance was not absolutely required, I had no wish to observe. The pain involved was evident by the loud moaning, wailing, and shrieking that filled the house in intermittent time periods. (Aunt Bess decreed that Priscilla should give birth in the house, not the cabin. Why, I am not sure, but father allowed it.) No apron thrown over Priscilla's head would have muffled the noise. Aunt Bess sent for me, demanding I come once the old woman had sight of the head. I still wish I had not complied. The room smelled terrible, and was stuffy and hot, yet no one allowed the window to be opened. The baby burst forth once the head was out, and appeared to be covered in lard, and bald as a marble. I was informed this is normal. It squalled and was plenty red in color. I nearly retched when they cut the cord. Priscilla seemed only mildly interested in the goings-on, yet I allow as the poor girl was exhausted and relieved to still be among the living. It seems a poor design indeed for such a large headed creature to pass through such a small aperture.

Sammie was fetched and told to wash and come inside to have time with Priscilla. I cannot recall ever seeing him go up those stairs before. He took them at a run, two steps at a time.

Aunt Bess has named the baby Bertrand, after her mother's father. But he will be called Bertie. He will be a Carter and not a Roberts, taking Aunt Bess' married name, as by law this new babe is her

205

property. She has promised Priscilla that this child will only work in the house, or perhaps drive the carriage, or train the horses like Sammie. Aunt Bess has promised she will never sell the babe. He will not go to the ground to do the hard labor of plow and hoe.

Sammie says naught, but it must go hard with him, or so I imagine. I might not have thought so, not so long ago. I confess it might not have even occurred to me. This is the way it has always been in my lifetime. I knew not else. But my eyes have been opened by my dear Major. Things I accepted as proper now seem worse than improper. But these are laws. And those who the law benefits, seek to preserve that benefit. The benefits are great. Not just labor but the great wealth created by that labor. I am of that class, my brother, my mother, my dear father, my dear Aunt. And those who the law harms? Must they accept it as their lot and pray for a better day in heaven? Because in this day they have no power to change law, no, not any more than my horse or dog.

I sound like Major Schmidt. He has turned my thoughts radical, but these are the days of radicals are they not?

April 18, 1781

Little Bertie has charmed us. I fear he will become

most spoiled. We do hand him off right quick to Priscilla when he squalls, which is but rarely. His cheeks are fat like a chipmunk who has found a stash of acorns. We are all clownishly making fools of ourselves in his presence so that Bertie will grace us with his smiles and his newly acquired skill of laughter. Even Beast has done the silliest frolics to get the babe to squeal and laugh. I have done Bertie's likeness in charcoal, one for father, one for Aunt Bess, and one for Priscilla and Sammie to have in their cabin.

We have had sad news of our neighbor Jefferson. Mr. and Mrs. Jefferson have lost yet another babe. This one, Lucy Elizabeth was but five months of age. Little Bertie is not my child, yet such news fills me with fear. Without speaking of it, I know each of us has entertained the same fear and hold our little Bertie even tighter. In such times as these, Bertie's presence is a blessing and joy to us.

Henry, as a babe, was my toy and my burden. I oft tired of his presence. I recall no such fear of losing him as I do Bertie. Now, I do not think of Henry as a burden. I admit that sometimes, when I see him sitting tall upon a horse, I take a bit of pride. He has spent nearly every day of his life in my presence and mounted on our horses. He used to be timid, and his complaints were constant and wearisome. Well, he is yet unafraid of using his tongue! How he does continue to grow into those giant feet and hands. I think one day he will be a tall and handsome man, if no great horseman.

Father and Isaac have started to teach Henry the skill of driving. I used to drive Beauty in the small cart that Father bought for us, but I much prefer to ride, as by cart one is limited to roads.

Father will not let me drive pairs. And now he and Isaac teach Henry. I believe Henry prefers to drive rather than ride. Father says Henry is strong enough and will be stronger with time, and that driving a team is too taxing for a woman. When I press, he says one day he may purchase ponies for my pleasure, but not presently when funds are scarce. It seems wrong that Henry should be allowed, and I am not. Though Henry says naught, this new advantage pleases him.

Henry and I still ride out. We have ridden through the abandoned barracks. It is a desolate sight. Beast takes joy in chasing the rats from the ruins. He catches none. Henry and I have tended to the prisoner's graveyard outside our gates. It seems a small task of care I can perform in the Major's absence. I do it because I know he would approve.

No letters yet from my Major. Father tells me that the prisoners did arrive in Winchester, and it appears they will reside there 'til the end of war.

Buck writes to say that Frenchman Lafayette marched 1,200 to Yorktown. Lafayette is but 23 years old and won the respect of General Washington enough to be given a command. The young man,

who loves the General like a father, has made it his
goal to capture the traitor Arnold and present him
to Washington for hanging.

Buck did write that Lafayette has both rich-
es and connections in France, that he did help in
adding the power of France to our fight. Buck grows
confident that with our clever tactics, and France
fighting on our side, victory will be ours.

On our domestic front, the yellow cat has been
prowling about. He and Cleopatra have had a few
dustups. Henry has suggested that we will soon have
tawny kittens. I countered that every time I have
spied them anywhere near each other, much spitting
and hissing ensued. Henry said, "Miss Louisa, seems
to me that be routine in the courting process."

I replied, "I wouldn't know about that."

He made a sly smile, "You and me, we watched
more than once down there at the breeding shed.
Lots of argumentation twixt the mare and stallion.
Mares, after a great deal of noise and fuss, they come
round when they ready. And when they ready, that
old stallion he ready too."

Henry was being cheeky. I felt his comments
were pointed, though I was not entirely sure. I
had no recollection of argumentation with Major
Schmidt, and certainly none in front of Henry.

I huffed with indignation, "Whatever are you
getting at?"

Henry played coy, "Me? Nothing, nothing at all.
'Cept we gonna' have tawny kittens. That's all."

June 12, 1781

I have been numb for days. Yet the numbness wears gradually back to feeling. I believed doom was near, but as I braced for the final blow, nothing. Yet now that I begin to feel again, I mourn. And so, I take up quill and ink to set things down on paper. The record I make has both historical import and medicinal benefit.

Oh, my beloved Major! I never thought him my enemy. But then I had not fully felt the war yet. To see him there with bloody Ban, well, to take my most precious possession, it was the breaking of me. Or so I thought at the time. Yet here I am still breathing eight days later. The sun still stubbornly rising. My plight matters not to the greater forces. I have read scripture about the sparrow and the numbered hairs upon my head. I do not believe them.

I suppose I should begin my telling at a logical place and move forward in time to this moment.

I shall begin with our Virginia Assembly fleeing Richmond. Aunt Bess was enraged to find that the Assembly reconnoitered in Charlottesville. Aunty understood this would draw the enemy to us. She was correct.

On May 21st, Governor Jefferson sent word that we should remove our best horses to safety. Where indeed would that be? Much discussion ensued. But nary a move was made.

On June 2, Governor Jefferson's term expired as Governor, and the Assembly adjourned without replacing him, to meet the following Monday. That would be June 4th. Father drove the wagon into town early that morning to pick up supplies, while Isaac rode Fox, as father had sold him to one of the visiting Assemblymen.

After they were well and gone from home, a strange man came at a clip into the yard and nearly flung himself off his horse at my feet, Beast barking incessantly in alarm. The man was in such a state that at first, I did not understand his words, what with the ruckus of my dog who I grabbed by his scruff. Aunt Bess and Priscilla with her squalling babe were drawn out the back door by the commotion and added to the chaotic atmosphere. Sammie and Henry too came from the barn.

The man was asking for sanctuary from the British.

Sammie took charge while the rest of us appeared paralyzed.

He said, "Mistress Carter, that cellar got its first refugee. Quick as a cat, git."

He commanded Henry. "Henry, get that dog down to the cellar, and shush him. He bite someone, they'll kill him."

Sammie turned to me, "Louisa, I got to hide this man's horse. You git down there, too."

Sammie took the lathered horse and swung up while all about me fled, Henry dragging Beast.

211

I stood my ground and yelled, "Where you taking that horse?"

Sammie sounded perturbed, "Louisa, I ain't stealing no horse. I'm hiding it in our burying place. Ain't no white man going to look there. Now git!" Sammie spun the horse on its heels and rode away at a canter.

Beauty, my Beauty, was unprotected. I decided right then that I too, would go to the burying place with Beauty, to hide with Sammie, even though I had never been allowed to step foot there before.

I slung the tack onto Beauty, knowing Aunt Bess would be sending Henry out to drag me down into that cellar.

Soon as I stepped out with Beauty to the mounting block, two shabby men on pitiful nags came flying into our yard.

One leaped down and came at me, saying, "Now ain't that polite of ya', getting that horse saddled fer me?"

The scoundrel put his foot in my stirrup and swung up on my startled mare. I growled, "Dismount this instant!"

He said, "No'm, I'll be taking this one in the name of your King."

I simply grabbed the crown piece of the bridle and pulled it sharply toward me and plumb off Beauty's head. The bits hit her teeth cruelly before the whole bridle fell away as she flung her head in the air and ran backwards. The man still held the reins,

and his mouth opened in horror. I yelled, as loud
and as crazy as I could, 'haw!' while flapping my
arms about."

Beauty who was unnerved, spun away from me,
at about the same time as the man, foreseeing the
trouble he was in, tried to dismount. With his right
leg in mid swing over her back, the force of the spin
flung him through the air. He landed hard upon his
back, all the air was expelled from his lungs, and
the back of his head hit the packed dirt of the yard.
Beauty took off at a gallop, disappearing around the
bend. I found myself rooted like a tree, holding her
bridle close against my chest, the reins, that had been
ripped from his hands, were hanging at my feet, the
buckle broken. I wondered for a moment if the man
was dead. But he was groaning. Alive.

It took a moment to realize the yard was filling
with men and horses. The sound of men making
plans, making decisions, hummed like a hive of bees
around me. Deciding, no doubt, what to do with
me. How I should pay for the injury caused to their
soldier.

Henry appeared from nowhere and stepped in
front of me like a shield. How had he left the cellar
undetected? But there he was. The men seemed to ignore me at first, getting off their spent horses to steal
what they could find in our barn. They would find
our finest riding horses, though few in number.

Henry hoarsely whispered, "Good Lord Al-
mighty, we are saved! Miss Louisa!"

I looked up, and Henry stepped to the side, and there before me stood Major Schmidt. My knees went to water about the same time that he grabbed me tight and pulled me into himself.

He put his mouth to my ear and hissed. "Louisa, listen to me carefully, this man who commands me, his name is Tarleton. You know of whom I speak?"

I nodded into his chest.

He continued, "He is a ruthless man."

I did then say, "Why are you here?"

The Major again whispered into my ear, "Prisoner exchange. I am to guide these men through this country that I have come to know."

I said, "You must escape."

He said, "They shoot deserters, dear one."

The Major stopped whispering and said, "Give me the bridle, Louisa."

I tightened my grip. Then heard another voice. It was Sammie riding toward me, riding the Assemblyman's horse, with Beauty freely walking loose at his side. He also said, "You got to give the Major the bridle, Miss Louisa."

Again, I found myself asking the same question, "Why are you here?"

Sammie said, "Beauty, she fetched me. She come flying up that shortcut trail like her tail was on fire. I had just come out to look through that peephole Master Roberts keeps cut, and I saw the yard was filling up, and there you stood. Beauty, once she found me, she turned back around and headed right back down that trail. I got to follow her then, didn't I?"

Sammie got off the Assemblyman's horse and walked it over to the soldier who had been flung off Beauty and was now at least sitting upright. He said, "This un's a safe ride." Sammie helped the man to his feet and held the horse while the man stiffly mounted, cursing under his breath.

Sammie commenced giving orders. "Henry, fetch Fashion quick like, fore someone else grabs her. I'll be leaving with the Major."

Major Schmidt and Sammie exchanged a glance. Sammie said, "I 'spect I can go to do for the horses, that is, if they's still offering freedom."

The Major nodded. Sammie said, "You and Henry guard Fashion for me whilst I fetch my gun and pack a bundle."

Major Schmidt said, "I'll take Beauty."

All I could say was, "No."

Major Schmidt said, "They will not let you keep her. And if I take her, then I will do everything I can to keep her alive and bring her back to you. Give me the bridle, Louisa."

The Major peeled my fingers away one by one, and then bridled my sweet mare who stood at our side, wary and nervous.

Sammie returned and so did Henry with Fashion. Sammie swung up on Fashion who looked terrified. He said to me, "You tell Priscilla, it all gonna' go right in the end. You promise, Miss Louisa?"

215

I nodded, as it was all I could do. Henry was now at my side, and I found myself reaching for his hand, as I had not done since he was a small child. He took a firm grip.

It was not until that moment that Tarleton presented himself.

Major Schmidt said, "Colonel may I introduce you to my intended, Mistress Louisa Roberts."

The devil Tarleton spoke to me. "Mistress Roberts, we thank you for your good horses, few as they may be. Please accept our spent mounts in exchange. Another time I would linger, but sadly, we must rush away."

Then he turned to Major Schmidt. "Are we sorted?"

Major replied, "Colonel, the grey mare is best left for me to ride as I know her well. Baxter there did learn the hard way."

Tarleton pointed at Sammie on Fashion, "And why should the slave get that fine beast?"

Major Schmidt said, "She is fine, indeed. I own that one, and just last year broke her to ride, but she is green as grass. Sammie can manage her, but few others could."

Tarleton then cast his eyes about the place and narrowed his eyes as he spied Aunty's false privy. How he spotted it, I could not say. Henry noted it too and gently increased the pressure on my hand.

Tarleton said, "It appears we have run our fox to ground Major. I've no time to dig him out today, as he is of no real import. Sadly, I think we must give up the chase, jolly as it was. Let's be off."

He then doffed his hat and said, "Good day, madame."

Major Schmidt and Henry exchanged a brief embrace, the tears flowing down Henry's cheeks. Then the Major pulled me tightly into himself and once again whispered into my ear, "I will do what I must to bring Beauty back to you. Until then you must endure."

His kiss was warm and pressed hard against my lips but was brief. And then he mounted my beautiful and loyal horse, and he and Sammie rode away with all the other men, looking over their shoulders but once. Henry and I stood still and silent as stones, as we once again watched soldiers march away, this time taking our horses with them.

14

Prince alerted Eloise that someone was at the front door. It had to be someone he knew as his barks turned into excited twirling and whining.

It was Betsy with an enormous Poinsettia.

"I bought too many of these for my small condo. Surely, we can find a place for this somewhere?"

Eloise had been incredibly moved by Louisa's last entries. She was sad for Louisa. She was frightened for her and for Major Schmidt and for Sammie and for Henry, sweet Henry, and for the horses, Beauty and Fashion. What would become of them all? She felt anxious about what was likely to come. Loss and mourning. She knew something about those things.

The recent journal entries had motivated her to dive back into her research. This time she was reading an interview given in 1847 by former Jefferson slave, Isaac Granger, which had led her to another amazing find.

She ushered Betsy in mindlessly, while enthusiastically telling her of her discovery.

"You have to hear this, a 1949 audio recording with a former slave, Fountain Hughes. Fountain was the grandson of Wormley Hughes, the Monticello gardener and grandson of Betty Hemmings. It is an otherworldly experience to hear his voice and it transported me into Louisa's story in a different kind of way."

Betsy sat down at Eloise's kitchen table, nodding. She recognized the name Wormley Hughes as one of Jefferson's slaves.

Eloise hit the play button.

They listened until Fountain said with conviction, "If someone told me I would have to be a slave again, I would take a gun and end it."

Eloise turned it off.

Betsy said, "Good Lord. I'll bet Sammie would sound just like that, his accent, his tone, and certainly his passion to be free."

Eloise nodded, "It's like we just heard Sammie speak from the grave."

"I came over here to bring Christmas cheer and here I am, nearly in tears. It makes me think of the latest transcriptions Dabs sent. Terrifying. It made the war real."

Eloise said, "I can't stop thinking about Henry's bravery protecting Louisa in Tarleton's raid, and Louisa losing Beauty."

Betsy said, "Louisa's account made it personal."

Eloise added, "I saw this coming. Not just Tarleton's raid on Monticello, but this. Isn't that weird?"

"Well, Dabs and I have observed how you have tuned into Louisa. But we feel a connection to these people too. Between the journals and our sleuthing, we have literally unearthed a hidden history that allows us to get to know these people, or feel that we do. We know what is to come, generally. We know about the death of Buck. I assume the journals will reveal the details. But we don't yet know what will happen to the rest of the family. Unless you've had another one of your prophetic dreams?"

"I don't see how my dreams are prophetic when they are about the past. But, yeah, I did have another dream. I saw Beauty, my over-active imagination at work again, I assume. Don't put too much stock in it though. My imagination went off the rails over Major Schmidt. I'm not always right."

Betsy sighed and shifted the poinsettia plant, which was sitting on her lap.

"My immediate need is more pressing; can you please take a moment to imagine where I should put this plant?"

"That's a stunning poinsettia. Gosh, thank you."

"Where's your tree?"

"I didn't get one."

Betsy picked up the poinsettia and carried it to the living room, Eloise trailing behind her. She placed it to the side of the fireplace.

"How about there? Or we could put it in the foyer?"

"It looks good there."

Betsy gazed at Eloise sympathetically, "It's not much fun to decorate for Christmas by yourself. I got a tiny little tree and decorated it, because I love to see my old ornaments. But it would have been more fun to have had company."

"I guess you're just as alone as I am."

Betsy said, "I have a feeling you've a box full of ornaments around here somewhere. I'd love to see them."

"In the closet under the eaves, upstairs."

"Lead the way. I have oodles of time."

And so, Betsy followed Eloise up the stairs, to a guest room. Eloise dragged a large box out of a closet. It was neatly marked in her mother's hand. "Christmas ornaments" with large red stickers on all the sides of the box that said, "FRAGILE" and other stickers that pointed, "THIS SIDE UP."

Betsy observed, "Even marked, I'll bet your mother had to hang over the movers to be sure these weren't tossed about."

"Are you sure you never met my Mom?"

The two women then sat on the floor as Eloise brought out one ornament after the other. Some were clearly old and expensive glass figures. Some had their years marked on them. Eloise carefully lifted out a stack of trays that made both women say, "Aw." They were tiny ceramic horse figurines.

Eloise exclaimed, "As a child, I loved these. Especially the unusual colors."

"Which ones?"

"Well, let's see. The dun. That one there, the palomino. The appaloosa. This one, the gray one, would be the color of Beauty."

Betsy said, "They are all in perfect condition. You must put up a tree so we can display them!"

Eloise said, "We used to get a live tree and on New Year's Day Mom and I would watch while Dad dug a big hole in the ground and planted it. They made a row eventually."

"A lovely memory. But for now, my recommendation is that we take this box downstairs and go find a little tree. I saw just the spot for one in your living room."

Eloise picked up the dun and playfully cantered him up an imaginary hill. She was glad to see him again.

"Okay."

Betsy drove them to her favorite place. The two of them walked among the rows of greenery, the air fragrant, music playing, families milling about with restless and excited kids. If Betsy had not been there enthusiastically examining each tree for size, shape and freshness, Eloise might have felt saddened by it all, might have even bolted. But she didn't. Being confronted by all things Christmas reminded her of happier times and all she had lost. The journals had left her feeling sad, and dredging up memories of Christmas' past was sweet yet painful. Then, there was all the recent drama with Prince, losing him, seeing him, losing him, seeing him, having Joe say she was too crazy to consider allowing her to keep him, then Dabs being the one to win the prize. Prince would be his dog. That should have made her happy, but it made her feel pathetic. She was pathetic. None of it put her in the Christmas spirit.

But Betsy was excited and drew Eloise along with

her enthusiasm. Betsy, who lived alone with her cat, had sought Eloise out. Eloise remembered her mother's advice, that sadness was normal but that the cure was to do something for someone else. Betsy was doing something for Eloise, and Eloise could, in return, do something for Betsy. She could be a good sport about it all.

Betsy said, "I used to always find myself purchasing a tree that was much too large. But no more. The one I bought this year, I thought so small that I would need to place it on a table. But once I had it delivered to my condo, well, it was larger than I thought and still perfect for the space."

Eloise asked, "Marilyn doesn't bother it?"

"Marilyn watched me decorate, and I may have seen her check out her reflection in a glass ball, but that's about it."

Eloise mulled over that a moment and said, "Lady Jane might not be so respectful."

"I hadn't thought of that. And you have so many delicate and pristine ornaments. I'd be just heartsick if the kitten broke any of those. But, what about Prince? He can be a bit, shall we say, boisterous."

Eloise shrugged, "One time our dog lifted his leg on our tree."

"Oh no! I hadn't thought of that."

"Only happened once. A misunderstanding. Jock said he thought we had installed an indoor toilet for him."

Betsy laughed, "Prince *is* housebroken and smart. I'm sure you can explain to him that an indoor tree is not the same as an outdoor tree. As far as Lady Jane, surely others with kittens have a way to protect their trees."

Eloise pulled out her phone and did a search. "It says here to wrap the trunk of the tree with foil and then place orange and lemon peels around the base along with pinecones sprayed with apple-cider vinegar. Also, no tinsel. It also recommends jingle bells on the lower branches as an alarm."

Betsy said, "Oh my."

"Are you still sure I need a tree?"

Betsy looked disappointed. "How about a couple of small table-toppers? Just to showcase those marvelous little ornaments. We can put them high enough that Lady Jane can't climb them. Let's go inside and look at the other Christmas decor. My treat?"

Betsy really was totally into this. Eloise said, "You love Christmas, don't you?"

"I suppose I do. But what I'm most looking forward to is your dinner party. Pinky and Buzz are fun, and I want to meet Ralph and Bev. I'd like to help. I hope you don't mind me inserting myself."

"Are you kidding? I don't know what I was thinking offering to host a dinner party. I'm completely out of my depth. I mean, I hired a cleaning service, and I put up a wreath. Other than that, and admiring my Mother's taste in furniture, well, I ran out of steam. One minute I'm reading "How-to-entertain" articles on the internet, and the next minute I'm overwhelmed and want to call the whole thing off."

Betsy's face lit up. "Never fear dear. You let me help.

I adore just this kind of thing. Let's find those table-top trees and get them decorated. Then let me tell you my other ideas for your party."

Betsy was a woman on a mission. She found two tiny trees, bags of pinecones, jingle bell ornaments, stands, felt "skirts" and then the best find of all, LED garlands of tiny carrots and apples. You'd think she had won the lottery. Her enthusiasm was infectious, and Eloise did feel better just watching her.

The LED garlands were cheap. Betsy bought all they had. They ran on batteries.

When they checked out the cashier said, "I told my manager to put those out. See, they're leftover inventory from Easter. But I knew someone would buy them for Christmas."

Betsy chimed in, "We're going to decorate these two little trees in an equine theme, with the most beautiful little horse ornaments."

The woman said, "My daughters would go nuts. They have a bunch of those tiny plastic horses. They leave them all over the floor. Man, it hurts if you step on one though, 'bout as bad as my son's Lego's."

Betsy and Eloise managed to get the trees into Betsy's car where they no longer looked tiny. They barely fit in the back even with the seats down.

When they got to Eloise's, Prince escorted them into the house with great enthusiasm, nose in the air inhaling the fragrance of pine. Then there was much discussion as they moved the little trees all around the living room and dining room multiple times before coming to a final decision on placement. They wrapped foil around the bases, placed the tree skirts, put out the pinecones as barriers, and hung the funny carrot and apple LED garlands and switched them on. Now it was only the addition of the jingle-bells and the precious ornaments to be hung, for the tree project to be complete.

Once they were up, Eloise and Betsy stood back to admire their handiwork. The trees were charming. Eloise congratulated Betsy as being a skilled designer.

Betsy did not sit upon her laurels long. "Pancakes in the morning? I want to help you plan the menu and I also have some fun things to add as ice breakers and activities that will liven up the party."

Eloise said, "I was hoping to talk about the journals, and our reading for Extreme Readers."

"Well of course. That too dear, that too."

When Betsy left, Eloise realized she was no longer feeling sad or anxious, but she was exhausted.

* * *

When Eloise and Prince got to the barn the next day, she saw that Bev had directed Miguel to set up a course of jumps in the hayfield. The field was fallow, so it didn't matter if Eloise and Red chopped it up a bit. Most of the lines were unrelated distances, with a skinny and a drop carved out of a ravine, but all set low to encourage Red and not to challenge her too much. Bev had even had Miguel gather tree trimmings to improvise a brush jump.

Bev had tacked up Jethro to ride out with Eloise, a first. Jethro stood placidly in the middle of the field, Bev sipping on a can of soda and watching. Bev bellowed directions at Eloise every time she got close enough to hear.

It was a nice feeling at the end of the session, to walk side by side with Bev once around the field to cool down.

Bev said, "Next month, this mare needs a real cross-country school. She ain't seen no water complex. Caroline needs hers out and about soon too, afore we get to the Spring calendar. I figure I can take Jethro here along for a chair and lend you girls a hand."

"Sounds like fun, although I haven't even met Caroline."

Bev had a sly smile on her face but said nothing.

Eloise probed, "So, Caroline plans to compete her horse in the Spring?"

Bev ignored her. Instead saying, "You want to take Red Devil? Keep her company?"

"You'd let me do that?"

Bev looked away for a moment, but Eloise suspected it was because she was smiling. When she turned back around her face was expressionless, her tone serious. "You got to get yourself up to date with dues and such. You got to do that SafeSport thing online nowadays."

"Sure. Sure, I can do all that."

Bev changed subjects again. "Doc, he and Jethro get along real good."

Eloise was genuinely surprised. "Get out! He came?"

"Break of day most mornings."

"How in the world?"

"Same as Caroline."

"He hasn't mentioned it, not once!"

"Well now Missy, Doc's a grow'd man. He don't need your permission."

"Of course not, but why?"

Bev added cryptically, "Maybe Doc's still got a few surprises up his sleeve."

Once Bev and Eloise were back in the barn, and their horses put up, Bev surprised her with a bag with a bow on it.

Bev handed it to Eloise, "I been going through my stuff, and I fully intend to give away or throw away most of it. These ain't your memories, they's mine, but still, I thought you might like 'em."

Eloise opened the bag to find an old photo album.

Bev said, "I just left in the ones I thought you might like."

Eloise opened the album to see three people jumping a timber jump.

Bev said, "Hunt team. Pretty sure we won that one."

Eloise said, "That's you?"

"I believe you know the other two riders, too."

"No. Yes. Oh my God. They look so young."

Eloise flipped the page to see her parents dressed in formalwear, Jock in a tux, champagne glass in hand, and in her opinion, inebriated. Her mother had a funny upswept hairdo and appeared to be holding a cigarette. Shocking.

Bev said, "Hunt Ball. Not sure what year."

The next photo was from the same event, but with Bev and some man, clearly older than all of them.

Bev said, "Travis."

"Your husband?"

Bev snorted, "We never tied no knots. But we did have a helluva' good time. He could hunt a pack of hounds and sit a horse like he was born in the saddle."

Eloise said, "I sense a good story."

Bev shook her head. "Not every story needs tellin'."

Bev added, "Album's yours now."

Eloise was astounded, "I'll cherish them. Thank you."

Bev switched gears again, "Mighty kind of you to offer me a seat at your Christmas Eve dinner."

"You better still be coming! I want you there. I asked Doc, but he had other plans. But I have Betsy and Pinky and Buzz and Ralph Jameson coming. I'm counting on you."

"Now don't you go gettin' your panties in a twist. I don't know any of those folks and likely would stick out like a sore thumb."

Eloise explained, "You've met Pinky. And Ralph was a friend of Mom's. They went to high school together. He handled all her financial business at the bank and takes care of my money. He and Jock evidently didn't get on though."

"Was he the little fella who was kinda' light in the loafers?"

Bev was incorrigible. "Bev, I can't believe you said that."

"Elly did always say as he was smart as all get out. Maybe I do need to meet him."

"You promise you'll come?"

"Don't make me sing no Christmas carols."

"Cross my heart. Deal?"

"I was fixin' to stay here and get drunk." Bev waited a beat for impact then added, "Okay, you got you a deal."

* * *

The big dinner was on Christmas Eve. Eloise could hardly believe her eyes when she looked at her guests seated around the table. They had done it. Betsy gave the blessing and made it brief, but before they tucked into the feast, Buzz called for a round of applause for Eloise. And she couldn't help but feel proud. Buzz had carved a picture-perfect turkey. Eloise was proud of her mashed potatoes and gravy too. Betsy had brought roasted veggies with nuts and cranberries. Bev had brought home-made apple and sour cherry pies.

Eloise felt the presence of her mother, a happy presence, warm and approving. This is what her mother had tried to tell her. This was it. Simple as it was. And although in one sense Eloise felt detached from the scene, it was also sharply in focus, and she seemed to take in everything and everyone.

Bev and Ralph engaged in discussion, Ralph laughing, his mouth full, chewing and grabbing a sip of wine to be able to respond to Bev, who had one corner of her mouth lifted. Prince was under the table, collecting

napkins off the laps of the diners, while Lady Jane batted at the fringe on his tail, while Pinky and Buzz were
entertained by Betsy telling a story.

She had gathered nearly all her friends. Doc was
missing, but also Dabs. Thinking of Dabs gave her a
small pain in her chest. This fact surprised her, then
warmed her. She missed him.

The weird moment passed, and Eloise found herself
smiling into her glass of wine, thinking to herself that
she had just had her Charles Dickens moment.

After everyone had finished dinner, Betsy directed them to look under their plates. Each person had a
poem to read.

Pinky started with hers but was giggling too hard
and had to hand it to Betsy, who began again from the
top.

Betsy read; *"I have a Christmas album, with lots of
festive HITS, I like to play it nice and loud, and decorate
my..."*

Betsy paused and everyone yelled out "TITS!"

Betsy shook her head and yelled back, "CHRIST-
MAS TREE!"

Ralph commenced twittering. Which made everyone else crack up again.

The readings continued, some silly some cute, some
lewd.

Eloise read hers last:

Snowball — by Shel Silverstein
I made myself a snowball, as perfect as could be.

231

I thought I'd keep it as a pet and let it sleep with me.
I made it some pajamas,
And a pillow for its head.
Then last night it ran away,
but first—it wet the bed!

Everyone applauded and Eloise suggested they have dessert and coffee in the living room. Betsy's next planned activity was a lottery style gift exchange. Everyone had brought an untagged, wrapped gift of low monetary value and placed it into a pile. As desserts and coffees were served, Betsy walked around with a bowl and people drew out a number. Each person would then draw a wrapped gift from the pile in order, or instead of pulling from the pile, could steal any previously opened gift. If your gift was stolen, you could steal any opened gift, or draw an unopened gift from the pile. The theft could go around and around until each gift had been stolen three times. Eloise remembered this game. They had played it at barn parties.

The giant box of jellybeans was clearly from Ralph. There was a coffee mug with "Mr. Peabody and his Wabac machine" that read, "Smarter than the average human." There was a red pillow that read, "Naughty." There was a snow-topped ceramic cabin where you put incense inside, and smoke came out the chimney. That got passed around until it found a home with Ralph. Eloise had put in a lap rug with Jane Austen quotes on it as her gift, hoping it would go home with Betsy, who did in fact end up with it. And one gift (that had to be from Pinky) was two glasses and a kit for making giant Margaritas. Buzz made sure that went right back home with them.

Throughout the fun, Prince sat on top of Eloise's feet, and Lady Jane curled up on the sofa between Eloise and Pinky.

Even as the evening came to an end, the magical aura remained. Eloise refused to let anyone do more than load leftovers into plasticware to take home with them, even though she had everyone offering to help in the kitchen. As she said goodbye at the door to each guest, she noticed that Ralph gave a business card to Bev, and that Bev winked at him.

Eloise felt especially grateful to Betsy. Eloise may have been the official hostess, but Betsy had acted as the party planner, and her drive and enthusiasm had made all the difference. She could hardly admit to herself that Betsy reminded her a tiny bit of her mother, but there it was.

All Eloise wanted to do was curl up in the bed with Prince and Lady Jane and rest on her "laurels" this one night. Eloise knew she would have all day tomorrow to clean and get organized and pack. The day after Christmas, she and Pinky would hit the road to deliver Prince to Dabs, fulfilling their promise to Joe. She could barely believe that once again she would have to say goodbye to Prince. But she also felt a strange thrill when she thought about seeing Dabs. She briefly imagined all of them together, curled up in one of those four poster beds, then felt embarrassed at the thought.

* * *

Eloise woke up on Christmas morning in the dark, Prince tucked up against her side and Lady Jane next to her left ear, purring.

She started a pot of coffee. Then after caring for the kitten and feeding Prince, she tucked into leftovers, finishing off her feast redux with cherry pie. Once she had cleaned up her wreck of a kitchen, she would go have a Christmas ride on Red. She hated leaving Red for the week, but Bev assured her the mare would still be broke to ride when she came home.

Eloise had not even thought about Jock. And so, when his name came up on her phone, it startled her.

Jock's voice sounded far away, "Merry Christmas, Lulu!"

Eloise flopped down on her sofa, Prince curled up on the floor, and Lady Jane cried to be picked up, so she picked her up.

Eloise said, "Hey, merry Christmas to you too."

"Thanks sweetie. Hope you're having a good holiday."

"Best in a long, long time."

"Here too. You go first."

"Well, I had a dinner party here last night. Cooked the turkey myself."

Jock laughed, "Will wonders never cease?"

"It was fun. We played the gift exchange game like we used to do at the barn. And tomorrow, my friend and

I are driving to Virginia to deliver Prince to Dabs. You remember, the big hairy dog?"

"The one you had to give back?"

"Yeah. It's a long story, but he is being rehomed for good this time. He gets to live on a farm and be a companion to a special friend of mine. You might even remember him from eventing days, Dabs Carter."

"Boyfriend?"

"Maybe." The cozy image of being in bed with Dabs and her pets flashed in her head and she was embarrassed to think Jock could almost see it too.

He suggestively said, "Ah. Things *are* looking up then."

"Yes. Horses, dogs, and friends. My kitten is thriving too. So, what about your Christmas?"

"Sounds like yours. It's good to have a home again."

That simple statement softened Eloise's heart. Jock had suffered losses too. Betsy had called Eloise's Christmas memories lovely. And they were. They shouldn't be a cause for sadness. She said, "You know, you were a really good Dad. I bet you're a great stepdad too."

Jock took a moment to respond, clearly touched, he said, "Thank you Lulu."

"It's not up to me to say what kind of a husband you were, or business partner. Or friend. But to me, as my Dad, you were the best."

There was only silence on the other end. She added, "And when it comes to riding, there's only one Jock Robertson."

His voice was soft. "It's sweet of you to say so. It's been my passion all my life."

Eloise had more to say though. And it seemed like the right time to say what she had been too much of a coward to say directly to him up until then. She said, "But you haven't been honest with me. Not Eloise the adult. Not Eloise living on her own and grieving all she has lost."

There was another long pause, and then far, far away a weak and tinny voice that was hardly recognizable as Jock said, "Lulu your mother and I, we tried to make things as smooth as possible for you. Maybe that wasn't the right thing, not to be honest with you. And maybe we weren't honest because the truth was too painful for us, the adults. So, we cushioned ourselves by pretending we were shielding you, when maybe it was because we were protecting ourselves."

Jock continued, I wasn't sure how I was going to survive. I had no money. I had to get back on my feet. But things are finally turning around for me. I knew you would be fine. Your mom left you well-funded. The rest would just take time. And look, I was right. You've always been amazing at landing on your feet."

Eloise said, "I guess getting spun off of Whiplash all those years, I was developing a life-skill."

Jock said, "It's not the fall that counts, it's what comes after. Remember what I used to say? Get up, and get going, because the clock never stops."

"Yes."

"Remember what I taught you about riding to the big jumps? You remember?"

Eloise did remember. She said, "Have a plan, be ready to adjust the plan, but don't let anyone undermine your decisions. Don't pussyfoot, commit and go for it."

"That's my Lulu."

"Jock, you are a great coach."

"I'm sorry for the times where I wasn't as great as I should have been."

Eloise surprised herself, "I forgive you. I forgive you both. I do. But I'm not going to pussy-foot. I asked for one thing and one thing only. I leave it up to you to untangle the tangle of knots you've created. Adjust your plan. The clock is ticking."

Jock simply said, "Eloise ..."

"Send Whiplash back to me. Find a way. And for now, enjoy the holidays. Enjoy your new family. And Dad ..."

Eloise paused a beat, long enough for Jock to say, "What?"

"Don't screw it up this time."

"Ouch."

"It's not the fall, it's what comes after. Such wise words Dad. So wise. Merry Christmas. Carrots to Whiplash from me, love you."

Eloise hung up before he could answer. And then she cuddled her kitten and thought about what she needed to pack for the week in Virginia.

She didn't get long to think about packing though,

because as soon as Eloise hung up the phone, it rang again. This time it was Dabs.

Dabs said, "Merry Christmas. Sorry I missed your big soiree."

Eloise said, "I wish you could have been here. I cooked a turkey! It was beautiful, and it wasn't too dry either."

"Ah, well, that's a victory. I'm sorry I missed out."

"Betsy has been so much help, too. And we talk about the journal entries a lot. Especially Tarleton's raid. Did you have any idea that Tarleton himself had been to Ivy Creek?"

Dabs barely answered before Eloise broke in and added enthusiastically, "I have custody of your new dog, by the way. You are going to love him!"

Dabs laughed, "Well now, you could never be a spy. You just told me it's a 'he' and not a 'she' after making a big deal out of it all being top secret."

"Oops."

"Anything else you want to let slip?"

"Nope. Nada. Pinky would kill me."

Dabs said, "I can't wait to meet Pinky. Something tells me this will be a fun week ahead. I've planned some good meals, likely not as fine as the one you did, though. I've also been working like a man possessed on the journals. I'm starting on the last journal. Or maybe I should say the last one I know about. I'll save transcribing the last entry for while you are here. It seems to be fitting that you be here for the finish. Hopefully we finish on a positive note, although it is a war story. It's all I have for your Christmas gift."

"Dabs, that is a wonderful gift. There are only we few, we happy few, we band of brothers and sisters who have read Louisa's story. It's the best gift ever."

Dabs said, "Ah, Shakespeare. Well, until tomorrow then. Drive safely."

15

Pinky had on a pink beret and wore heavy chain necklaces over a black sweater-dress. With this she wore black tights with pink suede booties. Eloise thought, but did not say, that Pinky looked more like someone's idea of a 1960's hip Parisian than someone dressed for a long car trip.

Pinky bubbled with excitement, "Oh, please let me drive first! I love a road trip. I brought a bag of red licorice. They taste like a flavored strip of latex, but they are great entertainment."

Eloise was putting Prince and the kitten (in her sherpa bag) in the back.

"Anything you say, Pinky."

Pinky slid in, buckled up, put the key in the ignition, and ripped open the bag of licorice, put one in her mouth without biting down, just letting the thing hang there like a melted red cigarette. Pinky could make even a ridiculous image seem cool. But Pinky was cool, especially after she put on her oversized sunglasses.

Pinky said, "You said this old car has a CD player."

Pinky dug out a stack of CD's from her bag and

handed them to Eloise. While Pinky started the engine and backed out of the garage, Eloise thumbed through the stack. Before Pinky had put the car into drive, Eloise had selected the first CD. As soon as it came on, Pinky turned up the volume, grinned crazily with the licorice pressed between her teeth and slapped Eloise hard on the thigh.

Pinky pulled the licorice from her mouth and pointed it toward the road, "Engage thrusters! Prepare for blast-off!"

Travelling with Pinky was going to be different in every way from travelling with Betsy.

They began working their way through the CDs as the car headed north, including the soundtrack to Hamilton. Pinky knew most of the words, bobbing her head and singing along to the rap-tempos, banging on the steering wheel for percussion. After that CD was finished, the drive got more subdued. The dog and cat had settled, and all was quiet in the back seat.

At the first gas stop they threw away what was left of the red licorice. Eloise thought to herself that she would never put another one of those toxic, red-dyed things in her mouth again. It felt cleansing to have gas station coffee. The kitten had a break from her carrier, helpfully taking a whiz in the dirt, and Prince had taken care of his business. Eloise took her turn at the wheel.

Pinky exclaimed, "I love a road trip!"

"Yeah. You said that."

"But I didn't say *why* I loved a road trip."

"But now you're going to, I take it?"

"Because it's the most amazing place for a therapy session. Like, you got some stuff to work through. And I have nowhere to go. Plus, I am a terrific listener. Well, maybe not terrific, I can get distracted. Hey look, next exit has completely nude girls! Oh wait, where was I?"

"Ha-ha, very funny."

Pinky took a slurp of her coffee, "Let's get this session started. Any news from dear old Dad?"

"Jock."

"Okay, Dear old Jock."

Eloise had no way to escape, nothing to do but keep driving, and no reason not to bring Pinky up to speed. It didn't need to be a therapy session. Did it? Eloise felt her stomach tighten.

She told Pinky about her Christmas chat with Jock. About thanking him for being a good Dad. But she had also let Jock know that she knew he had not been truthful with her. Jock had then accused her of the same thing. Eloise pointed out to Jock, he now had everything he wanted. At least for now. If he didn't blow it. But he still owed her one last thing, Whiplash.

Pinky looked thoughtful. "Could be good news for you. He may not need Whiplash now that he's closed his deal. He used your horse to get this woman's kid competitive success. He squeezed all the value out of the horse. You helped pick out the new horse who takes it from here. And now Jock needs to keep the new wife happy and the kid winning, and convince her to spend more money, all in the name of her child, right?"

Pinky had a devilish look on her face when she added, "Of course, not totally all self-less for the kid, right, since she'll enjoy the other benefits of Jock belonging to her, um, stable."

Eloise groaned and rolled her eyes.

Pinky wagged her finger, "Jock has a job to do that comes with being a gold-digger. She won't do him any good if they divorce. I'm going to assume she's got a good pre-nup."

"I'm sorry, you went too fast past the bit about how this is good for me."

"You still want your horse back, right?"

Eloise drew the word out slowly, "Yeeees."

"And Jock said you could revisit the subject once the foal was weaned."

"Whiplash legally belongs to her. Jock has no reason to ask her to do a favor for me. No, she has no motive to return my horse. Horses can be a fever that's tough to shake. Jock knows how to feed that fever and keep it hot. Whiplash was put to that use and is still being put to that use."

"Well, I'm no horsewoman, but I think there's another kind of hot you seem to be ignoring, and I don't just mean sex, I mean anger, revenge. Stuff like that. I'm going to guess, her ex ran off with his much younger secretary, or something like that. She's going to be sure to take Jock out and let everyone know the sex is great, best in her life."

"Oh, Pinky, please don't make me put my fingers in my ears. I'm driving."

Pinky said, "Jock's going to be busy working to keep his job once things cool down, and she wonders what the heck she just did."

Eloise said, "This has nothing to do with me. Can we focus on the horses, please? Jock has likely promised continued success with the horses. He's going to make that kid a star. And he might do it too. But it's not like rubbing a lamp and having a genie pop out. Eventing is a tough game and dangerous. Stuff happens. That kind of pressure can be exhausting, and it depends on the kid as much as the horses."

"He delivered so far, right?"

"Yeah. That's the thing. He is good at what he does. I was once his project. And it took some years, but once-upon-a-time, I was on my way too."

Pinky squinted, "You aren't coming down with a fever, are you?"

"No."

"You need leverage. You could throw some heavy guilt his way. It can be effective as a tool of manipulation, slinging that sort of stink that you have on Jock, what with your mother's illness and death, and whatever Bev has on him.

To be honest, it creates major resentment when it sticks, though. So, man, you can only walk away after that. Those kind of slings and arrows make deep wounds and not just to the one on the receiving end."

Eloise scowled. "Wait, weren't you recommending I throw guilt at him to get what I wanted?'

"Moi? Not me. I was just talking. But tell me, do

you want your mare back or do you want to repair your relationship with your Dad, um, I mean Jock?"

Eloise was silent. She was about to say she just wanted Whiplash back. But it stuck in her throat.

Pinky said, "It sucks that your parents divorced, that your Mom died so young. Life can sure beat us up."

"Whiplash is the only living thing left from my life."

"Your life is not over, Eloise."

"My happy life."

Pinky's tone stopped being light, and she held up a finger to add emphasis. "That's where you're wrong. That happy thing? You've barely scratched the surface. Sure, you had this fairy-tale childhood. Some of us thought it only existed on the Hallmark Channel. But for God's sake, you just turned twenty-one."

Eloise caught Pinky's eye before turning her own eyes back onto the road. "Boy, you weren't kidding about the therapy session. I think I'm ready to hear you say that our time is up now."

Pinky laughed, then hit the door-lock button and it made an ominous chu-chunk noise.

"No way. Tell me more about that fairy-tale childhood. I used to love those sappy movies on Hallmark."

Eloise thought Pinky couldn't be serious. But when she glanced at her, Pinky's expression was soft, young, expectant. She really did want to hear more.

Eloise told Pinky about the magical Christmas she got Brighty, and how Jock dressed up as Santa for their musical barn ride.

Pinky listened intently, with brief interjections like, "Wow." and "Cool" and "How fun was that?"

Then she told Pinky about horse shows. They'd bring dinner and eat on the grounds on Friday after setting up and riding. On Saturday night there was a competitor's party. It was early mornings and late evenings and cheering each other on. Eloise described the exhaustion of the drive home, of getting the horses put up when they arrived.

"This went on for years?"

"It was our business. Jock had students to coach and at least one horse he was competing. Our barn was full of women who adored their horses and adored my parents. Well, in retrospect, mostly they adored Jock. Jock is talented and handsome and funny. It was our life. It was my life until I graduated from High School."

"Golden."

Eloise agreed, "Golden."

Then Eloise added, "Until it was all taken away."

Pinky said, "Gut punched."

They drove in silence for a while. It seemed the therapy session had finally ended, but Eloise still didn't feel good.

Pinky said, "I think I have an opinion."

"Is that a news flash?"

Pinky said, "Jock is Jock. Talented, handsome, charming, but enough of a scoundrel that your Mom wanted him gone. Bet he left a trail of pissed-off people here at home besides yourself, too."

Eloise could only mutter assent.

"Good news, bad news, is everyone's childhood ends. I had a crappy one, so for me it was good riddance. You had a great one, that at least gives you some great memories."

There was another long pause.

Then Pinky continued, "You've been telling yourself this is about Whiplash. I get that the horse is a symbol of what was. I still think you are going to get her back someday. But it won't change anything. Because, what seems clear to me is that your Mom was the center, she was the real power and force that held you guys together and made everything work. It just might be that no one knows what the hell to do now that she's gone. It's not Whiplash. It's not Jock. It's your Mom. That's a hole no horse can fill."

Eloise's throat and chest ached, her nose began to run, and her eyes burned. Pinky was too goddam good.

She croaked, "Is the session over now?"

Pinky found her bright and mocking tone, "Sure. Now you have to sit and listen to how screwed up I am, which is aplenty and beyond repair, so get comfy."

Eloise said, "Thank God."

* * *

Pinky had the wheel as they pulled up the rutted driveway of Ivy Creek. Eloise put the rear window down halfway so Prince could hang his head out. The excited whining had begun.

Pinky was leaning forward and peering at the landscape, "Wow, so this is it. This is where it happened."

Eloise thought she felt just like Prince. The excitement was building up inside of her. She said, "And it would all be lost if Dabs had never found those journals, if Louisa had not written it all down."

Pinky added, "If you hadn't joined Betsy's groupies."

Eloise swallowed, "Now are you starting to understand the magic of reading? Don't you want to read all the journals now?"

Pinky was bounced in her seat by a rut in the road, and yelped, "I'll wait for the movie."

The house came into view and Prince's whining got louder as if to say, "Drive faster!"

Eloise put her fingers in her ears until she had to take them out to point to Pinky where to park. Once parked, she couldn't get out of the car fast enough to let Prince out.

It was "Deja Vu, all over again."

Prince took off running around the side of the house. Eloise picked up the Sherpa bag and followed him. Pinky followed her, almost running into the back of Eloise as she came to a sudden stop.

Pinky came alongside Eloise, "Why are we stopping?"

"Look."

There stood Dabs, silhouetted between the big sliding barn doors, Prince standing on his hindlegs with his feet on Dabs' chest and Dabs rubbing Prince's head vigorously.

Pinky said, "Oh man, I'm gonna' cry."

Prince jumped back from Dabs, did a few twirls then ran toward them barking, then veering off, tucking his

butt, doing crazy zigging and zagging around the barnyard.

Dabs walked up to Eloise, her Sherpa bag hanging
at her side and gave her a bear hug, then extended a
hand to Pinky.

Pinky said, "We meet at last."

Dabs said, "At last."

"Prince? I'm confused."

Pinky said, "You like the dog we picked out for you?"

"For me?"

Out of the Sherpa bag came a piteous "Mew?"

Eloise said, "Confessions to come. Let me take care
of Lady Jane."

Eloise put the bag on the ground and unzipped the
top, right about the time that Prince had circled back,
panting heavily. He poked his nose into the bag, and
then looked back up at Eloise as she lifted out the kitten. Lady Jane was still tiny, but no longer the hazy-eyed
neo-natal. She was bright and alert and complaining
about being left out of the party. Eloise held her up like
the scene from "The Lion King" and said, "Behold!" all
for the benefit of Dabs.

Pinky caught on, and sung a line from "The Circle
of Life."

Dabs chuckled, "Did you plan that?"

Pinky said, "Nope. I swear."

Eloise laughed, then said, "This kitten is about to
pop. Then she walked over to the shrubbery and put
Lady Jane down in the dirt. Even with an audience,
the kitten promptly dug herself a spot and emptied her

bladder and then her bowels, and then went through an elaborate burying procedure.

Dabs said, "I just finished feeding the geriatrics their mush. Let's get your things inside, then you've got some 'splaining to do."

Dabs fed them Chili with cheddar biscuits. Lady Jane ate and then made a nest in Eloise's lap, purring loudly. Eloise felt the same sort of contentment as her kitten.

Pinky was telling Dabs all he needed to know and answering all his questions about Joe and Prince. She reassured Dabs that Joe had signed the surrender papers. Prince was his dog.

Dabs turned to Eloise. "Is this okay with you, Eloise?"

"You know something? It is. As long as I can still come up to visit."

He said, "I'm counting on it."

Prince had put his wet, sloppy chin on Dab's thigh, and Dabs had placed his hand on the dog's head.

Eloise thought to herself, Prince gets it. He's always gotten it. He wants to be here. He has loved me, but he knows that this is where he belongs.

She said none of this out loud. Instead, she just said, "Merry Christmas, Dabs."

* * *

Pinky and Eloise were in the bathroom upstairs brushing their teeth at the same time. Pinky rinsed first, tapped her brush against the edge of the sink and then put it in the plastic glass next to the sink.

She said to Eloise, "Why didn't you tell me?"

"Tell you what?"

"Dabs is some kind of hot."

"You sound like a thirteen-year-old when you say stuff like that."

"When he walked up and hugged you, I think I went all googly-eyed and weak in my knees."

"Don't be silly."

Pinky said, "He's a cross between rugged and dreamer. Like Matthew McConaughey."

"He doesn't look a bit like Matthew McConaughey, or sound like Matthew McConaughey."

"Oh, yeah, he does. He's got that soft southern accent and that calm vibe."

Eloise rolled her eyes and went elsewhere. "I hope Prince will be okay staying in Dabs room. I mean, last time Prince stayed up here with me."

Pinky lifted her eyebrows, "Bed assignments aren't my business."

Eloise ignored the remark, saying, "I'll leave my door ajar."

Pinky said, "I'm closing mine. And no matter who is roaming the halls tonight, I plan to ignore it." She winked.

Eloise gave up.

"G'night, Pinky."

* * *

In the morning, Pinky walked into the kitchen saying,

"I could have slept later, but my nose got me up. And it's not just the siren song of that coffee you're brewing. I smell bacon!"

Prince trotted over to Pinky and bumped against her thigh, as if directing her toward a chair, while the kitten flew across the room, skidding into the pantry.

Dabs and Eloise were sitting at the breakfast table, empty plates pushed to the side, heads together over some paper.

Dabs looked up first. "Good morning!"

Eloise said, "Did you sleep well?"

Dabs jumped up. "Sit. I've left the biscuits in a warm oven, along with the pan of bacon. How would you like your eggs?"

Pinky, instead of sitting, had poured herself a mug.

Dabs was still talking, "Cream, sugar?"

Pinky said, "You are as eager to please as a Labrador Retriever. Cream please. And two eggs over easy." She turned and winked at Eloise in an exaggerated way, then scooped up the kitten who had ventured back out of the pantry, "My, my you are getting brave."

Pinky sat down next to Eloise with the kitten in her lap.

She said, "You two looking for a buried treasure?"

Dabs was breaking eggs into a hot pan, he turned, "We kind of are."

Eloise added, "You won't believe it, but Dabs and I might be related."

Pinky raised one eyebrow, "Scandalous."

Dabs asked, "Do you like the yolks runny?"

"Yes."

Lady Jane was kneading Pinky's lap and purring.

Dabs soon presented Pinky with a plate of eggs, bacon, and biscuits. He set down a butter dish and a honey dish, saying, "The honey comes from a neighbor."

Pinky said, "I assume you both have eaten?"

Eloise laughed, "Hours ago. I was sitting here when the sun came up."

Dabs said, "I haven't beaten Eloise to the kitchen ever."

Eloise said, "We've cleaned stalls and turned-out horses. Eat up and then join us on a walk. I want to show you the cemetery and then the slave burial grounds."

Pinky said, "Didn't you say it was haunted?"

Dabs said, "I suppose it depends on what you consider haunted. Eloise and I are entranced with the story of this young woman, though some of her journal is light and funny, it's still a sad story."

Pinky nodded, "We all gotta' die. Although vampires don't. We all like a story about a person who gets a pass. But, okay, no vampires in this story, at least so far. But we all love a love story, right? I just hope it has a happy ending. The love story part."

Eloise said, "How about we print you a copy and you can read it tonight? I'd like you to catch up to where we are."

Pinky shook her head. "That sounds too much like school. I hated school. I'd rather you tell me the story yourself."

Dabs asked, "You don't enjoy reading?"

"Ugh. No. It's never come easy for me. I mean, I can read and all, but I'm slow."

Eloise asked, "Are you Dyslexic?"

"Maybe. Who knows?"

Dabs said, "Tell you what, tonight after dinner, we'll have dark chocolate and port wine, and I'll read the journals from the beginning. If my voice gets tired, Eloise can take a turn. I'll start at the beginning, and we can do a bit each night. I've still got to finish transcribing the last journal, and I'll keep working on it, and leave you and Eloise and Betsy in suspense. I check in with Betsy every day. Once we get you caught up, Pinky, we can finish the journals together."

Eloise nodded. "Let's get Pinky caught up quickly because that last entry was ..."

Dabs put up a finger, "Don't spoil it for Pinky."

Eloise sighed, "I guess I'll make it."

Pinky pressed her palms together in thanks. "Awesome! This is going to be so cool. And in the cemetery, I can have a meet-up with the cast of characters."

Dabs said, "We don't know exactly where they are. Apart from Buck."

Pinky said, "Bet they're all there though."

Dabs nodded, "Likely true."

Pinky said, "It's a courtesy call. Seems like the right thing to do, being that it's my first visit to their home and all. Southerners put a lot of stock in manners. Even trailer park folk like me."

Eloise and Dabs exchanged a small smile.

Pinky waved a biscuit at Dabs. "These are to die for."

Dabs thanked her, stood up, and fetched the coffee pot to give Pinky a "heater-upper."

Pinky asked, "So, how is it that you two guys are related?"

Dabs said, "Turns out, Louisa's mother was a Robertson. So, there may be a direct connection to Louisa for Eloise. But me? Not much to go on except that Major Schmidt's mother was named Frederika and my mother was named Frederika."

"Okay, I get it. Louisa Roberts is dropping all these clues and you two are following her lead. At the end of the line, there's a pot of gold."

Eloise said, "Maybe not gold. But we keep getting tidbits that apply to us personally. So, yeah, the journals are a treasure. It was a total surprise that in one of the last entries, Louisa writes that her mother was a Robertson."

Pinky said, "That's freaky."

Eloise nodded. "I agree."

Pinky said, "You know what else is freaky? Both of you ride horses. And that crazy bit where Dabs and you crossed paths in the past but never met each other. Freaky. Dabs even met your Mom! Freaky!"

Pinky had sopped up the egg yolk with her last bit of biscuit. Dabs noticed and said, "There's another biscuit."

"Wow, I did that plate in like a farm hand. Must be the fresh air."

Eloise said, "You haven't gone outside yet."

Pinky answered, "Must be the expectation of all that fresh air."

Pinky offered to do dishes, but Dabs put his foot down.

Dabs cleared the table and set the dirty dishes in the sink, put the stopper in and ran some hot water before announcing, "We are NOT doing dishes. We are going to pay that courtesy call, as per Pinky's suggestion, like the proper Southerners we are. We will introduce Pinky to the folks on the hill, who quite possibly are our ancestors."

* * *

Eloise put Lady Jane into her Sherpa bag and left her in her room, while they walked to the cemetery. Before joining the others downstairs, Eloise put in her backpack one item she felt compelled to bring, a box with a clay pipe and tobacco bag and pipe cleaner, still intact and wrapped in a towel for transport. It was what she had removed from the hillside on her last visit. The hillside that was at one time, a slave graveyard.

As they began walking toward the cemetery, Eloise said to no one in particular, "Do you know about the Elgin marbles?"

Pinky said, "Marbles? Like what kind of marbles?"

Eloise did not laugh. "How about King Tut's curse?"

Dabs interjected, "I think I know where this is going."

"Well, I have no clue."

Dabs explained, "Lord Elgin of Great Britain, stole the marble friezes right off the face of the Parthenon in Greece, and shipped them back to the British Museum. I've seen them. They're still in the museum, although Greece has been trying to get them returned for ages."

Pinky said "Still clueless here. Moving on. What's King Tut's curse?"

This one Eloise answered, "Death and destruction to anyone who dared disturb the boy King's tomb."

Pinky then asked, "Okay. I'm catching on now. What happened to those disturbers?"

Eloise said, "Well, Lord Elgin's nose fell off. "

Dabs laughed out loud, but Pinky did not.

She said, "Get out! For real?"

Eloise shrugged, "I think the medical reasoning of the day was syphilis."

Pinky said, "Ew! What about the guys that opened the tomb?"

Eloise had Pinky's full attention, "Lord Carnavon never made it out of Egypt. He died in a Cairo hotel."

Dabs interjected, "Pinky, don't look so impressed. Their deaths had nothing to do with curses."

Eloise added. "Yeah. Probably not, but the legends continue for a good reason. The thing is, stealing from temples and graves is an assault against those who can no longer defend themselves."

Dabs looked serious now.

Eloise said, "I've had time to think about it Dabs. And to think about your Mom. And it's also that Louisa and her journal entries got to me. It's not like everything is clear now. It's not. But what I do know is that we don't belong in that slave cemetery, and that it was wrong for me to take this box. I have it in my backpack to return."

Dabs said, "What's this got to do with my Mom?"

"Maybe your Mom was protecting it?"

Dabs mused, "Was it being protective? I don't know, Eloise. If that was her intent, why not tell me?"

Eloise said, "Once you tell a secret, is it still a secret?"

Dabs did not reply.

They turned off the road and headed up the trail, the trail that Eloise now thought of as the shortcut trail. It was no longer the shortcut trail. It was the *only* trail. Nature had fully reclaimed the cart path to the cemetery."

Eloise said, "It seems that your people and possibly my people, once claimed to own those whose remains reside on that hillside. For the enslaved, the only release from bondage was in death. For the descendants of their oppressors to go there, and take something, well, it dawned on me, I was thief, just like Lord Elgin, just like Lord Carnavon."

Dabs used his feet to press some dead bramble canes to the ground along the path, cautioning Pinky of the thorns.

Eloise said, "Maybe your mother decided the best protection for those who are buried there was for nature to reclaim it, and the secret burying ground to remain a secret. And what if she had promised to someone to keep that secret?"

They climbed the path in silence until cresting the rise, breaking free of the wooded path and vines and brambles to appear outside the stone walls of the family cemetery.

Pinky was struck by the view. "Wow, look at that. Makes that rough climb worth it. That's beautiful Dabs. Has that lookout always been there?"

"Yes. Well, a very long time. It's been maintained all my life."

Eloise said, "Let's visit Buck's grave."

The three of them walked through the broken gate, Dabs and Eloise knowing exactly where to go. Pinky stood by their sides, not knowing, not yet, the significance of Buchanan Elijah Roberts.

Eloise knelt and ran her fingers lightly on the carved lines that had been revealed to be his proper name.

She said, "Buck, you broke your father's heart. You broke your Aunt Bess' heart. Your sister, your brothers were afraid of you. Pretty sure Priscilla's Bertie was your son. Did you meet him? I hope you have found redemption, and peace, I do, but from what I read, I'm not sure you have. And for that I am sad for you."

Dabs said, "Amen."

And then they heard a cracking noise, and a branch fell from a tree inside the cemetery not twenty feet from where they stood. It was not a large branch, but it was large enough to make Pinky shriek, "Good God!"

Eloise stood up. "Okay, that was freaky."

Pinky swatted Eloise on the arm, "Don't go stirring things up like that!"

Dabs chuckled a little uncomfortably. "Let's go return that box."

The three of them headed outside of the stone enclosure and began the search for the way down the hill to what they now knew was indeed the slave graveyard. Eloise took the lead. She knew how to orient herself by the location of the head of the short cut trail.

But when she got to the place on the road above the graveyard, she hesitated.

Dabs said, "Do you want me to return it, Eloise?"

Pinky said, "Give it to me. I'll return it."

Eloise raised her eyebrows. "You mean that?"

Pinky was dead serious, "No slave owners in my dirt-poor pedigree. All dirt-scratchers and moonshiners from the hill country. I got plenty of racists in the attic, but I expect those folks buried down there never knew any white folk who weren't. I won't go back and bother any of them once I return what was taken. I can promise them that."

Dabs nodded and said, "Do you want me to lead the way?"

"Will I get lost?"

Eloise said, "Go straight down that line there, and then in about two hundred feet, drift a little left. You should see an Angel."

Pinky's mouth dropped open. "I don't want to see any Angels today, thank you very much!"

Dabs explained, "There aren't any headstones, just a statue of an Angel pointing toward heaven. She's not entirely uncovered, but you'll see her hand and we uncovered a bit of her arm. Just place the box there. I think that would be fine."

Eloise took the backpack off her back and handed it to Pinky, who solemnly put it on, took a few steps down the path and turned to look back at the two of them, before continuing.

Pinky was not gone long.

She said, "Okay. I saw the hand. I sure hope it was an angel, because any other possibility was too creepy to consider."

Eloise said "Thanks, Pinky."

"I put the box right at the base, and I said a little prayer."

Dabs said, "For those buried there?"

"Oh yeah. But I also asked for a little intercession. I mean, angels are famous for intercessions, right?"

Dabs asked, "Hmmm? And what did you ask for?"

"Kinda between me and the angel, but geeze, someone needs to get the ball rolling around here."

Pinky handed Eloise the empty backpack and began to walk toward home. Dabs looked at Eloise, and she just shrugged.

16

After supper, everyone, pets included, made themselves comfortable in the parlor. Dabs produced the promised port, chocolate covered caramels, and oddly enough, peanut butter cups. The house was chilly, so Dabs brought in lap rugs, and the kitten and Prince got up on the sofa and tucked themselves between Eloise and Pinky, nesting in the blankets. Dabs and Eloise took turns reading to Pinky from the journals, starting with the first entry. Eloise was eager to get Pinky caught up so they could move on to the newest transcriptions. Dabs appeared more interested in giving Pinky proper entertainment. He was good too, his voice measured and smooth as silk.

Eloise found she was as engaged in the writings of Louisa Roberts as the first time. And she noticed that Pinky was completely silent, her mouth slightly open, her gaze unfocused, her fists holding the edges of her lap rug. Dabs had a rapt audience.

But even though Dabs and Eloise took turns to save their voices, Eloise felt fatigued after her turn reading. That and the port wine had relaxed her to the point of drowsiness. As absorbed as they all were in the journals, no one noticed that Prince had left the room.

It wasn't until he jumped back up next to Eloise on the sofa, that she realized he had left. Prince had something in his mouth.

Eloise interrupted Dabs by asking, "What's Prince got?"

Pinky commanded the dog, "Drop it!"

Prince spit out the dolly into Pinky's hand.

Pinky stated, "Prince got a dolly from somewhere."

Pinky then handed it to Dabs, who frowned and said, "Well, I'll be damned. It's another one of those rag dolls, like the one he found before. Look, this one's wearing pants. I suppose it was meant to be a boy. Might be a black boy."

Eloise asked, "Why do you think that?"

Dabs passed the doll to Eloise.

Pinky began to apologize for the dog. "Sorry. He has this thing he does. I hope it won't bug you. See, he finds stuff, and then you hide it, and he finds it again. He's gentle though. I mean, I've never had him destroy anything, but he does get stuff spitty."

"Not to worry, Pinky. He brought me a doll last time he was here for a visit. Then he brought me an old key on a leather fob. It's weird though because I have no idea where he got any of that stuff."

Pinky brightened, "We can ask him."

"You're kidding, right?"

Eloise said, "She kind of is, and she kind of isn't. He's pretty smart."

Pinky looked over Eloise's shoulder at the doll. "This dolly looks really old. The face is so faded that you can barely see it. But look at the hair. Isn't that cool? It's a bunch of little knots."

Dabs said, "First thing I noticed. It's not like the other doll."

Eloise said, "They look like little horse braids. In embroidery it's called a French knot."

Pinky looked astonished, "How do you know that kind of thing?"

"Don't be impressed. I know nothing about embroidery. I only know what it's called because once, when my mom was teaching one of our clients in the barn how to braid a mane, the woman said the braids looked like the French knots she did in embroidery. These knots *do* look like horse braids."

Pinky said, "I was pretty sure it wasn't because you were sitting up at night doing fancy needlework."

Pinky said, "Let's see if Prince will show us where he's finding all these goodies."

She let Prince sniff the dolly and said, "Go find dolly!"

Eloise laughed, "Here we go again with the Lassie routine."

Prince jumped off the sofa and twirled around twice.

Pinky held the doll up high and waggled it, then turned to Eloise to say, "You got a better idea?"

"Nope."

Dabs stood up and crossed his arms, looking doubtful.

Pinky tried to get even more excitement in her voice, "Go find Dolly. Go find Dolly!" Prince ran out of the room, stopping in the hallway to check to see they were going to follow him.

Pinky grinned, "The hunt begins!"

The three of them exchanged an amused glance before falling in line behind the dog.

Prince disappeared like a flash up the stairs.

Pinky calling after him, "Go find dolly, Go find dolly!"

Eloise was having a flashback of when she and Pinky told Prince to "Go find Turbo!" They sounded like idiots. But then, Prince did find Turbo. Or at least Prince found the goop that Turbo was licking off the asphalt.

When they got upstairs Prince was nowhere to be seen. But the empty room to the right of the landing had a door pushed ajar.

Pinky pointed to the door, "Was that door opened before?"

Dabs said, "I don't think any of the doors are ever fully closed."

They proceeded into the room quietly. When Dabs and Eloise stepped into the room, Pinky was silently pointing at the tail that was peeking out from beneath the dust ruffle on the four-poster.

Pinky picked up the dust ruffle and peered under the bed, "Did you find a dolly?"

Then she observed, "He's rooting around in a big wooden box."

"I thought I'd moved all of Mom's boxes up to the attic."

Pinky called, "Come Prince, come on out of there."

The dog wiggled backwards with something in his mouth. Pinky took it from him. It was another old rag-doll. This one had on a dress with an apron.

Dabs got down on his knees and peered under the bed, then stood up. "I'm going to drag it out from under there."

Dabs reached under the bed and began to pull. It was awkward and large and clearly heavy. Once he got it all the way out onto the rag rug, it was clear it was not a box at all. At least that was not its original purpose.

Dabs exclaimed, "The mattress is gone, but this is an old trundle bed. Someone's lined it with plywood to store stuff."

Eloise pointed to the contents. "Are those more journals?"

Dabs said, "I don't think so."

He picked up one of the oversized and thin "books" and opened it to find sketches. Mostly charcoal. He showed it to Eloise and Pinky. The one they were look-ing at was a sketch of a boy of about ten or twelve. Un-derneath the drawing it said, "Bertie."

Eloise put her hand over her mouth.

Dabs said, "Portfolios."

Eloise whispered, "Bertie. Our Bertie?"

"It could be."

Pinky said, "Someone I should know?"

Dabs nodded, "You will soon enough."

Eloise stared at the sketch. "He survived babyhood."

Dabs said, "He did. His features ..."

"Familiar?"

"Could be me. But I'm imagining things. I wish there was a date on this."

"Or at least Louisa's signature."

Dabs said, "But at least we know, this is Bertie."

"But is it our Bertie?"

Pinky was busy pulling out a large plastic zippered bag chock full of legal pads.

The bag said, "Rambo."

Eloise noticed, "Your mom saved the bag. That's my favorite brand of horse blankets."

"Mom never threw anything away. Looks like she had a purpose for it though."

Pinky said, "Look at all those legal pads. All those notes? What's that all about?"

Eloise and Dabs said in unison, "Freddy's scribbles!"

Dabs added, "I've got to let Henry know we found them."

Eloise said, "Henry. I'd love to meet Henry."

Pinky noticed that Dabs answered Eloise by reaching for her hand. The two were holding hands, again. Maybe the angel had been listening to her request.

* * *

Eloise was in a deep sleep, the kind where you feel paralyzed, when she realized someone had gotten into bed with her. She lived alone, and Prince was no longer living with her. Although her eyes were closed, she was instantly flush with panic, her heart pounding. She calculated it was someone big enough to cause the mattress to sink and the bedframe to squeak.

But then she heard a long sigh followed by deep slow breathing. Good grief, a rapist wouldn't climb into bed with you to go right to sleep. She was not at home. She was not alone. It was Prince.

Her late-night visitor then stretched and rolled over on his back and placed a wet sloppy beard on her shoulder. Eloise placed her hand on Prince's sternum and caressed him. Good dog Prince had wanted to be with her. Eloise took a long breath and willed her heart to slow down. Prince was supposed to be making the transition to sleep with Dabs. But in a few short days, Eloise and Pinky would be leaving and Prince would be staying. She should enjoy these last few nights with the security, warmth, and comfort of her bedpartner, Prince.

She was beginning to drift back to sleep. She rolled over onto her stomach, one hand touching Prince, the other fingertip touching the soft fur of Lady Jane. A muffled "thud" from outside her room woke her back up, enough to motivate her to get up and make a trip to the bathroom. Prince sweetly got up with her as escort. But on the return trip back to her room, Prince did not follow, but instead stood in the hallway and made a breathy, nearly silent "woof."

"You whispered. That's very considerate of you, seeing as it's the middle of the night and everyone is sleeping except us."

Prince did it again, except this time he only opened and shut his jaws with a snap that seemed impatient.

Then he turned and headed toward the stairs. Eloise assumed he was bed hopping again.

"Back to Dabs then?"

But he did not go down the stairs. Instead, he disappeared into the bedroom where earlier he had been thieving dolls.

Eloise followed the dog, only to be surprised to find Dabs sitting on the floor wearing a cashmere dress coat over tee shirt and sweatpants. He was looking at one of the many legal pads filled with "Freddy's scribbles." He had placed the small bedside lamp on the floor next to him.

He looked up, surprised. "I woke you. I'm sorry, I'm afraid I knocked the lamp over. It's marble, so it landed hard."

"No. I heard it, but it was Prince that woke me. He jumped into bed with me."

"Oh. Sorry. I never noticed he had left the room. I guess I got absorbed. I apologize for both of us then."

"You couldn't sleep?"

He shook his head, "No."

"Been at this long?"

"Too long to confess."

Eloise said, "Nice dress coat."

"Seemed like a warm choice as I don't actually own a bathrobe."

Eloise said, "Cashmere?"

Dabs nodded.

Eloise said, in all earnestness, "Very professional. For an attorney, I mean." Eloise pointed to the stacks of legal pads, all now in rows on the floor. She said, "I guess journal-keeping runs in the family."

Dabs said, "I just wish Mom had been as meticulous as Louisa. Kind of stream of consciousness. No dates. All on legal pads swiped from Dad's law firm. And they are tough to read."

"Tough? Do you mean illegible, cryptic, or disturbing?"

He said in a grim tone, "All of the above."

"Sorry. I know the feeling. I had those letters in my closet. They also were 'all of the above.' I felt like I didn't know the people who were writing them. I mean, I know my Dad and my Mom, and now Bev. But only the bits of their lives that included me. And then, really, not all of that either, only the bits they wanted me to know. Strange, isn't it?"

Dabs nodded.

Eloise asked, "Do you want to tell me about any of it?"

Eloise then saw what Pinky had seen when she first met Dabs. She realized too, that she had always seen it. Why had she denied it to Pinky? What made her push back? Dabs *was* ruggedly handsome, even in his odd fashion combo of cashmere dress coat over his tee shirt and sweatpants. Eloise took in the whole of Dabs, including the bottom edges of his pant legs which had those sticky seed heads stuck to them. Clearly, he had worn them out to the barn and then to bed. That's what happened when you lived with horses, and she found this tiny detail endearing.

Even distressed, Eloise thought there was something self-assured about Dabs, so comfortable in his own skin, so honest, something she couldn't say about herself. And something else too. He was not entirely of this time, but oh, so of this place. That was something Pinky couldn't see, couldn't know. But Eloise did, and found that aspect of Dabs enticing, foreign, intriguing. But also, intimidating. He was in so many ways, much, much, older and wiser than she was.

It was only a moment later that a shy Lady Jane appeared at the door, tail held aloft. She spotted Eloise and trotted over to her, closing the circle as they all sat down.

Eloise asked Dabs again, "You can say no if you don't want to tell me about your mom's writings."

"But I do want to tell you every little thing. I just haven't absorbed it all myself. For one thing, you were right. She knew of the slave burial ground. She knew about Buck. She knew about well, everything we know now and then some. It appears she was working it out in these writings, too, as rambling, and incoherent as they seem. She was not ready to share with me or the world what she knew, at least not yet. But she fully understood the value of it all, due to that, she could not destroy anything, or throw anything away. She believed in the wrong hands, the story would be used to defame the family and the state. And one of those she feared most would defame the family was me. So, instead, she hid things from me. Besides, in her mind, I was different."

Eloise shook her head. "You? Different? And how would you defame the family, or the state of Virginia? I don't understand."

Dabs shook his head again. "I'm not sure I understand either. But she did know that I was not interested in mythmaking or an apologist for the antebellum south. But that doesn't mean I don't love Ivy Creek or my home state. I haven't gotten through all of this yet, but here's one fascinating new twist. In the history of our family, I am different. Mom had this bizarre notion that I had broken a curse, or perhaps I should say that she had broken a curse."

"Curse?"

"I know, it sounds crazy, it is crazy but evidently, there hasn't been a legal male heir to this place since Buck."

"All female children?"

Dabs nodded, "Only one child, all female, all named Frederika. Remember those baby curls I found, pressed inside a worthless old book? They were marked 'Freddy.' I assumed that meant they had been my mother's. Freddy, it seems never was a name of a male child. But there was a string of Frederika's, including my maternal Grandmother, who I never knew. Now I wonder, looking at those curls, which Freddy?"

Eloise only nodded.

"Mom writes, it was all because of Buck's curse. Something along the lines of, 'if he couldn't be master, then there would never be another master at Ivy Creek.' So, no male heirs. None."

"Your mother wrote that?"

"And more weird stuff she was working out in her head over I don't know how many years. I like to think in time she would have shared all of this with me. But her health declined. No one plans for that do they?"

"I guess not. But this curse thing, so, when you were born?"

"Curse broken. Not that it makes any difference. This old place, what's left of it, belongs to me, the only child. And I was not named Freddy. As you well know. I was named after my Dad."

"Do you think Henry knows about all this curse business?"

"No doubt. Henry knew mother better than anyone else left alive. I'd like to ask him about it all, but I already made Henry cry by mentioning mom had died. He had forgotten. I'd don't want to upset him, but at least I can tell him I found those 'scribbles he told me about."

Eloise said, "I'd like to think he's connected to our Henry in the journals."

"Henry is a Carter, not a Roberts."

Eloise said, "Like you."

"Like me."

Eloise said, "He won't be around a lot longer Dabs. I'd like to meet him if that's possible."

"I'd like that too. I'll see if we can do that."

17

It was cold and rainy the next day when Eloise and Dabs went to see Henry. Pinky elected to curl up on the sofa with Prince, watch a movie on her phone, and miss the excursion.

Henry's granddaughter was expecting them. She answered the door while calling over her shoulder, "Here they are Grandpa. I told you they'd be right on time."

Henry was wrapped up in one of those old-fashioned Afghan crocheted blankets, and wearing a zippered hoodie, his walker sat next to the sofa. There was a fire blazing in the fireplace.

He called out, "There's my young Dabs, and who is this lovely young Missy?"

Dabs said, "Henry, may I introduce Eloise Robertson."

Eloise gave Henry her hand. Henry's hand was large and narrow, with elegant long fingers, warm and dry to the touch.

"I'm so happy to finally meet you, Henry. May I call you Henry?"

"You may. Now, you sit right close because I don't

hear so good. My, you look real familiar-like. You ain't been by here before?"

Dabs leaned over to Henry and said, "Eloise here competed in those events I used to ride in. She's one heck-of-a horsewoman."

Henry's bushy grey eyebrows went up. "You don't say? I used to help Freddy drive the van and handle the horses. Maybe that's how I seen you before. Dabs here always did have a passel of young ladies hanging about him in those days. 'Member that, Dabs?"

Dabs looked embarrassed. But nodded.

Eloise said, "Well, I'm afraid I was not one of those young ladies. But recently it came to me that, maybe I did see Dabs ride in a symposium. At least it could have been Dabs."

Henry raised his eyebrows again. "Would thata' been down in Florida? Nice German lady teaching?"

Eloise nodded.

Henry's face lit up, "I seen you there. I sure did. I never forget a face, not me. Ain't life odd that way?"

Henry's granddaughter brought mugs of coffee and a plate of cookies and set it down next to her grandfather where he could easily reach it. She said, "Grandpa, yours is the lightweight white mug. Not too hot or too full."

Henry looked up with his eyes without moving his neck.

"She my angel. These here cookies, well, they an old family recipe. They is made with molasses. Freddy and me, we raised on these."

Dabs took a cookie, "I was too."

They enjoyed cookies and coffee for a minute before Dabs said, "Henry, I did find Mom's writings. She filled a whole bunch of those legal pads from Dad's office."

"You don't say?"

"You were right of course, about Mom's scribbles. Mom had plenty of stories to tell from slavery days, of curses and ghosts and family secrets. You believe in those things, Henry?"

Henry nodded, "Ain't I lived long enough to see things?"

Eloise said, "Those other journals we found, the real old ones, well they tell about a young slave named Henry."

Henry hardly reacted, seeming more interested in his cookie and coffee.

Dabs added, "There were some boys in the story, all sons of the master. Named Henry, Isaac, Samuel."

Eloise said, "Let's not forget Bertie."

Henry said matter of fact, "Colored boys."

Dabs added, "Those journals made me think, maybe I found where our two lines crossed, yours and mine."

Henry calmly said, "Is that so?"

Dabs said, "Do those names mean anything to you?"

Henry chuckled, "Virginian's use the same name over and over 'til you'd think they'd wear 'em out. That why you is Dabs like your Daddy. Your Momma, she come from a line of Freddy's that go back nearly to the Garden of Eden."

Henry's granddaughter was in the kitchen, but they

could hear her laugh. She poked her head into the room and said, "Grandpa, you are sharp as a tack today. You're cracking me up."

Henry's lips curled slightly, "I's saying it true. They's a genuine lack of creativity in these parts when it come to names."

Dabs said, "Bertie's not that common, though."

Henry said, "Was my Daddy's name. It's all down the line as I recall. Same as all them other names. So, where do we cross, Dabs?"

"I think you came by Carter because, well, it sounds wrong to say this, but the person who owned Bertie's mother was a Carter, but the babe was sired by the young master of the house, whose last name was Roberts. I think I may be from his line too, not through Dad, but through Mom. But I still got more digging to do there."

Henry still looked calm. "I 'spect all that's true."

Dabs said, "Our common ancestor is likely a fellow named, Buchanan Elijah Roberts. He went by Buck."

Henry echoed Dabs, "Buck."

Dabs said, "I'm guessing, that's not a name that was given out again."

Henry was solemn for a moment. Then he said with another lift of his eyebrows, "He one of them haints rambling around inside them stone walls?"

Dabs answered, "If there is such a thing, then I think Buck would be one, yes."

Henry sighed deeply, "Them slavery days was bad. But them days after slavery, they was mighty bad too. Life is a vale of tears. I glad to live when I did and to have a friend in Miss Freddy all my days. When the Angel comes for me, I'se ready, 'cause I sure like to see folks I loved who went on ahead, yes, I surely would."

Henry's granddaughter joined them and asked, "You tired Grandpa?"

"Not yet. I hates to see Dabs and Miss Freddy leave, cause at my age, I knows it might be my last sight of 'em."

No one corrected Henry.

Henry added impishly, "Now, Dabs, don't you worry none about that curse neither. Freddy done broke it when she had you. I reckon you two will get you a house full of children once you get started."

Eloise felt her face heat up. But Dabs looked as serene as Henry.

Henry grinned naughtily, "And if you wants to use them old names, I gives my blessing. I guess they ain't wore out yet. You can call one Henry."

Then Henry giggled.

Dabs said, "I always did like that name."

"I dreams a lot, Dabs." He was beginning to sound tired. "I dreams in a way that I ain't never done before. I keeps having the same dream over and over, too. They is more real than you sitting right here. And I sees folks I ain't never seen in my lifetime. But I knows them. I believe I seen them colored boys, Henry and Isaac and Sammie and Bertie and some other folk, white folk. We's had a good ole time, too. One of them colored boys is right good on the fiddle, but the old white feller he be better than good. And we's walked through a field of horses, with our dogs. Then I hears womens calling to us to come on inside for dinner, but to wipe our feets good first. And I knows we got us something good to eats, so good my mouth it start to water. Then I wake up with a powerful hunger. I ain't yet made it into that house to that feast. I knows the day I do, I ams in heaven sure."

Eloise's mouth dropped open.

Henry's granddaughter said, "Grandpa, you sure you aren't tired? When your voice sounds like that, I know you're tired."

And Dabs said, "Henry, I'll be back next week for another visit. We'll go on now if you need a nap."

"All right then, Dabs." Then he looked at Eloise and said, "Dabs is alright. I know'd him all his life. Go on then and get started. You don't got to ask no one's permission."

Henry reached for Eloise's hand with his large warm hand, and gave hers a squeeze, and she found herself gently returning it.

When Dabs and Eloise got back into the confines of his truck, Dabs said, "I hope he didn't embarrass you."

Eloise shook her head. "No. But, Dabs, there at the end. The bit about the dreams?"

"Yeah. How did he know about the fiddle?"

Eloise said, "And he said Sammie. You did say the name Samuel, but never Sammie."

"He's a sly old fox, our Henry. He won't ever say, but I think there's nothing Mom knew that she didn't share with Henry. He even mentioned the curse."

Eloise looked incredulous. "You think he made all of that up, about the dreams?"

"Not exactly. But all those folks in his dreams, I expect he knows them all. Just as well, if not better than we do."

Then Dabs turned in his seat with upturned lips and said, "While it's not a requirement, I perhaps should mention, I wouldn't mind having a passel of children, just in case you were wondering."

Eloise thought she should have delivered a clever come-back, but was speechless.

* * *

After Dabs put a chicken pot pie in the oven. He and Eloise forced Pinky out of her nest to join them for a walk. The sun was dropping, and the wind was blowing so they made it a short one. Prince bounded alongside them as they made their way to the marker for the Hessian graveyard. Pinky was surprisingly silent as they described in detail their visit to Henry and all he had shared with them, except the bit about urging them to get started on a family. That tidbit they kept to themselves.

As Pinky read the marker, Prince leaned into her, and Pinky placed her hand on his head. Eloise and Dabs exchanged a knowing glance. History was repeating itself, again.

They walked back into a house that was fragrant with the aroma of chicken pot pie. Eloise fed Prince and Lady Jane, Pinky set the table, and Dabs brought out a CD he had purchased of traditional Scottish ballads. He popped it into a portable player and put the CD cover down in front of Eloise.

Eloise asked, "What made you want to listen to Scottish ballads?"

Dabs said, "Scottish music was popular at the time the journals were written."

Eloise tipped her head. "Mournful tunes like the violin music in my dream?"

"Yes."

Eloise said, "I thought I would never forget the melody, it was so distinct, and sad, but I did. I forgot it almost immediately."

Pinky said, "Forgot what?"

"The music in my dream."

Pinky said, "Music? Wow. I don't think any of my dreams ever came with a soundtrack."

Eloise said, "Well, this one did. Violin music."

Dabs shrugged, "Mostly, I thought it would be nice to have music to play for your visit that was of the time and would evoke the mood of the journals. As Pinky just put it, a soundtrack."

Eloise studied the cover on the CD case, while the strings came on and "Loch Lomond" began to play. Dabs leaned against the counter and crossed his arms, his head lowered, focused on the violin as the sound filled the room.

Pinky began singing along when it came to the well-known chorus, "I'll take the high road, and you take the low road."

The bagpipes joined in and all three of them were ready to join in with the next chorus. Dabs had a beautiful voice. They quieted to listen to the lyrics of each verse and then joined the singing for the chorus.

When the song finished, Pinky was wiping a tear from her eye while laughing, saying, "Oh my God, are they all that sad? Keep this up and y'all are going to have to pick me up off the floor."

"Afraid so. Danny Boy is next up. Steel yourselves."

Again, it opened with lush violin, then flute and finally bagpipes. Dabs opened a bottle of wine and poured them each a glass, and they listened and drank and wiped at their eyes.

When Danny Boy finished, they listened to "Wild Mountain Thyme." Pinky was not yet on the floor, but Dabs went and got a box of tissues.

Dabs passed the box around and said, "Major Schmidt wouldn't have known the first two, but that last one he might have known. This next one Major Schmidt also might have known, it's very old and was popular then."

Eloise picked up the cover to look. "'The Parting Glass.' Ah man, another song for weeping."

The timer went off and Dabs put on his oven mitts and pulled out the pie. It was no ordinary looking pot pie from the frozen food aisle. It was deep-dish pie with an artistic crust with cut out leaves of pastry adorning the top.

Pinky said, "That's stunning! Dabs, did you make that?"

Dabs shook his head as violin music filled the room along with the aroma of steaming chicken pot pie.

Dabs was telling Pinky about a bakery in Charlottesville that specialized in pies, both sweet and savory. This was their highly rated Coq Au Vin version of pot pie.

Dabs was saying, "It has bacon and maple syrup in it and of course wine. I hope you like it as much as I do."

Eloise only half-heard the conversation because the music had grabbed her ear. She closed her eyes and tried to block out everything but the music, because she might have been wrong. She might have simply been wishing to find that melody so hard that she was grabbing for anything like it. But no. This music brought back the scene from her dream in blurry bits, like the sight of the tear-streaked face of the violinist, and his long fingers moving the bow across the strings.

When the song ended, Eloise opened her eyes to find both Pinky and Dabs had stopped talking and were looking at her.

Dabs said, "Beautiful, wasn't it?"

Pinky added, "Stop, okay. You guys, this music is just crushing me."

Eloise asked, "Can we play that one again?"

Pinky said, "Isn't there some kind of happy pie-eating music we can play during dinner?"

Eloise looked past Pinky at Dabs. "I think that's the song."

Dabs said, "From your dream?"

"But I want to be sure."

Dabs went to the CD cover to find what the track number was for "The Parting Glass" and then selected in on the player. The lush violin notes began again.

Pinky said, "Oh for Gawd's sake. I'll cut the pie and think happy thoughts while you two are momentarily transported into dreamland. But don't stay long. That pie should be eaten hot."

Dabs had once again reached for Eloise's hand.

When the song finished, Dabs turned off the player. "I can see why you would remember that one, 'But since it fell unto my lot, that I should rise and you should not, I'll gently rise and softly call good-night and joy be to you all.' Only someone sweet and good leaves his loved ones like that."

Pinky said, "Please, I am trying to stop crying."

Dabs said, "Celtic Women do an amazing rendition. Eloise, you might have heard their version. It's been used in films too."

"I must have."

Pinky brightly said, "Eat."

There was no problem with the food still being hot. Eloise had to blow on her forkful before she could put it in her mouth. Pinky was raving over it and saying Buzz should do a version.

Eloise enjoyed it too but felt unsettled.

Pinky noticed. "Earth to Eloise. What is going on up there?"

Eloise said, "Did I say, the old man in my dream was Major Schmidt? I mean, who else but Henry played the violin? And he was crying. He was burying someone he loved. And it was in your slave graveyard. Louisa wasn't there. Or maybe she was, riding up there uninvited because she couldn't stand not to be there. I put myself in her place in my dream. It was me who rode up. I saw the whole scene through the ears of a chestnut horse. I realize it all came from inside my head, stuffed full of the journal entries. So, I guess I have heard the tune somewhere and put that in my dream too. My brain must be filling in what we don't know."

Pinky said, "Who's to say where dreams come from? It's like your conversation with Henry today, he could have been telling you about a dream, or he could simply have been telling you something he wanted to tell you, and that's how he decided to tell you. Doesn't mean the message is less real. I for one, want to hear more about this dream of yours. Whatever you tell me, hey, I'm going to believe you." There was no mocking tone in her voice.

Dabs asked, "Who were they burying?"

A tear ran down Eloise's cheek.

"It was Henry. It had to be. He was younger than they were, but he passed before they did. His death broke their hearts. It hit me hard too. Silly isn't it, because I know of course that he has been dead and likely buried up on that hill for a very long time, but for whatever reason..."

Dabs said, "When I reminded Henry that Mom had died, he cried, although surely somewhere in his mind, he knew it, just like we know all the people in the journals are long dead. But for us, the Henry of the journal, well, his passing, and the loss and grief of Major Schmidt and Louisa has just been felt, fresh and raw, and made poignant with the playing of "The Parting Glass."

Dabs had just made something very confusing, clear to Eloise. Grief, buried grief, old grief, could find a way to re-emerge, and feel fresh and raw, and sometimes all it took was a trace of perfume or the sound of a violin. And there was something right about that too. These were real persons whose lives mattered, enough for strangers to mourn.

* * *

Dabs brought in lap rugs again as they settled in for journal readings. Lady Jane and Prince took up their places between Pinky and Eloise.

"I apologize for the chilly room. I'd light a cozy fire, but sadly none of the fireplaces are deemed safe."

Pinky smiled impishly. "Well, a hot body next to you is just what's needed in a cold house." Before anyone could say a thing, Pinky quickly added, "Prince is keeping us nice and toasty, isn't he Eloise?"

Eloise nodded in agreement while stepping on Pinky's toes with her foot, well hidden by the blanket. She realized she could thank Aunt Bess for that little trick. Pinky endured the toe crushing without a blink.

If Dabs was embarrassed, he did not show it.

He said, "I think we can get caught up tonight if we are willing to make it a longer session. I'm nearly done transcribing the last of the journals and I'm eager to share them. We catch up tonight. Tomorrow we advance."

Pinky said, "Only if we can finish off that bottle and the rest of the chocolates."

"Of course. Just pace yourself so your blood sugar doesn't spike then plunge, wouldn't want you to pass out before we finish."

Dabs handed out the drinks and the chocolates and began to read, his voice rich and calming. Eloise's tummy was warmed by the wine and her head was fuzzy. Lady Jane was purring and kneading her thigh and she wanted nothing more than to slide down under the blanket and drift away. She could dream of Louisa and Major Schmidt, and all the others as they lived their story here in this very house. She would recline right here in the parlor, like a ghost and observe. And observe she did, while still under many different influences. This place. The journals. The music. Old Henry. Dabs reaching for her hand and Henry saying they didn't need anyone's permission.

It was late when they finished, the room still but for the sound of Dabs' voice telling the story of Tarleton's raid on Ivy Creek. It was there that he stopped. Only Dabs knew what came next.

Pinky said, "Is that what you call a cliffhanger?"

Dabs laughed gently. "Betsy and Eloise have been hanging. You Pinky, only have to hang until tomorrow evening. The journals continue."

Pinky said, "I'm so stupid. I've got so many questions."

Eloise said, "No sane person would ever mistake you for stupid. Ask whatever."

"Don't forget that the only war I know about was the war between the states. I don't know anything about this one."

Dabs chuckled, "Well, maybe we'll get to that war on another day. But what can I tell you, as far as Louisa's war?"

"So, I knew that Benedict Arnold was a traitor. But I had no idea it was because he attacked Virginia. I guess that's why George Washington wanted him hung."

Eloise added, "Well, he turned his coat earlier, and tried to end the war by giving the British West Point. We caught his accomplice and hung him. Arnold got away."

Dabs nodded. "But he led the attack on Richmond, successfully too. Marched right down the middle of main street unimpeded. Jefferson and the assembly fled to Charlottesville. Arnold famously tried to ransom off the city in an exchange with Jefferson. Jefferson refused, so Arnold burned the city."

Pinky said, "Rat."

Dabs added, "Traitor lived to be sixty in Britain, too."

Pinky asked, "Okay. We're square on Arnold. Who was Tarleton?"

Dabs said, "He was intent on capturing Jefferson, but was foiled by our own Paul Revere-style midnight rider, who rode hard and fast to Monticello, and warned Jefferson with only minutes to spare."

Eloise added, "Jack Jouette. He saw Tarleton's men

at a tavern and listened in a window to hear what they were up to. He really was a hero."

Dabs explained, "But there's more. Tarleton became known as 'The Butcher' because of the Waxhaw massacre. Men surrendering, who were asking for 'quarter,' were slaughtered. Of course, the men doing the slaughtering were American Loyalists led by Tarleton, who by the way, was trapped under his dead horse at the time. He claimed innocence. I'm not sure I believe him. He was brutal throughout the conflict."

Eloise added, "He was horrid to his horses. Horrid. Literally rode them to death. Slit the throats of those he could not steal."

Pinky shivered, "Okay. We hate Tarleton, but love Henry. What's not to love about Henry? Louisa loves him too. She just didn't understand how much. Major Schmidt is opening her eyes to what she couldn't see."

Dabs said, "Agree. Don't you think it often takes someone from the outside, someone with perspective, to open your eyes? How people and places and things you can't see because they are too familiar to you, an outsider can show you?"

Pinky shrugged, "Like Dorothy in The Wizard of Oz, yeah. But it took a good knock on her head to set her straight."

Eloise said, "Speaking from experience, I don't think head-knocking is recommended."

Pinky said, "I wouldn't be so sure about that."

Both Eloise and Dabs gave her odd looks.

18

The next day they stood in a windy field scanning the acres of grass that had been a prisoner-of-war camp, trying to imagine the way it had been hundreds of years before. Major Schmidt and other prisoners had filled those fields with huts and lanes, gardens, and chickens and even a makeshift theater. When the prisoners had first arrived, all they found was heavy snow and roofless and incomplete cabins.

Dabs said, "I've known these fields all my life, but I'll never see them the same way again. Funny how the familiar can suddenly feel foreign."

Pinky shivered, pulled her jacket tighter and then crossed her arms. "Is it ever warm here?"

Dabs pulled his knit cap off his head and handed it to Pinky. "Here, maybe this will help. It is lovely here both Spring and Fall. Summer can be miserable. Hot and humid. The winters have actually gotten milder, nothing like the winters of my youth, and certainly nothing like that terrible winter of 1779."

Eloise turned her gaze from open fields of grass to the large horse farm at the end of the road. She too was scanning the landscape, but in a different direction. She asked, "Is that an indoor arena?"

Dabs smiled. "I was waiting for you to notice. Yes, that's where I learned to ride. And by that, I mean, where I learned to ride properly. Mom put me on a lead line way before I was old enough to take instruction. Later, Mom and I kept our best horses there in the winter so we could keep training."

Eloise said, "It's so close."

Dabs nodded, "An easy hack in good weather."

Pinky now had the large knit cap down low over her eyebrows, pink braids sticking out over her upturned collar. She asked, "Can you ride horses in those fields?"

Dabs nodded, "Around the edges."

"Eloise, I can picture you and Red out there."

Eloise said, "What *I* picture are men in worn out uniforms and boots, trying to build shelters. They felled whatever trees they found. They were cold, malnourished, and ill. They looked to their superior officers to help them survive, and there is so little that those officers could do. One of those officers was someone we know."

Pinky said, "Hey, look again and maybe you'll see Native Americans'. They got to that field way before those soldiers. But I like that it's been kept a field. One you and Red could ride around."

Dabs added, "Eloise, if you ever want to bring Red up, there's more than the fields, there's that indoor arena, good coaching, real jumps, and great hacking. You wouldn't have to keep her with my geriatric herd."

Pinky enthused, "What a cool idea!"

Eloise said, "Nice, but she's not my horse."

Dabs led them back to the historical marker for "The Albermarle Barracks" and read it aloud.

Then he said, "Let's go to 'The Corner' for a hot meal, then I'd love to show you Mr. Jefferson's 'Academical Village.' The delicacy of the house is a hot donut right out of the fryer with a scoop of ice cream on top."

Pinky grinned, "I'll let you in on a secret about Eloise. She can destroy a donut."

When they finally returned to Ivy Creek, exhausted from touring, but well fed, there was the immediate matter to attend to of getting warm. Pinky was not only frozen through, but her feet were killing her. Hot showers and toes up were in order. Dabs went out to bring in his herd.

When Eloise came downstairs warmed up from her shower and bundled up by wearing double socks, a turtleneck, jeans, and a hoodie, Prince trotted up to greet her. She could hear music playing from the kitchen but heard no voices. Prince gave her a head bump on her thigh, but instead of leading her to the kitchen, turned into the parlor. Eloise found Pinky was face down on the sofa.

"Pinky? You okay?"

Pinky groaned and turned her head, "You guys are killing me. Can I just sleep here, and you can wake me up tomorrow?"

"Ah, too much fresh air?'

Pinky groaned again.

Eloise said, "Dabs is making Beef Stroganoff. And you don't want to miss the new journal entries. I've been waiting for you to get caught up, now you are, so this is the big night. Dabs has dropped a few hints about how we won't be disappointed. Your presence is required."

Pinky looked unimpressed, but agreed, "Uh-huh. Okay. Got it. Wake me up when dinner is ready."

* * *

Dabs directed them to the sofa for an after dinner "delight" to accompany the next journal reading.

Eloise said, "I don't know about dessert, Dabs. That dinner was delicious, but I think I ate too much."

Dabs shook his head, "Oh, you'll find room. Trust me. So, get your lap rugs arranged, the dog, the cat. Don't move. I'll be right back."

When he left the room, Pinky sighed, "You sure you two don't want the sofa and the blanket?"

"Nope."

Pinky shook her head, "Y'all are slower than molasses in January."

Dabs came back carrying a tray. "My deadly, but delicious, doctored high-test coffee, topped with whipped cream and caramel sauce. Don't light a match anywhere near it."

Dabs once again left the room, returning with a sheaf of papers. The new transcriptions. He settled into his chair and took a big slurp of coffee that left whipped cream on his top lip.

Pinky and Eloise had likewise started on theirs. It was sweet and flavorful. And yes, clearly alcoholic. Dabs was right. Somehow, they both found room for his coffee.

Eloise and Pinky were soon feeling warm, both inside and out.

Dabs began to read.

June 17, 1781

I have a confession. I have ripped away three pages of this journal and turned them into ashes. Yes, I have done that before. But in those cases, it was to polish my prose. I am too proud of my skill with pen and paper. In this case it was not pride but shame. Major Schmidt did tell me that I was braver than I knew. He thinks me a strong person. But I am not brave nor strong. I will try with greater temperance to describe the aftermath of Tarleton's raid.

After all the soldiers had ridden away, after Henry and I had seen the last of Major Schmidt, Beauty, Sammie, and Fashion, after the last cloud of dust had settled, my legs gave way and I sat in the dirt. I'm not sure exactly what happened next as I hugged my knees to my chest and put my head down and closed my eyes. But I was put to bed in my shift by Aunt Bess. Though it was warm outside, I was cold and trembling. Father allowed Beast to climb up into the bed, vermin, and all, and even lifted the covers and pushed him into my body and placed my arm atop him. It was only due to Beast that my body ceased to quiver. It was an internal chill unlike anything I have ever known. My heart seemed intent to beat its way out of my chest like a fly banging against a pane of glass, looking to escape. But while I had Beast pulled tightly against me, I could feel the slow beat of the dog's heart, and it was as if my heart regained rhythm by listening to Beast's heart. Aunt Bess brought hot broth, but I had no interest. After it cooled, I fed it to Beast and watched him lick the mug clean. Father came bedside and gave some soothing speech and promised me the daughter of Beauty. He does not seem to think much of Major Schmidt's pledge of return. Father's words did indicate, though he did not say outright, that the idea of Major Schmidt coming back, to be a part of Ivy Creek, to be my intended, that these were hopes best laid aside. Major Schmidt now rode with those whose intent was our destruction. We had suffered losses in this day. These losses were like to be permanent.

It was Henry that I wanted. I asked Father to send him up. And when he arrived, he brought his violin and took a seat. He played some tunes and did not attempt to engage in talk, and I fell asleep. When I awoke, Henry was still there in the chair, though his head had dropped, and his violin was in its case.

I woke him by gently calling his name. He did

startle. I said, "Henry, I think I am dying." I cringe to write those words, but I did say them.

Henry retorted, "No you aint. I feels mighty bad too. But we both of us got to survive these trials."

I felt angry when I replied, "Why? Why do we?"

Henry frowned and snorted before saying, "Major Schmidt say he coming back, and if he says he is, he gonna'. You want me to have to say, 'Miss Louisa jumped off a cliff 'cause you rode off with her horse?'"

I was shocked. It took me a moment to recover. I said, "You think me a shallow and selfish mistress, don't you?"

Henry said, "Priscilla, she been crying her eyes out. Me? I been mighty sad. Likely I'll never see Sammie no more. Your Aunt Bess, she crying and crying and wringing her hands, course we all real glad she built that cellar. Major will come back if he among the living. I hope your Daddy live to a hunnert, but it worries me no end thinking on him being gone someday. Once he gone, Master Buck won't tolerate the Major staying here noways, nohow. I'll belong to Master Buck then. I don't like to think on that. No, I can't have you jumpin' off no cliff."

Henry has never spoken so frankly to me in my life. Nor so harshly. Nor so like a grown man. He had first been my babe, then just a little boy. I was astonished to look upon him sitting there, chastising me. It silenced me rather than angered me, as I felt too weary in my bones for ire. It did occur to me then, that I had not passed on Sammie's message to Priscilla.

I said, "Did you give Priscilla the message from Sammie?"

Henry said, "Them words was for you to pass on."

I sighed, "I suppose I cannot die today, though I should like to."

"No Miss Louisa, you sure can't."

Henry got Priscilla from the kitchen house where she was working. She brought Bertie with her. I could tell for sure she had been weeping as her eyes were badly swollen and red. I made her sit, and the babe was rooting at her breasts, so Priscilla pulled down her dress and let the babe suckle.

I said, "Sammie told me I was to be sure and tell you that this is all going to come right in the end."

Priscilla made no response. She looked to be made of stone. I'd never seen Priscilla like that. She of the wails and moans.

I confessed, "I'm not sure I believe him or the Major. What if this is the end?"

Priscilla did meet my eye boldly and held it with a look that I can only characterize as disdain. It was not her face that I saw in that moment, but Sammie's.

She said, "Miss Louisa, men talk like they know what's coming. They don't know better than you nor I. I got little chance of seeing Sammie again."

All I could say to Priscilla was, "I'm sorry."

And she got up and said, "You mean that?"

And I nodded. But I got the feeling that Priscilla did not believe me. She and I were not looking for comfort it seemed. And neither of us gave it nor found it.

Priscilla left me to my complete and utter misery, still brittle, still ill and shaken to my core. But not dying. Henry was right. We had a duty to try and survive these trials, although at that moment I had not the stomach to try.

July 2, 1781

Father and Isaac have been caring for our refugee horses. The horses are a sorry lot. They have no names; they have no history. Four geldings. They were covered in dried sweat, galled and footsore. They are fearful. The dun has weeping rope burns about his front pasterns.

Isaac has trimmed their hooves and brushed them clean. He daily treats the rope burns with his special ointment and keeps the wounds clean and bandaged.

Father says the horses are young and that the young are resilient, and so they would recover with a 'tincture of time.' We will never be compensated. Beauty and Fashion can never be replaced. But these four, once recovered, can be sold for some amount of money. We know at least that they are broke to saddle and bridle. Father has asked me and Henry to spend time working with each one each day. I am to regain their trust in humans, handle them and work them from the ground in simple obedience drills. Although father generally names the horses, he has given me the task. Something inside of me rebels at this task. I think they shall not be named. I refer to them by their colors. Dun. Bay. Brown. Black.

I have had two gentlemen callers. Absurd. As I never cared for these boys before, what makes anyone think that my mind would have been changed? Both had served in our state militia and were now home. I told each one they should get back into the fight. Once they had departed, I asked Aunt Bess to see to it that they did not return nor did any others get the notion to come calling. I prefer to spend my time in the stables with the four refugees and with Isaac, Beast, and young Henry.

Truth be told there is no place where I feel at ease. I have not been much interested to write in these pages. I have not been at my drawings. I have no horse to ride out with Henry. Beast and Henry and I do walk to the cemetery, but we do not go inside the walls. I do not dare traipse into the slave burying grounds though I was prepared to hide Beauty there. I try mightily not to think of Major Schmidt, nor his promises. I try not to think of what Sammie did for us that day. How he returned because Beauty led him back. Aunt Bess and father do not speak of my precious Beauty. They do not speak of Fashion either or the others. But Henry does. It is only Henry to whom I can unburden my heart.

Henry and Beast and I were out in the barn. He said, "Major gonna' keep his word."

I cried in frustration, "Major Schmidt was supposed to be in Winchester, out of the fight."

"You told me he got changed."

"Exchanged. That's what he said."

Henry stiffened defensively. "However you say it. I be glad of it. Miss Louisa, what you think would have happened if Major Schmidt been up in Winchester when Bloody Ban come into the yard?"

I did not answer, because the thought was not one I wished to entertain. But Henry was not going to let it go.

He said, "I'm gonna' tell you. When that soldier done got around to hauling himself off the ground, he would have made you pay mightily."

I turned away from Henry and began to groom the Dun. I began to peel the horny excess of growth off the horse's chestnuts, fussing that Isaac should have taken care of this chore when he trimmed their hooves. They were tough and protruded off the inside of each leg. But layer by layer I pulled them away and tossed the bits on the ground where Beast instantly devoured them as treats. I was not going to think or talk anymore about what Henry was saying. I did not want to summon the scene back into my mind.

But it was too late.

Henry was unrelenting, saying, "I thought sure you was going to get a whipping, if not worser than that. I heard tell of things much worser than that done to womens. I was mighty scared for you."

I felt ashamed as I said, "You put yourself in front of me."

"Miss Louisa, I thought maybe we were both gonna' die. People they die in war. And I hear tell that Ban fellow, he the devil. He killed men that was beggin' for their lives."

"I heard the same."

Henry continued, "When I saw Major, well it was like seeing an Angel coming to deliver us from evil. Most beautiful sight of my life."

I felt myself sway a bit. I feared my legs might not hold me. It did pass through me like a chill. I hoarsely whispered. "Oh Henry, you realize, that is like to be our last sight of him! The last we ever see of Beauty, too!"

I could not hide the panic in my voice when I said in rising tones, "What shall become of us? Buck may try to take you from me from pure meanness. If that should come to pass, then I will be alone."

Henry looked me steady in the eye and said, "We's gots to look out for each other, Miss Louisa. No matter what. That's what we gots to do."

Fine words. But we could make no promises to each other. Father and Aunt Bess would not live forever, and Buck would take control of all about me, including Henry, and including myself. He

*could sell Henry to a slave trader the same way he
had urged father to sell Sammie. He would do it too,
just to punish me, knock me down a peg.*

*And for the first time in my life, Henry took me
in his arms while I wept. All our lives, I had been
the one to hold him, from a tiny babe on. He was
my little Bud no longer. He had bravely placed himself in front of my person to meet with Bloody Ban,
believing that day we might die, that he might die.
That had been my tiny Bud. Now Henry. Henry
my protector. Henry my friend. I clung to him and
wept, and knew his worth, perhaps for the very first
time.*

August 15, 1781

*Aunt Bess and I have paid a social call to Mrs.
Jefferson. We are glad to have her back in Albemarle
and safe. Aunt Bess did make her a gift of our own
clover honey that is especially fine, and she politely
received us and served tea and biscuits.*

*Mrs. Jefferson did lose her babe Lucy Elizabeth
this past April. This terrible blow that all mothers'
dread is not her first. She did lose her son Jack. her
daughter Jane, another son who did not survive
birth, and now little Lucy Elizabeth.*

*Mrs. Jefferson had not the spark of liveliness
that I recall being her nature. But she is finally able
to rest and recuperate from this horrific year, where*

she has been in constant peril. She fled Richmond in January from childbed, and then Monticello in June, living in a rough cabin until last month with her two little ones. Patsy is but eight, and Polly is but two. I pray she can regain her health which is much damaged. Jefferson too is returned to Monticello, which is still an unfinished house in need of his attention, along with those persons most dear to him. I did observe the entry hall at last has a floor.

Mr. Jefferson has not fully recovered from breaking his arm from a fall from Caractacus, another trial of this most trying year. I did not learn of the details of the fall, but it was while at their own Poplar Forest in Bedford where they had found shelter while Cornwallis and Tarleton did their worst.

I did recount to Mrs. Jefferson our encounter with Tarleton and the misfortune of seeing our common friend, Major Schmidt riding with him, of losing our Sammie and our best horses, including Beauty. Since Jefferson did know Beauty well, I asked her to please let Mr. Jefferson know. He was fond of her too.

Mrs. Jefferson reminded us that Cornwallis had not only stolen Mr. Jefferson's breeding mares but slit the throats of the foals before burning her Elk Hill to the ground. Oh, the horror!

Aunt Bess had soothing words to say. "We must not lose heart now. One day this shall be behind us, and victory will be sweet. But you, dear lady, must rest and recover your strength so when that day comes, we shall celebrate together."

Later, as Isaac drove us back down the mountain, she stated grimly, "Mrs. Jefferson is not well."

And I said, "Yes. I did observe that also."

"It is well Mr. Jefferson stays at Monticello. He must not leave her side again."

I did not answer, but I certainly could read her thoughts. Aunt Bess thought Mrs. Jefferson's life in peril.

September 18, 1781

I have had nothing to report in my journal until today. A rare missive has arrived from Buck. Aunt Bess is aglow as it begins by boasting of her foresight. He avows that his stockings are the envy of all, and he guards them jealously. Many are suffering fearsomely from the ill effects of wet, blistered, or chilled feet. His greased boots too have held up fine. Most of the soldiers have marched to shreds what once passed as footwear. He also bragged on his gun. When supplies are scarce, he has been able to shoot a squirrel or a pigeon and roast up something to eat. Buck knows how to make do whilst living rough.

Buck's important news was of war. He claims, with righteous tones, that the fates have interceded on our behalf. The British have made decisive tacti-

cal blunders. *We have the quarry trapped.* Although by "we" he neglects to say it is the French who did the trapping.

Britain and France had a battle at sea outside the bay, the French warships led by a General De Grasse cleverly drew the British out to sea so that other French ships coming south from New York, bearing cannon and supplies and soldiers to our forces, could slip into the harbor. De Grasse then sailed away from the Brits, abandoning them in the Atlantic, and headed back into the harbor of Yorktown to meet new French naval forces, and together sealed off the Bay.

Cornwallis now had no way to escape or resupply by sea. The British navy, damaged and defeated, sailed to New York, thinking to do battle there instead. When they arrived, the Continental and French armies, Washington, and Rochambeau, had marched south to Yorktown!

They had no one to fight in New York but each other.

Cornwallis cannot escape by sea, and now he also cannot escape by land. Lafayette, another Frenchman, has sealed off that route.

So, we Continentals' sit, and let the French and Brits fight each other.

But I am being sardonic. Though it seems a war between Britain and France, we are indeed involved. Washington is now in his home country of Virginia, and the war is still waged for American *independency. Buck now serves under a Captain Olney, a foreigner from Rhode Island. Buck has grudging respect for Olney as the man has seen much fighting and did return to the fight after being wounded. Olney serves under the command of La-fayette. Whatever the outcome, one thing I know for certain, Buck will not come home speaking French.*

I wrote that I would not name the refugee hors-es. But I could not prevent Henry from doing so. He has informed me that the Dun's name is Cider. Henry is quite smitten with him. He thinks "Cider" a rare beauty. Cider is small, sickle-hocked, with a Roman nose, tiny ears that point at each other and ropey scars that thicken his pasterns. I admit he does have a kind eye. His black mane and tail were thick and corded with knots. Henry has tediously untangled every hair. Then he took our good apple vinegar and washed the hair and skin. The tail and mane and forelock are now luxurious, soft, and full. Henry is rightfully proud of the results. Cider seems to think Henry is God. He follows him around like a pet dog. We have never owned a Dun. Father says the color is unknown in a blooded horse, and by that he means an English Thoroughbred or Arabian horse. Father says this color, with its odd black stripe down the spine, comes from the Moorish breeds. I suppose Cider once came from the Spanish held parts of this continent. If he could talk, what a tale he could tell.

Henry did also demonstrate to me his skill with

making and using a wisp. He has perfected braid-ing straw and Cider did tolerate well its use, which comes in a steady sort of slapping against the hide, followed by a swipe with the brush. Henry informs me Major Schmidt did teach him this. It does seem to bring up the oils in the coat. Cider has pretty dapples coming.

Out of the blue, Henry asked, "You think Master Roberts would consider Cider for keeping?"

I did not want to get the boy's hopes too high. I said, "Father says they will be fitted up in the spring to be sold."

Henry frowned, "They's all prisoners of war. Like Major Schmidt. But as we don't know where they come from, they can't be sent home after the war, or changed like regular prisoners. I sure is glad they don't know they be sold. If they knew that, I fears they'd give up on life. But I knows one thing certain, Cider, he wants to stay."

I said, "Is that a fact? Cider told you that?"

He turned and looked at me in that moment, and oddly enough, so did Cider. It was a long and probing look from both, which made me feel that it was I, not they, who was being silly. Of course, Cider wanted to stay. Was I blind?

Henry made sure I understood. He said, "Just as clear as did Major Schmidt. They come here as prisoners, but they wants to stay as family."

Tears instantly burned in my eyes. I said, "I will speak to father. Surely, we cannot keep them all, but I will see if he will allow Cider to remain."

I repeated Henry's words to father. We did laugh, though gently. But then he granted Henry's request, and his eyes did shine. I let him have the pleasure to announce his decision to Henry.

* * *

Dabs had done the entire reading himself, never asking Eloise to take a turn. He put down his papers.

"I think I've pushed my luck keeping you two awake, even with my special brew you two look comatose."

Eloise yawned and said, "Cider brought to mind my collection of horse Christmas ornaments. One is a dun."

Pinky sounded sleepy when she added, "Henry got to keep Cider. A gift of love from Mr. Roberts to both Henry and Cider. From the powerful to the powerless."

Eloise felt her throat tighten. She wasn't sure why.

Eloise and Pinky supported each other as they wobbled to their feet. Prince and Lady Jane were displaced and looking disgruntled about it. Pinky wrapped the blanket they had tucked over their laps around her shoulders, gave Eloise and Dabs the peace symbol and left the room, the blanket trailing behind her.

As Pinky made her way up the stairs she sang, "I gently rise and softly call, Good night and joy be to you all."

She had remembered "The Parting Glass" song.

Dabs said, "Doesn't Pinky have a good ear? Such a clear, sweet voice too."

Eloise nodded, "That song. And that reading. Louisa finally understands that her little brother, Henry, well, she loves him, and he loves her. They could have died together, but they survived. They have a bond, forever."

Dabs leaned forward to give Eloise a goodnight kiss, just as she leaned forward to pick Lady Jane up from the floor. Eloise's head hit Dabs on the chin.

Both straightened up, apologizing, feeling awkward and embarrassed. Dabs did not try for another kiss, just at the moment that Eloise thought perhaps he would and found that she wished he would. Instead, Dabs tried to pick up the tune where Pinky had left off.

He sang in low tones, "Of all the comrades that e'er I had, they're sorry for my going away."

Then he asked, "What comes next? Pull it up on your phone."

Eloise did. She sang back to him, "And all the sweethearts that e'er I had, they'd wish me one more day to stay."

Eloise held up the phone, and they sang together, "So fill to me the parting glass, and drink a health what e'er befalls, then gently rise and softly call, Good night and joy be to you all."

19

Pinky found Dabs and Eloise at breakfast, heads bent toward each other deep in conversation. Pinky helped herself to a cup of coffee.

She said, "Dabs, whatever you put in your witch's brew last night gave me the weirdest dreams."

Dabs said, "It was only coffee, Amaretto, rum, cream and sugar."

Eloise laughed, "A bang-up dose of stimulants and depressants all in one cup. Tasted yummy, though I doubt any of that affects dreaming."

Pinky shook her head, "Please explain why all these strangers in my head kept going on and on, about stuff that made no sense."

Dabs said, "Ah, you are now under the influence. Not of alcohol. It's Louisa and her writing. She gets in here," Dabs tapped his head, "And even though I stopped reading the journal out loud to you, she just kept talking."

Pinky looked over the rim of her mug at Dabs and blinked a few times dismissively.

Dabs switched topics. "May I fry up some eggs for you?"

"Thanks, but I think I'll just sit very still and drink coffee."

Eloise said, "Dabs and I were just discussing how to spend the day. There's Monticello. I'll bet you've never been."

Pinky held up a finger, then looked under the table. "Just a sec. What? Oh. I'm hearing some protest from my feet." Then she lifted her eyebrows while still peering under the table. "What did you say?" She looked shocked and said, "'Hell no, we won't go?'"

Pinky mouthed, "Sorry." And then looked over her shoulder. "Wait, what? Okay."

She shook her head, and announced, "My ass just joined the protest. Evidently, today it will be staging a sit-in. But, hey, you crazy kids do whatever."

Eloise and Dabs exchanged an amused glance. Then Eloise said, "Dabs, why don't we stay put and help you organize that stuff you found in the trundle bed?"

Pinky said, "I might lend a hand there, as long as I can catch a nap or two."

And so, it was decided. They would work in the spare room to organize the notebooks, sketch books and dolls.

About thirty minutes in on that project, Pinky took Lady Jane and went back to bed. They didn't see her again until that afternoon when she took Lady Jane out for a potty break, made a pot of tea and a plate of warmed up buttered biscuits and disappeared back into her room, kitten in tow.

Eloise knew that Pinky was tired, but also suspected Pinky was providing her an opportunity to be alone with Dabs. Time was short. Time was fleeting. Time alone with Dabs and with Prince well, it was a gift.

Eloise and Dabs took Prince out for a walk, and as they walked, the sky darkened to an odd glow, like twilight, but hours too soon. Prince got the zoomies which entertained them both, and then the rain began. By the time they got back into the kitchen, they were drenched, their faces wind burned, and their fingers and toes stiff and numb with the cold. Wet boots and jackets were left in the laundry room, which was nice and warm from the water heater. Dabs found an old towel and gave Prince a good rubdown which further excited him and sent him charging around the kitchen. Then they changed into dry clothes, and Dabs and Eloise began another organizing session.

Eloise and Dabs sat on the floor. The sketch books were fragile. Handling one had caused breakage of the paper edges and flaking of the binding. The legal pads they divvied up in piles according to little clues about age like the condition of the paper, and edges. But it would take context drawn from reading them to place each in approximate date order.

While Dabs read an entry out loud that described a family event, an event that Dabs remembered and was working to place in time, Eloise found herself running her finger down one long side of the trundle bed. She interrupted Dabs to ask, "What are all these holes for?'

"For stringing rope. The mattress went on top of tightened ropes. A sort of flat hammock. Someone came along later and added the wooden platform on this one. That's what made it so heavy."

Dabs read out loud from one of the legal pads. His Mom's hunt horse had heard the huntsman's horn, jumped out of her pasture, and joined the chase, finding the hounds before the huntsman did. His mother was a good storyteller, and they were laughing.

Eloise asked, "It was a mare? Was it chestnut?"

Dabs smiled, "As a matter of fact, it was."

Eloise looked back at the bedframe, trying to imagine the lines of rope woven from hole to hole, back and forth to create a secure decking for a mattress. And as she ran her finger along a sideboard, she hit a spot that had a deep scratch, and she found herself following the indentation with her finger. She tipped her head to examine the spot more closely.

"Dabs?" And found that she couldn't say more. She spit on her finger and rubbed at the spot. Dabs stopped reading. There was a stillness in the room, still but for the beating of her heart that filled her ears.

Eloise said, "Sammie. It says Sammie."

* * *

Pinky made her way downstairs in time for dinner still clutching the kitten.

"I smell something good."

Dabs said, "You must be starved. You barely ate a thing today. I was just about to pull the casserole out. Turkey Tetrazzini. Same bakery that does the pot pie."

Eloise asked, "Are the feet happier now?'

Pinky nodded, "Feet, ass, etc." then added, "Let me take Lady Jane out."

Eloise said, "Take Prince too. He just ate."

Pinky and company rejoined the party, and soon they were seated in front of a hot plate of pasta and a tossed salad. Dabs did a generous pour of white wine.

Eloise was explaining to Pinky, "And then I wet my finger and ran it over the marks, and wow! 'Sammie' carved into the side rail. Hard to describe how it felt, but my finger traced where he had carved his name. Sammie, our Sammie."

Dabs cautioned, "Hmmm? Our Sammie? Don't forget what Henry said. We southerners use the same names over and over."

Pinky said, "How cool! Like one of the cast members just sent you a bonus scene, or outtake. I mean, the story is almost over."

Eloise said, "Pinky, this isn't a movie or a novel, This is history."

Dabs said, "I guess the journals, the ones we have, well, we *are* almost finished."

Dabs smiled, then got up and offered second helpings. Eloise was quiet for a moment while Pinky polished off her plate.

Then Eloise said, "Dabs, do you know how it all ends? I mean, in the journals?"

Dabs added more to all three plates, then sat back down.

"I know what you are going to hear tonight. And

I've almost finished what you will hear tomorrow. But I won't do the last bit."

The room grew quiet while the three of them ate every bit on their plates.

When they sat back in their seats Pinky asked, "Dabs, can I at least load the dishwasher?"

"Nope." Then added, "Ladies, please retire to the parlor so I can serve you the petit-fours I brought from the bakery."

Pinky groaned, "You've got to be kidding. I love petit fours. I can't say no, not as long as I can have hot tea with mine, but I'm serious when I say, *un-doctored* hot tea."

"Would you like Earl Grey, English Breakfast, or Sleepy-time?"

Eloise and Pinky nearly shouted at the same time, "Sleepy-time!"

Eloise noted that Dabs had shifted into his Virginia Gentleman persona. The one that always made her feel he was so much older than she was, so old in fact, that he was from another century.

Once they were settled, nibbling petit-fours, and sipping tea like proper English ladies, Dabs began to read, his voice low and softly accented.

* * *

October 21, 1781

Henry and Beast and I now took a daily walk to the

cemetery. The routine, even without horses, gave us some semblance of normalcy. Without the exertion of a walk, much internal agitation developed within myself. I also have come to depend on Henry for company. So, I try never to miss our mid-morning ramble.

This day, Henry and I had breasted the hill and made a loop around the walls of the cemetery, then entered through the iron gate to visit the grave of mother. We paused to consider our angel that stands watching over her, pointing toward heaven.

Henry said, "That angel powerful good."

I agreed. "She's watching over mother, protecting her."

"I don't remember my mother. She down yonder." Henry pointed to the hillside where the slaves bury their own.

"Isaac and Sammie used to take me. We takes a stone to add to her stack, to shows we don't forget. I ain't been in a long time. I guess I got to add a stone now for Sammie."

I said, "I didn't know that, about the stones."

"They tell me she was real pretty."

Henry looked up at our angel and said, "I think my mother ought to have an angel guarding her. She don't even have her name writ down on her grave."

I answered weakly, "Perhaps at some future brighter day."

Henry looked me in the eye, then looked down at the ground. "What you remember of my mother?"

I confess I had to think on it a moment.

I said, "She sewed all the clothes. Tidiest stitchery you ever did see. She could embroider too. And she never wasted an inch of cloth. Kept all the scraps to make quilts and dolls. Even made dolls to look like the servants."

Henry nodded, pitifully unsatisfied. I had fallen short. But at that moment truthfully, it was the only detail of Maisie that came to mind. Henry did not ask to visit his mother's grave and I did not offer to go. I had never stepped foot into the slave burying ground. Father had told me that although he owned the land, some places did not belong to him.

Henry and I turned and headed back out the iron gate. And then Henry froze, Beast froze too, and the hackles did rise upon his shoulders and neck, a low growl rumbled in his throat.

The view through the peephole was its usual aspect. The back of the house, the barn, the fields, all framed by trees and hedges and vines, cut clear to make a view. And then I focused on what they saw. A wagon. One I did not know. A flurry of activity about it.

Henry exclaimed, "That be Beauty tied to the back!"

And he spun on his heels and yelled, "C'mon, Louisa!"

He cut across the path and headed down the shortcut trail. Beast soon overtook him as I struggled to catch up. My, how Henry did fly. I fell so far behind that once I reached the bottom of the trail, Henry had gotten well away. Beast ran back to me, as if to urge me on, but I ran out of air and gained a stitch in my side and had to break to a walking pace.

When I reached the wagon, Henry was untying Beauty. The back of the wagon had been lowered, and Major Schmidt was in the wagon, propping Buck up into a sitting position. Both men were gaunt and in filthy rags. No one seemed to notice me or Henry. Priscilla was standing with Isaac at the head of Buck's horse, who was hitched to the wagon. My senses were assaulted by a powerful stench I cannot describe.

Aunt Bess was speaking tenderly to Buck, and father was struggling to compose himself. Father called for Isaac, who was instantly at his elbow. I saw a need to take Isaac's place with the horse, as Priscilla could not manage the horse with Bertie on her hip.

I placed my hand on the bridle and saw for myself that the horse was trembling in its knees. It was our own poor sweet Friendly. He would not try to move another step. Of that I felt sure. How I longed to see him safely in a stall, bedded deeply in the straw to rest.

Buck did cry out then, "Priscilla!"

Priscilla obeyed. I could not hear what was said. Isaac and father used their arms to make a chair, and Buck did manage to grip them around their necks a horrid grimace upon his countenance. Slowly and with great care they removed Buck to the house.

Bess said to Priscilla, "Go fetch Master Buck a clean shirt from his wardrobe. Heat water for his bath. We have much work to do."

Which left Major Schmidt and me, since Henry had removed Beauty to the stable.

Major Schmidt said, "Please help me get Friendly into the barn."

I said, "Unbuckle the harness, then let me do the rest."

Major Schmidt's hands were trembling as he did so.

Henry came out then and stepped toward the Major. "Lean on me Major. Got to lie down now. You home. You done good. You lean on me. Louisa and me, we can take care of things now."

Major Schmidt lifted a hand and patted Henry on the head like one would a favorite dog. Henry put an arm around his waist and took Major Schmidt's hand that had rested on his head and placed it on his own shoulder, and the two made a crazy jagged trail toward the Major's cabin.

I unhitched Friendly, pulled off the harness and let it fall to the ground, then led him to a stall, forking him a manger full of hay, filling a bucket of water for him. Beauty was down in the deeply bedded stall next to him, her nose resting on the ground, her eyes closed. A lump was lodged in my throat. I knew I was needed inside. The horses were safe. They had made it home, because of Major Schmidt. I heard Henry's voice in my head speaking as if he stood at my side, "You done good Major, you done good."

Inside the back door stood Priscilla, Bertie on her hip, a bucket in her hand filled with the wretched rags that had been my brother's clothes. She said, "Mistress said I was to burn these."

I nodded. "They are full of vermin and stink."

Priscilla said, "The stink, it comin' from Master Buck."

I asked, "Buck see the babe?"

She scowled, "Uh-huh, He says, 'Bertie Roberts' and I says, no, he be Bertie Carter. He belong to Mistress Carter. Then he say to Mistress Carter, all playful-like, 'Maybe I buy him. Make you some money, Aunty.'"

I said, "Don't 'low him to bully you, Priscilla."

Priscilla narrowed her eyes. "Don't 'low him?"

Priscilla had Bertie on her hip, the bucket in her hand. Her eyes were narrowed and full of ire. For a moment I admit, I was afraid of her.

The look vanished, replaced by the Priscilla I knew. She said, "S'cuse me Mistress Louisa, I got to burn these and then bring more hot water and towels to Mistress Carter."

October 23, 1781

Once we got Buck settled into father's bed down-stairs, Priscilla brought in hot water and soap. Isaac undressed him and bathed him and carefully cleaned the wound. It is in his groin area. I have not seen it, but there is no doubt from the smell that it has gone putrid, and my brother's life is in peril. He asked for water, and Aunty made sure he took it by small sips. She promised him a strong broth once he had rested.

He slept for hours but in the dark of the evening he was in agony and calling out. I thought I should go to him. Do what I could. When Beast and I came into the room, father and Aunt Bess were at his side. Buck's face was bathed in sweat and Aunt Bess was wringing a rag out over a basin, trying to cool his brow. He seemed not to notice, as he writhed about and yelled. I found myself holding Beast by his scruff and shrinking against the wall. I should not have stayed, but I could not go.

Buck was raging nonsense. He yelled at father, "You preferred her litter of mongrels. You, Sir, are a disgrace. You killed mother. It is you who kill me too, sure as if you had pulled the trigger!"

Bess tried to soothe him. "Buck darling, these are deliriums. You must not believe these fevered dreams. Please."

Father tried to place his hand upon Buck's arm, but though seemingly weak, Buck threw off his touch. He said, "You gave him the instrument of my destruction. You gave it."

Aunt Bess rebuked him with, "Buck!"

Father said, "I gave what?"

Buck spat out, "Sammie fired upon me with my own gun. The very one he used to clean and oil with envy. Everything I had, he wanted. Everything was mine, not his, not one God-damned thing was his. He was property. He should have been put on the block as soon as I caught him. But now he resides in hell, dead."

At this an icy chill came upon me. It was as if my blood had drained from my head down into my bare feet. I turned my gaze to father and Bess. Their faces had gone slack and ashen. They both backed away from the bedside.

Buck was hoarse, his voice raspy, yet I still made out the words, my attention rapt.

Buck said, "Colonel ordered fixed bayonets. We were there to end the war. It would go down in history. The storming of redoubt number ten."

Buck drew a ragged breath and continued, "Over the top, and in, and damn it to hell, there stood Major Schmidt. It must have been the Devil himself who placed him there. I knew my duty was to run him through, and I meant to do so. Damn it to hell. I hesitated. I hesitated. Your black bastard Sammie shot me 'for I could do my duty. Shot me with my own gun. Why, it was the Devil certain who placed him there to spoil my moment of glory. And now I shall die, and the Devil shall try and collect his prize. Well, he ain't going to get it."

Bess tried to argue with Buck who looked wild-eyed. She said, "Nonsense. We have the Doctor coming. I think it will be painful, but I expect he shall clean the putrid flesh away and set you once again upon a path of healing. I've seen such wounds before."

Buck narrowed his eyes again at father, his face slick with sweat, "You would not whip him, you would not sell him, you would not even chasten him. And then you give him my gun?"

Father took the abuse without comment.

Buck turned his face away, but then turned back to look at father. He raised his voice spitting as he spoke, "The Devil may come for my soul, but I will bargain mine for yours instead. May you burn in hell. You have murdered me."

And then he howled like a wild animal.

Father looked up then and saw me. Aunt Bess too. Aunty ordered us out, "Both of you, leave. Leave now!"

Father said, "Bess, I cannot let you alone with him in such a state."

And she pointed her finger at father, "Listen to me brother, you will, and you must, and you will take Louisa with you."

And so, father and Beast and I repaired to father's study. We sat in shocked silence, slack jawed and miserable.

At length, father put his head on his desk and covered it with his arms and sobbed. Beast went and put his head upon father's thigh. Finally,

323

father's hand found my dog's head and stroked it slowly and quieted.

I said, "Perhaps Major Schmidt is correct. We do not deserve to win our freedom."

Father collected himself. "Buck is wrong. I loved him always. I loved your mother too. Buck is wrong. Been wrong. Like some demon got hold of his soul. I am not a perfect man. I have my own demons. But no matter how we quarreled, I never ceased to love my son."

Then shaking his head, and mumbling he added. "All my sons."

Then he looked up at me, looking alarmed I think at my own state, and said, "Can you not seek rest?"

I shook my head "No."

Father would not leave his office to rest but begged me to do so. Before going upstairs, I did go back to father's bed to check on Aunty. I opened the door slowly, coming in a step with candle held high. The room was dead quiet, I could hear the night sounds coming through the crack of the window. I could hear Beast panting with worry at my side.

Aunt Bess looked up at me, her face streaked with tears. She simply nodded and waved at me to leave. And I backed away. I went up the stairs but of course could not sleep. I did not remove my cloth-ing. I watched my window and watched the sky gradually lighten. I got up before the sun, the moon still visible in the dawning.

I crept downstairs and tip-toed back to father's room. Aunt Bess was still very much awake, still sitting in the same chair bedside. Buck's form was still. Father was yet in his office, waiting to be summoned.

Bess rose and stretched and came to me, leading me by the elbow into the hall. She whispered. "Poor lamb. Poor tortured soul."

I felt my hand go to my mouth.

Aunt Bess said, "I had not the courage to tell your father yet."

My knees went weak, and I sought support from the wall.

Aunt Bess said, "I held his hand and asked him to please forgive. But he could not. He would not. I will not share his last words. They will go to the grave with me."

I could do nothing for my brother, nor my father, nor my Aunt. I thought of my precious Beauty. I could at least check on her welfare. I stepped into the barnyard to find Henry waiting for me.

"Miss Louisa, Beauty, she gonna' be alright. She always been tougher than she look. Isaac done poulticed her feet in flannel bandages. She real skinny. She ain't gonna' wear a saddle for some time neither. She got saddle galls bad."

I had started toward the barn, Henry trailing my heels, but I turned to say, "She won't be wearing a saddle ever. She more than earned her time."

Henry nodded. And although Henry had tried

325

to prepare me for the sight of my poor girl, it still cut me to the quick. That, and the sight of Major Schmidt, standing in the stall with my horse, Isaac at his elbow. When they saw me, they both looked fearful. Although I had said nothing, I am sure they could tell by my face that I carried the burden of bad news. Yet they did not ask for news of Buck.

Major Schmidt stood before me a stranger. He had not shaved in some time, but beneath his beard, his face wore new deep lines on either side of his mouth. His beautiful long lashed eyes were deeply creased in the corners, the lines traced with grime, his eyes underscored by shadows. His clothes were rags. Though it had not been half a year since last I saw him, he had aged twenty.

Beauty turned to see me, and softly whinnied. I went to her, put my forehead to hers, and stroked her dear face. I had no more tears to shed. I tried to thank the Major but could not get words out.

He said, "We have time to speak of this later." And I nodded, grateful.

The Major nodded at Isaac and Henry, who receded into the barn. I'm sure Buck's horse looked as bad as Beauty, but I did not follow.

Major Schmidt led me away toward his cabin, away from the house. We did not speak until we were inside. All thoughts of propriety abandoned, he closed the door and we sat at his table.

Before he could speak, I answered the unspoken question, "Dead. He is dead. And Sammie too."

The Major nodded, then added, "I had hoped for a miracle. It was six rough days on the road. I wish I had been able to save Buck's life, truly. But Louisa, Sammie lives. I lied to Buck. I thought it best to lie. Sammie fled. Buck was too hard hit to note his escape. Buck and I barely made it safe behind the lines. By that I mean into the Continental's camp."

"You took Buck from the battle?"

"I did. Buck's need was urgent. I took him and I surrendered. What a sight we must have made. I had his arm around my neck and half dragged him to his lines. We had to cross open land. Me in my coat, Buck in his. Once in your lines, I turned my coat inside out. Sammie and I were two of seventy men set to guarding a redoubt when the Continentals tried to take it. Sammie and I, we were among thousands holed up in Yorktown. Buck, there with Washington, laying siege to Yorktown, was also among thousands. And yet fate placed us there in that redoubt to face each other. Is that not a wondrous thing? Sammie fired. That is true. He fired to save my life. I don't believe he meant to kill Buck."

"I feel sure Buck did mean to kill you."

Major Schmidt made the smallest gesture of his chin, and said, "He told me so."

"Buck thinks Sammie dead."

"I swore to it. May God forgive me. I said I saw him run through the gut. I thought if Buck thought Sammie dead, Sammie would be free at last. Oth-

327

erwise, Sammie might be a hunted man for the rest of his life."

"Father must be told. Aunty must be told."

Major Schmidt said, "I told Priscilla. She had a right to know. I saw her up to the house. I'm awfully tired now, Louisa."

The Major's admission did cut at my heart, but still I pressed on, "But I must know, how is it that you came to bring him home? Buck held no love in his heart for you."

"After I crossed the lines with Buck, I caused a scene. I put Buck down as gentle as I could and called for help. He had gone cold and limp and could not speak. Once we got him to the field surgeon, I asked to surrender myself to his superior officer. I met first with and aide to Captain Olney.

I explained that I had lived with and worked for your family as a prisoner of war. That I hoped to marry Buck's sister and become an American. That I had honored my obligation to my Prince but felt no such obligation to King George. I told him I had no more stomach to fight Americans. He found my story remarkable. Once Olney was informed, he evidently shared it with Lieutenant General Lafayette, who shared it with General Washington."

"Buck went along with this?"

"Buck knew none of this until I was permitted to see him, and I told him of my plan to take him home. He was not so far gone then, you see. The surgeon told him he would survive with good care. But

I told him if he stayed in camp, among the diseased, the filth and the dying, he would surely die of camp fever. I did believe that if he could get home, I might save him. I wanted to save him for your father and for your Aunt Bess and for you. I still think that if I had been able to get him home sooner, he might have lived. I am sorry I could not.

Major Schmidt continued, "I was called to an interview by a staff member of Washington's. I provided useful information regarding Cornwallis, and the state of things, everything I knew. I then had a night of rest, and during that night, much came to pass.

Horses being in short supply, I asked to retrieve Beauty, and was allowed under a white flag with escort to retrieve your horse. Sammie was there. He had guarded Beauty with his life. You should understand most of the horses had been slaughtered for meat. I am sorry to report that Fashion was taken by Tarleton, to his position at Gloucester Point. I do not know if she yet survives

I waited patiently for the Major to continue. "They did procure a rough wagon for me to bring Buck home. I had Buck's horse Friendly to put to harness, and I tied Beauty to the back. I was given a letter of transit, should I be stopped."

The Major paused yet again, holding his palm to signal me to wait. "That letter! That is a tale. I was called to Washington's tent to find the great man himself writing it in his own hand. I was astound-

ed that he would attend to such a detail. It seems redoubt nine and ten had been taken. Cornwallis had failed in a desperate attempt in the dead of night to escape across the York to Gloucester Point. Fate had intervened with a rain of biblical strength that destroyed all hope for the British.

Washington was in no mood for glory though. His only stepson, kept safe for his mother's sake through these long years of war, had joined him for the closing days of the siege. Jack Custis had caught camp fever. Washington feared for the young man's life and wished fervently to return him safe to his mother.

This made my mission more poignant to the great General. He said, he hoped Buck would live to see me wedded to his sister. But that if such an outcome was not the divine plan, that Buck's father should know of his future son-in-law's devotion."

I shook my head, "This is hardly to be believed."

Major Schmidt nodded, "I was sorry to deceive the great General regarding my devotion to Buck, but it allowed me to bring Buck home.

The Major looked thoughtful, "In one detail I was gratified, Buck trusted me to do as I pledged. His trust allowed me to bring Beauty home. It allowed me to come home to you. For I can see no picture of home without you in it. That is, if indeed you still agree, Louisa."

I had little real feeling at that moment. Should

*I be ashamed to write such a terrible thing. But
I did place my hand over the Major's, and he did
then place his other hand over mine. He said, "We
will find joy again someday. I will do what I can to
make it so if you will allow me."*

*The Major lifted my hand in his two hands, and
lightly kissed it. Then I helped the Major remove his
boots and found a quilt to pull over him on his dusty
bed. Before he closed his eyes, Cleopatra was heard
loudly mewing at the door. I let her in, and she
jumped up on the bed, purring and curling herself
against the Major's neck. The Major was already
asleep.*

* * *

Dabs had done the entire reading, his voice grown raspy
toward the end. And when he stopped, when he put
down the last sheet of paper, no one could speak.

Finally, Pinky said to Dabs, "How long have you
known?"

Dabs said, "Since Christmas day."

Pinky said, "What a depressing way to spend Christmas."

Eloise said softly, "Sammie killed Buck."

Pinky added, "Sure didn't see that coming."

Eloise added, "With Buck's old gun. Biblical."

Dabs said, "I guess we know how the legend of curses and 'haints' got started now. And even though I don't
believe in any of that stuff, I do believe in tragedies and

331

trauma. I even feel sorrow over Buck's untimely end. He was a young man."

Pinky sat up a little, rousing the kitten. "Major Schmidt is a Saint. He kept his promise to Louisa, and tried his best to save Buck, a man who was going to run him through with his bayonet. I think I have a crush on him. If something bad happens to him now, it will do me in."

Eloise looked at Dabs and frowned. "You know though, don't you? You know but you won't say. Geeze Dabs, you could have been a spy or something."

Dabs said, "I have more transcribed, but that seemed like a place to stop tonight."

Pinky said, "No wonder you bought all that music to cry by. I mean, maybe I'm not crying over Buck. He was an asshole. But good Lord, that was sad for his family. I am worried about Major Schmidt." Then Pinky turned to look at Eloise and brightened, exclaiming, "Your dream!"

Eloise tipped her head, "What about it?"

Pinky exclaimed, "Major Schmidt was the old guy! Oh, that makes me feel so much better. He lived to be an old guy. Okay, now please describe how he looked. Other than the eyelashes, Louisa never says."

Dabs began to chuckle.

Eloise said, "It was a dream, Pinky. I got the tune back only because I heard it on the CD, and who knows, that may not even have been it, you know, power of suggestion and all that. And you know how fuzzy dreams are. They kind of evaporate once you wake up. Besides, all of it likely came from my overactive imagination."

Pinky said, "Give it a go. You can make shit up and I won't be the wiser for it anyway."

Now Dabs had tipped his head forward into his palm to hide his smile. Eloise, who was used to Pinky, tried to oblige her.

"Um, okay. The guy in my dream was crying. So, I must have seen his face. I noticed his long fingers on the violin. He had grey hair, pulled back."

Pinky nodded sagely, "Long fingers. They go with long arms and long legs."

Eloise said, "Mostly I was struck by the music. And the sadness of the moment. That's what dreams mostly are made up of, emotions."

Pinky tipped her head and asked earnestly, "It wasn't Joe, was it?"

Eloise looked surprised at the question. She said, "It wasn't. Wow. It definitely wasn't."

Eloise felt some real relief and joy at that thought.

Pinky looked satisfied and simply nodded.

Dabs sat back up and stretched. "I admit I was relieved to read that Sammie survived. I expect we may never know what becomes of him. Sad, he has left behind Priscilla and the rest of his family. I hope he got his freedom."

The three of them stood and Pinky handed Eloise her kitten, excusing herself to head up to bed while Dabs and Eloise walked to the laundry room to retrieve coats and head out to the barn to check on the old horses and give the pets a chance to relieve themselves.

The coats had not only dried but were slightly warm.

Eloise picked up her kitten and walked with Dabs to the barn, while Prince bounded ahead of them into the dark, toward the one security light that was on over the barn doors. The ground now sported a thin but pristine layer of snow, their boots soundless as they walked, fine flakes continued to fall. The barn doors were stuck, and Dabs had to give them a hard pull to get them open.

Then he flicked on the lights and the old horses gave a gentle greeting.

Dabs pointed to an empty stall and said, "Indoor toilet for the kitten."

"Lady Jane, how posh! And just think, your namesake may have once peed right here in this very stall!"

All was well. Before Dabs pulled the big door shut on their way out, the light of the moon reflected off the new fallen snow, creating a magical scene.

Eloise said, "I'm sorry tomorrow is our last day. The journals are magical. Can you believe what we learned about George Washington?"

"A total surprise."

"I'm a little jealous that you know how it all ends."

Dabs shook his head earnestly. "But I don't. I don't know how it ends. I've left the ending for us to experience together."

20

The next morning, there was a decidedly different vibe in the kitchen. When Pinky came downstairs, Dabs and Eloise had done the barn, eaten breakfast and Dabs was loading the dishwasher.

Eloise was feeling unsettled. The trip would soon be over, the journal finished, and yet she felt no sense of closure. Ugh. She hated that word. Closure was a fantasy. Maybe death brought closure. But not to those still living.

As soon as Dabs spotted Pinky, he got chatty, while Eloise said nothing. He buzzed around the kitchen getting Pinky the usual, a mug of coffee with cream, then after cracking two eggs into a skillet, pulled a pan of hot biscuits and bacon out of the oven.

Dabs said, "Eloise wants to go hike back up to the cemetery. There's a beautiful blanket of snow on the ground. It should prove a pretty walk. It's warmer out today."

Pinky said, "Warmer? How's that possible?"

"Well, warmer is not the same thing as warm, but the wind has died down, the sun is out, and it just feels a lot more comfortable. Don't you think so, Eloise?"

Eloise said, "Um, I guess. I'm sorry to be out of sorts. I couldn't sleep last night."

Dabs said, "I kept Prince with me all night. Maybe you're still adjusting to sleeping alone."

Pinky took a sip of coffee then said, "Yeah, well, that *is* a shame."

Eloise glared at Pinky, then picked Lady Jane up off her lap, the kitten giving a squeak in protest. "Not alone. I had Lady Jane purring into my ear all night. I think it's just that the journals are coming to an end, and tomorrow we say goodbye."

Dabs said, "Eloise, we keep going over this. It's not goodbye."

Eloise shook her head, "It feels like goodbye to Louisa and Major Schmidt and Henry and…" Eloise stopped speaking.

Eloise had noticed Pinky and Dabs exchange a meaningful look. She was being a drag on the party. Time to shut up.

The hike, as it turned out, was not cold, but restorative. At least for Eloise. Prince shoveled his snout through the snow, twirled, rolled, charged ahead, and circled back at speed. It was impossible to remain glum in his presence.

They paused at the top of the path to admire the view through the woodsy picture frame, Mr. Roberts' "peep hole."

Eloise said, "A timeless tableau."

Dabs added, "Of course, in Louisa's time, there would have been slave cabins and outhouses in view."

Pinky narrowed her eyes and said, "See how far back the ground has been graded out? Grading without machines must have been a helluva' job."

Eloise said, "What? What are you pointing at?"

Pinky continued. "The man who cut this peep-hole, I bet he set those cabins back, so the picture wasn't spoiled. Likely put them against that tree line, along with the privies. Hid it all from this cultivated view."

Eloise asked, "But, that's too far from the house for an outhouse. Especially in cold and wet weather."

Pinky said, "You think Aunt Bess was traipsing out to an outhouse in bad weather? No way. They used commode chairs and pots, and the slaves emptied them."

Dabs said, "Pinky has a good point that the less attractive dependencies might have stood behind that front line of the barn, out of sight."

Pinky nodded. "It came to me just now by looking at the flat land. From here you can see the line where the graded area stops."

Eloise said, "I guess the kitchen house had to be closer."

Pinky nodded, "You don't want dinner getting cold. Bet it was attractive. Like matched the house."

Dabs was nodding. "Good observations."

Pinky said, "Dabs, I know what you need. You need a metal detector. You see these guys who do that sort of stuff, find all kinds of cool things."

Eloise said, "What kind of things?"

Pinky said, "I don't know. Buttons. Shot."

Eloise asked earnestly, "Where do you suppose Aunt Bess put her cellar?"

Pinky said, "A false outhouse was good cover for her shelter/cellar. An outhouse needs ventilation, but so does an underground cellar. A ventilator coming out of the ground is a dead giveaway of an underground something."

Eloise said, "Louisa made it sound like Tarleton spotted something."

Dabs said, "Yes."

Eloise asked Pinky, "Do you think we could locate the cellar?"

Pinky said, "It's buried, caved in years since. Someone would fill it up for safety reasons. Wouldn't want people or livestock falling in. But under all that fill dirt would still be the rock wall and a flat hard packed floor that would give it away as a cellar. And maybe if you're lucky, some metal canning lids or some such that could be picked up by a metal detector."

Dabs said, "There are endless discoveries to be made here, but I simply do not understand why my mother left everything hidden away to be lost to history."

Pinky said, "I do. Let the dead and their secrets stay buried, right? Especially when it's embarrassing or shameful stuff. Course, digging up old bones is interesting. Lots of folk just pray they're long gone by the time someone comes along and does it."

Dabs and Eloise walked through the crumbling gate into the cemetery.

Pinky said, "I think I'll wait out here. That branch

falling was creepy. But now that I've heard what happened to Buck, the curse and all, it's gone way past creepy."

Eloise said, "But now that I know what happened, what he said, I feel less creeped-out."

Pinky shook her head, "If anyone is a ghost, it's Buck. And he's one pissed off ghost, too."

Eloise nodded. "But he's not the only soul up here. Besides, one man's curse is another man's blessing. More than one man I imagine."

Dabs said, "Agree. I've been thinking of all that, too."

Eloise said, "Buck may be a lost soul, but in this cemetery somewhere lies our Louisa and our wise and gentle Major. Somewhere is our beloved Mr. Roberts and devoted Aunt Bess. Knowing they are here, well, it's a comfort. Come on, Pinky. They'll protect you."

Pinky looked nervous, but she stepped in, and Eloise put her arm through Pinky's. They headed to the empty plinth, then to what they presumed were the oldest grave sites.

Dabs used a gloved hand to brush the snow away to examine the stones.

Eloise said, "Buck's death meant that Louisa, not Buck, would inherit Ivy Creek. It would be her children, her daughter, after she was gone, who owned this place."

Dabs added, "And a succession of daughters that came after."

Pinky nodded, "Generations of women. Pretty unusual."

Dabs added, "Buck's death was likely a great relief to

the slaves of Ivy Creek. The lives they made here were made better by that death."

Eloise looked surprised, "Exactly my thought. Buck had no power to curse anyone but himself."

Eloise with her arm linked through Pinky's, visited each grave, even Buck's. They did so silently, making a trail of footprints through the pristine snow.

It wasn't until they were away from the hill and headed back to the house that Dabs announced brightly that he had ordered Chesapeake Bay "She-Crab" soup, a Virginia specialty. He needed to run to town to go pick it up along with a batch of spicy cheese straws. They would enjoy one last night of culinary excess.

* * *

Later, full of outstanding crab soup and cheese straws, they settled in for the final reading. Tomorrow, before they left, they would transcribe the final pages of the journal together with Dabs in his study. They would cross that finish line together. But tonight, was the penultimate moment.

Dabs had gone once again to his favorite bakery and purchased freshly baked gingerbread to serve with tea for their last reading. The spicy gingerbread was the perfect counter to the rich soup and offered comfort, sweetness, and warmth to the setting, scenting the air with sugar and steam and ginger spice.

Eloise and Pinky and Prince and Lady Jane made their nest on the sofa with lap robes and let Dabs' low tones tell the story. Eloise wanted to savor the last bits, cling to each word, knowing it was a slow parting she was engaged in, with people she loved, but who would never know her, let alone love her in return.

* * *

October 27, 1781

Aunt Bess arranged everything. Father seems incapable at present. Major Schmidt has been of tremendous aid to us, though he is but a shadow of his former self. We assembled in the yard, Isaac driving the wagon with Buck's mortal remains in a pinewood coffin. The priest led the procession and then father and Bess, and then I and the Major next. Henry walked at the side of the Major at his request. Behind us came the overseer and his wife, behind them the field hands and all the other laborers, some I know, and some whose names I do not know, but whose faces are familiar. They sang their mournful dirges as we walked along, one man singing a line, and the others echoing that line, slow clapping of hands set the beat. The walk to the family cemetery is long enough, the road narrow enough, the horses slow enough that our steps were short and measured. My mind struggled to comprehend how we came to be on this slow march up the hill to bury my brother.

Buck and Sammie were two sides of the same

*coin. Yet one had killed the other. One was banished
forever. They were boys of the same father. There
is no longer a reason to ignore this fact. They were
raised on the same ground to be companions. One as
master, one as servant. Buck was always the leader,
Sammie his loyal accomplice, as boys there was no
subservience, no discernable discord. The ease was
natural, the affection genuine. They were full of
bedevilment, riding at breakneck speeds and leaping
their horses over the fence rails. They stole our dinner
pies cooling on the porch and gorged themselves.
They helped themselves to father's brandy and drank
themselves sick. They fished in the creeks, they took
their dogs out at night to catch possum and coons.
From a distance, you could not have told one from
the other. They walked with much male swagger,
even then as boys.*

*Things went badly awry once Buck enrolled at
William and Mary. Sammie went as his body servant. What a place it must have been with Patrick
Henry calling his country to rebellion in righteous
tones. Buck had Sammie play the jockey, and sure
enough, wagers were made and won with father's
good horseflesh. But while Buck met with tutors,
Sammie could not. In Williamsburg, Sammie was
nothing but a slave. I expect Buck, to make such
things clear, played up the role of master in front of
his classmates. Buck was in Williamsburg to begin
the transition from boy to man. One side of that
coin was his destiny. The top side. Heads. Sammie*

was to be reminded his place was forever to be the bottom half of the coin. Tails.

Sammie must have heard enough talk of tyranny and freedom to feel the same stirrings as Buck, but from a different prospect. He saw Buck turn from racing and gambling and drinking to the enthusiasms of rebellion. And it was there that Sammie must have made his own commitment to rebellion. When Dunmore flew from the city, so did Sammie. But how could love for one another be so soon forsaken! Not just forsaken but turned to poison. Sammie must feel the pain of this moment, even from afar. It would be unnatural for one so connected to be unawares. Buck was dead. Today he would be buried.

I felt a sharp pain in my chest. I heard myself exclaim under my breath the most fervent yet ridiculous desire. I said, "Sammie should be here!" My knees felt weak in that exhalation, but I felt the Major's hand firmly under my elbow.

Major Schmidt hissed, "Sammie can never be here again. He is a fugitive. You must not utter his name. Not where any can hear it."

I nodded but my eyes were hot with tears. Banished. Forever. Murderer. Fratricide it was called. Buck had played an equal if not greater part in his own demise. Of this I had no doubt. The Major was right. But it was not right. None of this was right.

Isaac stopped the wagon at the gate, put the brake on and hands appeared to take Buck to his

*final place. Buck would be buried against the stone
wall, a plot as far from his father and mother's resting place as could be found. Father had so decreed.*

*The priest began his readings. I do not recall
what was read, just that I became aware that none
of the servants had come inside the stone walls.
They remained on the roadbed next to the wagon.
Heads were bowed, respect was shown, but no one
had come to the gravesite. Even Henry had stayed
outside the gate to stand next to Isaac.*

*I only noticed then that Priscilla was not in
attendance.*

November 1, 1781

*Major Schmidt has been fevered, and Aunt Bess
and Priscilla have been given new purpose to
restore him to health. They moved him upstairs into
Buck's room and check upon him constantly. Yet, I
am ordered not to disturb him, though I steal in
for visits when I am unobserved. He coughs and
shakes. It is as if his body, having fought great
hardships and survived, has finally the luxury of
surrender. His frame, always slender is nothing but
bone and sinew now. He looks much as did Tarleton's horses when they were abandoned here after
a seventy-mile pressing ride at speed. With five plus
months of care and rest, those begin to thrive. I trust
Major Schmidt will do the same.*

The Major mostly sleeps, but wakes for Aunty's strong broth, Isaac's baths and shaves, and Henry's serenades on his violin. The Major's own precious instrument was lost at Yorktown. He prefers to imagine it sold rather than burned as firewood, but he cannot say what happened. He refuses to take up Henry's instrument. I know money is scarce as hen's teeth, but father has promised to find the Major a fine replacement. I feel it unnatural for the Major to be without his violin. Father has written to Jefferson for aid in the matter. Jefferson's aid will also be needed to gain official permission for the Major to remain here. He is a prisoner-of-war yet again, as we have no treaty signed and he did fight at Yorktown, though his surrender came before that of General Cornwallis, who did surrender the day after the Major and Buck left.

I miss riding. Henry too. We do not even make our walk now. In Spring we shall sell the horses left by Tarleton's men. Of course, excepting Cider. In summer, the new group of three-year-old horses will be brought up from pasture to be trained to ride or drive.

Until then we have one cart horse to pull the wagon, or we are left to walk, as the overseer has naught but plow horses and his mule. Beauty I will not ride again. Her feet will grow and harden, the galls are dry and crusted over, but whether she will grow hair back on the spots is doubtful.

I have sweet grass hay before her always. But her eyes have changed. She has grown old.

Aunt Bess has tried to teach me to knit, but my heart is not in it. I take Bertie instead and leave the knitting and spinning to Priscilla and Aunty. Aunt Bess and Priscilla bake tarts with dried fruit from our cellars, apples, and cherries. They make hearty stews with salted meats and root vegetables with buttered biscuits. We are blessed that none of our larders were destroyed or thieved, none of our buildings fired. Jefferson's mountaintop was also spared, though Elk Hill was destroyed.

Aunt Bess does fawn over Bertie. She and I were left alone in the parlor, father had retired to his office, and Priscilla was busy cleaning up after our supper. Aunty was rocking the babe, when she said quietly, "Bertie is the spitting image of Buck."

Reflexively I said, "Do you not mean Sammie?"

Aunt Bess looked down at the babe, and then back at me. She calmly said, "Are we not tired of the ruse, all of us?"

Her words did carry meaning beyond their sparse number. All those terrible things that Buck said in rage against father? All that he had said about Sammie? All that was said that night that Aunty called delusional? It came to me in that moment, that none of it was delusion. That Buck in his enraged and fevered state had spoken true. It washed over me again in part measure of the terror of that night.

I asked earnestly, "What Buck said that terrible night, Aunty, those things he said, what of it was true?"

Aunt Bess said nothing but continued to rock the babe and gaze upon its face.

I asked, "Buck was his father's son, then?"

That caused Aunt Bess to draw a sharp breath and lift her chin in a defiant gesture. Still, she kept her voice low. "It was not right for Elizabeth to poison Buck's mind against his father. But the Robertson's are a hard and unforgiving tribe."

I was shocked silent for a moment. I had never heard one bad word spoken against my mother in all my life. I had nothing but good memories of my mother. Mother did always speak of her family well. The Robertson's were Tidewater Virginians' and early settlers with land grants from long ago. Her death was a great blow to us as she was the center of our home and beloved. Buck had been gutted by her death. It was no secret that he was her favorite. But to hear Aunty speak of her so filled me with a deep rush of anger that welled up inside me in an instant."

"I'm sorry to say so Louisa, but it's well-known Robertsons' are prone to violence, the women no less than the men."

I shook my head and whispered, "You blame my mother?"

Aunt Bess sighed deeply, "It is inappropriate for me to question what ruptures the sacred vows between a man and a woman. But it was wrong for your mother to draw her son into that chasm. I grieve so for the loss of both, but my poor Buck! He was never the same after Elizabeth's death. I do believe he saw himself as her champion. You and I are more resilient than the menfolk. Yes, it is true. And your father, he is thrice wounded, no more than thrice, for he also loves his dusky boys and Sammie might as well be dead."

And there it was. A confession of sorts from one who could not say it full. Thrice wounded? I had to wonder what that meant. Then it came to me. Aunt Bess was including Maisie. She must have been.

"Buck spoke true."

Aunt Bess shook her head vehemently. Saying softly, "No. No. No."

But then said, "But, yes as well as no. Louisa you are not blind, surely? Where in the world do you think come these shaded complexions, everywhere you go, from village to houses all-about? Some are sired by overseers, by visitors, sure, but also masters young and old. It is near considered by the men hereabouts their right. Some women do not mind sharing the marital duty with another, but instead see it as respite from the burden, and a chance to recover from childbearing. But not your mother. Maisie knew to keep clear of her. Your father refused to sell Maisie or the boys. That would be the crux of it."

I answered, "I am a fool."

Aunt Bess shook her head again. "You are just now leaving the age of innocence. I was once like you. But men are not like us. Think of that old stallion your father takes such pride in. He may not have a tooth in his head, but he will breed whatever mare he can regardless of color or size or age. Men are made in much the same mold. It is their nature, and women have as little choice in the matter as those mares in the field."

I disagreed. "Men are not horses. Men can know what an oath taken before God requires. And women, as well as the mares in the field, do take part in the proceedings."

Aunt Bess narrowed her eyes at me, "Men who can assign themselves privileges, will do so, and believe they deserve them too. Women have little choice, and a slave woman has none. Men will deceive themselves by calling it our duty. And so, you see my dear, women find power only in the realms they are afforded. For me it was in flight. And I was lucky to have a place to which I could flee."

Looking at my Aunt Bess, I could see she would not say more. This had been her life among the Carters. Why she had to flee, the real story, the full story, would never be shared with me.

Aunt Bess continued, "Women must be canny. But there are many things from which cleverness cannot shield us. And in those instances, acceptance is a blessing. See here this perfect child."

Aunt Bess lifted the child who squeezed tight his

eyes and puffed out his reddening cheeks. We both instantly recognized the humor in the rosy puffed out cheeks of this perfect child. He was soiling his clout.

The tension was broken by our laughter.

November 6, 1781

Major Schmidt's fever has not abated. I could tell by the look on Aunt Bess's face that she was afraid. And to see her afraid, filled me with terror. Aunt Bess sent Isaac to town for the Doctor. The act filled me with both fear and rage.

Our Doctor was a quack. He seemed to know nothing curative, but always tortured the ill and dying. I would never forgive his treatment of mother. And he always bled the patient. It was his treatment of choice for balancing the "humors." Why blood was always the humor in excess, made no sense to my mind. Although, on occasion, he added to his bloody practice the torture of purging until all was expelled. This too, "balanced" the humors. I should never do such a thing to a dog, let alone a person.

I had been sitting with the Major and trying to keep him cooled down with a rag dipped in cold water. This attention Aunt Bess did allow. He did cool, but then heated back up. His eyes were bloodshot, and he did say they burned. When the Doctor arrived, as predicted he recommended a heavy

bleeding. How I hated the man. I did try to stay
and hold my dear Major's hand whilst the Doctor
took the fleam and cut into the vein of the Major's
other arm. But the sight of the bowl filling with his
blood made me flee the room. Aunt Bess followed
me out and made me sit upon the stairs and put my
head down upon my lap and draw deep breaths.

Henry brought out the bowl and carried it out.
Poor boy looked ill himself. Bess sat there with me
for an hour or so, and the Doctor emerged dramati-
cally pronouncing, "The danger has passed."

Aunt Bess praised the Lord, but I narrowed my
eyes at the man. He said, "Miss Louisa, I have saved
your intended."

I echoed his words, "Saved him?"

"He will need a solid month or two of rest and
Mistress Carter's good cooking. Then he'll be right as
rain. You'll see."

Aunt Bess gave my leg a jab and said, "We are
eternally grateful. How I wish you had been able to
do so for our dear Buck."

"As do I, dear lady."

Father was waiting for the Doctor at the bottom
of the stairs, and I knew well that the Doctor would
take his fee as well as a libation.

I fed Major Schmidt some broth and he was
desperate to sleep. Aunt Bess seemed convinced the
Doctor was correct and that the danger had passed,
as indeed the fever had broken. Aunty brought extra
quilts up and we tucked him in tightly to trap his

351

body heat as now that he was no longer feverish, he complained of the cold. Priscilla put another log on the fire, and I could feel that even the floors were warmed by the blaze.

Since the danger had passed, Aunt Bess insisted we all retire for the night and rest ourselves.

I was awakened by Beast whining. Buck's room is near to mine, and I assumed the Major had called for aid.

I lit my candle by my fire and hastened to his room in my shift. He was in evident distress. I did my best to aid him in the use of his chamber pot, averting my eyes as he managed the last bit by himself. The candle on his bed stand did throw his face into dreadful shadows that sent a chill down my spine. I asked him to lie flat and I would cover him better. I took his hand to place it under the quilt and it was cold as ice. His eyes met mine and I gasped out loud as he gripped my hand in a pleading sort of desperation.

The look in his beautiful large dark shining eyes, still heavy with lash, held a look of defeat.

He said, "I am so very cold." I had a sinking feeling then, that all was lost.

Without thought I released his hand, nearly throwing it away from myself. I pulled my shift off over my head, peeled back the quilts, and slid my body against his.

The Major did raise his eyebrows in shock but said nothing. Instead, an icy hand lifted and curled against my back as I pressed myself into his body and pulled the quilts over us.

I whispered into his ear. "When I thought I should die, my blood went cold, my heart tried to escape my chest, but Beast got up into the bed with me. He did save me with his heat. He warmed my blood; he slowed my heart. We must do the same. You must take my heat."

With that statement, Beast jumped up on the bed. I said, "See, he comes to your aid. We both shall give you our heat. We shall make you warm."

Beast lay on the other side of the Major, stretched his full length, his head turned and rested on the Major's shoulder, his eyes calmly staring at us both.

Major Schmidt closed his eyes. His cold, cold hand, I took from my back, and placed between my thighs. I had no thought other than to find the warmest spot on my body to warm his icy hand.

I said to the Major, "Do not move. Conserve."

He whispered, "I move only in my mind. It is a sweet dream. If I die, I die a happy man."

But then his eyes closed, and he slept. And after a while, I slept. Even the dog slept.

I don't know when the Major awoke. But Beast had removed himself to the rag rug in front of the fire, and the Major had shifted my position onto my back. His hand was still placed between my thighs but felt warm and was moving. His lips were warm and dry upon my neck and seemed to move with his hand and soon his whole body was moving.

I am a woman who has observed the breeding of horses, I had no doubt about the predicament I now found myself.

Except I did not care to extricate myself. That is the truth. The Major's hand went where no hand, including my own, had ever been, and I allowed it. I could feel his heart beating strongly against his shirt. My heart answered his. My body answered his. It was nature at work. Just as Aunt Bess had lectured.

I said, "The Doctor will boast that it was he who saved you."

Major Schmidt answered, "But you and I will know the truth."

"Should I flee the room. Or shall I stay?"

"Do you want to stay?"

I said, "Oh yes. But no. Now that I have saved you, I do not want to be the cause of your demise."

Major said, "What if I promise not to die?"

"The Doctor left instructions that you should rest."

"I shall be a good patient and stay in bed."

The Major had left off kissing my neck and had started on my breasts. My heart was racing. I said, "You realize that once done, this cannot be undone. I will not let you leave me for your homeland. I will not let you take another. You are trapped here with me for the duration."

"Is that a promise?"

I said, "Only if you promise the same."

He whispered most solemnly, "Then I promise."

"And you are sure it will not overtax you?"

He nuzzled into my ear saying, "I shall go slowly so as not to be overtaxed."

And he did.

Afterwards, for a frightening moment, I thought I had killed him sure. I said, "Please tell me you are well."

This did make him softly laugh into my hair, his breath nice and warm. He whispered, "Fear not."

And then he fell instantly back to sleep.

I could see through the window that the sky had lightened in an alarming way. The Major had quite trapped me under legs and arms that though gaunt were heavy with sleep. But at least they were now warm. And I too was warmed from toes to fingertips and everywhere in between though aching slightly, as I assume was to be expected. I covered him thoroughly with the quilts and tucked them lovingly around him, watching him briefly to confirm to myself he was indeed still breathing, and marveled at the idea that the Major, the beautiful brown-eyed, long-lashed Major, was mine.

I picked my shift up off the floor, slipped it over my head and gathered my gutted candle. Then Beast and I made our way out to the hall, at the ill-timed moment that Priscilla was coming up the stairs and nearly on the landing.

We exchanged a quick glance but exchanged not a word.

21

The three geriatric horses were ambling in their odd Conga line across the barnyard toward their snow-covered pasture in the early morning light. Behind them walked Eloise and Dabs, blocks of hay under each arm. And orbiting the whole parade was Prince, very happy dog.

When Eloise and Dabs came in, pulling off snowy boots, looking rosy-cheeked and companionable, they found Pinky working on breakfast and Lady Jane scampering around the kitchen, freed from her Sherpa bag.

For once, the three of them ate breakfast at the same time. Lady Jane was sitting in Eloise's lap being pushy about sharing egg from her plate, and Prince was chewing on a gnaw-bone under the table.

Pinky said, "I realize we've got to translate the last of the journals before we can leave, but I don't want to get going too late. Who knows what kind of weather we'll hit."

Eloise said, "Transcribe. It's 'transcribe."

Pinky frowned, confused, "Yeah. That's what I said."

Pinky turned to Dabs, "Dabs, I put all of Prince's

medical records on your desk in your office. All the paperwork from Good Stewards too. You need to transfer the contact information with the registry for his microchip. Other than that, he's up-to-date."

"Thanks, Pinky. I don't know how to thank you enough. Now it won't feel quite so lonely around here."

Pinky nodded. "Prince is a lucky dog."

Dabs said, "You got up early this morning. I hope you slept well."

"I did, but not before having some more crazy dreams. And it's not like I'm dreaming about Louisa or Major Schmidt or Henry. I'm trying to sleep while people come in and out of the room, and they're trying to be polite and all, but they're whispering to each other. Does kind of wake me up and all. At one point, some girl was fooling around in the fireplace, and I know those don't work anymore."

Eloise said, "That's kind of creepy."

"It didn't creep me out. Like I said, they were whispering, so as not to bother me."

Dabs said, "Housekeeping ghosts?"

"Exactly! Polite ones too. Nothing like that Buck guy up the hill."

Dabs wiped a crumb from his mouth and rose to begin clearing plates. He said, "Well, I won't know what to do with myself after we finish reading those last transcriptions. But let's not put this off any longer. I'll just fill the sink with hot water and let the dishes soak."

Once the table was cleared, they headed to Mr. Roberts' office; well, it was Dabs' office now. Lady Jane ran past them down the hall and went sliding along the wood floor before running into the study and hiding behind the door. Prince galumphed after her. Pinky closed the door after they were all in, wagging her finger at Prince, "No one leaves the room until we're done. You got that?"

Dabs pointed at chairs, "Eloise, I think it best that I sit here and read the journals out loud while you type them up, that is unless you think Pinky the faster typist."

Pinky threw her hands up. "Don't look at me."

Eloise sat down at the desktop computer while Dabs leaned over her shoulder, tapped at the keyboard, and opened a blank document, typing in a name and hitting 'save.'

"I'm used to Louisa's handwriting and odd spelling by now. If I need to slow down, you just say so. Don't worry too much about typos and such. It's easy enough for me to clean up the document later."

Pinky said, "Ow!"

The two turned in time to see Lady Jane climb up Pinky's jeans.

"Go on you two, just ignore the fact that Eloise's kitten is turning into a hellion."

Eloise smiled, "As all healthy kittens should."

Dabs snapped on the light on his special embroidery lamp then pulled the magnifying glass in front of the journal. He carefully used his little tool to open the journal and find his place. He then sat down in a chair that reminded Eloise of the chairs in Doc's office. They had little wheels on them. Dabs wheeled his chair close to the manuscript, and even with the magnifying glass, he was leaning in closely. Eloise held her fingers over the keyboard and felt like a musician waiting for the conductor's baton to move. With a clearing of his throat, Dabs began to read.

* * *

November 9, 1781

It was mid- afternoon, and I was looking forward to warming up by the fire and changing into my warm slippers before dinner. I also meant to bring Major Schmidt his dinner and keep his company while he ate. We had a delicate topic to discuss.

Once I made the landing, I could hear commotion in the Major's room. I hastened my steps and walked into his room without announcing myself. In my defense, the door was ajar. Aunt Bess was directing operations like a field general.

There stood Aunt Bess, her troops included Isaac and Priscilla, Bertie on her hip. Major Schmidt was propped up in bed and part of the conference. And upon the floor by Major Schmidt's bed in a state of filth and disuse was a trundle bed.

Aunt Bess was exclaiming, "That mattress looks as if the cat had kittens on it. Surely it has creepy-crawlies. Priscilla, you must give it a boil and a good scrub with lye soap. Isaac, once it is dry, I give you the task to re-stuff it. Henry can bring his things up tonight and make-do with what he has until we make him a better mattress and there, look at how the ropes sag. Isaac, please tighten up those ropes, or Henry will find his backside falling through to the floor."

Major Schmidt caught my eye and was suppressing a sly smile.

I asked Aunt Bess, "What's all this now?"

Aunt Bess said, "There you are! Here, take this rag and wipe down the bed frame, and watch for spiders. Isaac killed one. There may be a nest, and they are disturbed and fleeing."

Henry appeared behind me carrying Lady Jane.

Aunt Bess said, "Henry, you don't mean to bring that cat!"

Henry looked stricken.

Major Schmidt interceded, "My apologies Mistress Carter, but I told the boy he could bring his pet. I rather miss Cleopatra, but Lady Jane will do. Besides, she will keep the spiders at bay."

Aunt Bess drew a deep breath and exhaled, "Well, you must take her out when you rise each day Henry, and for goodness' sake, please shut the door at night. I don't mind a cat, but I would rather not share my bed with one. They always carry vermin."

Someone placed a wet rag in my hand. So, I did as I was told. I squatted down and began to wipe the woodwork on the trundle bed. On one end I paused as I came across child-like carving in the wood. "SAMMIE."

No servant, that I knew of, had been taught to write. But there it was.

I said, "Sammie slept in this bed?"

Isaac was the only one to answer. "Yes, Miss Louisa. Way back when they was small boys. Don't you 'member?"

Now that Isaac brought it up, I realized I did, though the memory was vague. But now the scrawled carving of his name took on new meaning. Someone had taught Sammie his letters. I did not bring attention to the carving, and would not, not while Aunt Bess was standing there.

Isaac volunteered more, "Master Roberts, he say Buck used to have the night terrors when he was a tyke. Mistress Roberts, she move little Sammie in here and them terrors come to a stop. After Sammie come up, she and Master Roberts got good rest."

Major Schmidt finally joined the conversation, "I have nightmares from time to time myself. I don't think any less of a boy or man for it."

Henry piped up, "Maybe once I'm here you won't have 'em no more."

Aunt Bess said, "Well now Henry, that's the least of your duties while you are up here. You're to wait upon the Major. Isaac, please teach Henry how to do all that a manservant is required to do. I'll let you decide when to trust the boy with a razor! But he can certainly do everything else the Major will need of him. Can't you Henry?"

Henry looked pleased with himself, still holding

361

his cat against his chest, who was purring loudly. "Oh yes Mistress. I just got to go get my violin and my quilts and my corn husk pillow. Can I bring my pillow? It do make a rustle when I roll over. That won't bother you Major, will it?"

"No, you bring that pillow Henry."

Isaac knelt next to the bed to work the ropes tighter but was shaking his head. "Mistress, this bed needs to be restrung. If I go to tightening, they gonna' give out."

"Oh dear. Henry, it may hold you, skinny as you are. At least 'til Isaac can restring it for you."

Bertie began to squall, and Priscilla said, "Bertie's clout is soaked through."

Aunt Bess ignored her, "Shall we have dinner then?"

And then she said, "Louisa, you may bring the Major his meal on a tray."

Henry objected, "Ain't that my job?"

Aunt Bess couldn't suppress a small smile. "Henry, you may carry the tray."

And so, Henry carried up both my dinner and the Major's. And then thankfully, was called away by Aunt Bess to eat his dinner in the kitchen with Priscilla and Isaac and little Bertie. He did so reluctantly, and not until he had helped prop the Major upright with pillows and tucked a large napkin under his chin.

The Major suppressed a grin directed at me over Henry's shoulder, then earnestly thanked Henry.

Once Henry was gone, I said, "You are looking quite restored Major."

"Dearest Louisa, I am brought back from the brink. I have much to live for, it seems."

I deflected, "The stew is delicious. Although Aunt Bess goes heavy with the onions. I think I shall leave mine for Beast."

The Major said, "Aunt Bess is shrewd, is she not?" And when he said it, he raised his eyebrows, making his meaning clear.

I said, "Henry has been placed on sentry duty?"

He nodded, "Indeed."

I added, "Aunty will not want a wedding too close to Buck's funeral."

The Major did surprise me then. He whispered hoarsely, "How I will burn for you until then."

The stew in my stomach did churn as if the room had tilted like a rocky boat. I had to wait a moment to settle.

"Then I expect you will stay perfectly warm through the winter."

We both laughed, partly from nerves, and ate our stew in companionable silence and then I put both bowls on the floor and we watched as Beast licked them clean, onions and all.

November 11, 1781

I have taken the job of reading to Major Schmidt

*from the Gazette, although the paper has become
inconsistent in production and distribution, this
week our issue is current. Henry too, sits and listens
whilst doing small chores like combing the vermin
from the dog and cat. The dog and cat have become
fast friends, against all nature. Beast is a gentle
soul, though his size tends to signify otherwise, and
Lady Jane is an opportunist, who tucks herself into
Beast for warmth, tolerating his rude nudges and
tongue baths. It has turned cold and wet and so
we feed the fires and stay indoors. The animals are
mostly confined in the barns which makes extra
work for the servants.*

*I have been drawing again and it does help pass
the time. The Major grows restless. This is a good
sign.*

*I read aloud news of the passing of General
Washington's stepson, Jackie Custis, this past Monday, Nov 5th at Eltham Plantation, the home of
Lady Washington's sister. This did cause my dear
Major to cry out as if he had received a physical
blow. Washington had removed the young man
to the Williamsburg plantation and sent for Mrs.
Washington. It brought too sharp to mind our recent
trials. To Major Schmidt, it recalled the great man's
kindness. Major Schmidt had not shed a tear for
Buck, but one did make a track down his cheek for
this young man, a man he had never met.*

*He said, "I had hoped for the General and Lady
Washington a better outcome."*

I noted, that we are still at war, though York-town was a mighty blow, but Major Schmidt did reassure me that the blow was a death blow. Death would yet be a long and painful process. I trust his assessment.

Vile rumors travel regarding our Jefferson's near capture that fateful day in June. Jefferson provided for the safe escape of his family and guests, then made away himself at the dearest last moment. This is bandied about as cowardice! This cannot stand! Jefferson's term of duty as our Governor had expired and released our poor neighbor at last from his service to his state, to tend to his terrorized wife and girls. My dear neighbors had been forced to flee more than once from the enemy and in doing so lost a babe. Real cowards are those who make such claims. Such ingratitude can barely be borne.

I do believe Patrick Henry is behind this campaign of lies. He despises Jefferson. It is no secret. Aunt Bess is more enraged than anyone. I fear for anyone who dares slander our neighbor in her presence. These times are too perilous, the enemy yet too strong, to be cannibalizing our own.

Major Schmidt insisted, once Isaac had given Henry a tutorial, for Henry to shave him. I was not allowed to witness the first shave as the Major felt I would make Henry too nervous. I am happy to report that no blood was drawn. Henry is quite proud of himself. He declared that after the shave, he had meant to play his violin for the Major but that his hands were shaking too violently. He claimed they had been steady until he finished, and then they would not stop. I suppressed my laughter during this confession. Once Henry left the room however, the Major invited me to feel the smoothness of his face, and we did steal kisses until the door opened and interrupted us. Of course, it was Aunt Bess, and I think we must have looked terribly guilty as it took us a moment to compose ourselves.

December 1, 1781

Father and Isaac and I walked down to the breeding barns to discuss the young stock. Major Schmidt would have liked to go, but Aunt Bess put her foot down and Father allowed how she was correct. Though the Major protests that he is recovered, he does still cough and is painfully thin. No, Aunty will not let him lift a finger until he has no cough, and she is able to take the hard edges off his form with her good cooking. He finds that he is to be companion to Bertie. He is adept at the job, as completely charmed by the babe as the rest of us and does not even shrink from attending to soiled clouts.

Father and I were to evaluate the stock and make plans for the spring breeding. Father had promised me Beauty's daughter, "Contessa." She had given us quality stock, being the mother of Fashion, but as I would not ride Beauty again, I did require a horse. Father was loath to give her up, I could tell. I foresaw he would try and convince me to take another. But a promise is a promise.

I had filled my pockets with dried apples. Aunt Bess would not have approved them going to the livestock, but father never minded. Once the lead mare saw me, she came, the others followed, and soon we were surrounded. It was a cold day, dark and breezy with a light mist. But we had dressed warmly. My boots sank in the saturated grass. Father called each mare by name, then to me repeated her sire and dam, her grandsire and granddam, her babes and their qualities and weaknesses. He mused about what he would desire to improve in this new breeding. Isaac, quiet as always, took it all in with nearly imperceptible nods of agreement.

Father sighed, "Should you take Contessa, it will be a great loss to our program."

I countered, "We should find Fashion. She is the best we have bred. She may no longer be rideable, but if she is alive, we need her returned."

There was a long silence. I noted that Isaac was staring at the ground. My heart sank. "You do know something you are not saying."

Father said, "I sent inquiry. And I have had my answer."

I stood surrounded by our herd of broodmares, the rightful place to share such news. There stood our Fashion's mother, her Aunts, and their companions.

We humans were not the only ones to suffer from this terrible conflict.

I asked, "The truth please."

Father nodded; Isaac lifted his gaze to mine.

Father said, "Tarleton took Fashion to Glouces-ter Point where he commanded a smaller force. And there our forces boxed him in, preventing an escape up the coast, cutting off his supply line from any direction. Rather than watch the horses starve, he ordered them slaughtered."

I understood in that moment why bad news felt like a physical blow. It was hard to draw breath be-fore speaking. I said, "They could have let them loose to forage on their own, to have a chance at life. Such wanton wickedness. I shall never forgive. Never."

With trembling fingers, I began to pull dried apple from my pockets, handing them out to the beautiful girls coming to Contessa, I took a moment to scratch her withers and tell her how terribly sorry I was. She ate her treat and then nudged my pocket gently to ask for more. But I had given away all. We walked back through the field, the three of us, and the mares seemed to understand that our task was complete. They did not follow.

We walked down the hill to see the young stock, fillies on one side of the road, the geldings on the other. They were none of them broke yet to ride or drive, they would be our work to prepare and to sell in the future.

Father and Isaac and I leaned upon the rails

and considered them. Father said, "Our first job will be to sell that lot in the barn."

I did look shocked.

He reassured me. "All but Cider, that is."

I nodded, relieved, and he continued, "Then we begin preparing these come spring. But we must plant before we can harvest. Once the calendar turns, we must plan our breeding season. Louisa, I can only offer you Contessa if you allow me to breed Beauty."

Ah, there it was. Contessa was no gift; she was a trade. "Has Beauty not done enough?"

He put his arm upon my shoulder and drew me near, "Daughter, men are destined to do battle, and women to be mothers. It is no different in the animal world. Beauty must do her duty."

I lifted my chin. "And yet, not all men are soldiers, and not all women mothers." I brazenly met his eye.

He answered plainly, "We find ourselves at a time we must restore and replenish. The war might not be over in fact, but it is not too soon to begin the process of rebuilding. I've been negotiating on a young stallion of Mr. Taylor's. By his English stallion, but out of a sturdier sort of mare. He did two test breedings, and he swears they are heavier of bone than the sire, yet still comely and not coarse. I offer two mares in trade. "Bonnie" and "Gaily.""

I said, "Those are good mares."

"It would not do to cheat my good neighbor by

shifting off lower quality stock. Besides, we have too many by our own stallion, and he too many by his. We both require fresh bloodlines."

Then he added, "I will need Beauty."

I answered merely in a sigh. I noticed that Isaac had drifted away from us. Father said, "Buck's death has necessitated a change in my will."

I stupidly said, "Oh" as if this news had no bearing upon me.

"This enterprise, all these people here, when I am gone, they will now depend upon you."

For some reason this new reality had not occurred to me.

Father said "Your Major, he is not one of us. I had indeed made provisions to include him in our family, under the assumption that Buck would come into his inheritance, and you and the Major would make a home on land I cut out of the estate for you. We can thank Jefferson for the change in the law that permits me to do that. But with Buck's passing, all is changed. The papers I drew up for the Major are null and void."

I had little time to react as father put up his hand to stop me from responding.

"Major Schmidt has made clear his feelings in all aspects. And yes, I fully understand this system is not just. The conundrum on how to untangle us from the blasted system and remain intact from the struggle, well, it still eludes the greatest minds among us. I cannot trust that the good Major would

not reduce our income or our assets. He must not tear down what I have built. You must be the new guardian."

My throat seemed to constrict, and my voice was raspy. "What are you saying?"

"We have a responsibility to care for our own, just as they have a responsibility to labor for our general welfare. You know I do not use the lash. Those who will not work, I send elsewhere. I do not wish to be hated or feared. I would rather earn loyalty by engendering a will to please. You must manage as I have managed."

"I thought you did approve of the Major."

"I am quite fond of him. But our situation has changed. I had not expected this burden to fall on your slender shoulders. It would not be that way if you would choose a Virginian. You now have more to consider than just your own desires. If you choose the Major, then everyone and everything, will someday be yours to guard, not a common burden for a woman. It is not too late to reconsider your choice."

I exclaimed in shocked tones, "There is no going back now!"

An uncomfortable silence hung heavy for a moment. Father's face did redden as the full implication of my words hit him in full. I braced myself for his rage, which I had indeed earned. Instead, father did begin to laugh. He sputtered, "Well, then! So, that is the way it is? So much for your speeches on spinsterhood. We Roberts are a hot blooded tribe.

371

There is no use pretending otherwise. As much as I know of the Major, I do not blame him in this case. No, I do not fault him. Oh, my. My children are alike."

Father continued bending over and sputtering and honking like a goose. I felt most discomfited as I waited in horror for him to compose himself. I expect my cheeks were also red although I was quite cold standing there.

Finally, he straightened up and squeezed out the words, "Oh, please do not let Bess discover this. She believes she is a mightier force than nature."

Father gave me a sly look before saying, "We must not delay too long the marriage, eh?"

Stupidly, I nodded and said, "We are most eager."

Oh, that sent father into another fit of laughter as he pressed my hand against his chest and sputtered, "Oh, to be young again. Dear Lord, such memories." Then he dropped my hand and wiped a tear from his cheek.

He added, "Your marriage won't be the grand affair I had imagined. Buck is too soon laid to rest, and I thought for some days that the Major was to follow him. He still looks a scarecrow, but clearly you give him a reason to rise."

He began to laugh again at his ribald joke.

"Really father!"

Father wagged his finger at me and said, "I will keep your secret from Bess on condition you will give *me Beauty. Try not to get caught out before you are wed as it will cause a scandal."*

I was too aghast to reply. Father was using my unintended confession as leverage.

He said, "I will trade you Contessa for Beauty, but only after Isaac has fitted her up and made her rideable. Once I have Mr. Taylor's stallion, we shall get to the business of breeding. Beauty shall do her duty, and so daughter, shall you."

And he gave me a naughty wink and walked away still chuckling to himself.

December 30, 1781

I am married. The soulful-eyed Major is officially my own. I can hardly believe it.

I feel some discomfiture whenever I see father or Aunt Bess for, we are still under this roof and though they ask no questions nor make ribald jokes, I often feel they joke about us when we are not present. Whatever it is they say to each other, they know what we do these past nights, and I cannot shake the feeling that it is not allowed. To my journal alone I will say that the marital bed is a wonder and a delight. I leave it there to spur my own sweet memories should I read these words in the future. I do also assure whoever else may read these words, that we are indeed happy.

We had our wedding with our Christmas feast

that included a short ceremony that made our union legal and proper. All about us attended, from the lowest laborer to Mr. and Mrs. Jefferson, to witness our nuptials and to partake of Aunt Bess and Priscilla's prodigious baking. Isaac had spent days roasting meats until all was tender to the bone and glazed with his savory concoctions. We had fruits and nuts and vegetables baked in varied ways to round out the table. Father made sure there was no shortage of beverages. In short, our tables groaned with victuals of all kinds.

Henry played reels and jigs and the floorboards had a workout in our main hall as the dancing became more boisterous the later the hour. I had a dress altered from one of my old gowns. Priscilla's fine needlework added extravagant white lace and dark green velvet trim against the lighter green fabric, all per Aunt Bess' careful instructions. I even had new slippers of black velvet with embroidered leaves and flowers.

Although the Major has not fattened up adequately, he was still handsome in a dark frockcoat and green velvet waistcoat with new buckles on his shoes. His eyes were just as beautiful, his gaze as powerful in its effect upon my person. My knees did quake during our exchange of vows.

Father did give to the Major as a wedding gift, a new violin, selected by Mr. Jefferson himself. The cost must have been great. It was made in Italy, constructed from a special wood known for its rich tones. Major Schmidt was moved to tears. I confess some jealousy as he did not cry on receiving me! I also have competition for his caresses, as he does cradle the thing with tenderness. I wonder if instead of jealousy, I should be grateful. Is it his musical training that make his hands most dexterous? This is a question I ask no one, not even himself.

Father's other gift to Major Schmidt was Henry. Now, this is not as happy an acquisition for my dear Major except that the Major has every intention of granting Henry manumission should he desire it. In this present moment, Henry has expressed no desire to leave home. Henry will continue willingly as Major Schmidt's body servant. He has mastered the art of the shave without drawing blood and is proud of his new skills. I notice the Major's facial hair has gone quite grey. It is as if it has happened overnight. His head of hair, still thick, has threads of gray as well. He tells me this is not unheard of for soldiers who have witnessed horrors. I will not bring it up again.

Father has given to me a Ladies' maid named Dinah. And to the house an additional cook with the odd name of Fizzy (she tells me her given name was Phyllis.) Dinah has taken over Major Schmidt's recent quarters and was kind enough to take charge of Cleopatra and her paramour, the yellow cat, who we have named Danny, in honor of the hero of Cowpens, Daniel Morgan. The two cats have ceased their quarreling. Cleopatra's belly has rounded out conspicuously.

Fizzy should lighten Aunt Bess' burden. Although Aunty does not seem as grateful as I would have expected. Father has every intention of re-building our staff, so depleted during these terrible war years. When I asked Aunty if she did not care for Fizzy, she huffed that the girl was too yellow and too comely. I wondered aloud if father had se-lected her with Isaac in mind. This seemed to mollify her. She did say that a wedding did have that effect on folks, putting minds to pairing up every single warm carcass in the county. She then exempted herself, saying that she of course, felt no such com-pulsion. Then she seemed to consider things for a moment and said, "I will speak to your father about Isaac." So much for a lack of compulsion. I predict if both parties are willing, that Isaac will soon have a bride.

Dec. 31, 1781

Father tried to give us his spacious downstairs quarter, but neither of us agree. I have instead simply moved myself into the room that was for-merly my brother's and now is my husband's. How odd it is to write that. Father is to share with me the details and burdens of the running of Ivy Creek Plantation. Father includes Major Schmidt in dis-

cussions, but the Major understands that his role is junior to father's and strangely even to my own.

The Major has a role though, as he excels at animal husbandry, is an adequate scribe and book-keeper, and a good student although he admits little business acumen. What he does have is experience caring for the men in his charge and directing them. This makes the Major especially well-suited to see to the needs of our people. I think, he takes this task on willingly and earnestly.

It is this stubborn fixture of chattel slavery that will never cease to chafe at the Major's conscience. On this father has little to offer in the way of solace. It is a fact that was brought to my acute attention yesterday when we received an odd missive. But though we knew not the name or the place on the envelope, when father shared the contents, all rec-ognized the child-like letters that topped the single sheet of paper.

"SAMMIE ROBERTS"

Below was written in a fluent hand:

"Your former servant, Sammie has found employ in my stable. He is a hard worker and an excellent hand with the horses. He asks of me to inform you that he is saving his pay to purchase the female slave named Priscilla and her child Bertie, who he claims to be his wife and child, and who are the property of your sister. I hope you will arrive at a fair price for the two so that I can arrange transfer of funds, legal paperwork, and

*make travel arrangements. If you require further
assurances, I am happy to oblige. Please send correspondence to:*

*The address was Buffalo, New York, although the
author of the note wrote below the line, his business
was on the other side of the border in Canada but
as he often had business in Buffalo, he would receive
all communications there.*

*Aunt Bess sent Priscilla and Bertie to have a
rest, while she and father retired to his study to
confer. Major Schmidt and I were not invited to
this conference.*

*When the Major and I had our room to ourselves
we did argue.*

*The Major said, "Priscilla and Bertie should be
sent post haste to Sammie without requiring ransom
be paid. If any funds should pass it should be monies
sent along for their support. Any delay is outra-
geous!"*

*I said, "Ransom? That is most unfair. Should
father and Aunty not be compensated for the loss of
three servants? Aunt Bess surely cannot want to lose
Priscilla? She has spent years training the girl."*

*The Major's face darkened. "Your father's son has
asked to have his wife and child sent to him."*

*"Hush. That kinship can never be acknowledged,
you understand that fully."*

*"Louisa, we are in our bedchamber. Sammie is
your half-brother, and Bertie is your nephew. That
makes Priscilla your sister-in-law."*

I sighed and nodded, "Whilst that is true, let me also be frank, Bertie is no child of Sammie's."

The Major nodded vigorously, "Quite true. Whilst we are saying hard truths, let us say how that injustice came about. That Sammie takes Priscilla and her son now as his own ... "

I felt suddenly that my stays were too tight. I am ashamed now to write what I said. "Priscilla by law belongs to Aunt Bess."

My Major looked sorely disappointed in me. So, I put my hand up. "Indeed, Priscilla has chosen Sammie. Father did allow the match."

Then the Major asked me this, "Why do you think such a mating, between Buck and Priscilla took place?"

"Buck always found her attractive. I suppose Buck felt that it was his right. You know how he was."

The Major said, "Many a local girl would have been delighted to have made a match with Buck. He did not need to take liberties with his Aunt's maid."

I grimaced, "Buck saw Priscilla as sport. And if she brought a babe into the world, I'm sure he considered that he had done no worse than his own father."

The Major now hooded his eyes with his heavy lashes. "Do you hear your own words, my darling? Because now you scratch at the truth."

I said, "Oh." And then was silent.

Major Schmidt said, "I listened many hours to

the ravings of a dying man who writhed in pain and swore vengeance. I think I may be able to enlighten you on your brother's motivations, twisted as they were."

Then he took both my hands in his, "Buck took Priscilla not because he wanted her, but because he meant to inflict pain. Priscilla was not the object of his revenge and neither truly was Sammie, though he became the target of Buck's vitriol. Buck's dying words are clear enough. Buck was the heir, the boy who stood to gain everything. But there were things he could not claim that galled him. What ate at him so, was not just that your father turned to Maisie and left his marital bed, wounding your mother, but that the three boys he sired off Maisie, those boys who were born to serve, those sons, the lesser sons, your father dared to love. And in Buck's eyes, that love was rightfully his and his alone."

We were silent as I tried to make sense of the senseless.

"Your father still has three sons. He cannot give to them by law what they deserve. But he can see to their happiness."

I proclaimed with indignation, "My father is a good man, a kind man, a generous man. He always strives to do what is right."

And Major Schmidt agreed. "I expect no less from him. But he will only do what Bess allows him to do. She holds the power as Priscilla's legal owner. But as for his goodness, his kindness, his generosity?

Yes, my darling, I find him so. And I also find his daughter so, and more."

And then, although it was not time for bed, we made our way to bed. His dexterous hands did remove my dress and unlace and remove my stays and we lost ourselves in the moment, making all feel right, though nothing was made right or could ever be made right for Sammie, Isaac, Henry, or little Bertie. No matter what father and Aunty did decide.

We could try to look to their happiness. But that is not the same. And though I could easily forget that in every toss of the coin, I would land 'heads,' I knew my Major would not. He would not forget, nor ever stop forcing me to look fully at the injustice. Even as he could not mete out justice in our unjust land. I realized it would ever be a source of conflict between us.

And there was nothing I could do to change that.

22

Dabs' low, fluent voice stopped. Eloise held her fingers over the keyboard, but Dabs turned off the light on the magnifying glass and pushed the swivel arm away from the manuscript.

Eloise heard herself make a sound not unlike the sound of her kitten. It was not a mew, but a cry, short, small, and high pitched. She put her hands down on the desk and exclaimed, "That's it?"

Dabs said, "That's the end. I've shared everything I have."

Pinky said, "What a way to end it. It felt like real life. She didn't live happily-ever-after her wedding to Prince Charming. How could she? Just because the war was ending, it doesn't mean no more conflict."

Eloise said, "I can't help it. I feel cheated."

Dabs said, "I wish I had more. But maybe we should be grateful for what she did leave us. She was a talented storyteller. An amazing chronicler of her time. And especially educated for a woman of her era."

Eloise said, "Do you think Major Schmidt gave Henry his freedom?"

"Hard to know. But after 1806, freed slaves were legally required to leave the state of Virginia. Cruel. To be forced to leave your home. I think your dream likely correct, that Henry spent his life right here and was buried right here."

Eloise simply said, "Oh, poor Henry."

Pinky exclaimed, "I wonder about the other slaves. Did Ivy Creek ever free their slaves?"

Dabs shook his head. "There was still slavery here at the time of emancipation."

Eloise lifted her eyebrows, "And if Bertie did sire a line that continues to your present-day Henry, then Bertie was not sent north with Priscilla. He wasn't an infant in those sketches, if those sketches were our Bertie, that is."

Dabs said, "And we don't even know if Priscilla was reunited with Sammie."

Pinky weighed in, "I don't know Dabs. Priscilla had her spine stiffened by Sammie. I'm betting she went north."

Dabs said, "Without her son?"

Eloise said, "He was Buck's child. And Aunt Bess' property. Bess had promised to give Bertie a good life. Yes. I expect that's what happened. Bess cut a deal."

That thought left them silent, absorbing the likelihood. But of course, no one could be certain.

Pinky stood up; Lady Jane cradled under her arm. "What a way to end the trip. Eloise, time to pack it up and hit the road, girl."

Dabs stood up too. "I'll email everyone a copy. Betsy

will want to check in with me after she reads hers. Betsy and I always have a good jaw-fest."

Eloise thought to herself, "jaw-fest?" Good grief, who says stuff like that? Old people. That's who. It irritated her more than it should, but then she was feeling grumpy as she got up to go upstairs to pack.

Prince bounded up the stairs ahead of Eloise. He surely thought he was going with her. She hated that he wasn't going home with her. She climbed them slowly, her legs feeling leaden. Her emotions a jumble.

Once in the room, Louisa's room, Eloise shut the door. Prince watched her pack her few items. This was it. She had to say goodbye. She looked at the window where she had seen Louisa's shadow and heard her words. Or dreamed it all. She looked out into the barnyard, at the same sights Louisa would recognize. She did not want to leave, was strangely angry about leaving. But all good things must come to an end. They always did. Before opening the door, she leaned over Prince and kissed the top of his head, a moment of dizziness washing over her. He panted and grinned his crazy-happy dog grin. He was not sad. He was, after all this time, exactly where he needed to be. But he would always be her Prince. The thought caused a stabbing pain in her chest.

Eloise had one more goodbye remaining. She felt brittle emotionally. She opened the bedroom door and headed down the stairs, where she found Dabs waiting for her.

Pinky came down the stairs toting Lady Jane in her sherpa bag but stopped when she saw Eloise sitting on a step with her arms around the dog and Dabs standing on the landing below her, hand on the newel post. Pinky took a couple of steps back up the stairs and sat down, far enough to give Eloise and Dabs a bit of privacy, but not so far away that she couldn't hear what they were saying.

Eloise was saying to Dabs, "Yeah, I was wary at first. I thought maybe the journal was a fraud, used as catnip for you know, well, to lure me into a relationship."

Dabs shrugged, "You know now the journal is authentic, but, um, well, you weren't totally wrong about the catnip part."

"What?"

"Eloise, you're very pretty, have a great smile, great figure, and um, I had this feeling looking at your photo, that you were looking right at me, that the photo was meant for me. You of all people should get that, I mean, you fell for Joe from his photo. But, when I found out you rode, and the other pieces kept confirming in my mind that all this was meant to be, and well, maybe I got carried away. Destiny and all that sort of thing."

Eloise said, "I was an Extreme Reader and interested in all things related to Jefferson."

"True, but for God's sake, Eloise, why would I choose to share a rare historical find with *just* you? Charlottesville is full of scholars who devote their life to this time-period. I am confessing, trying to confess, that I wanted to use it exactly as you suspected, catnip. I wanted to use the journals just as you said. Maybe I thought it was the only way you would be interested. And I thought at one point, the prize was within reach. I wasn't all wrong, I mean right before you left last time… But I see I've been delusional, and I don't even have the excuse, as you did, of hitting my head. So, if you've changed your mind. If I'm just too much, well, I get it."

Eloise thought of present-day Henry, making his embarrassing assumptions, and suddenly realized, Dabs had made assumptions himself, and likely been telling others, too. Her brittle emotions, teetering between grumpy and tearful, tipped easily, and almost conveniently into anger. She said, "Oh my God. You said something to Henry, didn't you? He didn't get all those ideas about us on his own."

Dabs looked up the stairs at Pinky. The two of them made eye contact. Pinky lifted an eyebrow, and gave the slightest hint of a nod, encouraging.

He looked back at Eloise, "Henry has always taken an intense interest in my life. He's all I have left to call family."

Eloise then said, her voice rising slightly, "And Betsy, you and Betsy have been talking about this too? About me? About us?"

"Betsy and I talk every day."

Eloise now turned to look at Pinky. "Pinky are you in on this?"

Dabs answered for her. "Pinky and I have mostly spoken about Prince."

Eloise mouth hung open for a moment, "You got Prince. You have my dog."

Dabs sighed, "He's a wonderful dog. But falls far short of where I was aiming."

Eloise was feeling confused by her rush of emotions. She did not want to leave. But she had her rides on Red to get back to. She had a great job. She had friends, good friends. And here was Dabs, baring his soul, telling her what surely, she already knew. And in return, she was not able to give him anything in return except a scolding. The pull of Ivy Creek Plantation on her, well, it would be no pull at all without Dabs Carter. She knew that. She knew she wanted what he wanted. But she was just too chicken to go there.

Pinky got up, and breezily came down the stairs. Eloise and Dabs followed behind her as she made her way to the car. When she got to the car, she turned and put her hand out for the keys, saying, "I'll take first shift. I've got the jitters and I need to do something."

Eloise handed over the keys, and Pinky turned to Dabs, "Hugs. C'mon, don't be a stranger."

Dabs stepped forward and Pinky stood on tiptoe and as she hugged him, she said, "Keep the faith, bro."

Eloise, feeling hollowed out, her goodbye to Dabs still unspoken, stroked the head of a panting Prince who was beginning to look anxious.

Pinky said, "Don't upset the dog, Eloise.

Pinky turned her back on the two of them and slid behind the wheel settling` Lady Jane by Eloise's feet. The kitten was being quiet. When Eloise got in, Dabs was holding onto Prince's collar and waving goodbye, trying to look stoic, but failing. Pinky did a little toot-

toot on the horn and stuck her arm out the window to wave goodbye at Dabs, crossing her fingers, then flashing a peace sign.

Once they got down the bumpy driveway and onto smooth road, Pinky opened her purse and pulled out a full roll of toilet paper, tossing it at Eloise.

Pinky said, "Men. Right? They never seem to buy tissues. At least it's the soft kind of TP."

"I'm not crying."

"Not yet. You're slow. I'm sorry I couldn't wait for the dam to burst, but we needed to get the wheels rolling. At some point, you need to apologize to Dabs. But in the meantime, we've got eight and a half hours ahead of us, give or take with weather and traffic. Hey, and the Doctor is in, I'm ready to listen. This girl just needs candy first, though. Get on the GPS and find me some good road candy. You know who has the best, top of the line? The big Cracker. I'm going to get red whips. You want some?"

"Never again, Pinky, they're gross."

"Suit yourself. What do you want?"

Eloise leaned her head on the window. "Jellybeans. Cinnamon jellybeans."

Pinky exclaimed, "Easy-peasy. We all need a little sugar in our life, y'know? Speaking of sugar. What is it with you and Dabs?"

Eloise blurted out, "Dabs is such a weirdo!"

Pinky answered, "This from the woman who takes her cat on vacation."

Eloise's voice sounded weak, "Is that weird?"

"Yeah. Totally. But I renamed myself Pinky and died my hair to match. So, I got no issue with weird."

Eloise said, "Dabs talks like an old man, and gossips like an old woman."

Pinky said, "Yeah. But he's good to his animals, even when they are old and crippled up. He's stupid sweet on you too, falling all over himself cooking and running to town to find the next delicacy to try to soften your cold, hard, heart. Not to mention he's hot. But it's your decision, Eloise, yours alone. Although I don't get what's holding you back. And I do not get at all why you aren't crying right now, like buckets, saying goodbye to Dabs."

Eloise did not respond, but inside her head was the voice of Doc saying something about desire and being young. Henry had said, they didn't need to ask anyone's permission. So, what was her problem? Why not allow a little "sugar" in her life? She and Dabs had shared magical moments, a deep connection and attraction. But he was weird, wasn't he? Yeah. He was a strange and complicated guy. She had confessed a lot to Dabs about just how messed up she was. But not everything. She was a loser. That's what she did, lose. The best part of her life, her Lulu life, well, that was behind her. The safest romances for her were to be found in reading about the lives of others. Nothing in her messed up life could match the love she felt for the characters she had been following in the journals, the people she had fallen in love with, those who had long ago died. She loved them. She could cry buckets over them all. Especially, the man playing "The Parting Glass" on his violin.

Yes. Especially him.

* * *

It felt so good to be back at Bev's and heading out with the horses on a field trip planned by Bev. Eloise still felt a hollow spot in her gut, a sense of unfinished business from her trip to deliver Prince, but she tried to push it from her mind and focus on the present. This was where she was meant to be.

Miguel drove the trailer while Bev rode shotgun. Red and Jethro, and Caroline's horse, who Eloise finally learned was named, Chick-a-boom, or Chick for short, were in the trailer. The trailer was a four-horse head-to-head, with a side-ramp. Since they would be working out of the trailer, the horses were groomed, bandaged, and saddled with loose girths, with light-weight polar fleece coolers thrown over the top to keep the chill off. The plan was to bridle them in the trailer before they were led down the ramp for their cross-country schooling session.

Eloise had exchanged "how-de-do's" with Caroline, and now rode in Caroline's car behind the trailer. The meeting had felt jarring to Eloise. Caroline, Bev's "girl" was a middle-aged woman. Eloise had assumed that Caroline was someone just like herself. But she was nothing like Eloise. Caroline was blonde, with a wide smile, outgoing demeanor, and an accent that reminded Eloise of Betsy.

Eloise had whispered to Bev, "I thought you said,

Caroline was a girl?" Bev brushed past her loaded down with bridles saying, "Well, she ain't no boy."

By the time Eloise was in the car with Caroline, she had made the mental shift. Caroline was no boy or girl. Caroline was a woman, old enough to be her mother.

Caroline said to Eloise, "Glad you took on that red mare." Caroline drew out the word "mare," with her accent making it sound more like "mayor."

Eloise nodded, "She's a good horse."

Caroline nodded back in a slow and thoughtful way, "She's a lot of horse. Bev did say you've got lots of miles, for one so young. She also said that your Daddy is a genius when it comes to running and jumping."

Eloise couldn't help but smile. "So I've been told. But I've also heard that kind of thing skips generations."

Caroline hooted, then grinned, "Well, I'm no genius at this game, myself. I've only gotten this far with sweat and tears and my share of blood."

Eloise replied, "To be honest, I'm excited, but pretty nervous about today. Jock would say that Red is 'hotter-than-a-two-dollar pistol, and she's already spun me off once."

"Don't let Bev hear you say that, and don't let that firecracker mare feel that you're nervous. Whatever happens, I expect we'll live to fight another day. Besides, I've been under Bev's care for three decades, and mostly, she keeps me from seriously screwing up."

"Mostly?"

They pulled off the interstate and headed into rolling piney woods. It looked familiar. Eloise said, "I know this place. I mean I haven't been here for years. But they used to hold competitions."

Caroline raised her eyebrows. "You don't look old enough to remember that. But yeah. Not for ages. It's not open to the public anymore. They don't need to let us come school either, but they like Bev. Still, we try not to leave a trace behind that advertises that we've been here."

Once they got parked, Bev began to bark orders. "Girls, get on your boots, helmets, gloves. Miguel, you know the drill."

Miguel put down the ramp and got out a mounting block from the trailer tack room. Red was vibrating in her slot, nodding her head up and down, peering down the ramp, trying to get her bearings. Chick looked bright, but sane. Jethro was pulling hay from his hay net and chewing placidly. Bev was booted and wearing a heavy pair of deerskin gloves. Then, for the first time ever, Eloise saw Bev put on a helmet.

When Eloise cut her eyes at Caroline, her unasked question got answered. Caroline said, "Farm rules."

Miguel bridled Jethro, tightened his girth, and brought him to the mounting block for Bev, standing at his head until Bev was up and had the reins. Then he bridled Red in the trailer, clipping the longe line to her snaffle bit ring, rattling the bit in her mouth, and speaking to the mare in Spanish.

He undid her chest bar and she barged forward out of her slot. She came to the top of the ramp, Miguel hauling on the line to stop her. There she stood, stock still with a faraway look in her eye.

Bev hollered, "Miguel, she got that look like she's about to jump out of an airplane, and she don't got no parachute, and you don't either."

If looks could kill, Miguel's narrow-eyed glance at Bev would have been lethal. Still, Miguel took his hand and grabbed a fold of Red's skin, holding it in a pinch. He said to the mare, this time in English, "Listen up you devil, you gonna' walk down this ramp like a lady wearing high-heeled shoes. Got it?"

Red pinned her ears and turned to look at Miguel, affronted. He let go of her skin and directed her attention to the ramp by tapping it with his booted toe. The mare gingerly tested her first step, and then walked down the ramp exactly like that lady in heels, small, mincing, careful steps.

Bev said, "Miguel, you longe that devil, 'stead of Eloise, cause if she blows, that flyweight won't be able to hang on."

Eloise was sure that the Spanish she heard while Miguel was longing Red was full of expletives.

Red put on a display. Eloise was glad Miguel had been given the job. The mare snorted and huffed, leapt through the air, and put her tail up like a flag. Red cut chunks of sod with her hooves out of the perfect ground. So much for "leave no trace behind."

Red still looked and felt too up when Eloise was told to get on. Miguel held the mare tight as she mounted and got herself sorted. And then they were off, with Bev in the lead, Eloise in the middle and Caroline behind.

Bev soon had them trotting. She yelled over her

shoulder, "Gonna' jog a couple miles first. Knock the starch out. Don't let that hot head past me. Point her nose right there at Jethro's wide ass. That'll block her."

Jethro did have a wide ass. Eloise focused on nothing else. She was already out of breath. It was nerves. Here in front of her was this old lady, up in her jumping position, her windbreaker, which must have been partially unzipped, was filling with air, making Bev look inflated like a balloon. Eloise was too nervous to laugh.

Eloise took a deep breath, tried to let go of the tightness in her belly, and began to take in her surroundings. She could now focus on more than Bev's ballooning jacket and Jethro's ass. She gave herself a scolding, 'You are Lulu Robertson, daughter of Jock, the genius, remember?' It was about damn time she owned that. Jock might be an ass, but he taught her how to ride. Eloise bridged her reins, pushed her heels down, and took charge of Red. And as she did, the fire-breathing devil beneath her began to settle. They trotted up and down hills until they came to a big field. Bigger than Bev's. And it was dotted with cross-country jumps including two water complexes.

Bev put up her hand, to indicate they were coming to a stop. Jethro was breathing hard.

"Me and Jethro, we get to spectate now. You two split up, go different directions, show me a nice canter 'round this field. About five minutes, with a couple short sprints, then come on back. Me and Jethro are making a plan."

The Red Devil was now mostly in control. And

when they reconvened back at Jethro HQ, Bev led a parade over to a small jump. Caroline went first and Eloise and Red watched. Then Eloise took her turn, and Red fought the bit and took a long spot, over jumping. Bev had her repeat it a few times until Red "cooled her jets."

They progressed around the field with little drama. It was chilly, but the sun was out, the air still, Jethro was the picture of calm patience as he stood with one hind leg resting, his eyes half-closed, soaking up the sun, while Red and Chick took turns over the small obstacles.

They even were successful trotting through one of the water complexes, wading in, and hopping out via a small bank.

It wasn't until they got to a ditch that both Chick and Red put the brakes on. Eloise rode through a hard spin, to the left, and her muscle memory, thankfully, kicked in, keeping her on the topside, although for a split second, she wasn't sure.

Bev barked, "Eloise, get behind Jethro, but leave one horse length. Caroline, you get behind Red. Jethro'll lead."

Caroline managed to only get out one word, "Bev?"

But they were off. Bev was in jumping position, her jacket billowing, kicking old Jethro into a canter, then a hand gallop. She looked over her shoulder and yelled, "Keep up!"

Down the hill they flew. Then up the hill and over a small log jump. Then straight at the ditch at what felt like way too much speed. Over the ditch went Jethro.

Eloise grabbed a hunk of mane in her fist, and jammed her heels down, she knew Red was going to jump it this time and jump it big. There would be no duck and spin, not with the old horse and old woman leading the charge. Behind her she heard Caroline expel a curse word. But when she looked over her shoulder, Caroline and Chick were still behind her. Caroline was grinning.

The three of them pulled up. Bev whooped, "Jethro and I still got it!"

Caroline said, "Bev, you old fool."

Bev said, "Worked, didn't it?"

Three relaxed and tired horses walked back to the trailer, where Miguel sat on the mounting block.

Bev shouted, "You stomp down them divots?"

Miguel nodded. Although, once she was back on foot, she went over to the grass, hands on her hips, to check his handiwork.

The horses had their girths loosened, been loaded back on the trailer, fleece-coolers over their backs, and their bridles replaced with halters. Then Caroline and Eloise got back in the car to follow the trailer back to the barn. Once the horses were unloaded, Caroline and Eloise would still have horses to groom and tack to clean, while Miguel would be cleaning out the trailer and unhooking.

The riding was always the smallest part of an outing with horses, even if it was the meat of the matter. Eloise felt like a limp dishrag. But she was proud of her riding and proud of Red. It had been a successful first outing for the young horses. All due to Jethro and Bev. Bev. What a trip she was.

On the drive home, Caroline kept shaking her head, muttering, "Bev's not supposed to be riding or jumping, but she's still got it. Stubborn as the day is long. I know better than to try and stop her. She never ceases to amaze me, even after all these years. Although, she'll pay for that tomorrow. I mean, she's 86 years old, has arthritis and a bad heart."

That was all new information to Eloise. Not surprising. But new. Eloise felt like someone had squeezed her heart.

* * *

Eloise, showered, fed, and relaxed, logged back on to Extreme Readers.

Betsy wrote "It seemed an appropriate title to choose for our last read on Jefferson."

Dabs replied, "Twilight at Monticello."

Eloise typed, "Whoa! Last read?"

Betsy wrote, "Well, it will be our tenth book on Jefferson. We made a goal, and we will have met it. Of course, I expect you and Dabs, being our most extreme of this Extreme Reader's group, far exceeded our goal, you wild and crazy kids, you! No one will mind if you two continue to study the great man on your own. But I have a hankering to move on to memoirists from the American Civil War. Mary Boykin Chestnut's diary is at the top of my list. I'm going to lead another group on that topic, and of course, you all are welcome to join. But first, 'Twilight at Monticello', by Alan Pell Crawford to close out this study group. See you all here in three days' time to begin sharing reactions and insights."

There was a flurry of comments, exchanges, and praise for Betsy's leadership. The praise was genuine and deserved. Eloise felt a heaviness in her chest. Betsy was ending the group, this group. The study that had brought her Dabs and Louisa Roberts and the incredible history of Ivy Creek. Dabs had finished transcribing and sharing the journal. That was over too. Things that had come together into something magical and intense were now breaking apart. Eloise had been here before. Had fought it in ways that were not good for her or for anyone else. She was losing again.

The last read would be a sad one as they escorted Jefferson through his last hard years, as most last years surely were. Eloise thought of her mother and felt her eyes sting with tears.

Eloise looked online at the last portraits of Jefferson, especially the plaster mold made one year before his death. The plasterer was inept, nearly suffocated the old man, and did not use enough oil to pull the plaster cleanly away, peeling a layer of his fragile skin.

Poor man. Eloise studied the likeness made from that mask. Jefferson's face was a different Jefferson. He looked painfully thin, his eyes more deeply set, his mouth thinner, his hair wispy. All normal signs of advanced age. An honor not afforded everyone. This Eloise keenly felt.

Eloise made her way to bed, and Lady Jane cried to be put in bed with her. Eloise obliged, then wiggled her toes under the covers, and watched as Lady Jane engaged in a manic hunting display, pouncing, and scooting, and then returning to do more battle. But finally, the kitten wore out, and Eloise began her read.

* * *

The next morning, Eloise was in the basement kennels, beginning her walks, when Janet buzzed the intercom.

"Eloise, a delivery for you."

Eloise put the leash back on the hook and headed up the stairs. When she got to the front desk, there on the counter sat the biggest gift basket she had ever seen.

Janet had crossed her arms over her chest and raised her eyebrows. "Eloise, you never cease to amaze me. You clearly have an admirer."

There was one of those tiny little envelopes attached. Janet pointed at it.

Eloise opened it and Janet said, "Who's the guy?"

"Ralph. You know, the guy that owns Murtagh, the Scotty?"

Janet looked disappointed. "Ralph? Bummer." Then added, "What did you do that warrants this giant gift basket?"

"It's a thank you for a referral. I sent him a great client."

Janet nodded as if now all had become clear, she said, "One of your rich horsey-set, I take it?"

"Yup." Then, "I'll put this in the lounge. Help your-self."

"You mean it? It's from that cool gourmet shop around the corner."

Eloise said, "You can leave me the cinnamon jelly-beans."

Janet said, "Jellybeans? I don't think…"

"They'll be in there, even if he had to provide them himself."

Back in the lounge, Eloise took the plastic off the enormous basket. She unloaded the contents, threw away the packing, and pulled out the bottle of wine and the two glasses. The cinnamon jellybeans she put in her tote. Eloise knew exactly what to do with the wine and glasses.

Pinky arrived late. She had her hair piled on top of her head, a fluffy top knot of pink with two ornamental lacquered chopsticks with pink tassels protruding. To Eloise, at this point, the "do" was unremarkable.

Pinky was saying, "My life feels too quiet. No Prince, no having to get up every three hours for a kitten. No road trips planned. No holidays. I'm bored."

Eloise nodded, "Well, I can tell you all about my field trip yesterday with the horses and Bev and Caroline."

"With Caroline? Oh, goody. I want a full run down on this Caroline person. I mean, no one is too good for *our* Doc."

Eloise frowned, opened her mouth and then closed it.

Pinky said, "Whatcha' got there behind your back?"

Eloise realized then that she had been hiding the wine and glasses. "Oh. Ralph sent me a gift basket since Bev is now his new client. And well, I pulled this out for you, and Buzz."

Pinky took the bottle and said, "Oooh-la-la! I love this wine. Thank you!"

"I hoped you would. I put the other contents out to share in the lounge."

Pinky took some of the dog towels and carefully wrapped the glasses and the bottle and put them in her tote. "Sweet of you to nab this for us. Make sure you thank Ralph. He's a peach."

"Um. Pinky? Doc and Caroline? What the heck?"

"Oh Eloise, really? Where did you think Doc was on Christmas Eve?"

Eloise shrugged.

"You have absolutely the worst radar when it comes to romance. Or are you just willfully blind? Maybe you are just stubbornly resistant to change? Is that it? Well, time to wake up and smell the roses, or coffee, or whatever."

Eloise shook her head, "How would *you* know anything about Doc's love life?"

Pinky shook her head again. "What in the world do you and Bev talk about all those afternoons at the farm?"

"Horses. We talk about horses."

"Well, not me, I don't talk horses. Bev and I, we had a great chat. She sure is a hell of a lot of fun. Sometimes I do wonder about you Eloise, but I have noticed, your saving grace is that you have great friends."

"So, does that mean you and Bev talked about me?"

"Um, duh. It's what we have in common. And no, you cannot have the wine back. Besides, we said nice things about you." Then she winked, and said, "Mostly."

Eloise said impishly, "Never forget Pinky, I know your real name."

Pinky wagged her finger, "Ah, ah, ah, now, things revealed in therapy sessions..."

"I'm not sure that applies to people who aren't actually therapists. But, back to Doc, I have no right to know, but Caroline and Doc? Is it serious?"

Pinky touched her fingertip to her tongue, then touched her ass, and made a sizzling noise.

23

Eloise had a good day at work, and a good afternoon at Bev's, where Bev and she introduced the exercise of shoulder-in to Red. Eloise was tired and hungry when she got home, settling herself at the kitchen table with her kitten in her lap. She had a bowl of soup and her e-book on Jefferson, propped on a stand. But before beginning her read, she checked her email. At the top of the page was an email notifying her of a delivery. Lady Jane got put on the floor, and Eloise left her hot meal to find a thin box sitting on her front stoop.

Eloise brought it to her kitchen table and pulled the tab that opened the box. The contents were wrapped in bubble wrap. Once that was removed, she uncovered a thin black book, unmarked on the exterior. It opened stiffly and smelled faintly of ink and glue. There on the first page was written,

Dearest Eloise/Louisa:

"A story must be told or there'll be no story, yet it is the untold stories that are most moving."

403

(JRR Tolkien)
-DC

Eloise carefully turned the stiff pages to find that Dabs had assembled all the journal entries and had included some of Louisa's sketches and doodles. All thoughts of food, of her latest read sitting in its stand on the table, vanished. Instead, all she could think of was Dabs. Was this another "Parting Glass?" A farewell, meant to mark the end of a story? Or was it meant as one more tantalizing bit of catnip, meant to draw her back? He addressed his Tolkien quote to both her and to Louisa. Had he in his romantic fantasy confused them? And which of them was indeed "Dearest?" Well, she knew the answer. It was Louisa. She too loved Louisa, missed Louisa, and pined for Louisa and her words. Loved, missed, pined. All of it she found to be a sweet but slightly painful yearning. But not just for Louisa. She knew that to be true.

She again thought of Dabs. Dabs was, perhaps, a bit crazy. But in his defense, saner than she was. They were both under a spell. But wasn't it a lovely spell? What pained her was not the fantasy, not the spell cast by Louisa and her journal, but that the story had ended, the spell had broken. Her heart was aching now that it was over. And this was the message, she felt, that Dabs was addressing in his quote. The untold story was still untold. Was there another story to be discovered, together?

She understood the next move was hers. But she

wanted to give herself space, margin, quiet. Time to do nothing. Time to gird her loins for whatever came next. Time to make decisions she wasn't ready to make.

Eloise lifted the book once more to her nose to take in the aroma of ink and paper, then placed it on her bedside table. She went back to the kitchen and ate her cold soup but could not relax enough to read the book on Jefferson. She should thank Dabs for the gift. Of course, she should. But not yet.

Instead, she thought of Red. Every ride on Red was in a way a story, one she was creating. A girl and her horse. Each ride was a timeless bit of time, and a relationship that existed outside the realm of words. It was a private story, one not told in words. Louisa would understand. Dabs understood. This was who Eloise was, would always be. Lulu or Eloise, Whiplash or Red. She would never cut horses out of her life again. Red had helped bring her back to who she was.

Eloise found herself craving the cinnamon jellybeans she had stashed in her bag. She made a cup of hot tea, poured some jellybeans into her mother's crystal bowl, the one Ralph had given her, and then brought the bowl up to her nose and inhaled. The aroma of cinnamon was comforting. No matter where she was, no matter how many years passed, she was always going to be her mother's child. Nothing could take that away from her. The aroma of cinnamon would always evoke the ghost of Ellie Robertson, but now, at last, Eloise could bear it.

Eloise got into bed with Lady Jane, who was hiding behind the pillows, playing peek-a-boo. Eloise found an old Sudoku puzzle and an ink pen that was almost dry in the top drawer of her bedside table. She chewed jellybeans and drank her tea while placing numbers in squares. She gave up on it and placed it back in the drawer. By the time she had cleaned out the bowl, she had decided, not to decide about anything beyond brushing her teeth, as they were coated in a red-dyed sugar-plaque. Eloise brushed her teeth, and then although it was early, she got in bed, turned her face into her pillow and with the scent of cinnamon in her nostrils, fell fast asleep.

* * *

The clinic was running a dental special for the month to help generate business in the after-holiday slump, so Suzy and Doc were busy. But Pinky had so few clients that she was coming in late and leaving early most days. Eloise could leave work early too to ride Red.

Today would be another day in the indoor because the sky was iron gray, indicating more rain on its way. Still, Eloise felt optimistic. Yesterday's ride on Red had scratched the surface of a new level of sophistication from the saddle. Red was getting stronger, more obedient, and more relaxed in her reactions.

When she got to the barn, Eloise was surprised to find Miguel. She asked, "Bev okay?"

He nodded, "Bev said for you to ride. Then she wants you to go up and eat tamales with her. Tell her about your ride."

"Tamales?"

"Tamales and beer. Rosie make a special batch just for Bev. Not too hot."

Eloise said, "Rosie?" Realizing after she said it, that she was sounding like an echo.

Miguel smiled, "My wife. She clean and cook and run errands for Bev. Bev don't drive no more."

"Oh. I've never met Rosie. That sounds great. Thanks Miguel."

Eloise then repeated her ride from the day before. It was a good ride. Eloise felt that the cross-country fieldtrip had done something for Red that was not easily defined. There was a new relaxed focus to her work. Eloise went to the shoulder-in exercise and repeated it until she felt herself drape around Red and establish a steady connection between the two bodies.

Because of that good ride, she headed up the driveway to Bev's with a spring in her step. Yesterday, she and Bev had talked about the benefit of riding shoulder-in, and how it was essential, although basic; an exercise riders spent their riding life studying and working to master.

When she knocked on the door, "Rosie" answered. She was a plump woman with a huge smile. "Come on in. Miss Bev, she waiting."

Bev was sitting at the kitchen table, a big orange cat in her lap. Rosie scolded her. "Miss Bev, you don't want cat hair in your tamale."

Rosie cracked herself up and started laughing. Bev grinned back but pushed the cat gently from her lap. "Sorry cat, boss lady commands and we got to obey."

Then Bev said, "Pull up a chair. I had me a real hankering for Rosie's tamales. And she's a good sport to whip some up for me."

Rosie brought Eloise a plate of steaming tamales and a cold bottle of beer. Eloise was starving, and the tamales were delicious.

Rosie took note of the speed in which Eloise's tamales disappeared, and without asking, put two more on her plate. They were still wrapped in corn husks and piping hot.

Rosie looked at Bev and said, "Don't wash nothing, okay? I'll be back early with Miguel."

Bev waved her fork at Rosie, "You go on now. Eloise will keep me company for a bit, then I'm hitting the sack."

Eloise proceeded to give Bev a full report on her ride, and Bev showed a keen interest. Eloise felt Red had changed from the field trip in ways that had nothing to do with jumping.

Bev nodded sagely, "The more places you take her, the more she understands why you matter. You ain't no incidental person. You are her person, her leader, and she realized it when she got away from home. You mean something more to her now."

Eloise nodded. It made sense. But then she remembered to tell Bev about the impressive gift basket from Ralph.

Bev said, "Don't surprise me, him being grateful and all. Feller just got a pile of money to manage and scored all kind of fees. That's okay. It's past time for me to put my house in order. Was timely to meet him at your shindig. He's making me jump through all kind of hoops, though. Wears a body out worse than working around the farm."

Eloise nodded, "I get it. Ralph is persistent and kind of devious too, like he could have been a detective. He found out for me that Jock had sold Whiplash. Did it without me knowing about it."

"Ralphie there, he's a kind man. He got some bones of his own to pick with Jock, but he won't go for the jugular. He don't have a mean streak like me."

Eloise realized she sounded slightly annoyed when she said, "Why do you keep saying that about yourself? I don't know a lot, but you are about the kindest and most generous person I know. Why, look what you've done for me! Riding Red has been life-changing for me."

Bev made an odd face and Eloise said, "I'm serious. And I'm grateful."

"Nice of you to say so, but I done some things."

Eloise said, "Whatever you did to whomever, I'm sure they deserved what they got."

Bev gave a hoot and took a swig of her beer. "Likely true. Time changed my mind about a few things. Ralphie there, he may be smart, but he ain't devious. That title fits me better."

"What in the world did you do?"

"Clear this mess and get us an ice cream bar from the freezer, would ya'?"

Eloise did as she was told. Once Bev had taken a bite

of ice cream she said, "One time, I ground up a mess of my step-dad's drugs and mixed 'em into his coffee with an extra scoop of sugar, so's he wouldn't notice."

Eloise was, indeed, shocked. She managed to ask, "Did he deserve it?"

Bev nodded, "When he married Mom, he thought he had gotten a two-fer. But it was still wrong of me to do that."

"What happened?"

Bev said, "I moved into the spare bedroom here. I had dropped out of high school. Miss Annie here needed the help and the company, and I wanted to learn to ride the big jumps. She had some great horses, and she was a good teacher, too. So, it worked out fine. I done other stuff too. But that's all I'm going to say about that."

Eloise had a brief thought that the man may have died. Eloise said, "Bev, you sure have a story to tell."

Predictably, Bev said, "Not every story needs tellin'."

Eloise thought of Dabs. She thought of the inscription in his gift to her of the bound journal.

It was as if Bev could read her mind, she said, "So, this fella, Dabs. I hear he's handsome, rich and rides."

Eloise was speechless.

Bev said, "Old ladies like me, we get kind of nosey. See, I done had my flings. I don't got no regrets in that department. And they's real important memories to me. I'm tickled pink that lightning struck twice for Caroline. It's sweet to see. Them opportunities don't come along for everyone, not even once, so twice is extra special."

Eloise drew a deep breath and said, "Doc and Caroline. I hope it works out. I'd hate to see Doc get his heart broken. It's just, it's so hard when it ends."

Bev's brows lifted, "Why, everybody dies in the end no matter what. Some endings come sooner, and some come later, but while it lasts, it sure can be a great ride."

"Then every story is a tragedy, isn't it?"

"Baloney! Now, seems to me, you reading all them books, surely know it's more fun to read ones with juice to 'em. I may be old, but I still got a pulse. I expect you do too. Ain't natural at your age not to. Thing is, don't be writing your story without no juice to it. But, if you mean to say this Dabs fella' don't cut the mustard, then for sure, you take a pass. Annie used to say to me, be careful the company you keep. But heck, here you are, hanging out with a crabby old lady with a mean streak, who never finished high school, who is also nosey as hell."

"Bev, you're a treasure and I think you know it. It was my lucky day when I came to try Red for Jock. The luckiest day I have had in years, and I am forever grateful I said 'yes' to Jock and came."

"Well then Missy, maybe you oughta' consider saying 'yes' more often."

That comment sunk in. "I'm going to consider taking that advice."

"No pussyfooting. We made it over that ditch 'cuz we took it at a gallop."

Eloise was momentarily stunned. Bev and Jock. Same advice.

Eloise decided to wash up the few dishes, even

411

though Bev insisted that Rosie would do it. She just wasn't quite ready to leave, but she knew Bev was tired, so she told her to go on and get ready for bed while she put things to rights in the kitchen.

Before she left, she checked on Bev who was in bed with her cats, the television on.

Eloise asked, "You don't mind staying here alone? What if you needed something?"

"I got poor Miguel on a short leash. He'll tell you hisself that I bother him at ungodly hours day or night. Just let yourself out. I got the TV 'til I get sleepy."

Eloise wished Bev sweet dreams and let herself out.

24

February was replaced by March, and April was so near you could smell it in the air. To Eloise, April meant the smell of wet earth and unfurling new leaves. With the Azaleas and dogwoods and Cherry trees in bloom and the daffodils up, there was an explosion of colors, often clashing colors. Perhaps considered ostentatious by some, but not Eloise, and unsurprisingly, Pinky exulted in it.

Lady Jane had, it seemed, become a cat. Doc was still letting Eloise bring her to the clinic. Silly. There was no good reason LJ couldn't stay at the townhome. Each morning Eloise put her up in the cattery as soon as it was time to head down to the kennels. Eloise wondered if Doc thought of Lady Jane as her support animal. Of course, he had allowed Prince to come to the clinic, too. Prince had a better deal these days living at Ivy Creek. Eloise thought of him following Dabs all day, going out on hacks and hikes. It made a pretty image in her mind's eye. She was a bit jealous that the image did not include her.

Business had picked up but was still slow. The Dental special was over. The boarding and grooming business was light. Pinky reminded Eloise that things would rebound for Easter and then for Spring break and then came summer vacations. Until then, Pinky kept busy volunteering for Good Stewards with free baths, clips, and nail trims, and Doc kept her on a small retainer. But Eloise could sense that money was tight, and it did worry her.

Because the schedule had been light, Doc had been delaying his in-house exams until ten am. Everyone seemed to know why. He was spending more of his morning at Bev's.

This morning, Eloise was by herself and had decided to give the basement a spring cleaning. She managed to pull the washer and dryer away from the wall. It was disgusting. Dirt, hair, lint, dead bugs, and other unidentifiable lumpy black bits were piled up in the space, even a sock, which was hilarious as no human laundry got done in the basement to her knowledge. Eloise attacked the mess with a vengeance. She had nearly finished, her smock wearing the evidence of the battle, when Janet buzzed her.

When Eloise made it upstairs, the waiting room was empty and Janet and Suzy were shooting the breeze, laughing at something together.

Suzy said, "Good Grief, Eloise what have you been doing?"

"Working. And you?"

Janet guffawed. "Doc's here. Told me to send you up to his office."

Eloise said, "Thanks!"

Eloise was smiling as she turned around. What had gotten into her? She had been quick with her comeback, without even trying, and maybe she had even delivered it with a bit of swagger. She realized it was because she knew her worth. Perhaps the basement chores did not require a lot of skill, but they were necessary for the place to function. And she was proud of herself for taking the initiative and rolling up her sleeves.

When Eloise saw Doc at his desk, whatever remnant of a smile disappeared.

Doc stood up and came around the desk and held the back of his cursed rolling chair as if Eloise might repeat her head banging performance.

He said, "Sit."

The small gesture filled her with shame. But she sat, obediently.

Doc didn't mince words. "Bev passed this morning."

Eloise shrieked. Then covered her mouth. They would hear her downstairs. That's the first coherent thought she had. Her second thought was that she was damned glad Doc had made her sit, because even sitting she felt made of rubber. The tears began to flow down her cheeks.

Doc pushed a box of tissues toward her, and she helped herself.

"Old gal went in her sleep. Rosie found her, surrounded by her cats. Not a bad way to go. Rosie said the lights were all off, TV was off, and Bev just looked like she was having a good sleep."

Eloise blew her nose. She was crying, but not for Bev. She was crying for herself. She heard Louisa's voice in her head, she had lost the coin toss, again.

She said, "Bev was eighty-six. But I just found her. She lived right there all this time, since before I was born, but I just found her."

Doc said, "Good God Eloise, aren't we lucky we did? Unbelievable how much my life just changed on a dime. Because of Bev, because of you too. Life's like that. Bev might be gone, but she is utterly unforgettable."

Eloise nodded, blew her nose, and asked, "Everyone was there this morning?"

"Not everyone. You were here."

Eloise said, "Bev seemed fine last night. She watched me school over a course Miguel had set for me in the outdoor."

"Then she had just the kind of last day on earth she would have wanted. Yesterday, Caroline and I had a good morning with her too. She was full of piss-and-vinegar as usual. But you were the last person to get to spend time with her. Lucky, lucky you."

Eloise put her head down on the desk and cried into the crook of her elbow, so Doc didn't have to watch her face scrunch up into a red ball. Doc was right. Bev had lived her last days well. She was at home, still able to set a jump pole and shout wisecracks at Eloise. And she had eaten her dinner, watched TV, and then fallen asleep with her cats. But Eloise had just had her last afternoon with Bev. There would be no more. That story, the story of Bev and Eloise, well it was over. So, Eloise wept for her loss, not for the end of a life, well lived, on her own terms at that, of the loud, coarse, opinionated eighty-six-year-old Bev. Eloise cried for her loss, and the loss for the horses, the farm, Miguel, Rosie, Caroline, and Doc, who would all have to continue without Bev.

Eloise wiped her eyes, blew her nose, and asked, "What happens now?"

Doc said, "It's a good thing Bev hired Ralph, since he found Bev a lawyer who got her affairs in order. Bev had just told Caroline she was now 'good-to-go' and that she had left the farm to her. It's strange, isn't it? But it made perfect sense to Caroline."

* * *

Eloise passed the front desk holding Lady Jane in her arms.

Janet said, "Oh my God, Eloise. Did someone die?"

Eloise nodded, "Bev."

Janet's face went slack, "Wow. So sorry. I know you must be crushed. Doc too."

Even though Eloise had always thought Janet didn't particularly like her, she could tell that at this moment her condolences were genuine.

Eloise was strangely moved. She managed to say thank you. And then, as per Doc's request, she gathered her things, and put LJ back into her Sherpa bag.

Both Janet and Suzy were in the waiting room as Eloise headed for the door. Janet was no longer behind the counter but leaning against it. Janet put a hand on Eloise's forearm for a moment, saying, "I'm so sorry."

Then Suzy added, "Hey, condolences. Really sorry, Eloise. Was she a close friend of the family?"

Eloise thought for a moment, and then said, "I have an old photo album with photos of Bev with my parents, dancing at the hunt ball and flying over jumps. So, yeah, although until recently, I did not know it. She was, once-upon-a-time, very close to both my parents. And being with her was, in an odd way, a way to reconnect to my mom and dad. And, now losing her, well, it does feel like losing a member of the family. A long-lost member of the family."

Eloise was surprised at herself for the second time that day. She had never spoken to Janet or Suzy so honestly, right from the heart, about feelings she did not know she had, but owned them none-the-less. She wasn't looking for sympathy. She did not feel pitiful. She felt sad, but strong enough to realize she had been very lucky to have found Bev, regardless of the time being far too short.

* * *

Eloise owned a funeral dress. It was still hanging upstairs in her closet, her mother having purchased it for her. Because her Mom had been a planner, down to the small detail of what her daughter would wear to her funeral. She had worn it that one time only. She fetched it from her old closet and hung it up in her mother's closet.

But this was a different funeral. Little would be required of her at this one. Still, she sat on the closet floor, paralyzed. This funeral forced her to think of the other funeral. She had screwed things up, behaved terribly. She had told so many lies. She had spun a spider's web and then proceeded to get herself tangled up in it. It was a memory she hoped to repress forever. But here it was, trotting itself out for review, regret, shame. It had been the end of Lulu Robertson. The end of her relationship with her father. Or so she had once decided. But she had learned that blind bolts and digging a hole to hide in was not a good long-term plan.

Eloise looked again at the black dress hanging there. Here it was, springtime in Atlanta, and black was so dark. Yes, yes it was. Black was dark. What insight!

She needed to go to Bev's funeral. Eloise got off the floor and pulled out a skinny tan skirt, that had a thin black belt, a black blouse and rummaged around for stockings. All of it her mother's. She put the whole ensemble on. It looked okay. She could wear her mother's camel cashmere dress coat; it would feel and look good. Eloise pinned her hair up into a chignon with a tortoise shell butterfly clip. But of course, she would need to wear dress shoes. That meant once again negotiating heels. Her mother had plenty to choose from, some tan like the skirt, some black, and even a pair that were black and tan. Eloise chose those. Eloise had neglected to put on jewelry or make up, but it was too late. She had the presence of mind to throw a stack of tissues into her tote before leaving, pushing LJ away from the door with one pointy-toed pump as she exited.

Just turning into the parking lot of the place made her anxious. Eloise took a few deep breaths and walked in. She hung her mother's cashmere coat next to a larger version on the rack in the lobby. She brushed her hand against the strange coat, so soft. She resisted an odd urge to lift a sleeve to her nose. An older gentleman directed her to Bev's memorial service on the ground floor. He said, she could take the elevator or the stairs. Eloise felt remorse at being so late but smoothed her skirt, reminded herself to walk on the balls of her feet, and headed straight down the stairs.

Eloise looked down the stairs and saw a knot of people milling around the foyer, outside an open double door. She heard music. She was surprised to see Pinky and Buzz had come. Betsy too was there. Eloise was overcome with emotion. It swept over her like a wave. Eloise was feeling light-headed and reached for the railing, which was a good thing. The tall man standing next to Betsy, the one who had just turned around and started up the stairs toward her was a bizarrely, out-of-place, dark blue suited, tie wearing Dabs Carter. She wasn't sure how she did it, but she watched horrified as her mother's black and tan pump disappeared over the edge of the staircase, hitting the marble floor below with a "thunk." The next thing she knew she was enveloped in Dabs' arms.

She heard herself say, "What are you doing here?"

Which made them both smile as it was exactly what

Louisa Roberts had asked Major Schmidt when he had come to her rescue during Tarleton's raid.

"That's not an original line, Eloise.

"You look so different. So out of character, you in a suit."

He whispered, "Eloise, I was an attorney in DC, remember? But I can say the same for you, Eloise. You look quite sophisticated. Even wearing only one shoe."

Eloise said, "How did you get here?"

"I drove. Here, sit down on the stairs for a minute. You literally just fell into my arms. Which I admit, I did enjoy."

Eloise sat.

Dabs said, "Betsy gave me the news. Sorry to surprise you. I was afraid if I asked, you would say not to come. Easier to ask forgiveness than permission, right?"

Dabs had taken her hand as she sat down, and she found herself staring at his knuckles, studying the shape of his hands, feeling the roughness of his palm, her heart pounding, her stomach had gone squishy. She fought the impulse to kiss him. Heck this was a public place and a funeral. So inappropriate all of it. She had been feeling better about herself, but this was not okay. But Dabs had come all this way for her. And his physical presence here where it was so unexpected, well, it was lovely, and it was powerful. But she needed to get a grip.

Pinky appeared with the shoe in her hand. "Here Dabs, do the Prince Charming thing with the slipper."

And Dabs quietly did just that, holding the shoe while Eloise smashed her toes into the pointy end and then used her index finger to pop her heel in. Pinky was excitedly saying something so odd that Eloise couldn't make sense of it. She was frowning at Pinky, confused.

Pinky repeated herself, "You're a fainting goat. It all makes sense now. Eloise you're not actually a klutz. I mean, I've seen you on a horse. Well, okay, you fell off the horse too, so scratch that. But yeah, you are a fainting goat. That's it!"

Eloise got to her feet, Dabs supporting her by her elbow. She looked at Pinky, smoothed her skirt and said, "I'm pretty sure I'm not a goat."

Pinky and Dabs and Eloise got down into the foyer, someone appeared from inside the room to suggest they take their seats. Pinky staged whispered to Eloise, "Fainting goats are this weird kind of goat that if they have a shock, stress, or get startled, they just fall over, like 'boom!' Over they go."

They took their seats. Eloise saw Doc and Caroline in the front row. Ralph was there too. Miguel and Rosie too.

Dabs leaned over and whispered, "Pinky does have a point about fainting. Very Victorian, Eloise. But in those days, it was likely overtightened corsets. Pinky, I know nothing about goats, but might you mean the Vasovagal reflex?"

"Maybe. Looks like a fainting-goat-reflex to me."

Eloise focused on the music and the front of the chapel. She tried not to think about goats, fainting, or anything else.

There was an urn surrounded by flowers at the front

of the chapel. Three large photos stood on easels behind the urn. One was Bev jumping an enormous puissance wall. One was her sitting on a fence, smiling over her shoulder at the camera, while a group lesson of horses and riders in soft focus worked in the arena. And one that Eloise recognized as having come from the album Bev had given her, was Bev in formalwear, dancing at a Hunt ball, grinning widely.

A minister read bible passages, led them in prayer, and a hymn, and after a few remarks, introduced Caroline.

Caroline was the only speaker. She told a story but of course, only part of the story of Bev. The full story was left untold. Not what Bev endured as a kid, not the things she had done that she was not proud of. As Tolkien had written, the most moving part of Bev's story would remain untold.

Caroline said," Bev used to say Miss Annie had kept her from ending up in prison or worse. And she meant it. Well, Annie may have saved Bev, but Bev paid it forward, not just to me but to others too."

"Bev was a high school drop-out, but smart as hell, cagey, witty, tough, quick with a come-back, and suffered no fools. But the exterior was nothing more than defensive armor. Bev loved the horses, adored her cats, and mentored untold horsemen, instilling good technical skills, but also standards and a code of honor. She taught resilience and courage and to give a hand to those who needed it. She loved to jump the big jumps and the thrill of a gallop. Bev was fearless.

When I met Bev, I was a troubled teen. Bev told me I needed to come work for her, finish my high school classes and start riding the jumpers. I was to bring my stuff and move in. Not sure how she sold my folks on the plan, but she did. She wasn't easy to work for. God, she was demanding. She never negotiated. You did what she said, and you did it right away without question. If she didn't like the result, you did it over until she did. Her praise was sparse, but every nod of approval meant the world to me. She made me go to a local college. I had to show her every test, and every paper. If it was a B, she wanted to know why it wasn't an A. After a while, she started letting me compete the good horses, even convinced clients to put me on instead of her. Boy, did she have the horses and the know-how. Sometimes I was scared. I'm not fearless like Bev, but, if Bev said I could do it, I did it. I still don't know how I jumped some of those huge fences, or how I managed to get an A in statistics.

I fought Bev tooth-and-nail when she made me get a "real" job. I felt like she had fired me. But she had her reasons. I met my husband at that job. Horses took a backseat for a while. Bev said I'd come back to it. She was right. Bev saw me through some incredible highs, some very deep lows. There were times that I thought I couldn't go on. But Bev always said, "Girl, you just got to get up, dust that dirt off your britches, and have another go."

Caroline turned a moment to look at the photos, turned back and cleared her throat. "I have, I will, Bev."

Caroline had to compose herself before she could continue.

"Bev did live to see me have another go, she gave me the push forward, again, in her classic Bev style, and for that bit of mercy, I am grateful."

Caroline was looking directly at Doc, and Doc directly at her.

Caroline's words, the line about a 'bit of mercy' settled into a deep place in Eloise's mind and heart. Eloise felt it applied directly to her. And maybe to everyone. And if you could honestly show mercy to others, then maybe you also earned it in return. But who deserves it? Does it have to be deserved? And maybe the real challenge is to feel deserving. These thoughts came in a jumble, unclear, but teetering on an insight she felt she badly needed.

When the service was over, Pinky invited Eloise along with Betsy and Dabs, back to her place. Buzz had gone to pick up pizza. It would be a low key, paper plate kind of thing, but a chance to relax and toast the memory of Bev and a chance for Buzz to get to know Dabs.

Eloise had cried during the service and had a headache. She and Pinky spent a few minutes in the foyer again with the others who had come, most of whom Eloise did not know. She chatted with Miguel and Rosie, and then Caroline and Doc, who now stood at her elbow. Caroline made a point to tell Eloise that she was counting on her to come ride Red as usual. Then she added "no excuses."

They arrived at Pinky's to a chorus of excited barks from Ying and Yang. Eloise realized she still had no idea which was Ying, and which was Yang.

Soon, Pinky had her seated on the sofa with a glass of wine. Eloise took her first sip and nodded at Pinky.

"You like it?"

Eloise said, "Very much."

"The bottle from Ralph. Man knows his wine."

A knock on the door sent the puffballs back into a barking and screeching fit. Pinky stood up and pointed her finger at Eloise saying, "Sit and stay!"

Eloise giggled and said to Pinky's back, "That's not an original line."

As Pinky came around the sofa she said, "At least today you don't have that metal clip stuck on the top of your head."

Eloise realized this was her chance, her chance to quietly retrieve at long last, the clip!

Pinky opened the door and greeted Betsy and Dabs. Eloise shoved her hand down between the cushion and the back of the sofa and started to probe for the clip. Eureka! She pulled it out, and tightly palmed it.

Pinky took her guests coats and invited them to come into the living room and sit.

Buzz came in from the kitchen, wiping his hands on a dishtowel and greeting them enthusiastically. He grasped Dabs by the hand and said, "Man, you came down for this, for Eloise. That was good of you." Then, "Sit my friends, sit. I'm bringing you wine and an antipasto platter.

Buzz left the room and Pinky came and sat back down on the sofa, gesturing her guests to the club chairs.

Betsy said, "Pinky, I'm not sure how Marilyn and I will manage without you. I mean it's because of you she doesn't get hairballs and stays so, um, clean."

Betsy finished her sentence with a concerned look on her face. She said, "Oh dear. Did I let the proverbial cat out of the bag?"

There was an uncomfortable pause, then she added with narrowed eyes at Pinky, "You were supposed to tell Eloise."

Dabs stood up, and said, "Betsy, let's go keep Buzz company in the kitchen."

Eloise was staring at Pinky, the metal hair clip digging into her palm as she gripped it tightly. She managed to croak out pitifully, "You're leaving?" And felt her sinuses instantly clog back up.

Pinky said, "Wow, you look pale. Hey, on the bright side, you're sitting down so you can't do that fainting-goat thing."

Then she said, "Hold on with the tears a sec, at least here I can do better than a roll of TP."

Pinky got back up and came back with a box of tissues. Eloise did need to blow her nose and wipe away her tears.

Pinky said, "I was supposed to find a quiet moment to tell you. My bad that I hadn't done it yet."

Eloise blurted out with emotion, "You're my best friend. The best friend I've ever had. And you're leaving?"

Pinky grinned, "You're my best friend too, Eloise.

But geeze, I sure had to work damn hard for it, didn't I? But I love you too. I mean that. Not that you aren't a piece-of-work but then, so am I."

Pinky paused and then added "But hey, as much as I love you and Doc and grooming dirty dogs, Buzz got this incredible offer in Savannah. We may be living the 'American Dream' if things work out."

Eloise wiped her eyes again, "I'm happy for you two, it's just that everything seems to be going to shit for me. It's going to be so lonely down in the basement."

Pinky tipped her head, "Basement? I don't think so."

Eloise loudly blew her nose, feeling confused.

Pinky said, "Doc and I, we always like to see our rescues come out of their shells and blossom. We both get a charge out of that. That's how Doc and I became such good friends. He and I, we talk about how it's hard to know what you've got at first. We've seen some amazing turnarounds. Some have been living rough and are kind of shut down. Some take a little more attention than others. But the goal is always the same, to help them find forever-homes. Y'know?"

Eloise felt flushed. "I was a rescue?"

"Doc and I thought you were smart and funny but shut down. Like some of our rescues. Doc and I decided to try and give you a little extra attention. That's all. Betsy too was into you as soon as you two started talking books. But none of us had a clue what we were getting ourselves into. Then Prince showed up. 'Plot-twist!' He made things, um, interesting to say the least. But, I mean, when you kissed Joe? And had hidden the flier in your backpack? Sure didn't see that coming. You weren't just into delusions. You had this devious streak. Who knew?"

Eloise said, "Devious? And what? You know about plot twists?"

"I might have stolen that plot-twist thing from Betsy. Hey, I might get bored without you around. And Savannah is God-awful hot in the summertime, so don't think you can be shed of me forever. I'll keep showing up like a bad penny. But you don't need me and Doc and Betsy anymore to give you extra attention, although I expect they'll find ways to keep a foot in the door, too."

Eloise was still feeling flushed and confused.

Pinky said, "Don't waste that good wine. Drink up and dry your tears. I mean, how long do Betsy and Dabs have to hide in the kitchen?"

Eloise did dry her tears and drink her wine. She had to gather her thoughts a moment. Then she said, "I don't know how to thank you. You and Doc, Betsy, Ralph, and Dabs."

Pinky said, "It's been a hell-of-a-ride, the kind that makes it all worthwhile. I'll miss our time together in that basement, but I know you are going to be fine. Better than fine."

Eloise found herself reaching toward Pinky with her still balled-up fist.

"Whatcha' got there, Eloise?"

Eloise opened her fist, dropping the hair clip into Pinky's palm, just as Buzz walked in to say, "Dinner is served."

Pinky looked down at the hairclip, clearly recognized it, and laughed.

Eloise said, "Master had given Dobby a hair-clip, Dobby is freeeeeeee!"

Pinky shook her head, "What the hell?"

Buzz said, "Harry Potter!"

Pinky said, "You 'all know I don't read that stuff!"

Buzz looking exasperated said, "We watched all the movies, Pinky."

Pinky said, "We did?"

Buzz added, "Well, I take that back. I watched, and you fell asleep."

Eloise broke in, "The point is just that you're right, Pinky. I love you and will miss you terribly, but I'll be okay. I release you."

25

When Dabs and Eloise got to the barn the next morning, Doc was at the mounting block in front of the barn getting on Jethro, and Caroline was sitting on Chick.

Doc said, "There you are. There are donuts and coffee in the tack room. Help yourself."

Dabs said, "Thanks Doc."

Doc and Caroline rode out of the barnyard, side-by-side, chatting amiably.

Dabs said, "Makes me miss Dude. But c'mon, show me this red mare I've heard so much about."

Miguel was raking the barn aisle, having finished the morning chores.

Eloise asked, "You okay?"

Miguel nodded, "Going to miss the old lady, but me and Rosie are staying up at the house, looking after the place like she wanted."

Miguel put his pile in the wheelbarrow and with a nod goodbye, rolled it out the back of the barn to park it in the shavings shed.

Eloise and Dabs watched Miguel make his way down the aisle. Eloise said, "What happens now, Dabs?"

Dabs answered softly, "Whatever happens, it isn't up to us, is it?"

Eloise sighed. Things kept happening that were not up to her. That was true.

Red was hanging her head out into the aisle having heard their voices. She was bobbing her head up and down, eager to get out of the stall.

Eloise wrestled her into her halter, pushing on her chest to make her back up before she allowed the mare to come out.

Dabs said, "She's pretty. And I can see she's bright-eyed and bushy-tailed."

"Bev would say, 'full of piss-and-vinegar.'"

Once they got Red in the crossties, Dabs and Eloise grabbed a donut and a coffee. Eloise ate her donut quickly while Red fidgeted. She washed it down with a couple swigs of coffee. Then she grabbed a hoof pick and began her grooming routine. Dabs stood back and watched, eating, and drinking at a more leisurely speed.

Once Eloise got Red groomed and tacked up, she and Dabs walked the mare out to the outdoor arena with a longe line clipped to her bit ring. The air had a magical soft feel, so typical of Atlanta in the springtime. But Red seemed unaffected by the mellowness of the weather. She was agitated.

Dabs watched as Eloise followed the routine that Bev had demonstrated, of unbuckling the reins and tying them around the girth, and then sending Red out on the end of the longe line to warm up.

Dabs said, "You know, I have some nice leather side reins for longing I'd be happy to give you."

"Bev. She kept it simple. I don't mind doing it her way. But thanks, Dabs."

Red had no interest in paying the least bit of attention to Eloise. The mare demonstrated her athleticism, leaping through the air and kicking up her heels and whinnying loudly. Doc and Caroline came strolling into the arena, stopping to watch.

Caroline watched Red flag her tail and bounce around the longing circle and said, "Better you than me Eloise. Better you than me."

Doc and Caroline dismounted and led their horses to the barn. Red began to settle. Eloise felt like it was safe to get on. Dabs held Red while she mounted, and then sat on the mounting block to watch her ride.

At some point, Eloise noticed that Dabs had gotten up, and moved to the fence, where he and Doc were chatting. She found the sight freeing. Dabs and Doc were focused on each other. She left them to themselves. She felt herself internally relax and focus on Red. She let all the other worries and anxieties recede. Bev's voice rode with her, and the two of them carried on a quiet discussion in the background, connecting riding theory to the moving creature beneath her.

What was the purpose of developing lateral suppleness? Bend and stretch, instead of break. To become supple takes slow work. In the process of training, one develops strength along with suppleness, which leads to balance. Suppleness is built over time. It was protective.

433

It could not be forced. A worthy goal, never fully mastered.

The thing was, training horses, well it applied to humans too. It applied to Eloise. She needed to bend and not break, to be strong, and balanced. She had not realized she lacked mental and emotional suppleness, not until she had felt herself break. And the process to become supple? It was a process. It could not be forced. And its accomplishment could not be known until it was tested. And life continued to provide her with a multitude of tests, and the tests were not optional.

Doc and Dabs were full of compliments after Eloise finished. Red was no longer anxious or agitated but stood quietly with an open soft eye. They were being kind, but also, Red was wonderful. And riding was wonderful.

Doc invited them to join them for lunch in town, but Dabs declined. He had to get back to Ivy Creek, to the old house, the old horses, and a boisterous big black shaggy dog.

He was going home. And Eloise felt her heart break a little bit.

* * *

Eloise had finished mopping the floors, the dogs and cats were fed, and the only sound in the clinic was the coffee maker making a few burps as it finished brewing.

Pinky hadn't moved yet, but today was the day she was going to start packing. Pinky had worked her last day, gathered up her clippers and beauty supplies, but would be back for a going-away lunch at the clinic. Eloise would now be on her own in the basement. Eloise plopped down on the old brown sofa with her mug of coffee.

Doc arrived, and with him donuts still hot from the fryer.

Doc looked different. Or maybe it was just her imagination. But no. Doc had lost some weight. That was it. She couldn't think of a way to pay him a compliment without it coming out awkwardly.

He offered, "Nice and hot." And handed Eloise a donut wrapped in a napkin. She managed to thank Doc between bites of donut and sips of coffee.

Doc said, "I've got the new groomer and her daughter arriving any minute. I thought you could show them the routine.

Eloise was strangely disappointed that Pinky was being replaced so quickly.

Doc continued, 'Our slow spell is a good time for Brenda and Dolly to get used to the routines. By the way, Brenda's daughter, Dolly, is on the autism spectrum. Dolly has trouble with her interpersonal skills, but I'm told does very well with animals. I thought you could take the week to train her on kennels and see if she can manage. I think after a week we'll know if she can do your job."

Eloise stopped chewing her donut, her mouth gone dry. She set the remnant of donut down and had to take a couple sips of coffee so she wouldn't choke.

Doc wrinkled his brow and folded his arms across his chest as he said, "That kennel job has been a lifesaver over the years for a lot of people. I've had recovering addicts, people on probation, soldiers right out of active duty, and assorted others needing a temporary change of pace. But you do realize I hope, that for most folks, a kennel job is not a permanent career choice."

Eloise managed to say in a low breathy sort of tone, "You're firing me?"

Doc shook his head and smiled. "No. Never. I'm not firing you, Eloise. You're being promoted."

Eloise frowned, "To what?"

Doc smiled and nodded, "When you tell me, then we'll both know."

There was a knock on the front door.

Doc unfolded his arms, and said, "I'll unlock the front door and show them in." then turned in the doorway to say to Eloise. "I'm sure you will make Brenda and Dolly feel welcome, offer them coffee and donuts and chat them up before you go down to the kennels."

Eloise realized that at some level she already knew this was coming and found that she was not upset. She realized Pinky had already tried to tell her. At least she would not be down in the basement by herself. But beyond that thought a fog descended.

* * *

It was lunchtime before Eloise noticed she had a voice mail on her phone.

"This is Mr. Jameson's office. Mr. Jameson has asked if you can please stop by the bank today. He said it wouldn't take but a few minutes of your time as he simply needs your signature."

At first Eloise drew a blank. Mr. Jameson? Ralph. Gosh. What now? Eloise hoped Ralph was not going to keep her long, because the traffic out to ride Red would be brutal if she got delayed.

Eloise left work early, and she was grateful to be immediately ushered back to Ralph's office, where he directed her to a seat and pushed a dish of jellybeans toward her.

He said, "You must try these sour lemon flavor. They're in honor of Bev, sour as hell on the outside, sweet on the inside."

Eloise couldn't help but grin. She and Ralph each grabbed a handful of jellybeans and raised them in the air, as if making a toast. Eloise put her entire handful in her mouth. They were so sour her eyes teared up, but as she chewed, they turned sweet.

Ralph opened a file and slid it across the table to Eloise. He said, "Congratulations. You're a horse owner."

For the second time that day, Eloise felt like she might choke. Ralph let loose a barrage of titters. His high-pitched giggles sounded deranged as he handed her a bottle of water.

He said, "I've been wondering what you would do when I told you. Both Pinky and Doc were adamant that you be sitting down for the news. Oh, the expression on your face. Priceless. Go on, read it to me."

Inside the folder was a bill of sale, along with Jockey Club papers for "Whippersnapper Red" a Chestnut filly by the stallion "Whipper."

"Whippersnapper Red?"

He tittered again, "I believe Bev called her the Red Devil, but she did say it was the horse you've been riding. Bev signed over all the papers and left them with me along with that signed bill of sale. I loaned you the dollar by the way. Just sign where I stuck those red arrows. I'll make copies to file, and we're done."

Eloise signed the papers in a state of shock, handing them back to Ralph to copy. She asked, "Caroline knows?"

"Of course. Bev told Caroline everything. Now, go ride your horse before you get stuck in traffic."

Eloise rose from her chair, her mind a blank. When she got to the door she turned. She simply said, "Ralph."

He tittered again in reply.

She said, "I don't know how to thank you. You've done so much for me. And you can't know how much I needed this today. Thank you."

Eloise walked out to her car on a cloud. She needed to share all her news with someone. Well, everyone. Who should she call first? Her inner voice nearly shouted at her. Of course, it needed to be Dabs. Dabs. She would call Dabs. She was a horse owner again, of a red mare named Whippersnapper. She'd gone from Whiplash to Whippersnapper. Pinky was going to love that detail.

* * *

Eloise found Dolly sweet but incredibly shy. Dolly did not make eye-contact. Dolly hunched her shoulders and looked at the ground. Dolly spoke so softly that she was hard to hear.

But when Eloise watched Dolly interact with the animals, she saw a different person. Dolly relaxed, she chattered, she smiled.

Eloise found a quiet time working alongside Dolly to say, "Dolly, you're doing great, and I wanted you to know that this is an important job. Everything that happens here depends on you. You're central to the whole operation. Don't let anyone ever make you feel any less important because the job doesn't require a degree of some kind."

Dolly had kept her eyes on the floor but nodded.

Eloise went on, "And you clearly have a gift with animals. That's not something anyone can learn in school. You matter to each animal that comes here. I want you to be as proud of this job as I was."

Dolly picked up her head, but only made fleeting eye contact, but nodded, and whispered, "It's a dream-job."

Eloise wanted to hug her but knew that would be just too much for Dolly.

Eloise knew the animals in the kennels and cattery, the floors, the trash cans, the exam rooms, the laundry, and the morning coffee, well, they would somehow be fine without Eloise Robertson.

Pinky had been trying to tell Eloise. Doc of course

was required to be more explicit. Now Eloise knew in her heart they were right. It was time to go.

Pinky's farewell party at the clinic became a joint farewell party. Betsy came. Ralph stopped by. Doc had lunch brought in, cake and cards, hugs, and best wishes, to give Pinky and Eloise a fine send-off. Pinky had to leave the gathering early to meet the movers. Buzz was already in Savannah. As were the puffballs. At least Pinky knew where she was headed.

As everyone else went back to work, Eloise took off her smock, and tossed it into the laundry bin. It would not be Eloise who washed it or put it on tomorrow. Eloise was free. And although Eloise had no "promotion" yet to share with Doc, she did have something to look forward to.

Dabs had offered. Come for a visit. Bring the horse, bring the cat. Stay in Louisa's room. She had said "yes," because Bev's voice in her head said, "Girly, you ought to consider saying yes more often." So, Eloise had said yes, and had been excited to say yes.

And that is how she came to be sitting on a hay bale at the end of Bev's barn aisle, waiting for Dabs. She had packed her car with more than a backpack this time, in fact it was stuffed with stuff including Red's tack and supplies.

Miguel had set out three bales of hay, and two bags of feed. Red was booted, blanketed, bandaged, wearing a head bumper, waiting in her stall, pacing and anxious, as she knew this was no ordinary day, padded up in protective travel gear.

Eloise had no way to explain to Red, that so much had changed. But Red knew it.

Miguel had left the gate open for Dabs. So, the old diesel horse van made no stop as it loudly rolled up the driveway. Prince hung his head out of the passenger window, barking crazily. Dabs had hired a guy to help with the drive, and Eloise felt for him, having to share the bench seat with Prince. The poor guy had his hands over his ears while Prince barked and shrieked in excitement.

Dabs pulled up to the barn, cut the engine, and opened his door. Prince made a flying leap out the door, nearly knocking Eloise down. Then Prince tore down the barn aisle, then up Bev's driveway, then back to Eloise.

He looked right into her eyes as she told Prince in serious tones, "She's gone. I'm sorry." And although the words sounded silly, spoken to a dog, Eloise felt sure the dog understood. Because, hey, this was Prince.

He stared at her for a long moment after her words, his tail drooping, his body frozen, processing. And then he leaned up against her, sat down on her feet, and let Eloise rest her hand on top of his head. Condolences given; condolences received. He broke away again to roam, take in the smells and stretch his legs.

There was little time to greet Dabs or his co-pilot as both men made a beeline for the bathroom.

Eloise then had time to look over the old horse van. Dabs had assured her it had a rebuilt engine, new tires, and was still a solid citizen. It used to be his mother's. For years his hunt friends had used it twice a week during hunting season. It would be a roomy ride for Red, if a lonely one. She could have a double stall.

Dabs had hired a driver to share the burden since the van was a muscular and tiring drive. The trip had to be a turnaround to get his driver back home. Eloise would need to follow with LJ in the Sherpa bag and Prince in her back seat. The process was business-like and efficiently done. Seeing Dabs, feeling herself inwardly excited, yet outwardly mechanical, well it was awkward and unsettling. They only exchanged a brief hug.

An hour later, they were on the road. Eloise questioning herself. What did she want? What was her 'promotion' going to be? She thought of Henry saying she 'didn't need anyone's permission.' And yet she was not ready to kick into a gallop. Because there was still stuff, stuff that refused to be repressed. But she wasn't going to let herself break. No more stories, no more bolting, no more hiding away.

Lady Jane was protesting loudly in her bag which was not nearly as roomy as it used to be. Eloise had put a harness on LJ (which the cat hated) and packed a leash for LJ's potty breaks. The thought of LJ getting away from her at a gas station had haunted her dreams. And then there was Red. Eloise felt sure Red was nervous and unsure as she rode alone in the horse van, and she worried about the horse having a panic attack and injuring herself. Red had looked like she was heading into battle when Eloise had loaded her onto the van, she had her so covered in padding.

But at some point, a few hours and a gas station break later, Eloise had begun to relax. She was headed to Ivy Creek Plantation with her very own horse! The cat had given up crying. She and Dabs had taken the cat and the dog on leashes to a vacant lot next to the gas station to relieve themselves. Eloise was given a boost into the van from Dabs, via the "grooms door" to check on Red. Red let Eloise remove her blanket which had grown too warm, and she even took an apple from her hand. When Eloise offered her water, Red used her nose to splash water all down Eloise's front, even though she did not take a sip. All very saucy. Red was fine.

Eloise, stiff and tired, at last bumped down the rutted and pot-holed drive to Ivy Creek. Red tip-toed down the ramp like a lady in stilettos, just as Miguel had taught her to do. The old boys in the barn greeted Red loudly with enthusiasm as she was led in.

Dabs had deeply bedded the stall. Red made sure to both empty her bladder, and roll, flopping all the way over twice, before taking a good, long, drink of water. All was well.

Dabs stood by her side to watch, and had reached for her hand, and Eloise had taken it, and all the distance she had felt back in Atlanta disappeared in an instant. This was where she was meant to be. This odd, formal, older guy was who she was meant to be with. But not yet. The problem was hers to solve, to her own satisfaction. No one else's. Dabs didn't know her really. Not the way he needed to, had to. How was Eloise going to get from where she was to where she wanted to be? Because she was going to make that leap. She just wasn't sure when or how. Even that small commitment sent a thrill through her, right down to her solar-plexus. But it did not make her feel dizzy.

* * *

It touched Eloise to see how busy Dabs had been preparing for her visit with Red. He had mowed the neglected mare field that ran next to the gelding pasture, checked all the fencing, and nailed down loose nails and boards. He had discovered a ground hog hole that needed filling and had hired "critter-getters" to "remove" the ground hog.

Eloise asked him to please not give her any of the details because she was sure the groundhog was not caught in a "have-a-heart" trap and relocated elsewhere. Dabs had nodded and only provided the pertinent bit of information; Red was in no danger of being injured by stepping in the hole.

The next morning after Red and the others had eaten, Dabs went to put the old horses out first as usual. But they weren't having it. The conga line went astray. Instead of heading out to the field, they reversed course with unusual vigor, and ganged up in a pile in the barn aisle outside of Red's stall. She squealed and kicked and spun circles in her stall, the noise level elevating to pandemonium levels, increased by Prince barking as he tried to redirect the geldings. The wise old things ignored him completely.

Dabs and Eloise were laughing so hard they had trouble sorting the situation.

Dabs finally found dusty halters and said, "Eloise, I'll grab these two old fools, if you can grab Dude."

Eloise threw a lead rope around Dude's neck, soon discovering the halter she was handed was not only too small, but the buckles were frozen. So, she pulled on the rope and clucked to him, and he reluctantly followed.

All three geldings made it into the field, but then scrummed around the gate, waiting. They weren't going anywhere. Red was a neurotic mess, screaming in the empty stable.

Dabs winked and said, "This is going well."

Eloise wasn't going to put Red out without first covering her in all the body armor she owned. Not the travel sort of armor, but the turn-out sort. Dabs held Red with a chain over her nose, while Eloise put on four bell boots to protect her shoes and her hooves and coronary bands, and then topped those with four fleece lined boots that padded her legs.

Dabs said, "Shall we say a prayer, and then give it a go?"

Dabs led the fire-breathing Red Devil out to her field. He turned her around to face him once inside the gate, digging a treat out of his pocket. Red was too distracted to care about a treat. So, he slowly unthreaded the chain lead shank and turned her loose. Red twirled and took off at a gallop, but a short lived one as she turned and galloped back to the three old geldings she had just snubbed.

Dabs and Eloise leaned against the gate and watched. All three old geldings arched their necks over the fence and puffed themselves up to look as big and impressive as possible.

Dabs said, "Look at those old fools sucking in their guts and flexing their biceps."

Eloise laughed, "Well, she is pretty."

Red touched her nose to each of their noses in turn, breathing deeply, then bellowed loudly, striking her front hoof in their general direction, sounding like a trumpeting elephant. She turned her tail toward them, then put her head down and began to graze.

Dabs said, "Ooh. Rejection. Sorry guys."

Her admirers still followed her on the other side of the fence, entranced.

Dabs said, "I think they're going to be okay. I mean, rejection stings, but it is survivable."

Eloise smiled. She said, "Give it time. They can still turn things around."

Eloise watched with Dabs for a few more minutes, before agreeing to go inside for breakfast.

* * *

Dabs could not ride too close to Eloise and Red without the mare pinning her ears at Dude. While Red did not want Dude too close, she also did not want him too far.

If he lagged, she would stop on the trail, and wait for him to catch up.

By the third day, Red had narrowed the zone, allowing Dude to ride close enough that Eloise and Dabs could converse.

Dabs said, "I have long dreamed of this."

"What?"

"Riding next to you here, at Ivy Creek, ala' Major Schmidt and Louisa, with Beast, I mean Prince, romping along the path with us. We only lack a young Henry for history to be perfectly replicated. It feels good, doesn't it? I almost expect to meet Jefferson coming the other way."

They crested a rise and noted that the fields below looked like velvet, with the new spring grass, and wondered aloud if Louisa and Jefferson had stood near this spot, admiring this same view. They then turned back toward home, and the horses waded into the creek, which was this day knee deep and icy cold. Prince plunged in, paddled across, and got out on the other side, shedding water with a vigorous shake. They stopped the horses midway and let them drink and splash, mindful not to linger and suffer the same fate as Henry.

Dabs took Eloise to visit "old" Henry again. They enjoyed cookies and tea and listened as Henry told stories from his youth, stories Dabs knew well, but Eloise did not.

Dabs cooked, and Eloise chopped things up. And they stayed up late reading aloud from Freddy's "scribbles" which were sometimes interesting, sometimes disturbing, sometimes cryptic, but always colorful, providing laugh-out-loud moments.

Freddy, as it turned out, was a great storyteller (when she didn't lose the thread along the way). Dabs felt that these writings, odd as they were, were his way to introduce his mother to Eloise. And Eloise, being no stranger to "odd," was a safe and non-judgmental ear. Eloise was clearly charmed by Freddy. Dabs was sure that Freddy would have loved Eloise and so would have his Dad, Dabney Carter.

But still, at the end of each evening, Eloise cradled her cat against her chest, wished Dabs a good night, and climbed the stairs to go to bed. She was still holding herself back, although a strangely pleasant ache, not the heartbreaking kind, but something entirely different, was growing along with her certainty that she did love Dabs and she did want him. It was desire. And she was allowed. It was only her own permission she was lacking. She only had to say, yes. And she needed to find a way to say it. Although she climbed the stairs slowly, questioning her hesitation, she knew the time was not now. Not yet. But soon.

She fully understood that Dabs and Prince, watching from below, were disappointed, both of them. But that would not be forever.

26

Dawn was breaking. Eloise had beat Dabs to the kitchen, and so had Prince. She started the coffee, then headed out to the barn with Prince to feed the crew. Red greeted her with a low whinny as Eloise flicked on the lights. Prince led the way to the feed room. All four buckets of feed had been mixed. It was a quick job to dump the feed, and let the crew eat. She and Dabs would turn out, clean stalls, and have another ride on what promised to be a glorious spring day.

But when Eloise and Prince went to drop Dude's feed, he was flat out on his side and did not rise. Eloise knew the sad truth in that moment, because of the unnatural stillness, no flick of an ear, and his form seemed made of wood. Dude was gone.

Eloise's head swam. Her knees buckled. She thought, "The last thing you need is to tip over like a fainting goat and whack your head again." Her next thought was, "Pinky was right. She was a fainting goat."

Eloise managed to sit down fully and lean over to take a few deep breaths. Prince leaned into her protectively.

A voice inside her head said, "How can I tell Dabs?" She forced herself to rise, and as she did, she saw that Dabs was coming toward her, concerned.

"Are you okay?"

Her voice quavered, "Dude."

Dabs pulled out his cellphone and hit a number, telling someone it was an emergency and then hung up. He opened the stall door and Eloise followed, the two of them kneeling next to the body of Dude. Dabs was feeling for a pulse between his jaw bones, then holding a shaking hand in front of the old horse's nostrils. Stretched out in the stall, Dude seemed to take up all the space. He had been a big horse. Dabs sat down, pulled his knees up and hugged them, dropping his head between sagging shoulders, and taking two long breaths. Prince wedged his big hairy muzzle beneath Dabs' arm, forcing Dabs to hug him close.

Dabs lifted his head, composed himself and said, "He was fine yesterday."

Eloise said, "We had a beautiful ride."

"I didn't think he would be the first to go."

Eloise said, "The stall looks undisturbed Dabs. Like he just got tired and went to sleep."

Then she added, "Just like Bev."

Dabs said, "We got him as a three-year-old. Twenty years he has been here. For me. And Dad. Dad rode him when I left home."

Eloise had never seen a vet arrive so quickly. Prince went loping out to greet the truck, with a single "woof." A wiry gray-haired man got out, distractedly patting

Prince on the head. Dabs did not rise, although Eloise did. The vet had a stethoscope hanging around his neck.

"You must be Eloise. I'm Dr. Finn. I live right around the corner. Glad Dabs caught me before I headed out."

He walked into the stall and exhaled in surprise, "Oh no, it's Dude." Then knelt and put the stethoscope ear pieces in his ear, and the disc behind the elbow of the prostrate form. The barn was still but for a strange buzzing Eloise could hear in her head. Dr. Finn's face crumpled for a moment, the veil of professionalism dropped, as he was overcome with emotion. He gathered himself together quickly and simply shook his head.

He pulled the stethoscope out of his ears and draped it around his neck, placing a hand on Dabs' shoulder said, "I'm so sorry Dabs. I thought this old boy would go on forever. He's been such a sound and healthy horse. I remember the day he arrived like it was yesterday."

Dabs stroked the neck of his horse, then each ear, then traced the length of his face. It was as if he was memorizing the contours. Then he rose stiffly. He had not cried, but Eloise wished he would because instead he appeared to be in shock.

Doctor Finn said, "I've buried more than one horse for your Mom. I know where to tell Randall to put him. Randall and I can take it from here Dabs. Old Randall is likely sitting at his breakfast table right now and can come on soon as he sops up his egg yolk with one of Gail's biscuits. You go on inside. Go into the parlor. Sit down. Get some hot coffee. I'll call when it's time for you to join us for last words."

Dabs drew in another deep breath and then nodded. Dabs and Prince started for the house, while Eloise gave her cell phone number to Dr. Finn.

Dr. Finn said, "Sure am glad you're here. Poor Dabs has lost so much. This old horse has been a Godsend. That dog too. You did a good thing finding Dabs that dog."

Eloise managed to nod.

Then he added, "To everything there is a season." And again, he repeated, "Sure am glad you're here."

Eloise nodded, then thought of Pinky and her woo-woo wisdom, felt the push of Louisa's hand, or maybe it was the Guardian Angel on the hillside, or the Cosmos, or God only knows what, but whatever, this was her sign. She was here for a reason at this very moment to bend but not to break, to be supple in her mind and to be brave. In short, to believe in love, and mercy, as corny as it sounded.

Eloise made her way to the kitchen and poured two mugs of coffee. Just as she had known that Dude was dead. She felt it in her bones, that what Dabs needed from her right now, this moment, was a return of what he had given her at Bev's funeral.

She would bear the outpouring of grief that she knew was coming. The old Eloise would run and hide. But not the Eloise of today. She needed to compose herself, gird her loins, take the moment of white space, margin, silence, to steal herself, find her courage. She leaned against the counter.

But then she heard Prince. He was coming to

fetch her. Like Beauty had fetched Sammie. She heard Prince's nails tapping against the hardwood floor in the grand hallway as he trotted into the kitchen, mouth open, panting, he threw his head over his shoulder back toward the hallway, and then spun around and went to rejoin Dabs.

Eloise heard Sammie's voice in her head say, "I gots to follow." And so she did, spilling coffee on the kitchen floor from her unsteady hands, unsteady gait. Just looking at Dabs sitting on the sofa sent a shiver of fear through her body. She was light-headed again. She put the mugs down on the coffee table and sat down on the other end of the sofa, Prince wedged between the sofa and the table.

"Drink the hot coffee Dabs. It will help with the shock."

Dabs managed to take a couple sips. Eloise noticed his nose was running. She said, "let me get you a tissue." She realized, that once again Pinky was right. There would be no box of tissues in this house. She walked into the bathroom in his bedroom and spun the roll of TP until she had a fistful and carried it back to Dabs, who noisily blew his nose.

Eloise did manage to say, "You're a good man, Dabs Carter."

Dabs frowned and said, "But not apparently good enough to be loved by you." Here it was. She could not run and hide. A feeling of shame swept over her. She was frozen, like the proverbial deer-in-headlights, and would just have to take the blows.

Dabs said, "You don't love me. Not enough. But I love you, and I have been stupidly hoping, investing everything I've got, thinking just by persistence and patience, some miracle, you'd realize that this is it, Eloise. We are meant to be together. Why is it obvious to everyone but you!"

Eloise heard her own voice, small and far away say, "That's not true Dabs, I do love you."

Dabs narrowed his eyes and said, "Don't feed me bullshit lines. Not today of all days. I'm tired, my heart is broken, and I don't think I can bear it."

Eloise said, "You know, your inscription in the journal?"

Dabs looked confused.

Eloise continued, "I do have an untold story no one knows about. Well, Pinky sort of has me figured out. I never told her, but she's wise to me. I didn't want to tell anyone, ever."

Dabs said, "Maybe it's time, Eloise, because I can't go on like this."

Eloise said, "It is time. It's kind of what I've been waiting for. The right time, I mean. I already confessed the lies I told about Prince, and all that foolishness that nearly cost me more than just the dog. But I didn't tell you about what I did before that. How I torched my relationship with Jock. It wasn't all his fault. Although, he's still an ass. I have plenty of reasons to still be angry with him."

Dabs only raised an eyebrow in a way that made Eloise think of Pinky and wish fervently that she was there.

Eloise continued, "Where to start? You know how my Mom was a planner? While I was denying she was terminal, she arranged everything for her death. She had picked out her dress, packed her makeup, down to a bottle of her favorite nail polish. The coffin. The marker. The music for the service."

Dabs waited. Eloise took a breath, then continued, "Jock should have come. They were divorced, but he should have come for me. To be there for me if not for my wonderful, beautiful mother who died far too young. We had a perfect family. They loved each other completely because they loved me completely. Jock loved me more than anything in the world. I could not accept anything less. At Bev's funeral, it brought it all back. What I had done. The anger. The insanity."

Dabs said, "Your point would be?"

"Oh Dabs, I'm a liar and a fraud. I really messed up."

"What did you do?"

"I told a story. A beautiful story. All make-believe. I bought the largest blanket of red roses I could find to drape over Mom's coffin. Put a card with Jock's name on it and a mushy line for everyone to read. I won't even repeat what I wrote. Mom's coffin looked like she had won the Kentucky Derby."

Dabs couldn't help himself, he smiled.

"She would have hated it. But no one questioned it. People said stuff like, 'Oh Lulu, how beautiful! Oh Lulu, what a touching tribute to their love. Oh, Lulu, oh, Lulu, all day long. But that's not all."

Eloise took a swig of coffee before continuing. "I

told everyone who would listen how Jock was pleading for me to come to Ireland. Pleading. I laid it on thick. He was sick with grief and so depressed he couldn't get out of bed to come to the funeral. I said I had become concerned. As soon as I could make it over, I would go. Jock needed me. I told everyone that Whiplash was ready to go Advanced and he had so many horses in training he had asked me to be his assistant trainer. We would be a team. It's like once I started digging myself a hole, I couldn't stop."

"What happened after?"

"I got my passport. I shut things down. I booked a flight. I was strangely excited. People came over to say goodbye. I told them all goodbye."

Dabs said, "You were just going to show up unannounced?"

Eloise grimaced, "Yes. But someone squealed. Of course, they did. People were really concerned about him after they had heard my lies. He was so angry. But I was angry too. I unloaded on him, telling him that he needed to follow through on the promises I had told people he had made. I tried to manipulate him into following through on the lies I had told. I was angry at him for a lot of different reasons. And it all came spilling out. I stayed with Mom. It should have been Jock. It had been too much for me. We should have loved each other, and supported each other after Mom's death, and instead we were horrible to each other. We said unforgivable things. But he was jealous that I had the money, the house, everything had been left to me. And he wasn't going to send my horse back to me either. It was the only thing he had gotten out of the business. My horse. He was right about one thing though, that Mom wanted me to finish college and make my own life away from horses, and away from him. That was no lie. I had wanted to be with him, though, to be his assistant trainer. By the end of the call, I agreed with Mom. I told him I never wanted to see him again."

Dabs looked sympathetic when he said, "You're right about digging a hole."

"Oh, I kept digging. I vowed never to call Jock "Dad" again. He had forfeited that right. I put on my pajamas, put down the garage door, and turned off the lights. I did not go outside for three weeks. I ugly cried. I did not bathe or brush my teeth. I ate stuff I had put into boxes to toss or donate, stuff like canned veggies and saltines. I slept too much or not at all. I never wanted to see anyone again who knew Lulu. I never wanted to explain why I was not in Ireland with Jock. So, I sent Lulu Robertson on to Ireland, to be with her loving Dad, reunited with Whiplash. Lulu Robertson was never coming back to Atlanta."

Dabs' expression was blank, "You still lived in Atlanta, you still had to in fact, make a new life for yourself right where you were."

Eloise said, "No one came looking for Lulu. No one checked up on me. It was surprising how easy it was to drop off the radar while never leaving. I finished my degree like Mom wanted. Then, on my way home from my last day of classes, I spotted one of those little yard signs outside the animal clinic that said, 'Kennel Help Wanted.' It felt like a safe place to be, to fill my days. But the thing is, lying gets easier and easier. Manipulating people, making things up on the fly, turns out, comes natural to me. I can't remember what I told Doc in the interview, but I'm pretty sure a bunch of it was baloney."

Dabs said, "Did it ever occur to you, though, that all that pretending was not going to be a long-term solution for your misery?"

"No. That took a very long time."

Dabs said, "You took the job. You joined Extreme Readers, you sought out the company of animals and people at the clinic. You were looking for connections. People are not meant to live alone. We are none of us loners. Not really."

Eloise said, "But to get close, people would figure me out and as it turned out, I cracked anyway. That's the real Eloise. Damaged goods. That Joe incident, man, I was crushed that Pinky and Bev and Doc saw how messed up I am, because you're right, I'm not a loner, I love those people."

"Eloise, your friends rallied to your side. No one abandoned you, crazy as you may be. You undersell others as well as yourself. And I have to say, I was more than encouraged that when you bolted, you bolted to me. You saw that we were alike you and me. Even then. You saw a glimmer of hope, of the possibility for us to be together, a way out because that kiss was no lie."

Eloise nodded, "Except you still didn't know about how much I have messed up. The lies, the lies."

"Dear God, Eloise, you can be so incredibly self-absorbed. I have lost my Dad, my Mom, my marriage, my career, and today my old horse. Stop fixating on your own craziness and losses for one day. Besides, if you think your crazy is going to scare me off, well, you underestimate me. I know crazy. I was nursed by crazy. You read those journals. Those are my people, crazy, and mean, and deeply flawed. But I love them too. Love yourself, crazy as you may be, and then see if you have space in your heart to love me too."

Eloise asked, "Can you really love me? I'm not good like Mom. I'm Jock."

Dabs laughed, "Even Jock isn't all bad. No one is perfect, and while I don't want to disparage your Mom, did it ever occur to you Eloise, that you were not in fact an "Oopsie.""

"What's that supposed to mean?"

"Just saying. You said your mom planned everything, and I'm impressed by how thorough she evidently was, and Jock doesn't strike me as eager to marry young, or careful either. Seems to me that in this case at least, your Mom's plan worked."

Eloise was amazed to realize; he probably wasn't wrong. It was quite possible that Elly had done a bit of planning and manipulation to get Jock to tie the knot. Wow. Bev had told her that Elly and Jock were a match, but suddenly that meant something new.

Dabs said, "It's not uncommon to be relentless in pursuit of what we want. Unless we get too discouraged and give up from sheer exhaustion. That's where I am today, Eloise. I'm exhausted. Aren't you tired too, Eloise?"

She was. Very.

Dabs patted the sofa next to him, and Eloise scooted closer. Dabs took her by the hands.

"People here know me since I was a boy. I came back home to help Mom but couldn't leave after her passing, because I had given up on pretty much everything. I've lost so much, but the one thing that I still loved was this old house. But I was still alone and lonely.

Then, I became obsessed with this smart, sexy, funny young woman I met online. I stared like a fool at one photo. Eloise Robertson was a history buff, a reader, loved animals and was an incredibly good rider. My God, I had even briefly seen her ride, had met her Mom, and caught her horse. It was like a sign from heaven. I knew she had also suffered loss. And then, more signs, confirmation, that Eloise Robertson belonged here, may even have a blood connection to not only this part of the country but this very house. I constructed my own fantasy, my own plan, that I could fill that barn out back with horses, this house with children, and dogs, yes more dogs. And I would love you madly, 'til death do us part.

But see, I too am not as successful in life as I am in my fantasies. I have, like you, bolted from my failures. I bolted here. I hid out. I made a new plan. And it had you in it. And now if it doesn't have you in it, I too will feel mortified having to tell everyone the truth. Eloise Robertson does not love me. But I do not want to manipulate you into anything. As painful as truth is, as humiliated as I will feel, I'm braced for the worst. So, tell me the truth, and I will face up to my humiliation, my failure, my grief. I must ask you again, and I'll take it as your final answer, I will submit to the truth. Do you love me?"

Eloise felt herself float up to the corner of the room. She looked down at those two beloved idiots, masters of self-deception, sitting close, but not close enough. She loved them both, like crazy-real, not crazy-delusional. For goodness sakes, this was a moment she could make someone else happy, and in that moment of giving happiness to someone else, make herself happy too. She could give herself permission. She needed to kick herself into a gallop and fly at that ditch. She felt her mother's blessings.

She mustn't screw this up. Ha. That's what she had told Jock.

Eloise found herself back in her own body as she leaned in and kissed Dabs on the lips. It was not a friendly kiss, it was a kiss where she leaned into him with her hands behind his neck. He was startled. She pulled away and said, "I want you Dabs Carter. You and I are one crazy screwed-up pair of people. But at least we both know how damaged we are. And we might as well be damaged goods together."

"So, you *do* love me?"

"I do. Bev said I should try to start saying 'yes' more. And man, I'm not sure what's going to happen Dabs if I stop saying no and start saying yes. But Pinky was right, you are incredibly hot."

Dabs grinned, "Pinky thinks I'm hot? I'll have to remember to thank Pinky. Even if I find the compliment rather embarrassing."

"Oh my God Dabs, you sound like such an old man sometimes."

Dabs said, "I plan to prove to you I am not."

Dabs pulled her into his lap and they kissed, kisses that grew in intensity.

Dabs said, "I have dreamed about taking you to bed, relentlessly. We could console ourselves in that release and its sweet oblivion."

Eloise whispered, "I may disappoint you there too."

Dabs laughed, "Practice makes perfect."

Eloise said, "When we marry, you have to promise to fix the fireplaces. It's always so damn cold in this house."

Dabs slid his hand around her waist and pressed her into him again, kissing her mouth, her ear, her neck, working his way down her chest. He said, "If that was a marriage proposal, I accept."

Her heart was pounding, her body responding, as she pressed herself into Dabs. She said, "I attached conditions."

He said, "You're not entirely done with manipulations, are you? Good God, what else do you want?"

"The driveways. Someone is going to break an axle, and you need to make a road to the cemetery so it can be properly maintained."

"Done."

Dabs hands had run down her back, cupped her buttocks pulled her into him, then returned his hands to her breasts, then down her belly to the front fly of her jeans.

Eloise said, "Dabs, you can't unzip my pants now. Dr. Finn will be calling us any minute."

Dabs ignored her as he said, "You are going to be expensive to keep. I may have to go back to work."

The phone did buzz just then, and Eloise pulled away, slightly out of breath, but wagging a finger at him saying, "See?"

Dabs watched Eloise get up and move away and talk quietly to Dr. Finn. He needed to calm himself. After all this time, all this stress and strain, she was ready, now, now of all times.

Dabs returned to the room, pushing the phone into his back pocket.

Dabs began to laugh. "Remember when Henry told Louisa, 'Lots of argumentation between a mare and a stallion, but when the mare, she ready, the stallion, he ready too.' Well, damn it, Eloise."

Eloise said, "Sorry."

Dabs said, "I can wait. But only because I am deliriously happy and because I can tell you are too."

Eloise was pink in the face, a sly smile played across her lips as she glanced at him. The smile made a promise of "later."

There was a sad chore to attend to first. But not nearly as sad as it would be had he been left to face it alone. Surely there would always be loss, sad days, plenty more 'argumentation.' But someone he loved, who loved him back would be at his side and in his bed.

Eloise and Dabs packed a bottle and four glasses in her tote bag. They held hands as they walked. Prince trotting ahead, seemingly sure of where they were going. They passed Randall's flatbed trailer along the way.

It seemed there were many cemeteries at Ivy Creek. Dude would be buried next to other horses from earlier days of Ivy Creek Plantation.

Dr. Finn and Randall stood next to Dude's body and a pile of dirt alongside a backhoe in the corner of one of the hayfields. Dabs knelt one last time next to the body of his old friend and once again stroked his neck, his ears, his face. A tear rolled down his cheek and he brushed it away while Prince sat on Eloise's feet, leaning into her body, her hand resting on his head.

Randall pulled a Swiss-Army knife from his back pocket and handed it to Dabs, who used it to cut a fistful of tail hair as a keepsake. As Dabs stepped back, Eloise got out the bottle and half-filled each glass as she handed them around.

They raised their glasses in unison.

Dabs gave the benediction, "To Dude, a good horse." And then announced he would be reciting the last verse of "The Parting Glass."

Dabs looked at the body of his old horse with glass held high and Eloise thought to herself, she could nearly hear a violin playing the melody.

Dabs said, "But since it fell unto my lot, that I should rise, and you should not, I'll gently rise and softly call, Good night, (he choked slightly as he added,) sweet boy,

464

then composed himself to finish by addressing Eloise and Dr. Finn and Randall, with his glass still raised, "and joy be to you all."

Epilogue

Betsy had insisted on being the wedding planner, although Dabs and Eloise were having a tiny wedding supper, they thought they could manage without help, but Betsy said that would not do, and to leave it all up to her.

Betsy arrived at Ivy Creek with a checklist that would have made Elly Robertson proud. Jobs were delegated, a timetable created. The wedding was to be in the house. But it meant the house had to be in tip-top order. A professional house cleaning and yard overhaul was accomplished, including a grading of the driveway.

Dabs and Eloise had no intention of recreating the grand wedding of Major Schmidt and Louisa, how could they? Thomas and Patty Jefferson would not be guests this time, at least not in body. But Betsy had standards and she made them explicit. Eloise and Dabs would have a fine celebration. She and all who had lived through their courtship had earned it!

Buzz was arranging the menu and chose the caterers and the wines. Pinky volunteered for hair and makeup. Betsy selected flowers only asking Eloise a few questions before showing her what her bouquet would look like.

Betsy had suffered with Eloise in selecting the dress. (Nothing that would restrict breathing or blood flow, cause her to trip, and certainly no high heeled shoes!)

Ralph merely asked for an estimated budget for the entire affair and then had kindly dumped more in her account than she had requested. Then there were the accommodations. Dabs knew of an historic bed and breakfast nearby that was built in 1735. Dabs reserved the rooms. The cost of even this tiny wedding made Eloise's head hurt. Ralph assured her they could afford it, as he was now managing Dabs' money as well as hers.

* * *

Betsy and Eloise arrived back at Ivy Creek from their final shopping trip. They parked in front of the house, Betsy carrying the dress bag, and Eloise the two large shopping bags. It had been exhausting, but their work was done. As Betsy and Eloise walked to the house, Betsy was saying, "Don't forget, Dabs isn't allowed to see the dress. We want him to be surprised when he sees you come down those stairs on your wedding day."

Eloise was trying to think of a witty comeback when Prince came bounding out of the front door and down the stairs with a huge red bow on his collar, Dabs trailing behind.

Betsy ignored the dog and the giant bow. "Just set

those bags by the stairs, Eloise. I'm taking this to my room and having a toes-up."

"Would you like me to bring you a cup of tea, anything?"

Betsy looked over her shoulder, an impish grin on her face. "Thanks, but not yet, dear. Perhaps later."

Eloise looked down at Prince, waggling and panting, excited about something. Dabs caught up and took the bags from her. He said, "Prince has something for you."

Eloise saw it. In the middle of that crazy big bow, was tied the old, corroded key. It still had the dried-out twist of leather attached and wrapped around the leather was a bit of paper. It took a bit of doing but Eloise got the key untied from the bow, unfurled the note, and read it aloud. It said, "Dabs has snatched victory from the jaws of defeat and won his prize. Eloise must simply snatch something from the old jaws in the garret to lead her to hers."

"A scavenger hunt?"

Dabs nodded.

"The garret? Okay."

Prince let them lead all the way up the narrow stairs. The dog saw it first, and his hackles raised as he stiffened all four limbs and growled softly.

On top of a table, Dabs had set the Indian headdress of the Mountain lion, a rag doll placed in obvious peril under the canine teeth.

Eloise saved the rag doll, finding of course, another note.

"Another sort of treasure found. From the loving hands of Maisie? Next trace your fingers once again, along the name of Sammie."

Eloise headed to the bedroom where she knew the trundle bed was pushed back into its place. She knelt and pulled it out, and as it no longer had anything in it, it slid out easily.

There sat the old harness brass on top of yet another note. Before she read the note, she ran her finger over Sammie's name carved into the wood, and silently prayed he had lived a long and happy life in Canada with Priscilla.

Eloise read the note out loud, "Take this old dull brass, fetch an apple or maybe two, or four, to find a shinier bit of copper."

Eloise rose with the harness brass in one hand while still clutching the doll and the key with her other hand.

She said, "An apple or two, or four?" Then raised her eyebrows, as she understood, "The next clue is in the barn?"

Dabs looked a little nervous, "The apples are in the kitchen. Here, let's leave those other things here."

He set all three items and the notes on top of a dresser and took Eloise by the hand. She could tell he was anxious. Copper? She knew how the key and the mountain lion and the rag doll, and even the harness brass, were all part of their story. As was finding the tracing of Sammie's name. As was so much else they had discovered together through Louisa's journals and this wonderful old house and the land that was part of it. It was Louisa's story, it was Dabs' story, and now all this was their story.

But Eloise drew a blank when it came to shiny copper.

On the kitchen counter sat a large straw basket, the kind you might take on a picnic. It carried more than an apple or two or even four. It also had a bunch of carrots with the greens still attached.

In the basket was one more note.

"Horses give us wings. Because horses can fly."

Now she was really confused. But she took the basket over her arm, and said, "What a puzzle. Okay, to the barn, then!"

Prince was staring at the basket on her arm, so she handed him a carrot, greens, and all. Prince took the carrot and ran to the door. He knew exactly where they were headed and he charged out the door as soon as it was opened, heading to the barn, only stopping when he got to the big barn door, carrot in his mouth to wait for them. Eloise could tell he wanted to bark, but hanging on to his carrot instead, he whined for them to hurry up.

Eloise was sure to hand each of the old gents a carrot as she started down the aisle. Red heard her and called to her not to linger, but to hurry up with her treat.

And then another whinny joined Red's.

Eloise looked at Dabs in disbelief before rushing down the barn aisle. It could not be true. But it was.

Whiplash.

She threw open the stall door and nearly spooked her own horse, throwing her arms around the neck of the startled mare who soon realized there was a basket full of apples and carrots hanging from Eloise's arm.

Eloise was crying, Dabs, now standing at the open stall door, was wiping away a tear. Whiplash was soon slobbering apple juice all over Eloise, while Red had commenced banging on her stall wall, furious that Eloise and the basket of treats had bypassed her stall.

Dabs made a point of pulling a bunch of carrots and an apple from the basket and taking them to Red, as an apology, while Eloise peppered him with questions. He ended up snapping about six carrots in pieces and dumping them in Red's manger to placate her. Then he returned explaining,

"Jock suggested the scavenger hunt. I thought it was a good idea."

"Jock agreed to send her?"

"Jock and I got along like a house-a-fire. It was a little complicated, but we worked things out. We're like this now," Dabs crossed his fingers, "me, and Jock. He is pretty sure we are related, by the way."

Eloise rolled her eyes.

"Not to worry, by marriage only, not blood."

"I don't know how you did it."

"I charmed him by asking his permission to wed his daughter."

"Pretty sure that didn't do it."

Dabs pulled another apple out and fed it to Whiplash. "I might have used some gentle, friendly sort of pressure."

"What could you possibly use as leverage?"

Dabs smiled, all anxiety gone. He looked supremely confident, even smug. He said, "Not all stories need telling. Someone wise told you that once. But I will say this and then it's all I plan to say, it may or may not have had something to do with grandchildren."

Eloise found that she had dropped the basket as she and Dabs embraced, pressing themselves tightly into each other, but were interrupted, as Prince wedged himself between them, his mouth hanging open, his tongue lolling, with a deliriously happy grin on his face.

Acknowledgements

How did I come to combine the stories of a grieving young Atlanta horsewoman with Thomas Jefferson and a young woman in the 18th century?

Well, every story is a love story, a comedy. And every story is a tragedy. And as we struggle with "forgive us our trespasses" we also struggle with "as we forgive those who trespass against us." This struggle is apparent both on a personal level and on a larger, cultural, and historical level. We see this today as we look at conflict over how the history of America is taught, and how we, as Americans study and think about our founding fathers.

Thomas Jefferson wrote to his daughter Martha, "…and were we to love none who had imperfections this world would be a desert for our love." This thought was top of mind for me as I penned *Mercy Asked, Mercy Found*. Jefferson's own words helped me forgive him for his many imperfections, some deeply troubling, while at the same time, accepting his sublime accomplishments. Jefferson's vision for our country lives. His words still ring true. His words on the equality of man, and on religious freedom and tolerance are historically seismic.

And yet, in many ways he was no better than others of his class and time who had become wealthy from the labors of those denied their God given rights, denied by law, kept from those rights by violence, and by threats of violence.

Along with these serious themes I try to weave into my story my passion for horses, and for horse people. And along with horses there are always dogs. Dogs make me laugh; horses fill my heart with joy. But of course, they also both break my heart.

I want to thank Christine Ranallo for coaching me as I developed the concept for the story. Dr. Elizabeth Jacobs kindly read and commented on my first full draft. Fellow writer Susan Yaremko was my critique partner while I was composing, and Danielle Chiotti from The Manuscript Academy critiqued both volumes. A shout out to Marlene Butcher Whitaker's "Jeeter" who was one heck of a dog and an inspiration for Prince. Thank you to The Pharr Road Animal Hospital for hiring this English Major as a kennel maid all those many years ago. And of course, the horses and riding students who continue to inspire me and keep me sane. A prayer of thanks to a certain red-headed horse in my past who provided many a "near-death experience" but was the ride of my life in a good way too!

I want to especially thank Deeds Publishing for continuing to believe in my ability as a writer and for producing beautiful books.

—*Karen McGoldrick, January 2024*

Karen McGoldrick is married to a UVA grad, and lives in Canton, Georgia. She is the author of the series, "The Dressage Chronicles." She rides and teaches dressage and is a USDF certified instructor who has earned her USDF bronze, silver, and gold rider medals on horses she trained herself. She's lucky enough to still have horses in her daily life, a good dog, and a large number of books in her TBR pile.

www.ingramcontent.com/pod-product-compliance
Lightning Source LLC
Chambersburg PA
CBHW031025030726
47497CB00004B/1012